Gabriella

ALSO BY CARAGH BELL

Indecision
Regrets
Promises
Echoes of Grace

Published by Poolbeg

Gabriella

CARAGH BELL

POOLBEG

Published 2020 by Poolbeg Press Ltd
123 Grange Hill, Baldoyle
Dublin 13, Ireland
E-mail: poolbeg@poolbeg.com
www.poolbeg.com

The moral right of the author has been asserted.

A catalogue record for this book is available from the British Library.

ISBN 978-1-78199-762-8

Typeset by Poolbeg Press Ltd

www.poolbeg.com

ABOUT THE AUTHOR

Caragh Bell is from West Cork in Ireland. She lives there with her husband and five children. She has a degree in French and English and also dabbles in educational research. She loves quizzes, coffee, travelling and France.

This is Caragh's fifth novel, following on from the bestselling *Echoes of Grace*.

Facebook: Caragh Bell-Writer
Twitter: @BellCaragh
Instagram: @caraghbellwriter

ACKNOWLEDGEMENTS

This novel would not have been possible without Clémence, my au pair. She helped me get this book over the line and I'm eternally grateful.

I want to thank my husband John for putting up with my schedule which can be crazy.

To my wonderful children: Fódhla, Aoibhe, Lughan, Oscar and Feidhlim. You amaze me every day and I'm blessed to be your mother. I love you so much.

Thanks to my parents John and Ann. You have always supported me through good times and bad. You are simply the greatest. I will always be your best traveller.

Thanks to my siblings: Louise, Ian and Freyja. Love you all.

To my mother-in-law Kathleen and my father-in-law Eugene. Thanks for the love and encouragement.

To my colleagues at school (especially those who sit at my table) for being so great.

To Gráinne Collins for insisting that I go public with my novels. She is my 'favourite'.

To the *Southern Star*, who always treated me like somebody even when I was a nobody. The publicity is fantastic and I really appreciate it.

To Daniel O'Driscoll, my confidant and advisor. You're the best, Daniel.

To Gaye, thank you for editing and improving everything. I've learned so much from you already.

To Paula, Kieran and all the crew at Poolbeg. Thank you for being so kind and welcoming.

To the staff at Parson's School of Design in New York. Thanks for all the information.

To Patrick Kiely for all the help with my website. I would have been lost without your help.

DEDICATION

For Clémence
Merci pour tout

✦ Chapter One ✦

New York
2009

Gabriella stared at her reflection in the battered old mirror on the wall. Her brown eyes sparkled with silver glitter and took attention away from her Roman nose, which was slightly too large for her face. Big rose-coloured lips shone with gloss and her cheekbones glowed from the blusher she had applied minutes earlier. She would never be a supermodel – her frame was too curvy for that. Still, her dress made the best of what she had been given. It was a baby-pink chiffon affair, nipped in at the waist before flowing down to just below the knee.

Her bedroom was cluttered with clothes and magazines – a typical sixteen-year-old's domain with empty make-up palettes and curling tongs flung on the desk. It was a small room with an old brass bed and a patchwork quilt. She didn't have a laptop or a TV like other kids her age.

Gabriella Magdalena Ruiz Álvarez always made the best of what she had. Born in the South Bronx of Puerto Rican descent, she had grown up in a three-bedroomed apartment in Melrose with her family. Money had always been tight, but love had made up for it. She had never wanted for anything. Sure, she didn't get to go on excursions in middle school and her cell phone was always

1

four years out of date, but she didn't mind. Nobody made an orange cake like her mama. Nobody told stories like her grandmother.

"Gabby!" called her mother. "We need to leave in five."

"Sure, Mama!" she called back, hurriedly straightening her bodice and spraying some white musk on her neck.

It wasn't every day that she was invited to a high-society party. Her friend Celine du Maurier was hosting a Sweet Sixteen celebration at her mansion on Long Island. An unlikely friendship – she, an immigrant working-class girl from the Bronx, and Celine, the youngest daughter of the du Maurier dynasty. Yet they were very close and Gabriella loved visiting the palatial home of her friend.

It was through her own mother that they had met. Magda, Gabriella's mama, was a maid at the big house on Long Island. Hardworking and punctual, she had quickly become indispensable to the lady of the big house, Victoria du Maurier. Sometimes she had let Gabriella tag along when she was preparing for functions. It was then that the two little girls had struck up a long-lasting friendship. Celine, the youngest child, was often alone and craved the company of other children. Gabriella, with her open face and bright smile, had been the perfect candidate. Together they would play in the rose garden of the estate and Celine, being blonde, was always the princess whereas Gabriella, with her dark looks, was inevitably the wicked queen.

Then life got in the way. Celine was sent to school upstate and their playtime ceased. Still, Facebook was a blessing and afforded them the opportunity to stay in touch. When the invitation arrived in her notifications, Gabriella had jumped at the chance to attend her old friend's party.

Her mother was already outside when she swept downstairs. Her lined face looked tired and her dark hair was grey at the temples. She was dressed in her light-blue uniform and sensible black shoes. Gabriella couldn't remember the last time she had seen her mother take a holiday. She always looked exhausted and loved when her youngest daughter rubbed her shoulders at night. The main breadwinner, she had taken the job after the death of her husband Jorge, who had died tragically when Gabriella was a baby. No one spoke of the terrible accident that had robbed them of him. His photo hung on the wall by the front door, a handsome man with a black moustache.

"You look lovely," observed Magda, regarding her daughter.

"You're kidding me, right?" Gabriella raised an eyebrow. "I could really lose a few pounds."

"Young girls," tutted her mother, falling into step beside her. "Why do you want to look like skeletons?"

Gabriella laughed. "Not a skeleton, Mama, but you've got to admit that I could lose some of this!" She pulled at her waist to demonstrate her point.

"Men? They love curves," argued her mother. "Something to hold on to at night, *cariña*."

"That's what Lita says."

Lita, her grandmother, had lived with them for as long as she could remember. Gabriella had called her Lita since she was a baby, a variant of *abuelita*, the Spanish pet name for grandmother. Her dead father's mother, she was a wise old lady with a strong Spanish accent and staunch Catholic beliefs. She had emigrated from Puerto Rico during the Great Migration in the fifties with her young son, Jorge. She too had lost her husband at a young age and so worked as a seamstress to make ends meet. She had set up home in the South Bronx, a favourite of the Puerto Rican immigrants, and after a few years had established herself as a talented

3

dressmaker. Then, when Jorge had been knocked down by that truck, his wife Magda had taken her in.

Magda and Jorge had three children. Diego, the eldest, had twin boys and had a successful auto-repair shop two blocks over. He was thirty-two and resembled his father in every way, even down to the moustache. He often called over for dinner and slipped Gabriella twenty bucks when he could. Despite the big age difference between them, they were close. They shared a love of reality TV and Michael Jackson music. When Antony Morello had broken Gabriella's heart last summer, it was Diego who had confronted him and berated him. His tall frame and booming voice had been adequately intimidating for the teenage Antony who had begged Gabriella for forgiveness the same day. Diego was a great big brother – someone she could rely on when there was a crisis.

Teresa, the second child, was thirty and married with a little girl. Gabriella often looked after her nieces as her older sister worked part-time at the local supermarket. She and her older sister were very alike and shared lots of interests. It was Teresa who showed her what to do when at thirteen she became a woman. It was Teresa who sobered her up after she drank too much gin at Carlotta Madero's fourteenth birthday. She had held her hair while she vomited and forced her to drink gallons of water. Gabriella had made her sister promise not to tell Magda or Lita and she had kept her word. She was always on hand for advice and tagged Gabriella constantly on Facebook, usually in silly memes.

It had been a huge surprise when little Gabriella had arrived into the household. There was a noticeable fourteen-year gap and so Lita had stepped up to help as Magda needed to work. Consequently, she doted on her youngest grandchild and taught her all that she knew, including the skill of sewing. Lita had an old Singer machine and she instructed Gabriella how to use it. Her eagle eye spotted loose threads and uneven lines in a second. She demanded the best and, as a result, Gabriella was highly skilled for her sixteen years. Her pink party dress had been created in her bedroom under the watchful eyes of her grandmother. It had thrilled the old lady to realise that her *preciosa* had inherited her talent – she would never starve with skills like that.

"Come on, we've got to hurry," said Magda, increasing her pace. "You know how mad Victoria gets when I'm late."

Gabriella raised an eyebrow. "You're never late, Mama."

Her mother's unfaltering work ethic amazed her. She was pretty sure that she had never missed a day at the du Maurier mansion. Consequently, she was the head maid and ran the house like clockwork. Nothing happened without her involvement and she was adored as she was just and fair. She never abused her power and treated the staff with respect. Magda had passed this conscientious attitude on to her youngest child – Gabriella approached everything with the same diligence and dedication. She had realised at a young age that no one got anywhere in life without working hard.

The du Maurier mansion was an old plantation-style house in the exclusive Old Westbury on Long Island. It was a large imposing building with tall white pillars and two acres of gardens surrounding it. Frank du Maurier had purchased it in the early nineties to please his new bride Victoria, who hailed from Georgia. It resembled her family home and she adored sitting on the veranda in the summer with a pitcher of lemonade and some beignets dusted with powdered sugar.

Magda automatically entered the house through the servants' entrance at the side. Gabriella followed, her pink dress swishing as she walked. Bruno the chef waved madly at the young girl. He had been working for the family for years and had often fixed a bowl of delicious vanilla ice cream with chocolate sauce for Magda's little girl.

"The canapés look incredible," said Gabriella, gazing at the trays and trays of tiny mouthfuls ranging from blinis to tartlets.

"Her Majesty wanted fifteen different types," said Bruno, throwing his eyes to heaven. "I been up all night making these babies."

Gabriella smiled. 'Her Majesty' was what the staff called Victoria du Maurier, the lady of the house. Sure, she was regal-looking with her perfect hair and haughty demeanour. You could see why she was christened such a thing. However, she was feared rather than liked and the staff tried their best to avoid her acidic tongue.

Magda tied a white apron around her waist. "Go upstairs and find Celine," she suggested to her daughter. "We have a lot to do down here."

Gabriella nodded and kissed her mother's cheek. "Just yell if you need anything," she said fondly.

She found Celine in her bedroom, desperately curling her blonde hair.

"Oh, Gabby!" she said in frustration. "I wanted to put my hair up but it was all lumpy and now I look like a crazy Shirley Temple."

Gabriella smiled and calmly took the curling tongs from her friend's hand. "Let me do it," she offered, brushing out the ringlets.

Celine visibly relaxed and sat back on the chair. "Thank God you're here. I'm a mess. Daddy took me for lunch downtown and then I met Jennifer, a girl from Pilates, and suddenly it was four thirty and I hadn't even started my hair."

Gabriella grinned. "Oh, how awful," she mocked.

Celine giggled. "You got that right," she agreed.

She had a sweet face – similar to her mother's, but without the coldness. Her blue eyes were warm and her blonde hair fell to her shoulders. Athletic in frame, she was a talented equestrian, often competing in tournaments and dressage competitions. Being the youngest du Maurier child had its perks – she was spoilt by her father Frank and managed to escape her mother's sharp tongue by playing by the rules.

Charlotte, her older sister, was the main focus of her parents. Exquisitely beautiful with honey-blonde hair, big blue eyes and a willowy frame, she had excelled at school and was now in her third year of Harvard Law. She rarely came home, preferring to work weekends in her dorm, intent on being the best. Demure and soft-spoken, she reminded Gabriella of a modern Helen of Troy. She had a type of classic beauty that would stop you in your tracks. She and Celine use to steal into the older girl's bedroom when they were little and pinch her perfume and try on her clothes.

Celine both loved and envied her older sister. How often she would complain about being invisible and overlooked! She was a different child – similar in looks, but light years away in ambition and drive. She had her heart set on Art school, much to her mother's horror. "Lord, no, Celine," she would say, shaking her head. "You gotta do better than that."

Hugo was the only son and the middle child. He too was at Harvard, much to his mother's delight. Her own beloved daddy had been the state attorney back home and of course Frank was a partner at a city firm, so the natural choice for her one and only son was a legal profession. He shared Charlotte's height, but had his father's dark hair. What was really unusual was the light-blue colour of his eyes. His dark colouring only accentuated them all the more. Gabriella had met him a few times but, being four years older, he mixed in different circles.

"Okay, how's that?" Gabriella stood back and let her friend inspect her work.

Celine clapped her hands in delight. "Frickin' awesome, Gabby! You've saved my life."

"Now, let's get downstairs. Your guests are arriving."

Magda filled a pitcher with homemade lemonade and placed it on the table by the veranda. Bruno's canapés were doing the rounds and the big house was full of people ranging from teenagers to friends of Victoria's. The lady of the house looked impeccable as always, her cream suit crisp and pressed. Not a morsel of refined flour passed her lips and her glass of white wine was untouched in her hand. She nodded politely as a loud woman in a red shawl roared with laughter at some story she had related. Victoria du Maurier was the ultimate hostess. Her momma had taught her well: never let the mask slip. The fact that she found this woman boorish and unbearable was expertly concealed. Instead, she smiled at appropriate times and laughed when expected.

She thought Celine looked adorable in her blue dress. It had been the best choice. Her youngest child was appealing to the eye, but she lacked the grace of her older sister. How many times had she told her not to talk with her mouth full and never to have seconds at dinner. Frank, her husband, adored his 'baby' as he called her and often reprimanded his wife for being too harsh. *"Jesus Christ, Vic, let her run around the house if she goddamn wants to,"* he boomed. "She's only a kid."

Now, her eldest Charlotte was her protégée: the embodiment of the perfect daughter. Beautiful and smart, she had never caused an ounce of trouble. Soon she would graduate, with honours no doubt, and be the most eligible girl in New York.

Victoria smiled in satisfaction. She already had four young men lined up who were entirely suitable. She couldn't wait to host a society wedding and beat those Upper East Side bitches at their own game. With her southern drawl and sheltered country upbringing, it had taken years to be accepted amongst the society ladies of New York. They were as rigid as ramrods, there was no mistaking. Being Frank's wife and having tons of money had helped, but she always felt like they were sneering at her tendency to say 'y'all'.

Victoria pursed her lips. Those first few years had been lonely as hell. She had met the young Frank du Maurier at a Red Cross charity function in the late eighties. She had been sent to stay with her aunt for the summer and had caught his eye with her blonde looks and graceful ways. He was fresh out of Harvard Law School and looking for a wife. His mother had lined up dozens of girls, but Victoria had bewitched him and they were married within the year.

The du Maurier dynasty owed its success to Frank's great-grandfather, an ambitious Frenchman who had sailed the ocean after the First World War, determined to make his fortune. Inspired by the Statue of Liberty, he had set up a department store called Liberty Designs which specialised in women's fashion. The business went from strength to strength and was now a global brand. Frank, the heir, had rejected the offer of heading the company and had instead given the role to his younger brother, Maurice. Instead, he followed his dream of becoming an attorney with a fine income from the business to help things along.

The first few years had been tough. Frank had worked every hour he could to rise through the ranks at the firm and Victoria was often alone with baby Charlotte, an outsider amongst the society ladies.

Then Hugo came along, her only son. Dark-haired and blue-eyed, he reminded her of her own darling daddy, who had succumbed to bowel cancer right before the birth. Oh, how she had doted on her little boy, rocking him to sleep and kissing his soft skin. Then, as he grew, she realised that he was a quiet child. He was certainly not akin to the loud alpha male she had married. He didn't excel at sport and preferred to read, his dark head bent over a book. Frank would push him to play polo or even join the tennis club, but Hugo would quietly refuse. The only sport he enjoyed and participated in was sailing. Each summer he would spend hours on the water and, in the end, Frank had to be content with that. At the age of six he expressed an interest in music, asking to learn the piano. Victoria had hired a private tutor and Hugo had picked it up easily. By the age of ten, he was playing Chopin like a professional. She would often find him sitting at the grand piano in the library, his eyes closed in concentration as his fingers sped up and down the keyboard.

She had been musical herself when she was a girl. Her daddy had hired a tutor to teach her piano – an old man called Mr. Johnson. However, as she grew older, she let it slip. Without proper practice, her piano playing faded into the past.

Victoria pictured her son. He was a tough nut to crack. He certainly didn't tell her much. He always seemed so closed off which made it hard to read his true feelings. Sure, he had achieved a place at law school and was doing quite well. However, he always seemed such a loner. In senior year of high school, he had asked if he could apply to the prestigious Conservatoire in Paris. He would have to fly over for an audition. She remembered the conversation well. Hugo with his eager face, uncharacteristically pleading for permission and a horrified Frank, who had said no immediately. What kind of career would he have as a two-bit piano player? His only son would do law and continue his legacy. Victoria had not been so rigid – she wanted Hugo to be happy – however, she couldn't argue with Frank. There was no future in music. So, Hugo was told to forget about Paris.

How she wished that he would take her advice and date the girls she lined up for him. Yet it was always the same: he wanted to find his own way. He didn't need her guidance and advice when it came to matters of the heart.

There had been a few girlfriends. Little dalliances that went nowhere. One of them had been entirely unsuitable – her father worked at the docks – but thankfully it had ended on its own.

Hugo was deep, there was no denying it.

Charlotte glided past, her pretty blue dress floating behind her. Victoria grabbed her slender arm.

"Charlotte, sugar. Have you seen your brother?"

"He went outside, I think," she answered, looking over her shoulder to scan the room. "He filled a glass with whiskey and headed for the garden."

Victoria pursed her lips. "Whatever for? Why won't he mingle like the rest of us?"

Charlotte shrugged helplessly. "He's not in the mood, I guess. You know he hates parties." She squeezed her mother's hand and continued on her way.

Victoria took a small sip of wine. She would sort that boy out if it was the last thing she did.

Celine handed Gabriella a glass of lemonade. "Have some!" she said, beaming. "I put some of Momma's vodka in it."

"Vodka?"

"Why sure. Caroline says you can't even taste it when it's mixed with something else."

"Caroline?"

"That girl over there." Celine pointed to a group of impeccably dressed sixteen-year-olds over by the French windows. "Her momma's best friends with mine. Come on, I'll introduce you." She pulled Gabriella over to the small group and pushed her forward.

"This is my friend, Gabriella," she announced. "We grew up together."

A blonde girl smiled frostily and held out her hand. "Caroline Ashley Hamilton," she said stiffly. "Wonderful to meet you."

Gabriella shook her hand vigorously. "You, too."

The other girls followed suit, limply shaking her hand.

"Celine!" called Victoria from across the room. "Come here, sugar. Your grandma is on the phone."

"I've got to go," said Celine apologetically.

Gabriella smiled. "Take your time."

There was a lengthy silence. Caroline Ashley Hamilton looked at Gabriella with narrowed eyes. "So how do you know Celine?" she asked coolly.

"As she said, we've been friends since we were kids."

Caroline raised an eyebrow. "Childhood friends? That's funny. She's never mentioned you."

"We haven't seen a lot of each other lately, but we stay in touch."

Caroline made an 'oh' sound and sipped her drink.

"Your dress is awesome," said Gabriella, oblivious to the animosity. "Where did you get it?"

"Barney's."

"It cost a ton of money," added the dark-haired girl on Caroline's right. "It's Dolce and Gabbana, right?"

Caroline nodded. "Daddy bought it for me especially." She gestured loosely at Gabriella's pink dress. "And you? Where did you pick up your outfit?"

"Oh, I made it," answered Gabriella happily. "I love to sew."

"You made your dress?" Caroline snorted. "Who does that?"

Her companions laughed loudly and Gabriella blushed.

"I guess I don't have as much money as you guys," she said quietly. "My *abuelita* taught me to sew and that's how I get by."

"Poor you," said Caroline pityingly. "Still, I bet you fit right in where you come from. I don't think you see much of Dolce and Gabbana in Queens or wherever."

"I'm from the Bronx," said Gabriella stiffly. "Now, if you'll excuse me ..."

She attempted to back away but was halted by a shriek from Caroline.

"Look!" the girl gasped, pointing to the patio. "I just saw Hugo pass by."

The only Hugo Gabriella knew was Celine's older brother.

"So? What about him?" she asked.

"Mother has the deal in the bag," said Caroline, her eyes glittering. "That's my future husband, ladies. Make no mistake." She smoothed back her honey-blonde hair. "Now that he's at Harvard Law School it's only a matter of time before he goes into politics. I'll be Caroline du Maurier, the governor's wife!"

Gabriella looked at her incredulously. "What deal? What does your mother have to do with it?"

Caroline gave her a withering look. "This is how things work in our world. Marriages take place between two like-minded people and are very successful. Mother has had her eye on Hugo for years. She and Victoria have it all planned."

Gabriella shook her head. "Well, good luck with that."

"I don't need luck," flashed back the other girl, but Gabriella had walked away.

How could Caroline think she could snare Hugo du Maurier just like that? He was way older for a start and he always seemed so moody. Despite calling over to play over the years, she had never had much to do with him. He was Celine's older, more sophisticated brother who liked to play piano and sail his boat. He had driven them to the movies once in his dad's BMW, but that was about all she had ever had to do with him.

Draining her lemonade, she placed the empty glass on a tray. Celine was nowhere to be seen and she didn't really know anyone else. She had tried to make an effort with Celine's friends but it was impossible with people like that. Lita would often say that it was a sad state of affairs that young people nowadays knew the value of nothing.

"Are you okay?" mouthed her mother from the doorway.

Gabriella plastered a smile on her face. "Sure," she mouthed back. There was no point in telling her that she felt like an outsider in her homemade dress and cheap strappy sandals. It would just worry and upset her darling mama. Celine was nice, but her friends were hell. Opening the side door, she slipped out to the garden.

The moon was full in the inky sky. She gazed up in wonder at the glittering stars that littered the heavens. It was almost impossible to see the sky like this back home where the high-rise buildings and the smog inhibited her view. Strolling down the path, she headed for the rose garden. She and Celine spent hours within its high walls when they were kids. It had an old stone bench in the corner and large bushes dotted with red, pink and white blooms. Just as she approached the arched entrance, she heard Caroline Ashley Hamilton's jeering voice, commenting on the gardenias. Like lightning, she bolted behind the biggest rose bush and waited for her to pass.

"Of course, Mother always said that Frank married beneath him," said Caroline, rounding the corner. "We all know how backward those southerners are with their drawl and conservative views. Still, I'll have to put up with it, I guess. She'll be my mother-in-law after all."

Gabriella peered out a gap in the bush and saw Caroline light a cigarette with a flaring match. Her features were illuminated briefly and her diamond bracelet sparkled in the short-lived light of the flame.

"Do you guys want a smoke?" she asked her three companions. "I won't tell anyone."

They shook their heads.

"That Gabriella is something else, right?" Caroline blew a perfect smoke-ring. "I mean, what was Celine thinking? Who invites the help to a party?"

"Is she a waitress?" asked the brunette on her right.

"Not technically, but her mother is the maid." Caroline paused. "God in heaven, did you see her dress?"

Her companions sniggered loudly.

"Talk about horrendous. I wouldn't be seen dead in such a thing."

Gabriella shrank backwards in mortification. Lita always said to walk away if someone was talking about you behind your back. More often than not, you would hear something you wish you hadn't.

Emerging, she went through the arch and walked towards the stone bench, only to find that she wasn't alone. Hugo du Maurier was lounging on it, a glass in his hand. He put a finger to his lips. She nodded slowly and kept quiet.

Caroline's nasal voice cut through the darkness once more. "Plus, she could really do with losing a few pounds. Maybe cut back on the tacos or burritos or whatever. Could you imagine being that fat? It's just awful."

Gabriella hung her head in shame. Caroline's words cut right through her. It was as though the other girl was attuned to her Achilles' Heel. Not only had she mocked her dress – the dress she had designed and painstakingly sewn under the watchful eye of Lita – she had also confirmed what she already knew. She was fat!

A hand touched her shoulder and she jumped. Hugo was by her side, having abandoned his position on the stone bench. Her brown eyes, now filled with tears, met his blue ones and they stared at each other silently. He removed his hand and her shoulder burned from where he had touched it.

"Let's get back, you guys," came Caroline's voice. "I've got to find Hugo and make a play."

They walked away, their voices fading as they progressed towards the house.

Hugo brushed a tendril of hair away from Gabriella's face. "You're Magda's kid, right?" he said softly.

She nodded, feeling tongue-tied.

"I'm sorry you heard all of that. Caroline has always had a way with words." He smiled. "For what it's worth, I like your dress. Pink suits you."

Gabriella blushed and stepped backwards. "You don't have to say that."

"I mean it." His blue eyes regarded her steadily. "Don't let her upset you. You look great."

She sighed and strolled over to the bench. "That taco thing she said? It's just so typical. I'm not Mexican – my family comes from Puerto Rico."

Hugo laughed. "Caroline doesn't strike me as someone who knows where anywhere is. I'm pretty sure her knowledge of the world consists of Fifth Avenue and the Hamptons."

Gabriella smiled sadly. "She doesn't *need* to know about anything else. Her life is all planned out and everything will be easy. People like her don't need luck – they just stay privileged."

Hugo followed her to the bench and sat down beside her. His long leg brushed against her knee and she jumped.

"Well, I for one have a problem with her future wedding plans."

Gabriella giggled. "I know, right? She's convinced you guys will get married."

Hugo laughed out loud. "I really don't get why. We've never talked. Not properly anyway."

"Oh, it's all planned out. Your mom and her mom …"

He shook his head. "Not even. I can't see me and Caroline living happy ever after."

Gabriella said nothing. She could feel the heat of his thigh through the light fabric of her dress. This was the first conversation she had ever had with Celine's older brother. It felt strange and grown-up – he was at law school after all. Yet, here he was, talking to her, and seemed in no hurry to move away.

"So where do you live?" he asked.

"The Bronx," she replied guardedly. "Lita, my grandmother, moved there when my papa was little."

"I don't think I've ever been there," he said, frowning.

"It's not like here," she said honestly, "but it's my home. I've tons of happy memories. Do you know it's the greenest borough in New York?"

He shook his head and smiled. A cloud passed over the moon and for a moment there was only darkness.

"So, do you like law school?" she asked nervously, unsure of what else to say.

He shrugged. "It's cool. Pretty boring in places, but I guess that will get better."

"Harvard is so prestigious though."

"School is school. It meant more to Momma that I go there." He paused. "Harvard isn't the worst. Plus my big sister is around to get money off when funds are low."

"Are you guys close?"

He shrugged. "I guess. She always tells me what to do but that's how sisters are." His blue eyes met hers. "So what's your dream after high school? Are you a wannabe Caroline Ashley Hamilton? Have you got a suitable husband lined up?" His eyes crinkled in amusement.

She laughed loudly. "Finding a husband is not on my list of priorities." She smoothed her dress. "I want to be a designer. I want to make clothes." She hung her head, expecting scorn, but nothing happened.

"That sounds cool," was the reply and her head shot up.

His handsome face looked quite serious as he waited for her to continue.

18

"Lita taught me to sew when I was a little girl and I'm good. I know I'm good." She lifted the chiffon skirt of her pink dress. "Sure, Caroline mocked my dress, but she doesn't get how hard it is to make something like this with an old Singer machine by lamplight. I want to go to Art School and become a professional. I want to design gowns for princesses and actresses and countesses."

"Oh, you do?" He looked amused. "What about the plebs?"

She laughed. "I'm aiming for the big time, Hugo. I want to be a twenty-first century Chanel. I want to be the best."

"Her real name was Gabrielle, right?" he said thoughtfully. "That's a definite sign."

"God, I never thought about that." She laughed. "I won't be changing mine to Coco anytime soon."

He said nothing, but just took her hand in his. It felt cool to touch. Slowly, he traced her wrist with his finger and she shivered. She had kissed a couple of boys in the past, but nothing serious. Even Antony Morello had only got to first base. She had always been shy around the opposite sex. Hugo du Maurier was twenty years old – he was a man. He was the elusive older brother of her friend and he was making her stomach flip as he caressed her arm. She bit her lip and watched him trace concentric circles on her skin. Suddenly, there was a shriek from the main garden. He pulled back instantly and the moment passed.

"What was that?" she asked breathlessly, jolted and confused.

"I'd better check it out." He got to his feet. "It was nice to meet you again, Gabriella." He shook her hand formally. "I hope to see your name in lights someday."

She shook his cool hand and nodded. "Have fun at law school."

His expression darkened for a moment, but then brightened again. "I sure will."

Then he was gone.

Gabriella felt warm inside. For a moment, it felt like a dream.

Hugo du Maurier.

Smiling, she got to her feet and went back inside.

✎ Chapter Two ✐

2014

"Gabby!"

Oh, go away! I've had zero sleep.

"Gabriella Magdalena Ruiz Álvarez!"

She groaned. Footsteps thundered down the hallway and her bedroom door burst open.

"You have to get up! We need to try that dress. I'm going to be late for the photo shoot!"

Her roommate Isabelle Flynn stood at the end of her bed, hands on her hips. Her red hair was piled on her head and her green eyes were circled with kohl. To say that she was stunning was an understatement: Isabelle, or Zsa Zsa as she liked to be called, was simply the most beautiful girl Gabriella had ever seen.

"Okay, okay, I'm up." She sat up and yawned.

Gabriella and Isabelle had met during induction day at the famous Parson's School of Design on 5th Avenue three years before. Both were freshmen and wound up sitting together at the introductory lecture. Gabriella, bowled over by the other girl's beauty, asked if she was a model.

"Not yet," was the reply, "but I will be the most famous that ever lived."

Both ambitious, with greatness as their objective, they

went to lectures and soon became great friends. Of the two, Isabelle took a more relaxed approach to her studies, as all she wanted was to break into modelling. She attended audition after audition and won some minor jobs. Long days standing in the cold for little or no money tested her to her limits but like Gabriella, she had a dream – to make it. With her startling beauty and endless confidence, it was only a matter of time. Gabriella was convinced of it and so was she.

The stakes were higher for Gabriella. Parson's was a dream come true. It was one of the most renowned schools in New York. There was a sense of honour in being one of its alumni and she never let her grades slip. God had given her the opportunity to attend and she would get all that she could out of the experience. She rarely missed a lecture and pushed herself with steely determination. Inspired by past students like Donna Karan and Marc Jacobs, she vowed to graduate with top honours.

Isabelle, although beautiful, was refreshingly down-to-earth and made Gabriella laugh with her happy-go-lucky attitude to life. She regaled her with stories of her childhood in Philadelphia where she had watched *America's Top Model* religiously, vowing to be the next Heidi Klum. Her father, Patrick, was of Irish descent and credited his daughter's unusual colouring to his Celtic ancestors. Her mother, Elaine, resembled her only child in looks but instead of fiery red hair, she had dark-brown curls. She had modelled in the eighties but had given it up when she got married. Patrick was a stockbroker and there had been no problem meeting the demands of a third-level education for his only daughter.

Luckily, Isabelle lived in a rent-controlled apartment in the West Village of Manhattan. Her aunt had lived in the small two-bedroomed flat on Commerce Street for fifty years. Great-aunt Joanne had emigrated from Galway, Ireland, in the forties and obtained a rent-controlled lease for under four hundred dollars a month. After her death, her daughter Maeve had taken up residence so as not to lose the arrangement. The family knew that once a property became vacant, the rent control would be lost. However, Maeve wanted to move to Chicago, so when Isabelle decided to study at Parson's, she became the main resident and so prolonged the programme.

Magda had been trying to save for years to put Gabriella through college and when her youngest daughter received a coveted scholarship to Parson's, she was over the moon. The fees were paid for – she thanked God every day for that blessing – and Fifth Avenue was only an hour from home on the subway. She had to provide spending money for outings and books and she worked every hour she could to make ends meet. Diego and Teresa helped when they could. Gabriella was the first in the family to go on to third-level education and they were so proud of her.

So, Gabriella commuted from Melrose during that first year. The advantages were a hot meal every evening when she got home. Lita made sure she ate well and often helped her with her designs at night. Her grandmother was a wealth of information and guided her through each one of those early assignments with encouraging words and praise. However, Gabriella also felt like she was missing out. Living away from home was a rite of passage for a student – it frustrated her that she had to leave every evening and travel home to the Bronx.

Isabelle offered her a bed at her apartment whenever there was a party on and she gladly availed of it. Then, the next morning, the two girls would discuss the events of the night before over coffee and bagels.

On one such morning, Isabelle clapped her hands together. "I have it!" she said excitedly. "Next year, you've got to move in with me."

Gabriella had refused initially – she couldn't afford to pay rent – but Isabelle had insisted.

"If we split it, it's only fifty bucks a week, Gabs. Get a part-time job or something. Think of the fun we'll have."

So, in their second year of college, Gabriella applied for a waitressing position in a French restaurant called Brasserie Michel. The owner Giselle offered her two evening shifts a week. In no time at all, she was hailed as their best waitress and the tips were amazing. However, after a busy day at school, the hours were long. She would often return home and collapse into bed, her feet aching from running around.

She also worked in a gallery in Greenwich Village on Saturdays. It belonged to the artist Tara Jacob, an Irish painter and sculptor who was becoming one of the big names in the art world. It was a small building in the heart of the West Village and she adored meeting customers and talking them through the different pieces.

It was Magda who had set up the job originally. One night, when she was serving at one of Victoria's dinner parties, she had taken her chance. Tara Jacob and her husband Christian were invited as their only son Luca was engaged to the daughter of the house, Charlotte du Maurier. Magda had heard of Tara's success and found the woman to be approachable and kind. When Tara had excused herself to use the ladies' room, Magda had plucked up the courage to ask if there were any hours available for her student daughter.

Tara had set up an interview immediately – Magda's earnest face seemed genuine and she had utmost respect for

24

anyone who stuck their neck out for their kid – and soon Gabriella had a regular Saturday slot.

Luca was the main curator of the small space but he was due to go on honeymoon and it was necessary to have a trained replacement for the summer months. So, Gabriella was shown the ropes. Her first day was overwhelming, as most first days are. Two German tourists ambled in while Luca was on lunch. They displayed interest in a small painting and started to haggle. Unsure of how to handle it, she almost sold it for a discounted price until Luca himself came back and smoothly took over.

"You've got to push," he said seriously. "But never be pushy. Inspire but never force."

So, Gabriella became a regular fixture at the gallery, supplementing her income with shifts at the restaurant. She paid her rent, Magda subsidised her groceries and she still had some money left over for a hectic social life. Isabelle was always going to some party or some play and she would drag Gabriella along. Together they made the most of the city that never sleeps.

As a child, Gabriella had pored over stories of kings and queens, escaping into a fantasy land where she was the beautiful princess with the golden hair. She couldn't count the hours she had spent reading books and magazines about the royal houses of Europe. It was her dream to visit Versailles. Someday she would make it there.

It was Isabelle who had suggested creating a small business.

"You're so talented, Gabs," she said earnestly. "I know at least ten girls who would jump at the chance to get a dress designed by you."

"Really?" Gabriella had been doubtful.

"Really," Isabelle had said firmly.

So, she had taken the plunge and set up a Facebook page called Couture Royale, a name inspired by her love of royal history. It was slow to start but after a while a few orders came in for gowns. The trusty pile of *Marie Claires, Cosmopolitans* and *Vogues* proved unstable for clients when a podium was required for a fitting. However, she hadn't made enough money yet to invest in her brand. Her clients tended to be flat-broke students and she was too big-hearted to charge them a lot.

On top of her small fledgling business, she was also working on a portfolio of work. The real world beckoned and she needed a resumé of her talent to show the designers and companies she planned to target. It was imperative that she be taken on by a well-known fashion house and trained as a protégée. She knew the story – train under the greats and then branch out alone.

Isabelle's apartment boasted two small bedrooms and a tiny kitchenette. Even the bathroom was minuscule, but it was their home. Gabriella painted murals of seahorses on the white walls and Isabelle had a huge full-length mirror which covered the entire gable wall of her bedroom.

With limited funds, they made passable meals. There was an Italian deli on the corner that sold homemade ravioli and gnocchi for two bucks a portion. Coupled with a baguette from the local bakery and a glass of white wine, it made for a decent meal.

Now that their time was almost up, the real world loomed. Soon they would be cast out into the rat race. They both knew that they needed a lot of luck. Each night, Gabriella prayed to God that she would make it. She closed her eyes and begged her dead papa to guide her along the right path. There was no other option but to succeed. Otherwise she would wind up working in a supermarket like her older sister Teresa. That was a future she would die to avoid.

When Isabelle had asked her to design a dress for a photo shoot with a professional photographer, she had jumped at the chance. It was for Isabelle's modelling portfolio.

Paolo, Isabelle's agent, had called the week before, gushing about a perfume gig that required a red-haired girl.

"This is it, my darling," he said to an excited Isabelle. "It is the signature scent of Allegra Starr. They need someone beautiful and classy. You were born for this job!"

Allegra Starr, a veteran of the big screen, was launching a new scent for women. At fifty-two, her acting roles were few, so she used her money to invest in perfume and a clothing line for the mature lady. A redhead herself, she wanted a young girl similar in looks.

Isabelle had been poring over pictures of the film star, desperate to shine amongst the hundreds of applicants.

Gabriella had suggested dressing up in a gown similar to one Allegra herself had worn.

"Celebrities are so egocentric, Zsa Zsa," she said. "Flatter her."

So, Isabelle decided to emulate the iconic aquamarine dress that Allegra had worn to an Oscar ceremony in the nineties. It was a gown created by an up-and-coming British designer at the time who called himself Oberon. The dress Allegra wore that night catapulted him into the big time. After that night on the red carpet, everyone knew his name. Oberon became a brand overnight thanks to that one design.

"Can you recreate this?" Isabelle asked Gabriella hopefully, downloading a picture of Allegra in Oberon's iconic dress on Google Image. "The colour is perfect for my hair."

Gabriella bit her lip. It looked complicated with its

intricate beading and shimmery material. However, she couldn't disappoint her best friend. "Of course," she said assuredly. "Of course."

So, she had drawn countless sketches and sampled different fabrics, often working late into the night. She was determined to persevere until she was happy with the result. Even Lita had become involved, giving crucial advice when the material snagged or the stitches were uneven.

Finally, after hours of work, the aquamarine creation was complete and now hung on Gabriella's wardrobe door – a full-length figure-hugging sleeveless dress with a beaded bodice.

There was a final fitting to be done before sending her friend on her way, so she forced herself to leave the warm confines of her bed.

"Stand up there when you're ready," she instructed, pointing to the pile of magazines as she padded out to the bathroom.

I really need to invest in a podium, she thought, squirting some toothpaste on her brush.

"I'm ready, Gabby!" called Isabelle. "Hurry, okay? There's only so long a girl can balance on a pile of magazines."

Luca Jacob, soon to be husband of the beautiful Charlotte du Maurier, had his head over the new art brochure when Gabriella arrived at his mother's gallery. His blond hair gleamed in the ray of sunshine that streamed in from the skylight overhead. He really was gorgeous with his blue eyes and sallow skin.

"Hey," she said, dropping her bag by the desk. "Is that the new flyer?" She pointed to the colourful paper in his hand.

He nodded and circled a section of text on the back

28

page. "It needs to be edited," he said with a frown. "Who the hell wrote this trash? I specifically said to keep it short and sweet."

"That's a prototype, right?"

"Yeah."

"Then send it back." She typed her password into the Mac on the counter.

She was used to Luca by now. He was impatient and tough, but also loyal and fair. On her first day when she had entered his mother's gallery, unsure and nervous, they had liked each other instantly. Then over the months, he had mentored her and showed her the ropes. He was surprisingly good at his job as he had an amazing ability to sell without outwardly pressurising the client to buy. Gabriella learned many things from him and they had become firm friends.

"You want a coffee? I've just brewed some." He pointed to the machine. "I've got to leave soon. I'm meeting Charlotte for some sushi." He paused. "You're going tonight, right?"

He was referring to Celine's twenty-first birthday party which Victoria was hosting that evening. Magda had been stressed out all week about the champagne not arriving on time and the people who had not bothered to RSVP.

Gabriella nodded. "Celine emailed me a couple of weeks back. It feels like forever since I've seen her."

"Charlotte feels the same. L.A. is too far away."

"I can't believe that Victoria let her do that Art course. I was sure she'd end up at Harvard like the others."

"Nah," said Luca grinning. "Celine has Frank wrapped around her little finger. She had UCLA in the bag. Victoria had no chance."

"Two outta three ain't bad, right?" Gabriella smiled. "We sure as hell don't have attorneys in my family."

29

"I'd like to say the same," said Luca sighing, referring to his father, Christian Jacob, who was a partner at Joyce, Jacob and Firkin law firm.

Handsome and imposing, Christian resembled his son in many ways – both were tall with chiselled bone structure and sallow skin. However, when it came to personality, they were poles apart. Luca was like his artist mother, Tara – passionate and spirited. He lived life to the full and rarely thought about consequences. Christian, however, was rigid and haughty. He liked to be in control and couldn't handle his son's *laissez-faire* attitude towards life.

Luca's parents had met in the late eighties. Orphaned at a young age, Tara had lived with her strict aunt in Ireland until the age of seventeen. Then, she had moved to America, intent on starting a new life. Tara O'Sullivan, as she was then called, got a job as a waitress in an Italian restaurant. One evening, a young attorney called Christian Jacob ordered cannelloni and fell madly in love with the pretty waitress with the big blue eyes. He came to the restaurant every night until she agreed to go out with him. Then, after a few months, they eloped. Christian's upper-class French parents – Henri and Marcheline – were horrified at their only son's choice of bride. With her unconventional style and artistic ways, she was light years away from the suitable type of wife they had wanted for Christian.

Then rumours surfaced. Christian seemed to have an eye for the ladies and there was talk about Tara and her mentor, the artist Marcus Chensky. Still, despite all of this, the marriage survived, much to Luca's chagrin. It was no secret that he adored his mother and found his father cold and rigid. He also knew about his father's constant infidelity and couldn't understand why Tara stayed with him.

"It's dysfunctional, is what it is," he would say over and over again. "Leave him, Mom. Just do it."

But she didn't. Despite everything, she loved Christian.

Before becoming Tara's right-hand man at the gallery, Luca had played around, flitting from one college course to the next, never taking anything seriously. This had irked his father who was the product of a strict upbringing. His own father Henri would never have tolerated that kind of behaviour.

It was through Christian that Luca and Charlotte met. Fresh out of Harvard with a first-class degree and new ideas, she had been snapped up by his law firm.

After a few months, Christian had organised a partner's lunch and it was then that she had laid eyes on Luca and the rest was history. Christian adored Charlotte and was delighted about the upcoming wedding. She was, in his opinion, everything a woman should be. She was intelligent and refined – the perfect match for his son and heir.

Luca checked his cell phone before putting on his jacket. "That Russian guy, Kedinsky? He should call after three. He wants that bronze sculpture out back. Otherwise there's nothing to report."

"Great." She smiled. "I'll see you later."

He smiled back. "I'll be back in a couple of hours. Call me if you have any problems."

The day passed quickly. There were various customers ranging from French tourists to locals, all perusing the catalogue and taking their time absorbing each piece. She chatted amiably to each one, helping them if necessary and explaining the background of different sculptures. Luca had taught her well and her easy manner inspired one British man to buy a small watercolour of Central Park. Delighted, she wrote the title in the book and then marked it as 'Sold'.

Luca arrived back after three.

"I made a sale!" she blurted out in excitement. "Three hundred bucks!"

Luca whistled. "Not bad, Gabs. Did you write it in the book?"

She nodded. "I know it's not a fortune but hey …"

"Every sale counts." He nudged her playfully. "Although, try that sculpture over there the next time. It's twenty-five thousand dollars."

Gabriella made a face. "Yeah, yeah."

He smiled. "I called Mom and told her that we're finishing early today so we can head out to Long Island."

"Really? Did she mind?"

He shook his head. "Nah, Mom's great like that." He grinned. "It should be a good party."

"A perfect opportunity for you to get to know your new family." Gabriella grinned. "Not long now," she added, humming the 'Bridal March'.

Gabriella was referring to the wedding of the century, as Gabriella's mother Magda liked to call it. The minute Luca had proposed, Victoria had gone into overdrive, reserving the Four Seasons and booking the best string quartet that money could buy. Luca came from a prestigious New York family which had emigrated from Paris over a century before. Marcheline, Luca's grandmother, claimed that they were descended from the French aristocracy. They had properties all over New York, notably a huge apartment on the Upper East Side where the old lady lived since the death of her beloved husband, Henri. Luca ticked all the boxes for Charlotte's mother – breeding, money and, being the only heir, a promising inheritance. Sometimes his behaviour wasn't fitting. He tended to drink too much and liked to party. Still, that could be controlled once the ring was on his finger. Then her little Charlotte would be his wife and have access to all that wealth and position. It was all about getting the right publicity – nothing too extreme, but an announcement in the *Times* was a fait accompli.

Gabriella added two sugars to her coffee and Luca frowned.

"That stuff will kill you, Gabby," he chided. "You got to give it up."

She stuck out her tongue. "I like the taste and there's a lot worse I could be doing."

Luca sighed. "I can't save you."

He walked away and once again she marvelled at how two such good-looking people had found each other. Charlotte du Maurier, with her classic beauty, and Luca Jacob, who was simply irresistible.

Isabelle was on the couch watching a re-run of the *Oprah Winfrey Show* when Gabriella got home. Her friend's face was cleared of make-up and her hair was wet from the shower.

"How was the shoot?" asked Gabriella, dropping her bag on the floor.

"Awesome," she answered, stretching. "The photographer, Stan Beaumont? He's super-talented. He loved your dress, by the way. The colour really set off my hair."

"When will you get the prints?"

"I'm not sure. It depends how busy he is, I guess. Then I've got to email them to Paolo and I'm all set. I really want the perfume job, Gabby. I'm perfect for it!"

"You're still my plus-one later, right?" Gabriella poured herself a glass of orange juice and took a huge gulp.

"Sure I am," said Isabelle, yawning. "I'm pretty beat but there's no way I'm letting you go out there unchaperoned. We will stand tall against those Park Avenue bitches."

Gabriella smiled. Even though it was years since her experience with Caroline Ashley Hamilton, her words still cut deep. Oh, how she longed to meet those girls on a level playing field. She dreamed of meeting them dressed in couture with a Birkin swinging on her arm and the equivalent of the Hope diamond around her neck. Sure, it was materialistic and petty, but money was power. Everyone knew that.

"What time do we need to leave?" Isabelle stood up and switched off the TV. "I've got to curl my hair."

"Celine said to be there for eight thirty."

"I'm wearing that dress you made for the Christmas Ball. You know, the red one?"

Gabriella raised an eyebrow. "Then prepare to be scorned. They only rate French or Italian designers."

"Don't you worry about that," said Isabelle grinning. "We'll play them at their own game."

Gabriella blotted her lips on a piece of tissue and surveyed her appearance. She hadn't really changed over the years. Her nose was certainly too big for her face and she still carried a few extra pounds. She had accepted that she would never be skinny like Isabelle nor would people stop in the street to gape at her like they did with her best friend. Sure, she could diet all the time and reach her target weight, but it was impossible to resist Krispy Kremes and fries from McDonald's. She wasn't lucky like Isabelle who seemed to eat what she liked and never gain an ounce. What did her mother always say? Men prefer curves.

She stared at her reflection in the full-length mirror on the wall. Her black dress clung to her body, highlighting her best feature which was her tiny waist. All in all, she looked pretty okay – definitely better than in her pink ensemble all those years ago. The black colour gave her an air of sophistication. She was no longer a girl, she was a woman.

34

"Ready?" asked Isabelle, appearing in the door way. Her short red dress clashed gloriously with her Titian hair and her long legs seemed endless in her black heels.

Gabriella nodded.

It would do her good to get out. She had been working so hard of late. The restaurant was busier than ever after an excellent review in *The New Yorker* stating that the coq au vin was a must. Giselle had asked her to work extra shifts and then she had her thesis to finish. Luca was off to Dublin for his cousin's bachelor party, so Tara had asked her to man the gallery on her own next weekend. Craig, Luca's Irish cousin, was getting married in June and had asked Luca to be his best man.

She sighed. She could really do with a break. All work and no play was starting to take its toll. Her expression darkened. She was becoming like her mother.

ᨀ Chapter Three ᨂ

The du Maurier mansion looked the same as ever – large and imposing with a manicured garden and giant white pillars.

Isabelle whistled as they handed their coats to a young man in a black-and-white uniform.

"Classy," she said in awe.

Gabriella laughed. "It's pretty nice, I guess."

The young man also relieved them of the gift they had brought for Celine, adding it to a huge pile of gifts on a hall table.

They entered the drawing room which was crowded with people of all ages. A waiter with white gloves and a tray of champagne appeared and soon they were sipping flutes of Bollinger.

"What do Celine's parents do again?" asked Isabelle, placing her empty glass on the table and simultaneously grabbing a full one from a passing waiter.

"Frank, her dad, is an attorney but he has shares in the clothing brand too."

Gabriella glanced around the room and recognised Maurice, Celine's uncle: the CEO of Liberty Designs. He was standing by the fireplace with his wife Elena, a stick-thin dark-haired woman whose face shone from too much Botox.

Celine always talked about her aunt who spent her days at yoga and Pilates, spending the du Maurier money like water. "Momma hates her," she told Gabriella once. "She's so uptight."

Gabriella said nothing as privately she didn't think that Victoria was very different. Celine's mother never let her guard down and seemed adept at spending Frank's money efficiently. People in glasshouses and all that.

Celine appeared in a yellow dress, her blonde hair swept up into a chignon. Her skin was golden-brown from the California sun and her smile seemed whiter.

"Gabby!" she said affectionately, hugging her old friend close. "It's been so long. Thank God for Instagram."

Isabelle waited her turn and then kissed Celine's cheek. "Happy Birthday!" she said warmly. "We left your gift with the butler guy out front."

They had met briefly over the years due to their shared friendship with Gabriella. On the few nights they had encountered each other, they had clicked.

"You shouldn't have," said Celine, clinking her glass with theirs. "I've far too many gifts already. Most of them will be going straight back, that's for sure." She pointed discreetly to a frozen-faced woman in the corner. "That's Annabel Blythe Dalton, Momma's friend from bridge. She got me a pasta machine. I mean, I don't even cook pasta from a packet. Bruno cooks all my meals."

"Don't worry, we didn't get you any cooking utensils," Isabelle reassured her.

Charlotte appeared, looking as stunning as always in light-pink dress. A large diamond sparkled on her left hand and she looked radiant. "Can you believe my little sister is twenty-one?" she asked in her soft voice. "It's incredible."

Celine threw her arm around her older sister. "This is officially my favourite sibling ever."

"Oh?" Charlotte smiled.

"She got me tickets to the Coldplay gig at the Beacon next week. How awesome is that?"

"I got them at the office. They were complimentary," Charlotte explained. "Three tickets: one for me and Luca and, of course, one for the Birthday Girl here."

Isabelle gasped. "Now, that's a nice present. My life goal is to make out with the lead singer Chris Martin and inspire him to write a song about me." She closed her eyes dreamily. "Something with a red-haired theme. I'd be immortalised forever."

"I love the drummer," said Celine with a sigh. "I'm definitely going to try and get backstage."

Gabriella smiled warmly at Charlotte. "Not long until your wedding. Are you excited?"

"I'm too busy at the firm to be excited," she answered seriously. "I feel like I never switch off. We're working on a big case at the moment so I don't have time for wedding favours and flowers." She sighed. "Luca gets so bored with it all – my work, I mean."

Isabelle opened her purse and took out her iPhone. Accessing her emails, she shrieked. "*Gabby!* Stan sent some proofs. Holy shit, I look great!"

"She had a photo shoot today with Stan Beaumont," explained Gabriella to a bemused Charlotte and Celine. "For a big modelling contract."

"*Wow!*" said Celine, trying to see the small screen. "I'll bet you look awesome."

"The dress looks amazing," continued Isabelle, scrolling through. "Thanks, Gabby. I really owe you."

"Did you make that dress?" asked Celine, looking impressed. "That's unbelievable, Gabby."

Charlotte nodded in agreement. "I should have looked you up for my wedding gown," she said genuinely. "Vera Wang is proving demanding. I've had a million fittings already."

"It's got to be perfect," said Gabriella, patting her arm. "You're paying top dollar for the best. You couldn't go to your wedding wearing a nobody's couture."

"Momma would have a heart attack," agreed Celine.

"Still, I just don't have time for this bride stuff," said Charlotte. "Not with the Mackenzie case ..."

Isabelle brandished her phone at the group. "Hey, you guys. You've got to help me pick the best ones for my agent."

The four girls pored over her phone and gasped as each picture was better than the last.

"I love that one of you on the red carpet," said Charlotte. "I think that's definitely one to send."

Isabelle nodded. "Totally. I want to look like Allegra at the Oscars."

Celine scanned the room. "Where's Hugo, Char? He's supposed to be here by now."

"Hugo? God knows. He mentioned going sailing this afternoon, but I'm not sure."

Gabriella felt her cheeks redden. She hadn't seen him since that night in the rose garden. It was so long ago it was crazy to even think it mattered. Yet, she felt butterflies in her stomach at the thought of meeting him. How often she had scanned his Facebook profile, debating whether to send him a request? But she always bottled out. He was too old for her and probably didn't even remember her name.

"He'd better not miss my party." Celine looked fierce. "All he thinks about is that goddamn boat."

"Oh, he'll turn up," said Charlotte with a frown. "Momma's on a mission this time. She's not taking any risks."

"Risks?" echoed Isabelle. "About what?"

"Finding him a wife," said Celine, giggling. 'Now that Charlotte here is sorted, her next victim is our dear brother."

"Where's he working now?" asked Gabriella casually.

"Working?" said Celine incredulously. "Oh, he's not working. Quite the opposite. After graduation from Harvard he went AWOL. Disappeared to Europe with only a couple of emails home now and then."

"Momma went crazy," continued Charlotte, sipping her drink. "She had an interview with a firm in DC all set up. Now he's back and jobless so she's hell-bent on getting him settled."

"Europe sounds amazing," said Gabriella enviously. "I think he did the right thing."

"Yes, but not in Momma's eyes."

Maurice du Maurier appeared with a glass of scotch in his hand. He was taller than his older brother Frank but shared his dark hair and booming voice. When he had been offered the head position at Liberty Designs back in the eighties, he had jumped at the chance. Everyone had expected Frank to take over, being the heir and all. However, he had wanted a legal career and had opted out. This had been extremely fortuitous for Maurice as he had not been academic and had fewer options. Now, with the help of a cutting-edge team and a horde of advisors, the company was going from strength to strength.

"How's the Birthday Girl?" he said loudly, thumping Celine on the back. "Hard to believe you're twenty-one."

"Hi, Uncle Maurice," said Celine politely.

"How's L.A. going? You finished out there yet?" His face was red from too much alcohol and there was perspiration on his brow.

Celine shook her head. "One more year," she replied, backing away. "Then who knows?"

Charlotte smiled sweetly at her uncle. "Elena looks well," she said, referring to his wife. "Did she change her hair?"

"She's changed every part of her," Maurice said, swigging his drink. "I've paid for that plastic surgeon's new yacht, I'm telling you that for nothing." His attention shifted to Gabriella. "Now, who's this young lady?" he said, his eyes travelling up and down her body.

Gabriella blushed. "I'm Magda's daughter."

"I don't know who the hell that is, but no matter." He stared at her breasts. "Nice dress." Moving closer, he patted her bottom. "You're what I call a real woman. Not a stick insect like my wife over there."

Isabelle gasped. Gabriella stepped backwards, hot waves of mortification flooding her body.

Charlotte took Maurice's arm. "Let's take you back to Momma," she suggested smoothly. "Daddy's due home any minute and I know he wanted to discuss the catalogue for fall."

She led him away quickly.

Celine bit her lip. "Sorry about that," she said, "He's had far too much whiskey."

"Nothing to be sorry about," said Gabriella, brushing it off. "I'm just going to the ladies' room."

She exited the room through the side doors. The servants' restrooms were in the basement so she slipped down the back stairs. Minutes later, she splashed cold water on her face. Why did she feel like such an outsider? Would she ever fit in?

Luca was talking to Isabelle when she returned. His dark-blue suit was tailored perfectly to his long lithe body.

"Hey, Gabs," he said, smiling.

"Hey." She beamed at him. "Are your mom and dad here?"

Tara had mentioned earlier that she was thinking of popping in for drink. Privately, she thought that Luca's mother would bring a splash of colour to the party. Her flamboyant style and flaming red hair would lift the preferred bland pastels of the guests.

"Mom might be." Luca drained his whiskey. "Not Papa. He's too busy at work."

His handsome face looked dark for a moment and then regained its bright exterior.

"So, I hear that you're holding the fort at Mom's gallery while I go to Ireland."

Gabriella smiled. "I'll try not to sell any pieces at a discount."

"You're too soft with clients."

"I try not to be." She sipped her drink. "So, is your cousin excited about his bachelor weekend? Have you much planned?"

"Just a couple of things." He grinned.

"You guys are close, right?"

"Yeah, Craig's the best," he answered. "We shared a house together that time I went to school in Cork."

"School in Cork?" she repeated, confused.

"Sure, I did an English Master's a couple of years back. I've got to admit, I didn't finish it. Life got in the way." His face changed for a moment, a flash of desolation passing over his handsome features. Then, he took a deep breath and smiled again.

"Life?" she asked curiously, having seen his brief anguished look.

He waved his arm dismissively. "You know, liquor and women. Nothing serious. Craig was my roommate and we got really close. He was sweet on a girl called Samantha back then and now they're getting married."

"That's wonderful!" said Gabriella. "Are you looking forward to Dublin?"

Luca nodded.

"You'll have an awesome time," said Gabriella genuinely. "You need a break. You've been working so hard."

He smiled his heart-breaking smile and she blushed. "If you say so." He pointed to the doorway. "Hey, look! Hugo just arrived. The prodigal son has returned."

Gabriella inhaled sharply and turned around. There, in a dark-blue suit and white shirt, stood Hugo du Maurier.

Gabriella sipped her drink and kept her eyes cast down.

"Hey," said Hugo, joining the group. His dark hair was shorter but his blue eyes were still as unfathomable as ever. His tall frame suited his tailored Armani suit which was complimented by a crisp white shirt that was open at the neck.

Luca patted his back. "Watch your back tonight. Victoria has big plans for you."

"I heard." He smiled and Gabriella's heart began to thump. He looked far more relaxed than the last time they had met. Travelling must have suited him.

Isabelle held out her hand. "Hey there, I'm Zsa Zsa or Isabelle if you prefer."

He shook it politely. "Are you a friend of Celine's?"

"I guess. We met through Gabriella here."

His gaze fell on Gabriella and for a moment she couldn't breathe. "Hey, you," he said softy. "Nice dress."

She blushed. "Better than the last one, right?"

"I don't know about that." He moved closer. "Have you become a famous designer yet?"

She shook her head, touched that he had remembered. "I've got to graduate first. Just give me time."

"Graduate?"

"We go to Parson's," explained Isabelle. "That's where we met."

Hugo looked confused for a moment. "Parson's?" he repeated. "How did you …?"

"I got a scholarship," said Gabriella defensively. "I work part-time too. In a restaurant and at Tara's gallery."

Luca squeezed her arm. "She's my protégée."

Hugo regarded her with respect. "That's pretty cool."

"It's amazing. I've learned so much." Her eyes met his and she noticed that they were fringed with thick dark lashes.

Charlotte rejoined the group and Luca put his arm around her waist. "Do you want a drink?" he asked, kissing her neck.

"No, thanks," she replied. "I need to work in the morning."

"On a goddamn Sunday?" He pulled back immediately. "Jesus, Char!"

She reddened and hung her head. "Can we do this later? This is not the place."

Gabriella watched Luca down his whiskey and stride off to the bar for another.

Hugo kissed his sister's cheek. "You look great, Char. That ring is pretty eye-catching." Standing side by side with Charlotte, Gabriella could definitely see a close resemblance as they both had amazing bone structure and striking blue eyes.

"It's good to have you back," Charlotte said softly. "We missed you."

Hugo smiled. "It's good to be back but Europe was amazing. I lived in Berlin for three months and then Paris."

"Why did you come back?" asked Isabelle.

44

"I've got to get my life together," he said with a hint of regret. "Momma called me every day for the past month, demanding that I fly home. In the end, I caved."

Luca jerked his head. "There's a group of girls over there who haven't stopped pointing at you since you arrived. Especially the one in the green dress."

"That's Caroline Ashley Hamilton," said Celine, amused. "Be careful, Hugo. She's on a mission."

At midnight, they decided to call it a night. Isabelle had availed of the free champagne, but Gabriella had declined. For some reason, she didn't need or want alcohol. The adrenaline pumping through her veins had been stimulation enough. Plus she had a lunchtime shift at the restaurant the next day.

Of course, Caroline Ashley Hamilton had pigeon-holed Hugo for the rest of the evening, encouraged by a determined Victoria. It had been impossible to get near him after their brief conversation. Not that she stood a chance anyway. It was ridiculous to even think that someone like him would be interested in someone like her.

She wasn't proud of it, but when Isabelle had introduced herself to Hugo at the party, something had gripped her heart. How could he not be bowled over by her friend's beauty? She was like a goddess. Yet, he had been polite to Isabelle without flirting and then had turned his attention to her. Did that mean something?

Just as they were leaving, Caroline appeared in the hallway, her heels click-clacking on the marble tiles. Her blonde hair was curled and her short green dress sparkled in the lights.

"Gabriella!" she said in mock surprise. "Celine didn't mention that you were here."

Isabelle swung around straight away with narrowed eyes. "And you are?" she said icily.

"Oh, I'm Caroline Ashley Hamilton," she said haughtily. "Celine's best friend." She held out her hand. "Are you a friend of Gabriella's here?"

Isabelle pointedly kept her hands to herself. "I'm Isabelle Flynn." She raised her head proudly.

"Are you helping your mother out tonight, Gabriella?" asked Caroline. "Although, I doubt it in that outfit. Quite risqué for a maid."

"No." Gabriella's eyes flashed. "I was invited as a guest."

"Oh, you were, were you?" said Caroline, raising her eyebrows.

Isabelle glared at her. "Goodbye," she said pointedly.

"*Ciao!*" said Caroline with a knowing smile and walked off.

"She's a total bitch," said Isabelle with a look of disgust. "Just wait until we're really famous, Gabby. We'll eat girls like that for breakfast."

Gabriella took off her heels and winced. It was the next day and she had just finished a gruelling lunchtime shift at the restaurant. Lita was cooking a pork stew and had asked her to attend. She hadn't been home in weeks, what with work and school. Plus, her new business venture required lots of preparation and thought. Dress designs and fabrics filled her head constantly. She needed these graduation gowns to be the best ever. Then she could post pictures on her page and word would spread. All she needed was one person to take notice – one person who could catapult her into the big time.

Diego, her brother, was due with his kids and Teresa had promised to pop in after her shift at the store with her little girls. The small apartment would be filled with noise, laughter and love. Sure, they didn't have enough space around the old oak table, but it didn't matter. When Lita put the pot of stew in the centre, everyone just grabbed a plate and a fork. No one minded the lack of space or the mismatched crockery. It was natural and homely and comfortable, light years away from the stiff party she had attended the night before.

Gabriella frowned. Magda had been summoned by Victoria to oversee the clean-up so it was doubtful whether she would make it back in time. It was rare that she was forced to work on a Sunday. Now their family reunion would be incomplete.

Diego opened the door of the apartment with a big smile. "Gabby!" he said, pulling her into a big bear hug. "How are you?" His dark hair and bushy moustache made him look older than his thirty-seven years and he had developed an undeniable paunch in recent times. Still, he was a striking man with his dark-brown eyes and broad smile.

She kissed his cheek. "I'm good. Where's Lita?"

He pointed to the kitchen. "Finishing the rice. I offered to help but she told me to get outta there."

There was a delectable smell of plums coming from the kitchen. Lita had obviously added them to the pork stew. Gabriella inhaled the familiar smell of home and relaxed. It had been almost three weeks since her last visit. The last time they had broken bread together was for little Sophia's third birthday, Teresa's youngest child.

Gabriella adored her nieces: Penelope, or Penny as she was known, was eight and Sophia had just turned three. With their dark-brown curls and chocolate eyes, they resembled their mother Teresa. Penny wore glasses and always had her nose in a book. She was a serious child who stayed in the background. Gabriella had designed her white dress for her First Holy Communion the summer before. Lita had helped, of course, and the little girl had looked angelic.

Sophia was the opposite of her older sister as she loved to perform and sing. She adored the Disney princesses and had many of the costume dresses from the Disney Store. Decked out in Belle's yellow party dress, she would sing songs at the top of her lungs. Being three, she had limited language and often made up the words, but she could carry a melody and was hugely entertaining.

Diego had twin boys – Miguel and Salvador – who were both ten. Miguel was sporty and evidently the alpha twin. Salvador was bookish and loved when Lita would tell him stories of her childhood in Puerto Rico. Natalia, their mother, had long left. Unable to cope with two young boys, she had left her husband to care for them himself. Despite long hours at his auto-repair shop, Diego had done an admirable job of raising his sons. Lita had helped of course, but she was nearing eighty and found the twins boisterous and demanding.

Gabriella adored the children. She loved when they visited the apartment as they brought a vitality that only kids can bring. Noise and mess inevitably accompanied them, but no one minded.

"Is Mama back?" asked Gabriella, flopping on to the couch. "I can't believe that Her Majesty forced her to work on a Sunday."

"Not yet," said Teresa, walking into the sitting room. "I called her an hour ago and she said they were almost done."

Her older sister was simply beautiful with her dark hair

and bronzed skin. She looked almost identical to Gabriella except her nose was smaller and more refined. She was also slight in figure, unlike her curvy younger sister.

Sophia pulled at her mother's skirt and asked for an Oreo.

"Not before dinner, baby," she said, stroking her cheek. "Lita would kill me."

Teresa's husband Rico worked nights at a bottling plant and rarely made it to family events. This dinner was no different. They had met nine years before at a mutual friend's birthday party and married soon after. Gabriella had been flower girl at the ceremony. Gabriella often wondered what her sister saw in him. He was certainly handsome with his dark eyes and hair. Yet he seemed to have only two interests in life: baseball and beer.

Lita appeared, wiping her small hands on her apron. Her grey hair was wound into a chignon at the base of her neck and her small frame was clad in her habitual black.

"Gabby, *cariña*," she said, holding out her arms. "I've missed you."

Gabriella got up and hugged her grandmother, breathing in her familiar smell. She could feel her shoulder blades through the thin fabric of her dress. Age was certainly having an effect on her beloved *abuela* – there was no denying that she was shrinking.

"I've missed you too, Lita. I've just got to show you the orders on my Facebook page. Two dresses for graduation. Will you take a look at my designs?"

"Of course," said the old lady proudly. "I'm so glad you decided to put your talent to good use."

Diego cracked open a bottle of Bud. "Remember us when you're rich and famous."

Gabriella laughed. "We'll see."

Teresa came up behind her and began to braid her hair. "How's work going?" she asked.

"Busy. I had a shift at the restaurant today and it was just insane. The gallery is pretty crazy too. Luca is going to his cousin's bachelor party in Ireland next weekend so I'll be all alone."

"Make sure you don't neglect your studies," warned her older sister. "Remember how hard you worked."

"I won't," Gabriella assured her. "It will always come first."

Magda arrived home as they were finishing their coffee. Wearily, she undid her jacket and hung it on the rack. Gabriella jumped up immediately and offered her a chair. Lita disappeared into the kitchen to retrieve the plate of stew that she had kept for her daughter-in-law.

"You're late, Mama," said Teresa with a frown. "What took so long?"

Magda sighed. "Her Majesty gets bang for her buck. She insisted that I stay and serve dinner, having spent the day cleaning up after last night's party. My back aches from standing."

Diego poured his mother a glass of red wine and placed it on the table. "You shouldn't have to work on a Sunday," he said, shaking his head. "The next time she asks, you've got to say no, okay?"

Magda smiled sadly. "You know I can't do that. We rely on her. The best way is to say nothing and get on with it."

Diego snorted. "Rather you than me, Mama."

"Ah, she is good to us," said Magda loyally. "I rarely work on Sundays, you all know that."

"You look exhausted," said Teresa worriedly. "It is too much."

Gabriella rubbed her mother's shoulders and she let her head roll back in pleasure. "Thank you, *cariña*," she said, exhaling slowly. "That sure feels good."

Gabriella understood the aching muscles and exhaustion. She often felt like that after a busy evening at the restaurant. However, she was young and strong. Her mother simply wasn't able anymore.

"Did you see Celine today?" she asked, working out a taut knot at the base of her mother's neck.

"Why, sure. She was rounding up the gifts she wants to return. Frank is insisting that she stay on Long Island for the summer, but she wants to go to Europe like Hugo."

"Oh, how the other half live," said Teresa sardonically. "I've never been further than New Jersey."

"None of that matters," said Lita in her soft voice. "Happiness and family are what matters," Teresa. Look at how we love each other. Victoria du Maurier attaches importance to all the wrong things."

Gabriella continued to massage her mother's shoulders. Sure, she could see Lita's point, but money did make the world go round. Why couldn't she have both?

"Her Majesty has asked me to prepare for Frank's fiftieth birthday party. It will be a private dinner party for the family and a few guests." Magda sighed. "Bruno is in a flap already about the menu as she wants six courses."

"When?" asked Gabriella curiously.

"In a couple of weeks. She has invited Luca's family and some other important people I don't know."

"Wow, she'll put on a big show then."

Magda nodded. "She's flying in a crate of champagne from France. A special vintage. She really wants to impress Marcheline."

"Luca's *abuela*?"

"Yes, his grandmother."

Miguel came running into the room with Salvador in hot pursuit. "*Give me my goddamn Nintendo back!*"

"*Goddamn! Goddamn!*" chanted little Sophia, appearing behind them.

Lita gasped and made a Sign of the Cross. "*Sophia!*"

❦ Chapter Four ❧

A few days later, Gabriella was munching on a bagel as she watched New Yorkers rushing around through the large glass windows of the cafeteria at Parson's. She was sitting at her favourite pew which was a high stool facing out onto the street. It was from this favoured vista point that she observed people going to work and school, taxi drivers in their yellow cabs and the sea of commuters as they walked past in droves. Classes had finished and now she was just days away from submitting her thesis. Isabelle had promised to meet her but was running late, so she checked Twitter on her phone and scrolled down through the feed.

"Hey, beautiful," came a voice from behind her. She turned to find Noah Brennan, a fellow student at Parson's, smiling broadly, his backpack slung casually over his shoulder.

"Hey, you," she said, pulling an empty seat towards her. "Do you want to join me?"

He nodded and threw his bag on the floor. His baggy jeans looked like they would barely stay up and his Knicks shirt was loose on his slight frame. With his sandy-blonde hair and blue eyes, he looked like the cool member of a boyband or something you would see on a teen TV show. He, like Isabelle, had been in most of Gabriella's classes since first year, but it was only in junior year that they had become friends.

"You finished your thesis yet?" he asked.

She shrugged. "I'm almost there."

"You'll ace it like usual."

"I doubt that." She blushed.

Noah laughed. "Come on, Gabby. You've been like the model student since the beginning. Remember all those essays I copied off you in sophomore year? You made me look smart, I gotta say."

She sipped her coffee and grinned. "What are your plans for graduation? Todd Smith is having a party at his parents' place."

Noah made a face. "Todd? I bet he won't even have beer. I say we have our own party."

Gabriella said nothing. She didn't mind where she went. Parties had never really appealed to her as she hated being drunk and was always too busy with her part-time jobs to go too crazy. There was no way she could roll up to the restaurant, or the gallery for that matter, smelling of beer and looking like death warmed up.

"Where's Zsa Zsa?' asked Noah. "She goes to fewer classes than I do and that's saying something."

"Who knows? She promised that she'd meet me for a bagel, but it's a no-show."

Noah fiddled with a rubber band on his wrist. His sallow skin turned slightly red and he stared at his sneakers for a moment before clearing his throat. "So, um, I was wondering if you'd like to, um, go to the movies or something next Saturday …"

Gabriella, who was tweeting Teresa, wasn't concentrating. "Say again?"

Noah coughed. "I was asking you on a date."

Her head shot up. "A date?"

"Why, sure. The movies or whatever." He reddened again. "Unless you don't want to ..."

She paused and sipped her coffee once more. This wasn't the first time Noah had tried to initiate something romantic – he had tried to kiss her at a Frat party once – but she had always brushed it off. Why would he be interested in her when Isabelle was around?

His face reddened even more as he waited for a reply.

"Sure," she said eventually. "I'd love to go to the movies. Pick me up at the gallery after six."

He visibly relaxed and smiled broadly. "I might even take you for pizza."

"Cool," she said with a laugh, "but I get to choose the movie, okay?"

Saturday morning at the gallery was as busy as usual. Two prospective buyers called about a sculpture which required lots of talking and persuasion. In the end, neither of them bought anything. Then the inbox was full of emails regarding a small gallery Tara was planning to open in London. She was negotiating with a company in Canary Wharf who had a small space to sell. As yet, the price was too high and Tara was playing hardball. If she was going to crack Europe, she didn't want it to fail.

It was almost noon before Gabriella knew it. Pouring a cup of coffee, she added sugar and stirred. Luca's disapproving face appeared in her mind's eye – he hated when she added sugar to coffee – and she smiled. He had left for Dublin the day before in tearing spirits, determined to party like never before. Dublin was a vibrant city and a bachelor party was the ideal time to let loose. Plus, Charlotte's disapproval would be avoided as she was staying in New York.

His return flight was booked for Sunday as he had the Coldplay concert on Monday evening. When Charlotte had told him about the tickets, he had groaned. "I can't sit through that," he complained. "All that mushy heartfelt stuff? Can't you take a girlfriend instead?"

Cue a huge fight and Charlotte complaining that they rarely spent quality time together anymore. In the end, he gave in.

The door pinged and Tara herself appeared, striking in a yellow kaftan and silver sandals. Her long red hair was piled on top of her head, huge hoop earrings dangled from her ears and her blue eyes were painted with silver shadow.

"Morning, Gabby," she said, sweeping into the office. Her accent was American mixed with an Irish lilt. "Any word from my son?"

"Just a few photos on Instagram," replied Gabriella.

Gabriella activated her phone and leaned over the desk to show Tara a picture of Luca wearing a green hat and drinking a pint of Guinness.

"Oh look, that's Craig on his right," said Tara, pointing to a handsome young man with a bottle of beer in his hand. "He's a cousin from my side, you know. I'm so glad he's getting married to Samantha. She's a sweet girl. I met them in Cork a couple of years back, when Luca was at school there. Sam cooked dinner one night and we all hung out."

Gabriella nodded. "That's where he met Craig, right? They lived together?"

Tara nodded, her bracelets jangling as she flicked through the pages of the diary. "Luca was so different then," she reflected. "He was so, I don't know, aimless or something. He hooked up with this unsuitable girl who broke his heart and flunked his degree. It was a bad time for him."

"A girl broke *his* heart?" Gabriella looked incredulous. "But he's so lovely!"

Tara nodded. "I know, right? He was such a player, going from girl to girl. We could never keep track. Then suddenly, he fell hard for this girl called Lydia who frankly treated him like dirt." Her face darkened. "I told him to stay away from her but he didn't listen. I knew she was trouble."

"What happened?" Gabriella was intrigued. She thought someone like Luca, with his model looks and charm, could have anyone he wanted.

"Oh, she had a boyfriend yet insisted on stringing my son along. Then she took off to Paris and left him heartbroken. He came back to New York and pretty much pined for her. In the end, I had to push him to do a night course and help me here. It was the best move as he got his life back together, met Charlotte and is now a different guy."

"Poor Luca," said Gabriella, shaking her head. "I would never have thought. At least it's all forgotten about now, right?"

Tara bit her lip. "Well, I hope so. You see, Lydia, that girl, she's Samantha's best friend. She's also chief bridesmaid ..."

"And Luca's the best man," finished Gabriella, comprehension dawning. "That could be awkward."

Tara shook her head fervently. "It will be okay. He has Charlotte now and she's miles better. So what if he sees that girl again? He's totally over it."

The door pinged and a small Japanese man appeared.

"Tara," he said, bowing his head. "You free for talking?"

"You got it," she said, flashing her megawatt smile. "Just follow me into the office."

Gabriella winked at her boss. Mr. Fukui was a big client – he owned five hotels in Tokyo and was interested in purchasing sculptures for the foyer of each one. Tara stood to make a fortune if he committed.

"I'll bring coffee," she said and mouthed "Good luck!" as Tara closed the door.

She crossed her fingers for her boss. This sale would be a huge help for the London project.

Mr. Fukui left an hour later, having purchased the sculptures.

Tara kissed Gabriella's cheek and beamed. "Today is a good day," she said, clapping her hands in delight. "Mr. Fukui is just what we need!" Grabbing her Mulberry bag, she checked her phone. "I'll be back before six. Call me if you need me."

The door slammed shut. Gabriella fished a bagel out of her bag and took a big bite. It was past three and she hadn't eaten since breakfast. The only cheese in the refrigerator that morning had been Emmental, so she had smeared the rounded bread with mustard and shoved a slice inside. Humming a tune, she opened Instagram again. There was a new post: Luca had uploaded a picture of himself standing next to a sports car with a bottle of champagne and a small trophy with the caption #champion.

The door pinged and she hurriedly hid her sandwich under a pile of papers. Looking up, she nearly fell backwards. There, standing by a painting of Central Park, was Hugo du Maurier.

"Hey," he said with a smile.

"Hey," she answered blushing. "Can I help you?"

He walked slowly towards her, his hands in his pockets. His dark-blue chinos and navy sweater brought out the azure of his eyes.

She swallowed the piece of bagel in her mouth and took a deep breath.

"I was in the neighbourhood so I thought I'd call in."

"Sure, sure." She flicked her hair. "You looking to buy?"

He smiled again. "No, it's cool. I'm pretty broke after my trip."

He reached out and picked up the brochure that Luca had ratified a few days before. A lock of dark hair fell over his eye and she longed to brush it away. He traced his finger around the image on the front – a sculpture of a man with his head in his hands.

"It's been busy today," she said nervously. "We sold some pieces to a Japanese guy and Tara's really happy."

He said nothing. Instead, he continued to fiddle with the brochure, his head bowed.

"Um, Luca seems to be having a blast. He keeps posting pictures on Instagram." She felt like the words were tumbling out of her mouth.

"That's cool." He looked up and focused on her face. "You've got ..." Reaching out, he wiped something from her chin with one slow stroke. "Um, mustard, I guess?"

She stepped backwards, mortified. How typical that she would have food on her face! Her cheeks reddened. "Oh, thanks. I didn't know. How about the rest?"

He watched her in amusement. "You're all set."

Gabriella bit her lip. This had to be the weirdest conversation ever. He wasn't looking to buy yet he didn't seem in a hurry to leave.

"So, what time do you finish?" he asked suddenly.

"At six." She eyed him warily.

"Do you want to go for a drink or something?" he asked casually, running his fingers through his hair.

She cursed silently. Noah was due to pick her up for their date. "I can't. I have plans."

"Hey, no problem," he said lightly. "Some other time."

"Sure, some other time."

He stood up straight. "So, I'll see you around." His eyes locked with hers.

"I guess." She felt her chest heave.

He turned and walked away, his hands back in his pockets.

Gabriella exhaled slowly. Did that actually happen? Hugo du Maurier had called in and asked her out. Was it for real?

Her phone pinged and she accessed the message. It was from Noah, reminding her of their date.

As if she could forget. The date she had agreed to had prevented her from having a drink with Hugo du Maurier.

Immediately she felt guilty. It wasn't Noah's fault. He had asked her first and she never broke her word. Best to put Hugo out of her mind.

Noah picked her up as promised after work and they went to see the new *Spiderman* movie. Gabriella, despite only having a limited knowledge of comics and superheroes, enjoyed it. Happily, she munched on popcorn and sipped her Coke as Andrew Garfield jumped from skyscraper to skyscraper, shooting web from his wrist. Noah, who was a huge Marvel fan, was enthralled and kept whispering fan theories in her ear.

When the movie ended, they emerged out onto the street.

"So, do you want to get pizza?" he asked, linking arms. "I know a great place two blocks down."

"I'm pretty full after my popcorn," she said.

"Hey, come on," he said with a puppy-dog look. "You've got to give a guy a chance. Let me share a pepperoni with you."

She relented. "Oh, okay. Let's get some pizza."

The street was full of people as they meandered down the pavement. Women in sparkly dresses and expensive heels travelled in packs, their designer clutch bags in one hand and their cell phones in the other. An old woman sat huddled near a door, drinking from a bottle concealed in a brown-paper bag. Her small wizened eyes connected with Gabriella's for a moment before she turned away and started shouting obscenities at a man in a suit who was exiting a yellow cab. It was noisy and vibrant and quintessential New York.

"Did Zsa Zsa hear about that modelling gig yet?" asked Noah, guiding her through a pack of Spanish tourists.

"Not yet," she answered. "She checks her cell a million times a day. I mean, I keep telling her to keep her options open, but she's obsessed."

"I figure she'll get it," he mused. "I mean, she's got it going down – the red hair, the replica dress you made – she's exactly what they're looking for."

They stopped outside a small pizzeria. "After you," said Noah, holding open the door. "This place has the best calzone in the city."

She smiled and entered the busy room. The smell of oregano hit her immediately and, surprisingly, she felt hungry again. So much for her diet. She had vowed to lose at least seven pounds before graduation.

"*Buona sera*!" said a small Italian man, brandishing menus. "Follow me."

Noah walked her home, despite her insistence that she could manage.

"Hey, you've got to give a guy a chance," he repeated with a wink.

She felt uneasy. Sure, he had behaved like the perfect

gentleman all evening but she sensed that he was building up to something. Noah was nice and sweet and he wasn't bad-looking with his sandy-coloured hair and cheeky grin. Isabelle always teased her about him but she brushed it aside. She didn't have time for boyfriends and romance as she had other goals.

Hugo flashed through her mind but she pushed his image away. Now that was surreal and totally unattainable. Compared to Noah, he was a fantasy. She wasn't stupid enough to even dream that she had a chance. *But he called in to see you at the gallery,* said a voice inside her head. *He asked you out.* She shook her head and refused to even analyse it. Men like Hugo didn't bother with girls like her. Everyone knew that. Instead, they married trophy wives like Caroline Ashley Hamilton – girls with breeding and money. Certainly not an immigrant girl from the Bronx.

They reached her door and she took her key from her pocket.

"Thanks a lot for tonight," she said genuinely. "Who knew that *Spiderman* had such emotional depth? I shed a tear at the end."

Noah laughed. "I'm glad you liked it."

"Well, I'll see you around, I guess." She turned to unlock the door but he grabbed her arm.

"Hey!" he said, pulling her back. "Aren't you going to invite me in?"

Her brown eyes widened. "Zsa Zsa might be home ..."

"She's not," he said. "I just saw a picture of her on Instagram at a party in Harlem." "Really?"

"Yes, really. She's having a blast." He let go of her arm and moved closer. "I was hoping that you and me could, you know, hang out for a while."

Gabriella's heart began to thump loudly. His face was

inches from her own and she could feel his other arm stealing around her waist.

Throughout the years, she had not had much experience with the opposite sex. Lack of self-confidence was a factor and, of course, her busy schedule. A few kisses here and there was the extent of her expertise, although Brad Munroe had almost got to second base at senior prom. However, despite her naiveté, she could tell that Noah had intentions. Two seconds later, she was proved right when his lips locked with hers. He tasted of pepperoni and beer. His hand grasped her neck and pulled her closer, angling his face so as to deepen his kiss. His tongue flickered over her lips, urging them to open. Tilting her head backwards, she let him take control. It felt nice – pleasant, almost. Gently, he manoeuvred her backwards so that she was leaning against the wall. Then his other arm travelled downwards, cupping her breast and squeezing it.

"Oh!" she said, jumping. "What are you doing?"

He kissed her cheeks and nose. "Do you like it?" he said huskily. His hand moved around to her back and was soon cupping her bottom.

"Noah!" she said, yanking it away. "What's wrong with just making out?"

"We *are* just making out," he said, kissing her again. "What's the problem?"

She allowed him to kiss her but it didn't feel right. Why couldn't she just let go and enjoy it? As his hand roamed her body, she felt insecure that he would deem her fat and unattractive. She had big breasts and a sizable behind. When he touched her like that, it made her feel uncomfortable.

She put her hands on his chest and pushed him backwards. "I've got to go," she said quietly. "I have an early shift at the restaurant tomorrow."

His face fell. "Are you for real?"

She nodded. "Thanks for a lovely evening. I had a really good time."

She opened the door and walked inside, leaving a bemused Noah on the step. He was nice and perfect boyfriend material. Why then did she feel like she was kissing a friend?

The next morning she made pancakes for breakfast and forced Isabelle to join her.

"Ugh, I had way too many cocktails last night," complained her friend, taking a long swig of juice from the carton. "I don't remember getting back here, Gabby. Imagine that?"

Gabriella tipped two pancakes onto a plate and handed Isabelle the maple syrup. "Eat something," she said, adding more batter to the pan. "You'll feel better."

The sun was beating in the skylight of their small kitchen. Summer was well and truly on its way. The trees were green and full again, rejuvenated after the harsh snow of the New York winter.

"So, how was your date?"

Gabriella shrugged. "It was cool. We went to see a movie and then we had pizza."

"And?"

"He kissed me."

Isabelle clapped her hands together. "*And?*"

"He really went for it. I mean, touching me and everything."

"So?" Isabelle looked puzzled. "What did you expect?"

"I guess I'm not used to it. I pushed him away and came upstairs." Her brown eyes looked troubled. "Do you think I'm frigid?"

Isabelle laughed loudly. "Hell, no. He's just not the one

for you. If it feels awkward with a guy, then it's not meant to be."

"You think?"

"I think." She smeared some butter on her pancake. "Although you could play the field a bit, Gabby. You're too innocent. All work and no play is not a good idea."

"Play the field?" Gabriella repeated. "It's not that easy to meet guys, Zsa Zsa. I don't look like you."

"Looks have nothing to do with it. It's confidence – your aura. If you believe that you're a goddess, everyone else will think so too."

"Sure they will," scoffed Gabriella, putting sugar in her coffee.

"They *will*," insisted Isabelle. "People are attracted to positivity. Believe in yourself and others will too."

Gabriella chewed on her breakfast and watched her friend pour a generous second helping of syrup onto her plate. Maybe she was right. Maybe the problem lay with her own sense of self. She needed to play the field. Maybe Noah was the right path. Maybe if she gave him another chance ... he had texted three times already asking if she was okay. He was good and kind and they shared a lot of interests.

"Did you grill some bacon?" asked Isabelle, finishing the juice carton. "My appetite has come back."

Gabriella shook her head. "We're all out. Sorry."

"*Awww!*" Her friend moaned. "I can't eat pancakes and syrup without bacon."

Gabriella laughed. "Do you want me to go to the store?"

Isabelle shook her head. "I'll survive, I guess. Now, tell me all about the kiss. Every detail."

Miles away on Long island, Victoria du Maurier speared a piece of watermelon with her fork and chewed it methodically.

Her breakfast never varied – a bowl of fresh fruit, ice cold Evian and a small portion of fresh muesli with a dollop of fat-free yoghurt. The *Times* lay on the starched white tablecloth, waiting to be read by Frank, her husband.

Charlotte was due to call as Luca was still in Ireland. His flight was due in that night so she had suggested that her eldest daughter come over for the day. She rarely saw her anymore due to the huge workload at the office. She respected and admired her work ethic – after all, it was the reason for her success – however, sometimes she wished Charlotte would relax a bit. She barely had time to organise her own wedding. Thank the Lord she had it under control herself.

The Four Seasons in downtown Manhattan was the chosen venue. She had contemplated the Grand Ballroom at the Plaza, but Charlotte had preferred the Greenwich Ballroom of the other hotel. The dress was purchased and hanging in the spare room and the guest list was days away from completion. It was crucial that no one important be left out. This had to be the greatest society wedding of the year.

"Hey, Momma," came Celine's voice from behind her head. Her youngest child looked pretty in a yellow sundress and strappy white sandals. Taking a seat on the right of the large table, she took a croissant from the basket and spooned some honey on top. Taking a big bite, she groaned. "That sure tastes good."

Victoria pursed her lips. "You know you shouldn't eat that. It will go straight to your hips."

"I don't care," said Celine with her mouth full. "It's worth it."

Frank du Maurier arrived next.

Maria, a young Hispanic maid, appeared and he held out a cup. "Lots of coffee for me," he boomed, "and bring me some eggs and bacon."

"Of course, sir," she said, pouring him some coffee and then hurrying out.

"Eggs and bacon, Frank?"

"Sure, Vic. It's Sunday for Chrissake." He grabbed the *Times* and opened it. "Look at the goddamn Dow Flynn. What the hell?"

Celine refused coffee and opted for juice instead. "So, I have this lunch later, with the guys from the equestrian club. Can I borrow the BMW?"

Victoria shook her head. "You're not good with a stick, honey pie. Get Manuel to drive you."

"Aw, Momma, I want to practise. Everyone in L.A. has a car." She turned to Frank. "Daddy, can I borrow your car?"

"Sure, baby, you take what you want."

Victoria scowled and sipped her water. Why did he undermine her so? He spoiled Celine far too much. She found her daughter to be headstrong most of the time and he just indulged that behaviour.

"Have you seen Hugo this morning?" she asked her husband as Maria tentatively placed a white china plate with two eggs and three slices of bacon on the table.

Frank shook his head. "He got in late. He said he was going sailing today." He buttered a slice of toast and took a bite. "Maria!" he called, spitting it out into his napkin. "This toast is cold! What does a guy have to do around here to get hot toast?"

Maria reddened and, grabbing the silver toast rack, scurried away in the direction of the kitchen.

Victoria frowned. "We've got to do something with him, Frank. He's back two weeks now and has no intention of finding a job. He's almost twenty-five. Land sakes alive, Charlotte is only a year older and she's trying to make partner."

Frank took a gulp of coffee. "I'll make some calls. Harvey might have something for him at the Boston office."

"Don't forget," his wife warned.

"You got it."

"Why don't you get him a job at your firm, Daddy?" asked Celine curiously.

Frank shook his head. "It's better that he begin at the bottom in a firm where the du Maurier name means nothing. If he worked at our place, he would always be seen as my son. I said the same to Charlotte when she graduated and look at her now! She's practically partner at Joyce, Jacob and Firkin." He shook the newspaper. "She got there without any help from me. That's the right way."

Maria arrived with a fresh rack of toast and placed it on the table in front of him.

"That looks great," he said smiling at her. "Now some jelly and I'm all set."

"Try not to eat it all," said Victoria. "Frank, we talked about this. You need to cut down on refined flour."

Celine winked at her father. "Have a croissant, Daddy. They're just too good."

"Celine!" Her mother glared at her.

Frank laughed. "I'm good, baby. I don't wanna be unhealthy now."

Victoria pursed her lips.

❧ Chapter Five ❧

Noah called that evening. Gabriella's heart started to thump when she saw his name flashing on her phone. After a long walk and a chat with Lita, she had decided to give their relationship a try.

The old lady had listened and said, "Passionate, fiery love destroys, Gabby. Gentle love endures."

Even Isabelle had been adamant. "You'll die an old maid, Gabby. You've got to get out there and break a few hearts."

Taking a deep breath, she answered the phone. "Hey, you."

"Hey, Gabs. How you doin'?" His tone was guarded.

"I'm doing good. What you up to?"

"Oh, nothing. Trying to write a reference section and can't."

"That's the worst part of any assignment," she said, laughing. "Mine took forever."

There was a pause.

"So, do you want to go for a coffee later? The usual place?"

She could sense his trepidation.

"Why, sure." She bit her lip. "I've got to do a fitting with those girls for the graduation dresses but I'm free after four."

"Can I pick you up?"

"I can meet you there …"

"Let me pick you up."

"Oh, okay."

"See you later then."

"See you."

She threw the phone on the bed.

The two dresses she had designed for her classmates hung by the window, waiting for the final fitting before completion. She really didn't have time for coffee. He would probably suggest pizza after that and she had so much to do.

Noah called just after four, his hands shoved deep in his baggy jeans pockets. His sandy-coloured hair looked newly washed and he smelt of a musky cologne.

"Have fun, you two!" called Isabelle from the kitchen. She winked at Gabriella who glared at her.

The door slammed shut.

The coffee house they frequented was on the corner of 7th Avenue. The barista, a Caribbean woman in her forties, took their order and the machine hissed as she prepared their drinks. The small tables inside were full. The clientele ranged from students to bankers. Sunday was a popular day to go out for a coffee and so they were forced to sit outside on the pavement.

"This sidewalk is too small for tables," said Gabriella, squeezing into her seat.

Noah nodded. "So, my dad got tickets to Coldplay tomorrow night. They're playing at the Beacon."

Gabriella clapped her hands together. "Wow, lucky you! I love that band. My friend Celine is going too. Send me selfies."

Noah blushed. "Well, I got two tickets and I figured …"

"Are you serious?" She squealed in delight. "I'd love to go! Oh my God, that's awesome."

He visibly relaxed. "Women dig that Chris Martin guy, right? The singer?"

"Totally," she said fervently. "He's such a poet. Oh, Noah, this is so cool. I've just got to text Zsa Zsa."

He watched her type furiously, a lock of her dark-brown hair hanging over her face. She didn't need to know that his dad knew nothing about the concert. She didn't need to know that he had worked seven shifts in a row at Walmart to earn enough to buy the tickets. He knew that Coldplay were her favourite band and had been planning this for months. Gabriella had caught his eye from day one. He had noticed her straight away, with her dark looks and studious demeanour. She didn't go out and get wasted like the other girls. She didn't wear revealing clothes nor did she try to be cool all the time. She was real.

Isabelle knew how he felt and she had told him to go for it months before. It had taken him months to work up the courage – something always got in the way. Gabriella was either working or had a deadline or was making clothes. It was only when they entered their final month of college that he realised he had to act.

Kissing her had been everything he had imagined and more. He didn't like stick-thin girls who constantly watched what they ate. Gabriella was curvy and sexy and just how a woman should be. She often lamented the fact that she was on the bigger side and he didn't know why. She was perfect to him.

She was a descendant of immigrants, forced to leave their homeland in search of a better life. With his Irish ancestry and distant family still living in Donegal, he came from a similar background. Sure, he was a New Yorker, but he didn't feel like he had definite roots entrenched on American soil. Gabriella felt the same – he could tell that the minute he met her.

"What can I get you?" asked a young waitress with a pen in her ear.

"A mocha for me," said Gabriella, smiling from ear to ear. Isabelle had just texted back with green-faced emojis and a message saying #sickwithjealousy.

Noah ordered the same and fiddled with the sugar dispenser.

"Oh, would you mind if I text Celine?" said Gabriella. "We could hook up at the gig."

He opened his mouth to discourage her, but something stopped him. Insisting that they be alone might freak her out. Plus, they had assigned seats so the most time they would have to spend with her friends would be during the interval.

"Sure," he said, forcing a smile. "Whatever you like."

"Cool." She beamed at him.

"Say all of that again."

Luca's tone was low and controlled but Charlotte knew he was furious. She had been putting off the call all day. He had arrived back late from Dublin the night before, tired and hungover. What followed was a bad mood that typically lasted a couple of days.

"Well, Christian called and said that all the juniors have to work late tonight as the Mackenzie case is coming to a head ... so I can't go to Coldplay ..."

"Papa snaps his fingers and you run, is that how it is?"

"He's my boss, Luca. I've got to do what he says. Do you want me to make partner?"

"Not particularly, no."

"Are you serious?"

"Yes, I'm serious. I barely see you as it is. Now you're bailing on me. I don't even want to go to that goddamn concert."

"Oh, you've got to go. Celine can't go alone. Daddy would freak out."

He made a '*pah*' sound. "She's twenty-one years old, for Christ's sake. What does he think she gets up to in L.A.? Sleepovers and makeovers with her little friends?"

"You know how protective he is …"

"Then make *him* go. I'm sure he'd love it."

"Luca, you're being childish. This is so out of my control. Please go! Please. Do it for me, okay?"

There was a pause. "Fine. I'll go, but it's only for you."

"Thanks, baby. I love you."

There was another pause and Charlotte felt her heart thump.

"I love you, too." The line went dead.

The Beacon Theatre on Broadway was an old building on the Upper West Side of Manhattan. It had retained its old-world ornate look and with its rows of seats offered an intimate viewing experience for an audience.

Gabriella had worn her best dress for the occasion: a dark-pink dress that accentuated her small waist. Isabelle had helped her to curl her thick hair and pin it up at the side. Then, she had applied her make-up which was subtle and becoming with dark-brown tones giving a smoky look to her eyes.

"If you meet Chris Martin tonight he won't be able to resist," said Isabelle and Gabriella laughed.

"I'm the total opposite to his wife," she said, shaking her head. "I don't think he goes for busty Latinas."

"Now that they have 'uncoupled' or whatever, you're in with a shot."

Gabriella beamed at Noah as they waited in line. "I'm so excited," she enthused. "I've never seen them live. Thanks again, Noah."

He took her hand in his and squeezed it. She resisted the urge to pull back. Lita had warned her to thaw out a little. Still, it felt strange. It made them look like a couple. Sure, he looked nice in his navy jeans and purple hoodie. It's just that the spark was missing. Maybe there was no such thing? Maybe she had unrealistic expectations of men, stemming from watching too many romantic comedies on TV. Maybe this frisson, this bolt of lightning, didn't exist after all.

Suddenly the line began to move and she forgot everything else. "We're going in!"

He gazed at her excited face and felt ten feet tall. Working all those extra shifts had been worth it.

"Gabby!" came a voice from behind them.

Gabriella whipped around to see Celine barging through the crowd towards her. Her friend looked chic in torn jeans, a T-shirt with a picture of Shakespeare on the front and Doc Marten boots. Her blonde hair was braided at the sides and pinned up. Black kohl circled her eyes and hoop earrings dangled from her ears.

"Wow, you look amazing!" said Gabriella genuinely. "Did Victoria see you dressed like that?"

Celine shook her head. "God, no. She'd have a heart attack." She laughed. "This is how I dress in L.A. Pretty cool, huh?"

Luca emerged from the crowd behind her, his tall imposing beauty stopping women in their tracks. Dressed casually in jeans and a T-shirt, he looked younger than his twenty-six years.

74

"Hey, Gabby," he said, kissing her cheek. "You look nice." He turned to Noah. "Hey, I'm Luca."

They shook hands and Celine's hand flew to her mouth. "Oh, excuse my rudeness. I'm Celine."

Noah smiled shyly. "Good to meet you."

"Where's Charlotte?" asked Gabriella, looking around. "We've got to get moving. I can't wait for it to start!"

"She couldn't come," said Celine with a sigh. "Too much work at the office."

"She *wouldn't* come," corrected Luca bitterly. "There's a difference."

"So, you guys have a spare ticket?" Gabriella jumped up and down. "Zsa Zsa would love it! Can I buy it off you or something? She could be here in thirty minutes."

Luca shook his head. "No spare, Gabs. We gave it away."

"You did?"

"He should be right here," continued Celine, glancing around.

"Who?" Gabriella's gaze shifted to the crowd and widened when she saw Hugo du Maurier strolling towards them.

He smiled as he approached.

"Hey, you guys," he said to the group. "Sorry I took so long."

Celine pulled three tickets from her bag. "Okay, let's go." She joined the line and started to move towards the entrance.

Noah squeezed Gabriella's hand tightly, but she didn't notice.

Her mind was reeling. She certainly hadn't expected to see Hugo like this. He looked amazing in his navy sweater and dark-blue jeans. Luca was telling a story and every now and then, Hugo would laugh, his handsome face relaxed and happy. In a daze, she handed over her ticket and waited patiently for the others.

Noah leaned over and whispered, "I need to use the rest room. Back in a second."

"Okay," said Gabriella absentmindedly.

Celine joined her as she waited for Luca and Hugo.

"See you afterwards?" she asked, reapplying lip-gloss. "We could get a beer or something?"

Gabriella nodded. "Sure. Meet you out front."

The boys appeared, having handed over their tickets.

Luca slung his arm around Celine's shoulders. "The things I do for my favourite sister-in-law."

"I'm your only sister-in-law," she answered drily. "Who knows? You might even enjoy it."

Hugo moved closer to Gabriella. "So, are you a fan?"

"Absolutely," she said, blushing. "I listen to their music all the time."

"And your boyfriend?"

She went a deeper shade of red. "Oh, he's not my boyfriend. We're just, you know, hanging out."

"Hanging out? Is that what you kids call it now?" His eyes crinkled in amusement.

She bristled. She didn't want him to think of her as a kid. "No, we're not, you know, doing that."

He raised an eyebrow. "Doing what?"

"At least, it's not romantic," she continued, flustered. "At least, not for me."

He regarded her thoughtfully. "So, you don't like romantic?"

"No, I didn't mean that," she said. "I love romance. It's just ..."

He put his fingers to his lips and she stopped talking. "You're not in love."

Her eyes burned as she shook her head. "No."

"No," he repeated softly.

"Okay, you guys, let's make a move," Noah's voice interrupted the moment.

Gabriella jumped. Hugo pulled back immediately and melted into the background.

Before Gabriella knew it, she was being led towards her seat.

The band bounded onto the stage and the auditorium filled with guitar twangs and harmonious chants as they belted out old and new hits. Soon she forgot all about her encounter with Hugo and allowed herself to be swept away by the music. 'Viva La Vida' was the highlight, its upbeat sounds bordering on euphoric.

Noah watched her enraptured face as she swayed to the music. Maybe she would let him take her home and actually let him come upstairs this time. He longed to reach out and touch her neck, but he held back. He had to take it slowly. Otherwise she would bolt and he would be back in the Friend Zone.

Celine was talking animatedly to Luca when they emerged onto the street. Her bracelets jangled as she gesticulated dramatically, her cheeks flushed. Hugo was lounging up against the wall, texting someone on his iPhone.

"Hey!" said Gabby, running up. "How awesome was that?"

"As Momma would say: *Jesus H. Christ!*" Celine laughed. "I'll never forget it."

"Luca?" Gabriella turned towards him. "Are you converted?"

"Nah," he said, shaking his head. "Give me Calvin Harris any day."

Noah rubbed Gabriella's arm and pulled her away gently. "So, will we get some pizza or something?" he asked in an undertone.

She shook her head. "I think these guys want to get a drink someplace. Let's join them for a while."

He forced himself to say nothing. "Sure, sure. If that's what you want."

"Hugo! We're going for a beer. Come on!" Celine gestured to her brother who was still texting furiously on his phone.

He waved her away. "I'll be right there."

"We're just going around the corner on Broadway. It's called the Beacon Bar."

"I said I'll be right there." He flicked a lock of hair from his eyes. "Just go there already."

Celine stuck out her tongue and walked away.

Luca fell into step beside Gabriella. "He's been on his cell all night. Some girl he met in Berlin."

"Oh?" She felt her skin grow cold.

"Yeah, she's an artist with blue hair and piercings. They lived together for a couple of months." Luca laughed. "I keep telling him to invite her over. Just to see Victoria's face."

Gabriella smiled but her mind was racing.

Noah took her hand in his once more and she didn't resist. Encouraged, he moved his arm around her waist. Together they walked around the corner to the bustling bar.

Celine pushed open the door and they went inside. The barman nodded in salutation.

"Look, there's a table free over by the window," said Gabriella and they headed in that direction.

Soon they were ensconced in the blue leather seats.

Luca took out his wallet. "Right, first round is on me."

He turned to Noah. "You're twenty-one, right?"

Noah blushed furiously. "Sure I am. Since February."

"We're all legal," Gabriella assured him. "*Whoa*, look at the cocktail menu!" She scanned its contents. "I'm going to go for a Broadway 75."

"What's that?" asked Celine curiously.

"Prosecco and gin with some lemon."

"Hmmm, sounds nice. I'll have one too, brother-in-law."

Luca nodded. "Noah?" he asked.

"Just a beer for me, man."

"Right, what about Hugo?" Luca asked.

"Who takes my name in vain?" Hugo appeared behind him and smiled at the group.

"What would you like to drink? I'm buying."

"We're having cocktails," said Gabriella, beaming.

"I'll have one too," he said.

"The same as the girls?" asked Luca.

Hugo shrugged. "Sure."

There was a seat free next to Celine but he sidled in next to Gabriella. She didn't dare look at him but the minute he sat down every nerve-ending in her body came alive.

"So, did you like the gig?" he asked, tracing a beermat with his finger.

She nodded fervently. "It was everything I thought it would be and more. They're so talented."

"They're pretty cool," he agreed. "I love the piano on stage."

"I'd love to have talent like that," she said wistfully. "No one plays music in my family. Well, except Lita. She used to play guitar when she was little."

"Lita?"

"My grandmother."

"Why doesn't she play now?"

Gabriella shrugged. "I don't know. When she moved to New York, she left a lot of her old life behind."

"Do you have a big family?"

She shook her head. "Just me, Diego and Teresa. My papa died when I was a baby so I only have my mother Magda and Lita."

"Magda is incredible," he said. "The house would fall apart without her."

"Thank you," said Gabriella quietly. "I'm glad you think that. She works so hard, you know? I'm happy that she's appreciated."

Noah pulled at her sleeve. "So, do you want to leave after this drink? We could still get a pizza."

She shook her head. "I'm not hungry. Just relax, Noah."

He slumped back in his chair and scowled.

Hugo accepted a glass from Luca who had arrived back to the table with a tray of drinks.

Luca placed an identical cocktail in front of Gabriella and she took a sip.

"This tastes good," she said, savouring it.

"It does," agreed Hugo. "I'm happy I copied you now."

Luca raised his whiskey. "Cheers, you guys! Here's to mushy British music and good times!"

The group clinked glasses and drank.

"Thanks for buying," said Gabriella, winking at him. "This cocktail is awesome."

Two hours later they hadn't moved. After three Broadway 75s, Gabriella had changed to vodka. Celine's cheeks were flushed from alcohol and Luca was in tearing spirits. He was regaling them with stories from his cousin's bachelor weekend.

"So then Craig crashed the car and a tyre fell off." He laughed loudly.

"What was it?" asked Noah. "A race track?"

Luca nodded. "It's just outside Dublin. You get to race cars. I won in the end."

"Of course you did," said Celine, rolling her eyes.

Hugo beckoned to the barman and indicated another round.

Noah shook his head. "No, it's cool. I've got to split soon." He gave Gabriella a pointed look. "It's getting late."

She could feel Hugo's eyes on her. Taking a big sip, she shook her head. "The night is young, Noah. I'm not in a hurry."

"Gabby!" He already had his jacket on.

"You go. I'll get a ride home."

"Are you serious?" He grabbed her arm. "I thought I could walk you home."

She pulled back. "I never get to spend time with Celine," she said obstinately. "She's off to Europe soon."

"Gabby ..."

"I'll call you."

Hugo watched their exchange silently.

"Fine." Noah's face reddened and he nodded curtly to the others. "See you around."

And he was gone.

Luca whistled. "Pretty harsh, Gabs. That poor schmuck is in love with you."

Gabriella blushed. "Not at all. We're not officially a thing. Just leave it."

Celine clapped her hands together. "Well, I'm glad you stayed. It's not often we see you let your hair down."

"Let's do this properly." Gabriella unfastened the clips that held her hair up and let it fall loosely down her back.

It shimmered in the low lights of the bar and fell becomingly around her face. "Now I've really let it down." The combination of cocktails and Hugo sitting next to her had made her feel free. She felt like going crazy – she felt like letting go. Everything seemed heightened around her. Each sound was magnified, the beat of the music thrummed in her veins. The smell of lemon from Celine's cocktail filled her nostrils and her vision had filtered everything into a low, dusky light.

Hugo traced the rim of his glass with his forefinger. She watched him complete the circular task and then repeat in the opposite direction. Even though he didn't say very much, she felt relaxed in his presence. He was calm and, consequently, she felt calm too. Her life was always so busy – each day had a destination that she hurtled towards at full speed – that it felt nice to step back and breathe. Hugo, with his laid-back attitude and few words, allowed her to just be. She liked that.

Luca and Celine, two blonde heads, were sitting on one side of the table, deep in conversation about the latest Bond movie. Luca let out a yell and Celine threw back her head with laughter. There certainly wasn't silence on their side of the table. Biting her lip, Gabriella tried to think of something interesting to say.

"So, have you found a job yet?" she asked.

His expression darkened and she kicked herself.

"No."

"That's cool." She blushed. Oh, why did she bring that up? It was a lame attempt at small talk.

He noticed her distress and pulled himself together. Slowly the clouds cleared and he smiled again. "I've been sailing a lot. I have a little boat I take out."

"Sailing? I've never done it."

"Never?" he repeated incredulously. "Jesus, Gabby, it's the best feeling in the world. When the wind is right and you're skimming across the water and the only sound you hear is the water lapping against the hull, it's like nothing else."

She closed her eyes. "It sounds so peaceful."

"It's my favourite place to be," he said honestly. "Momma keeps on at me to settle down and get a job and get married. I just can't face it, you know?"

She kept silent, letting him speak.

"I went to Europe for some space. I couldn't go straight from Harvard into an office." He took a sip of his drink. "I still can't imagine it. Now, she has an interview lined up in Boston."

"Don't do it." She regarded him steadily. "Just say no. Hop on your little boat and sail away."

He smiled and it transformed his face. "Sounds great."

"So do it. You're an adult, Hugo. No one should tell you what to do."

"If only it were that simple." He brushed a tendril of hair back from her face. "I'll bet no one puts you under pressure."

She shook her head. "No one, except myself."

"Why is that?"

"Because the stakes are high. Because I don't have the advantages that others have. Because I want to provide for my family and give them a better life."

"Hey!" He put up his hands in protest. "Are you saying that we treat Magda badly?"

"No, no." She put her hand on his arm. "But she's too old now. She's bone-tired every weekend. I rub her shoulders and I can feel the tension. I want to give back. I want to treat her and take away her worries and buy her things."

"Do you think that would make her happy?"

"Yes."

"Things?"

"Why, sure. She never buys herself new clothes or make-up."

"Do those things matter? Really? It sounds like she has a loving family and healthy grandkids."

"God, you sound like Lita." She sat back. "Why not have both?"

"I just think you should give yourself a break. Celine says that you work every hour you can to make ends meet. Then you have school on top of that. You'll burn out, Gabby."

"Celine said that?" She glanced at her friend who was laughing loudly at something Luca had said. "Why? Why did she mention that?"

"Because I asked her about you."

"You did?"

"I did."

The barman gathered some empty glasses from the table and wiped it down.

"More drinks?" said Luca, getting up. "I'm all out."

"No, thanks," said Gabriella, shaking her head. "I'm only halfway through."

Hugo waved his hand. "Not for me either."

Celine did the same. "You seem to be drinking at double the rate of the rest of us, Luca. I see what Charlotte means now."

He whipped around. "What the hell is that supposed to mean?"

She sipped her cocktail. "You like your whiskey, that's all."

"So?" His blue eyes glittered dangerously. "What's wrong with that?"

Hugo glared at Celine. "Nothing. There's nothing wrong with it."

ᴄᴄ Chapter Six ᴐᴐ

An hour later, the bar shut its doors.

"It's too late for the subway," said Gabriella, frowning.

"Let's get a cab," said Luca.

They hailed a yellow cab.

"You guys take the first one," said Luca, opening the door for Celine and Hugo. "Long Island will take a while at this hour."

"Okay, thanks." Celine pecked his cheek. "Night."

"Night, Luca," said Hugo. Then he turned to Gabriella. "Goodnight, Gabby."

She blushed. "Night."

The taxi door slammed and it sped off down the street.

"Let's walk a couple of blocks," suggested Luca. "I could do with sobering up a bit before I see Char."

"Will she be up now?" asked Gabriella in surprise.

"She's probably still at the goddamn office with my goddamn father." He kicked an empty can in frustration.

"She's busy, that's all. Soon you'll be married and all will be well."

He said nothing but just shoved his hands in his pockets.

"She's probably getting things in order before she goes

off on honeymoon," she continued. "Just grin and bear it for a while."

Luca stopped dead. "I met someone. In Dublin. A couple of days back."

Gabriella's eyes widened.

"I met Lydia, a girl I was sweet on once."

"Oh?" It wasn't like him to talk about his feelings.

"She looked the same." He sighed. "I can't stop thinking about her, Gabs. What the hell does that mean?"

She said nothing.

"Is it pre-wedding nerves or something?" he continued. "I mean, I'm over her. I have been for a long time."

"That's what it is," she said reassuringly. "Nerves. Don't even think about it."

He hung his head. "She broke my heart."

"But that's all over now," she soothed, rubbing his arm. "You've moved on and you've a new life now."

"Seeing her again has really messed with my head."

"You've got to forget about it." She nudged him. "This Lydia isn't part of your life anymore."

"She'll be at Craig and Sam's wedding ..."

"So? Charlotte will too. Just play it cool. You're holding on to a memory. That's all. Just let it go."

He got to his feet. "Forget I mentioned anything. It's the whiskey talking."

She nodded. "And you had a fair bit of that."

"Ah, back off. Everyone comments on my drinking." He grinned. "I like whiskey. There are worse things."

"Yeah, like Dunkin Donuts," she agreed.

Gabriella woke the next morning with a pounding headache. Unused to drinking so much, her mouth was dry and her stomach felt queasy. Groaning, she pulled herself up and put on her robe.

Isabelle was in the kitchen.

"*Whoa!* You look rough," she said, taking in the tousled hair and panda eyes.

"I *feel* rough. I need to hydrate." She opened the fridge and surveyed its contents.

"We have some pomegranate juice," said Isabelle. "Second shelf."

Gabriella's stomach heaved. "I'm good." She grabbed a bottle of water and poured a big glass.

"So, how did it go with Noah? Any progress?" Isabelle peeled a banana and took a seat at the kitchen table. "Did he get his reward for the tickets?"

Gabriella shook her head. "He went home pretty early. I stayed out with Luca, Celine and Hugo."

"Oh, you did?" Isabelle narrowed her eyes. "And?"

"And nothing. We had drinks and went home." Hugo's face flashed through her mind and she smiled.

"What's making you smile like that?"

"Nothing. Just something Hugo said. He was telling me about his travels and it was so interesting –"

"What time did you get home?"

"Jeez, I don't know, Mom! Half two?" Gabriella rubbed her temple. "Luca and I shared a taxi and he dropped me off first."

"Thanks for all the video clips of the concert. It looked amazing." Isabelle looked wistful. "I wish I'd just get famous already so I can get VIP passes to these gigs for free."

"Now that's motivation. " Gabriella half-smiled and then winced as her head throbbed. "Have we got some Alka Seltzer? I think I'm going to die."

"I'll be right back." Isabelle disappeared into her bedroom.

Gabriella sipped her glass of water gingerly. The cold liquid definitely helped but it also made her stomach churn. She just had to get it together as she had a busy day ahead. Her tutor had emailed requesting a meeting at around ten, one of her customers for the graduation gowns was due at half two for a final fitting and she was supposed to meet Teresa for dinner in town. All she wanted to do was crawl back to bed.

"So, Paolo thinks I'll get a call today," said Isabelle, putting a packet of tablets on the table. "I've prepared myself for the worst. That's what Mom said to do. Prepare for the worst and then anything else is a bonus. I mean, it's their loss, right? If they don't hire me, I mean."

Gabriella reached out and squeezed her friend's arm. She knew that Isabelle's confidence was mainly bravado. She could see how much this job meant to her.

"I'm sure that you'll be successful. You're beautiful and your hair is naturally red. Allegra will see your star potential, no question."

"You think?"

"I think. Now, I need to go back to bed for a while. Make sure I wake in time to make that meeting with Michael Crantz."

"You've got one hour."

In the end, she cancelled the dinner with Teresa. It had been a gruelling day and she could barely keep her eyes open. Her tutor had final suggestions regarding the last chapter of her thesis and had been extremely positive. Sipping a large coffee, she had nodded dutifully but in truth she had barely registered what he was saying.

Then the graduation-dress fitting had been a disaster. Her client Monica had put on a few pounds and the sides had to be readjusted. Mortified, Monica had apologised. She had split with her boyfriend and become the cliché: comfort-eating cake and watching sad movies on Netflix. Gabriella, who was no stranger to fluctuating dress sizes, patted her arm. The dress would be perfect and she assured her that those pesky calories would not affect her on the Big Day.

Isabelle had gone to the movies with her cousin so the apartment was empty. Unable to face cooking dinner, Gabriella ordered some Chinese food and changed into her pyjamas. Drinking lots of alcohol was so pointless – nothing was worth how she had felt all day.

Noah had called, as she had known he would, and asked to meet. She had declined, claiming to be on death's door and promised to contact him before the weekend. He had then suggested to meet up the next day when she was feeling better. Again, she declined as she had tons to do. In truth, she didn't want to lead him on. The night before had clearly shown her that she liked him only as a friend.

Flicking through the channels on the TV, she settled on a rerun of *The Simpsons*. Her food was delivered ten minutes later and she was surprised to find that she was really hungry. Using chopsticks, she efficiently extracted noodles from the white carton and sucked them into her mouth. The grease left a shiny residue on her lips so she wiped it with a piece of tissue. Feeling better, she sat back and gulped down some water. Homer was drinking Duff beer on the screen and she laughed at his antics.

Suddenly her phone buzzed. She glanced down and saw a notification from Instagram. There was a follower request from Hugo du Maurier. Her heart leapt in her chest. She tapped the screen and gazed at his profile picture. He was smiling and there was a boat in the background.

His sailing boat.

Biting her lip, she pressed 'confirm' and she immediately

got the option to send him a follower request too. She pressed 'follow' immediately and the phone pinged, indicating that he had accepted.

He must be online!

With a beating heart, she accessed his profile and saw hundreds of photos ranging from boats to the Eiffel Tower. A message notification appeared and she opened it.

Hey you!

Her face broke into a smile.

Hey you too, she responded.

Seconds later he replied, asking what she was doing.

Eating some greasy Chinese food and watching Homer Simpson on TV.

She pressed 'send' and waited. He replied saying that he was watching TV too and that Victoria would rather die than let Chinese food into the house. She giggled.

They continued like that for a while – silly flirty messages about nothing at all. Then he asked if she was free to meet for a coffee sometime.

Yes. Just say when and where.

They arranged to meet in Greenwich Village the next day. He signed off and she did too. In a daze, she put the phone on the coffee table. Hugo had texted her and asked her out. What about that German girl?

She's in Germany, said a voice inside her head. *You're here. Go for it!*

Hugging herself, she couldn't stop smiling.

Hugo du Maurier.

What would Isabelle say?

Isabelle raised an eyebrow when she heard.

"Celine's brother? Really?" She poured some boiling water from the kettle into a large mug.

"Yes. It's very strange," said Gabriella from the sofa, raising her knees to her chin. "I mean, why would he be interested in someone like me?"

Isabelle laughed. "I wish you would gain some self-confidence, Gabby. Why *wouldn't* he be interested in you? To be honest, I can't see how *you* are into *him*. I found him a bit cold at Celine's party. Aloof, or something." She sat down on the armchair and stretched out her long legs. "That's the bit I find a bit strange. How someone as vibrant and passionate as you would like someone like him."

Gabriella sighed. "Because he's gorgeous and smart and kind. He has depth, Zsa Zsa. He makes me feel alive."

Isabelle frowned. "Then it's bye bye, Noah, I guess."

"I think so. I mean, it was never really a thing anyway."

Isabelle added some lemon to her tea. "When are you meeting him?"

"Tomorrow." Gabriella beamed at her friend. "What will I wear? I have to look amazing."

"I'll help you choose." Isabelle smiled. "What will Magda say? Her daughter going out with the son and heir?"

Gabriella started. "Oh, I won't tell her." She shook her head fervently. "I don't think that she'd approve." She pictured her mother's shock at learning of their date.

"But why?"

"Oh, Mama is rigid about such things. Hugo is from another world."

"I suppose it would make things awkward if it didn't work out. Her working there and all."

"*Whoa, whoa*, slow down!" Gabriella laughed. "We're only having coffee. No marriage yet."

Isabelle said nothing. She could see Gabriella's point. However, it wasn't Magda who posed a problem. Her disapproval wouldn't come close to that of Victoria du Maurier. From the little she had seen of the blonde Southern lady, she guessed that a young immigrant girl from the Bronx would not be a suitable match for her beloved son.

Hugo was sitting outside the café when Gabriella arrived. He looked amazing in a white shirt and navy chinos. His dark hair was blowing in the light breeze and his face broke into a huge smile when he saw her.

"Gabby!" he said, getting to his feet. "Great to see you."

She sat on the seat opposite him and smoothed her skirt. Her favourite green dress felt tighter than the last time she had worn it so she had skipped breakfast in order to squeeze into it. Her black high heels hurt her feet, but the added height made her feel sophisticated.

"Can I get you a coffee or something?"

She nodded. "I'll have a black coffee."

"That's it?" He gestured to the menu. "They've got muffins and croissants."

Her tummy rumbled. A giant chocolate muffin filled her mind and she closed her eyes.

"No, just a coffee is good."

"I'll be right back." He walked into the café.

Gabriella watched an old man sink his teeth into a bagel. She felt weak from the lack of food. Looking good was hard work.

The sun shone in the sky and the sky was as blue as she'd ever seen it. Tilting her head, she soaked up the hot rays and sighed. Sometimes it felt so good to be alive.

Someone tapped her shoulder and she started.

"Well, hello, Gabs. What are you up to?" It was Luca.

"Hey, Luca." She groaned inwardly. How would she explain this?

Hugo appeared with two cups. He stopped when he saw Luca and Gabriella couldn't quite read his expression.

"Hey, Hugo," said Luca, his eyes wide.

Gabriella stared at the ground, focusing on a piece of gum that had been flattened into the concrete. Hugo placed the cups carefully on the table and sat down.

"We're just having coffee." Hugo regarded Luca steadily. "Do you want to join us?"

Mercifully, Luca shook his head. "Nah, it's cool. I'm just heading back to the gallery."

Gabriella gave him a pointed look. "So, I'll see you Saturday."

"Sure thing, Gabs. See you." He smirked and waved. "Don't do anything I wouldn't do." Whistling, he ambled off, his jacket swinging off his right shoulder.

Hugo sipped his cappuccino. "What were the chances that he'd walk by as we were sitting here?"

Gabriella blushed. "I'll never hear the end of it now. He'll tease me forever."

As if on cue, her phone buzzed. It was a message from Luca with lots of heart emojis. She held up the phone.

Hugo laughed. "He's got way too much time on his hands," he said, shaking his head.

She laughed too and the tension dissipated. She barely noticed the time passing. Soon her coffee was gone and only a dark stain remained on the ceramic white cup. Even her hunger had disappeared. Being in such close proximity to Hugo gave her butterflies rather than hunger pangs.

She talked about her childhood and her family. She told him about her father and Lita. He in turn related how all his life he had felt like an outsider – that the role he was expected to play just didn't feel right.

She twiddled with her teaspoon. "So, stand up for what

you want. If you don't want to be an attorney, then don't."

"It's not that simple ..."

"Sure it is. Just say no." She reached out and took his hand in hers. His skin felt cool. "I said it before – just sail away in your little boat and be happy."

His blue eyes stared at her unfalteringly. "I don't want to sail away."

"You don't?"

"No, I don't."

"Why?"

"I want to be near you."

The world slowed down and the bustle of the village died away. He was staring at her intently.

"*Me?*" Her brown eyes were wide.

"You."

He stroked her cheek slowly with his spare hand and then caressed her full lips with the tip of his index finger. She watched him through half-closed eyes, her heart thrumming in her ears. Then he moved closer, his face inches from hers. His hand moved behind her and grasped the nape of her neck. As his lips drew closer to her, she waited in anticipation for him to kiss her.

"*Gabby!*"

A voice snapped her out of it.

Noah was standing by the table, his face thunderous. "What the fuck?"

She jumped and pulled back immediately.

Hugo stood up. "Hey, there's no need for that."

"Why are you here with him? You blew me off for *him*?"

Gabriella's eyes widened in shock. Noah looked furious.

"We're just having coffee," she said hurriedly.

"Sure you are." His tone was contemptuous.

"We are!"

94

"Yeah, right."

Hugo reached out and tapped his shoulder. "You'd better calm down."

Noah pushed him away and raised his fist. "You stay away from her, do you hear? Gabriella is my girlfriend, not yours."

Gabriella stood up immediately. "Noah, cut this out. I am *not* your girlfriend. We hang out, that's all."

"*What?*" He turned on her furiously. "*Are you fucking serious?*"

"*Yes!*" She stared at him defiantly. "We were never official, Noah. You know that."

"But you didn't mind pretending to be my girlfriend to get tickets, right? To go to Coldplay, your favourite band?"

She rounded on him, her eyes flashing. "That's not true and you know it. You offered me those tickets. I never asked for them."

He laughed sardonically. "You knew what you were doing."

She didn't answer. He was right. She had taken advantage of him.

"I'm so pissed with you right now." He kicked a spare chair and walked away.

She glanced around wildly, her chest heaving in distress. He was right – she was a terrible person. She should have just been honest and told him the truth.

"Sorry," she mumbled to Hugo, getting to her feet. "I've got to sort this out."

"Hey, you do that." He looked angry. "I can't believe you lied about you two."

"I didn't!"

"You said that it wasn't romantic. But he just called you his girlfriend."

"I'm *not*!"

He held up his hands. "It doesn't look like that."

"*What?*" Her eyes filled with angry tears. "Noah and I are *not* a couple. Surely you can see that."

"No, Gabriella. I can't." Hugo turned on his heel and walked away.

Part of her wanted to follow him and make him understand. Yet she had to make things right with Noah first. It wasn't in her nature to be hurtful and she could see by the look in his eyes that he was devastated.

So she took off after Noah, her high heels impeding her speed.

"*Noah!*" she called at the top of her lungs. "*Noah, wait!*"

He ignored her and walked faster. Her heels made a loud noise as she clattered along.

"*Noah!*" she yelled. "*Stop!*"

Still he continued.

Bending down, she yanked off her offending shoes. Breaking into a run, she caught up with him outside the subway.

"Noah!" She pulled at his T-shirt. "Please listen."

He stopped and turned to face her. His eyes were cold as he waited for her to speak.

"I'm sorry," she said breathlessly. "I'm sorry I let you believe that we were a couple. I didn't know how I felt."

"But you know now."

She nodded. "I know."

"Why? Because you like him, right? That rich guy?"

Her brown eyes met his. "Yes."

"Goddamn you both!" He spat on the ground. "You are a *bitch* and I never want to see you again."

"Noah!"

"Just leave me alone." He stalked off.

Miserably she put on her shoes.

Isabelle poured two large glasses of wine and cut a slice of cheese with a sharp knife. She and Gabriella were sitting at the table in their small apartment.

"Noah's hurt, that's all." Isabelle took a bite of brie and popped a grape in her mouth. "He'll calm down."

'No, Zsa Zsa. He won't. He hates me, I know it." She sighed. "Hugo obviously thinks I'm awful too."

Isabelle nearly spat out her cheese. "You're kidding me, right? He was the one who didn't give you a chance to explain. He could have messaged you or called you. I think he's the awful one."

Gabriella shook her head. "I get why he left. He thought that I was cheating on Noah."

Isabelle cut another slice of cheese. "Whatever you say, Gabs." She closed her eyes in pleasure. "I know I shouldn't eat cheese as I'm a model and all, but this is too good."

"You can eat what you want whenever you want," said Gabriella enviously. "I've never seen you put on a pound. Even after all the fries and doughnuts and potato chips. I can't even *look* at an Hershey Bar without putting on weight."

Isabelle shrugged. "It will catch up with me eventually. Hopefully I'll hear about that job first." She banged her fist on the table. "When will they call, Gabby? I'm obsessed. I know I'm the right person for the commercial. *I know it.*"

"Just wait," said Gabriella soothingly. "I'm sure you'll get it."

"I'd better." Isabelle looked fierce. "My mom always tells me not to put all my eggs in one basket but I've put every last one in there."

"Just relax. God will decide."

"God?"

Gabriella nodded. "God. He will decide and all will be well."

Isabelle laughed. "I forgot about your blind faith. Sure, sure. All will be well."

∽ Chapter Seven ∾

Two days later, Luca exited his grandmother's Bentley outside the du Maurier mansion. Jacques the driver closed the door with his white gloved hand.

"Thanks, Jacques," said Luca, slapping the roof. "I'm staying over so you can go."

"Have a good evening," said Jacques, tilting his hat in salute. "Call if you need me."

Victoria had invited Luca and Charlotte for dinner but he had come alone. His fiancée was working late at the office and promised to take a cab.

Again.

He sauntered up the steps and entered the mansion through the front door.

"Good evening, sir," said Magda from the foyer. "The family are having drinks. Just go on through."

"Hey, Magda." He smiled warmly at her. "Do you ever go home?"

She smiled. "Soon."

"Tell Gabby I said hi."

"You see more of her than I do." She smiled. "Have a good evening, sir."

"Call me Luca, please. Don't give me that 'sir' mumbo jumbo."

He entered the drawing room to find Celine and Hugo alone.

"Hey, you guys," he said, heading straight for the liquor cabinet. "Where's Victoria?"

Celine shrugged. "Doing her hair or something. Is Char with you?"

Luca shook his head and poured a generous shot of whiskey into a glass. "She's still at work."

Hugo stared at the floor. His mood seemed sombre.

Celine sipped her Prosecco. "Pity," she said lightly. "I could do with some company. It's been tough with Mister Personality here."

Hugo didn't react. Instead, he swirled his drink around and around.

Luca took a seat on an armchair. "What's up, Hugo? Lovesick?"

Celine laughed. "Over Helga? No way. That's over." She turned to Hugo. "It's over, right?"

He didn't look up.

"Oh no," said Luca, sipping his Jameson. "Not some German girl. I'm talking about someone closer to home."

"Oh?" Celine perked up. "Do tell!"

Hugo glared at Luca. "There's nothing to tell," he said pointedly.

Luca ignored him. "I saw him and Gabby having coffee a couple of days back. Real close and personal."

"Gabby? As in Gabriella?" Celine looked shocked. "My friend?"

Hugo rolled his eyes. "You have no life," he said to Luca. "Seriously."

Luca laughed. "I have a great life, thank you. I just thought Celine would like to know, that's all."

Celine gasped. "I thought you two looked close at the

100

Beacon Bar. I didn't realise you were that close."

"We're not," said Hugo hotly. "She's with that Noah guy anyway."

Luca raised an eyebrow. "I'm pretty sure she's not. She told me that she likes him as a friend."

"Really?" Hugo looked unconvinced. "So why does he think that she's his girlfriend?"

"I guess he really likes her." Luca shrugged. "All I know is that she definitely doesn't feel the same way."

"So, you and Gabby!" Celine clapped her hands in delight. "Interesting."

"There's nothing going on between us," said Hugo.

"Nothing going on between whom?" Victoria's voice appeared behind them and Hugo jumped.

"Nobody," he said and stared meaningfully at Luca and Celine. He sure as hell didn't want his momma poking her nose in any more of his business.

Luca nodded and winked. "Just some girl he met in Europe. It's all over now."

"Helga," added Celine helpfully.

"Lordy, I'm sure glad to hear that," said Victoria, standing in front of the marble fireplace. She was dressed in a light-blue Dior chiffon dress that fell below the knee. Her hair was in its habitual up-style and her manicured toes peeped out of Manolo Blahnik sandals. Glittering in the evening sunshine was her enormous diamond engagement ring. Such was its size, it fell sideways on her finger as it was clearly too heavy to stay upright.

"Where's Charlotte?" she asked, checking her gold watch. "Bruno is waiting to shuck the oysters."

"At the office," said Luca tonelessly.

"Your daddy works her too hard." Victoria pursed her lips. "That girl wouldn't have a wedding if it weren't for me. I have been around like a blue-assed fly sorting things out. She doesn't have time for anything."

"Or anyone," said Luca under his breath.

"Oh, Hugo," said Victoria, turning to her son, "I invited the Ashley Hamiltons to Daddy's birthday party next weekend."

"Party? I thought it was just a family dinner."

"Oh, it is, baby. Just a small affair."

"Why invite those people?"

"That Caroline is a good match for you, sugar."

"Match? This is the twenty-first century, Momma. I can find my own girlfriends."

Victoria's eyes narrowed. "Well, they're coming and I want you to make an effort."

Celine laughed and the tension eased a little. "Who have you got lined up for me, Momma? An heir to an oil company?"

"Don't sass me, young lady." Her mother frowned. "I'll just give Charlotte a call. We really oughta start soon."

She swept out of the room and Luca whistled. "She's on a mission, Hugo. If I were you, I'd jump in your little boat and take off tonight."

"You're not the only one to tell me that." Hugo got to his feet. "I'll see you guys at dinner." He walked off with his phone in his hand.

Hugo closed his bedroom door and threw his phone on the bed. His room was stuck in a time warp of his adolescence: *Harry Potter* books and *Star Wars* memorabilia were on the shelves and an old Snoop Dogg poster hung on the white wall. He was a minimalist and disliked having lots of possessions. When he had left for Europe after graduation, all he had taken with him was a small bag with essentials.

Graduation.

His face tightened.

Victoria and Frank had been so proud of their only son. Graduating from Harvard Law School, albeit without the top honours Charlotte had received, was exactly what they wanted. As he stood there, he felt the world close in. He didn't want to be an attorney. He had no interest in wearing a suit and working sixteen-hour days in a stuffy office.

No one listened to what he wanted as it was expected that he study law.

All his life, he had kept himself to himself. Unlike the sociable and extroverted Celine, he tended to stay in the background. Charlotte was a tough act to follow so he didn't even try to compete.

Now the pressure was on to find a job. Again, it was expected that he climb the ranks in a reputable firm and make his momma proud.

A part of him felt guilty for being so negative. He had been given so many wonderful opportunities. He had never wanted for anything in his life. Unlike Gabriella, who had two jobs and worked every hour she could to make a better life for herself, he'd had everything handed to him on a plate.

Gabriella.

He smiled. She was under his skin. Her apparent lack of confidence was endearing. She seemed so innocent in a world that was destined to change her. She had strength and drive and he admired her for it. Sure, she had been dishonest about that Noah guy, but he hadn't mentioned Helga either. Maybe after a few days all would have settled and he could try again. His time was limited in New York as his momma had an interview in Boston all set up.

Gabriella.

The same evening, Gabriella checked her phone for the

millionth time. It had been days and still no contact. Things had been going so well until Noah had turned up.

Isabelle was out again so she decided to make an omelette for dinner. A couple of eggs and some chopped tomato – a simple meal that filled a hole.

Humming an old Madonna tune, she cracked two eggs into a bowl and whisked them with a fork. She chopped a tomato and diced some chives. Heating the skillet on the hob, she added a knob of butter. It sizzled as it melted and swirled around the pan. The tomatoes spat and hissed when they hit the hot surface and she stirred them vigorously. Next the eggs and finally the herbs. A pinch of salt and pepper and she was set.

Grabbing a fork, she sat cross-legged on the sofa and took a bite. She had passed on the toast this time as she was a carb fiend and really needed to lose a few pounds.

The story of my life, she thought grimly.

In a couple of weeks, she would be a graduate. What then? Where would she even begin to find experience? New York was cutthroat and only the best made it. Sure she had always believed that she would be successful but, now that it was a reality, she wasn't so sure. She needed a lucky break – someone to notice her talent and give her publicity. She had sent photos of her original designs to all the main fashion houses both in America and abroad but so far nothing had come of it. She had even sent some of her work to Anna Wintour of *Vogue*. Nothing ventured and all that.

She knew fame and fortune wouldn't come easy. It didn't take a genius to work out that she would have to fight tooth and nail to get noticed. Her dream was attainable but she needed to focus. She would have to start at the bottom and work her way up. What was it that Lita always said? You can't make an omelette without breaking eggs.

She looked at her plate and smiled.

The door slammed and Isabelle appeared, her face shining. "*Gabby! I got it! I got the perfume job!*"

Gabriella gasped. "Are you serious? Oh, Zsa Zsa! That's awesome."

She dropped her plate onto the coffee table with a clatter and jumped up.

They hugged each other fiercely.

"Paolo called and said that Allegra loved the shots and asked to meet me personally tomorrow."

"No way!"

"*Yes, way!*" Isabelle whooped. "I have to be at the studio at seven."

"Who's shooting the commercial?"

"No one but Raphael Baptiste! The French director? He's won tons of awards. You must know him?"

"I'm not sure …"

Isabelle took out her phone and googled a picture. "There. That's him." She held up the phone revealing a black-and-white picture of a man with long hair and dark eyes. He had light stubble and full lips and was smoking a cigarette.

Gabriella looked impressed. "He's hot."

Isabelle nodded. "He does have that bad-boy look going on. Plus he's tall. I love tall men."

"So, this is all positive," said Gabriella in excitement. "This Raphael is pretty famous, right?"

Isabelle nodded. "Apparently he and Bertie Wells are great friends."

"Bertie Wells the actor?"

"Of course, who else? Anyway, there's talk that good old Bertie may feature with me in the shoot. Kind of like Clooney and Nespresso, an established star giving kudos to a new brand." She did a shimmy dance in delight. "Plus we all know that actors love models so who knows what might happen there. I googled him and he's single."

Gabriella giggled. "He's close to sixty, Zsa Zsa."

"Bertie Wells is A-list, Gabs. I don't care if he's eighty and bald." She stretched her arms up into the air. "This is it! I can feel it in my bones."

"Would you like an omelette?"

Isabelle shook her head. "I'm too excited to eat. I've got to put on a face mask now and paint my nails."

"You've got to eat something." Gabriella was firm. "I can whip something up in a few minutes."

"Oh, all right then." Isabelle hugged her again. "Raphael Baptiste! Imagine! I've got to call my mom."

An exuberant Isabelle headed off the next morning, only to return that evening wearing a glum expression. Gabriella, who was stitching the skirt of her client Monica's gown, regarded her in surprise. "Are you okay?"

Isabelle threw her bag on the table and flopped down on a chair. "It was a disaster."

"What? Why?"

"Well, Allegra didn't turn up for a start. There was no sign of Bertie Wells which makes me think that the rumours are false and everyone referred to me as 'the model', like I was a plastic doll or something. I kept asking them to call me by my name but no one listened."

Gabriella frowned at her friend's gloomy demeanour. "Did you shoot anything today?"

"Nothing. Raphael Baptiste turned up drunk half an hour before the end of the day and proceeded to tell me that he hated his life and he couldn't believe that he was now making commercials rather than movies."

"Drunk?"

"Wasted." Isabelle giggled. "Then he pulled out a ukulele and started to sing 'Where Do You Go To My Lovely?' in his French accent. There were about a million verses and we all had to sit there politely until he finished. Then he passed out."

"How did he look?"

"Dreamy. He still has the long hair and his accent is just too cute."

Gabriella laughed. "A productive day all round then."

"It was chaotic. I thought that at least we would have some rushes to look at by now." She yawned. "I'm going to take a shower. Do you want to order in some food? I'm thinking pizza."

Gabriella nodded. "I can do that. Go and de-stress."

She glanced around the room for her phone but there was no sign of it anywhere. Opening her bag, she rummaged around but again there was nothing. She had used it to text her mother earlier. Magda was busy with preparations for Frank's birthday party in a few days' time and needed some things from the city. Gabriella had promised to pick up the napkins and order the cake.

She walked into her bedroom and shook the quilt on her bed. Sure enough, her phone slid onto the ground and hit the floorboards with a thump. Picking it up, she unlocked the screen and noticed a message from Hugo. Her heart started to beat wildly as she accessed Instagram. It simply read: **What u up to?**

After days of wondering and waiting for something to happen, he had finally made contact. She bit her lip. What was she up to? Nothing remotely exciting really. Sewing dresses, obsessing about him and eating junk food. She didn't want to bore him with those details. She wanted to sound interesting and cool. She could tell him about Isabelle, hobnobbing with the rich and famous. That could work.

Well, not quite, she thought thinking of Allegra's no-show and the drunk Raphael Baptiste.

She typed in an answer.

Nada. U?

He didn't reply for ages. She went and sat on the couch with her phone in her hand, willing a message to appear. Anxiously she reread her message. It sounded fine. There was nothing in it that could be misconstrued as anything. Maybe it was a bit curt but she truly didn't know what to say.

Isabelle appeared with her hair wrapped up in a towel. "You ordered me pepperoni, right? Extra chilli?"

Gabriella gasped and her hand flew to her mouth. "Oh, I forgot to call them! Sorry."

"But you have your phone in your hand?" She looked puzzled.

"Hugo messaged me." She reddened. "I was waiting for a reply."

"Oh? What did he say?"

"He asked what I'm up to."

"That's positive."

"I guess."

Isabelle took a carton of juice from the fridge and poured a generous glass. "Would you like some?" she asked.

Gabriella shook her head and scrolled through her numbers until she found Four Star Pizza.

Just before she pressed the call button, her phone pinged.

"*A message!*" she yelled.

"Great!" mocked Isabelle with faux enthusiasm.

108

"He wants to meet up again. Tomorrow at the park."

Isabelle raised an eyebrow. "That's great and all but I've been working all day, Gabs. I'm frickin' starving. Just order the pizza already!"

But Gabriella wasn't listening. "What will I wear?"

Isabelle tapped her foot impatiently. "Gabby! You know how crazy I get when I'm hungry."

"I might wear my purple dress."

"Make mine a large pepperoni, okay? Gabby? Gabby?"

Gabriella was sitting there, smiling.

Isabelle sighed. She would just call them herself.

☙ Chapter Eight ☙

Gabriella arranged to meet Hugo at The Pond, the iconic body of water in the southeast corner of Central Park. It was a quiet spot, far removed from the busy streets of the city. When she arrived, she found him sitting on a black bench, looking out on the green water. He had his back to her as she approached, his broad shoulders and dark hair instantly recognisable.

In the end she had opted for a white sundress. Her feet were clad in strappy brown gladiator sandals that she had bought on sale from JC Penney's and her toenails were painted red. Gold and silver bangles adorned her wrists and her dark hair fell loosely down her back.

"Hey, you!" she said as she approached.

He stood up and smiled warmly. "You look lovely," he said genuinely.

"I'd hardly say lovely …"

"Lovely," he repeated.

He gestured for her to take a seat and they sat on the wooden bench. It felt warm from the sun. A little boy ran by, screaming in delight as his father chased him.

Neither of them spoke for a moment.

Come on, Gabby! Say something. Be brave.

"Why didn't you call?" she blurted out and blushed.

He turned to face her. "Why didn't *you* call?"

"Don't answer a question with a question." She grinned.

He smiled. "I guess I wanted to give you space. That Noah guy looked pretty mad and I wasn't sure if you guys were a thing or not."

"We're not," she said firmly.

"Yeah, Luca said." He took her hand in his and began to caress her palm. "I've been thinking about you a lot." He paused. "You see, I want to see more of you. I mean, only if you want to ..."

She squeezed his hand reassuringly. "I want to."

He smiled and his whole face lit up. "We could take a trip on my boat."

"That sounds cool." She struggled to keep her voice steady.

He threaded her fingers with his and she felt her breath quicken. Now this was electric – this was how it was supposed to feel.

"Maybe this weekend?" he continued.

She beamed at him. "I could get time off from the gallery."

Suddenly he stopped. "Damn, I can't this weekend. I forgot that I've got my dad's birthday party." He frowned. "Momma's been planning it for months."

"Look, we can do it another time."

"Sure, another time." A cloud passed over his features.

Time was limited. At the rate Victoria was organising his life, he only had a few weeks left. A month tops. He toyed with not saying anything. Gabriella didn't need to know that he was on borrowed time. Deep down, he knew that that was untrue. He couldn't start something with her without giving her all the facts.

"Gabby, I need to say something." He faced her.

"Yeah?"

111

"Remember I mentioned before how Momma wants me to get a job?"

"Yeah."

"Well, she has set up this interview and, the truth is, I don't know how much free time I've got left." His blue eyes met hers. "The thing is, I could be heading to Boston soon. To work there."

"Oh?" She stiffened.

"Momma is going crazy. She's insisting that I join a firm. She has it all set up."

She felt her heart sink. It was like he was dangling happiness in front of her nose and then snatching it away. Promising her a short-lived romance and a long-term heartbreak. Did she want to fall in love with a man who was destined to leave? She had to stay in New York – her future depended on it. Was it worth getting involved?

"That changes things," she said quietly.

"Really?" He looked surprised. "How come? I mean, it won't be for a couple of weeks."

"It's just I don't want to get close to you and then say goodbye." She couldn't bear the thought. "I'm not that kind of girl."

He regarded her for a moment, his face impassive. "No," he said eventually. "I guess you're not."

"I like you," she said with her eyes fixed on the ground.

"I like you, too."

"It's just I don't want to end up with a broken heart." She thought of the past few days – when he didn't contact her. It had taken over her life. She had checked her phone over and over, psyching herself up for disappointment after disappointment when there was no message. Her thoughts had been filled with his face and his voice and they hadn't even kissed yet. Perhaps it was better to leave it in fantasyland. Maybe it was safer to call time on whatever it was that was happening.

He reached out and stroked her cheek. "We could have some good times together, Gabby. You and me. Think about it."

She closed her eyes and allowed him to touch her. It felt like heaven. However, it was also surreal. He would have his fun and move on to a woman like Caroline Ashley Hamilton. She couldn't allow that to happen. She was too vulnerable.

"I don't think so," she said sadly. "You and me were always a dream anyway. We come from different worlds, Hugo. Maybe this is God's way of intervening and guiding us on the right path."

"God?" He raised an eyebrow.

"God." She pointed to the sky. "He knows what's best."

Hugo sighed. "At least give me today," he said in a low voice. "Give me one day with you."

"One day?"

"Just a few hours. Just forget about everything and enjoy today." He stood up and held out his hand. "One day, Gabby."

Her heart fought with her head. One day in his company was all she could think about. Yet, it made it harder to walk away. He obviously had no problem with a casual fling.

The sunshine blinded her for a moment and she shielded her eyes with her hand.

"I can't," she said honestly. "Hugo, you're a great guy but I can't. It's better that we break it now."

He held up his hands. "Fine, your call." Backing away, he turned on his heel and kicked a stone. "Have a nice day."

Isabelle arrived home that evening to find Gabriella curled up on the couch, her face sombre.

"Gabby! What's up?" she asked in concern, placing her bag on the table.

Gabriella stared at the TV screen blankly. "It's over."

"What? What's over?" She walked over and stood in front of the screen.

"Me and Hugo."

"You and Hugo? Were you guys together?"

"Not exactly."

"Then what's over?"

"The dream."

"Why?" Isabelle's green eyes were compassionate.

"He's moving away. To Boston. I called time before it had a chance. I don't want to get hurt." The disappointment made her heart sore.

"What?" Isabelle put her hands on her hips. "Are you telling me that you ended it before it even began? Why do you insist on being so mature and sensible all the time? Jesus, Gabby! You've got to live your life. You may have passed on something truly remarkable."

"Long-distance relationships don't work, Zsa Zsa – everyone knows that."

"You can make anything work." She made a '*pah*' sound. "You're just a chicken."

Gabriella shook her head. "I'm a realist. He would only end up breaking my heart. It means way more to me than it does to him."

"You don't know that."

"Sure I do. I'd just be a distraction until he leaves." She sighed. "Now enough about me. How was your day? As awful as yesterday?"

Isabelle smiled. "Not in the least. It was all pre-production stuff. Raphael was sober and gave us his vision for the commercial. Oh my God, Gabs, he's amazing.

There's talent oozing out of him. He spoke to us for about an hour and then left." She frowned. "I tried to get his attention, you know, flirt a little, but he didn't even look in my direction. Nothing."

"He's a professional," said Gabriella practically.

"So? It knocked my confidence a bit. I mean, men are normally putty in my hands." She spoke without vanity – she was merely stating a fact. Looking at her flawless profile and striking colouring, Gabriella could see why.

"Then Allegra turned up and I swear, her face was frozen as a popsicle. At least four gallons of Botox, I'd bet my life on it." Isabelle kicked off her shoes. "Anyway, Raphael wants me to stand on a rock and have the sea crashing around me …"

"Where?"

"Oh, in the studio. They'll CGI most of it. Then I'm rescued by a sailor and we sail off on his yacht. I think he's planning to hire a big boat upstate. I'm not sure." She giggled. "Allegra asked if she could cameo, maybe as a scantily clad mermaid in the background or something. You should have seen Raphael's face. He didn't answer. He just glared at her and walked away."

"So, when do you start shooting?"

"Well, Oberon is supposed to come on set to discuss the wardrobe. Allegra wanted him and him only apparently. The man's a genius but notoriously bitchy. I'm dreading it."

"Oberon?" She sat up straight. "*The* Oberon. As in the fashion designer?"

Isabelle nodded. "Allegra kept going on about how he was nothing until he met her and how she made him famous. How he was Jean-Paul Gaultier to her Madonna."

But Gabriella wasn't listening, her brain whirring. If she

115

could get Oberon to notice her, then he might take her on. This could be her big break. God was leading her on the right path. "You've got to let me meet him, Zsa Zsa. The man's a genius. Can I tag along as your personal assistant? If I showed him my designs maybe he would take me on as an intern …"

Isabelle held up her hand. "*Whoa!* Slow down there. His intern?"

"Why, sure. That's how it works. You become a protégée of a megastar and then branch out on your own. Dior took on an unknown Yves Saint Laurent and look what happened."

"Gabby," she said gently, "Oberon is one of the biggest names in the fashion world. Why would he take on an unknown student?"

"Soon to be graduate," Gabriella corrected her.

"Still, it's unlikely."

"Please?" Her brown eyes were wide. "I have a feeling in my bones that this could be it!"

Isabelle threw up her hands. "I guess it would be okay for you to tag along. I'll have to clear it with Paolo and security." She picked up her phone and texted her agent like lightning. "Just prepare yourself for disappointment. He has the worst reputation."

Gabriella got up, Hugo forgotten. "I'd better get something ready to show him." Determination flooded her body and her brain kicked into action. She would take her portfolio to the studio. It showcased all her best designs. Her favourite section was a modern take on gowns worn by Queen Victoria, Princess Margaret, Princess Grace and of course, Princess Diana. Her love of royals had inspired her and Isabelle looked enchanting in the various dresses.

"Sure. You do that." Isabelle sat on the seat she had

vacated. "I need to channel my Ariel from *The Little Mermaid* – you know, long red hair sitting on a rock."

Gabriella laughed. "Maybe Raphael is a huge Disney fan."

"I doubt that."

Raphael Baptiste stared at the skyline of New York from his window. The tall buildings squeezed together created a jigsaw effect and the dusky half-light made them seem imposing and sinister. He disliked cities, preferring the rural French countryside. It seemed like ages since he was sitting on his wicker chair by the wheat fields in his native Picardy. Life and his work brought him around the world and his downtime seemed to be less and less.

Raphael had been obsessed with cameras since he was a little boy. The great-grandson of the world-renowned photographer Louis Baptiste, he had grown up surrounded by the craft. Pictures of Louis drinking a carafe of wine with Picasso, with Hemingway in a Paris café and many other such moments dotted the walls of the ancestral home. Louis had mixed with all the greats, taking iconic shots of politicians, singers, actresses and artists. His trademark black-and-white portraits now hung in galleries all around the world.

The photography bug had then skipped a couple of generations – both Raphael's grandfather and father worked in finance – only to reappear in Louis' great-grandson. At the age of eight, Raphael had asked for and received a camera for Christmas. It was then he had realised that his life would never be the same again. Seeing the world through a lens gave him another dimension. He controlled what was put into the frame and he felt masterful and godlike. Louis' old dark room – an old attic

117

space which had been boarded up for years – was renovated and soon he was developing prints of various subjects ranging from his old nanny, Madame Dubois, to a lark singing on the branch of a tree. Raphael's father Pierre, bowled over by his only son's apparent talent, encouraged him to pursue a career in the Arts. With a name like Baptiste, he couldn't fail.

Raphael knocked back his whiskey and sighed. *Au contraire, Papa.*

He was a failure. A bona fide failure. How the mighty had fallen. Seven years before he had been at the top of his game, winning award after award for his direction in cinema. His remake of Jean Cocteau's 1950 film *Orphée*, an updated adaptation of the classical tale of Orpheus, had been a massive success. Then he had followed it with a biopic on Stalin, all at the ripe old age of thirty-one. With his long hair and dark eyes, he was like a French Jim Morrison – moody and poetic. Parties followed and a penchant for cocaine and models. He never seemed to have time to sleep.

Then came the flop. Arrogance and short-sightedness spurred him to take on a movie written by the son of a friend. Skimming through the script, he knew it wasn't up to scratch. However, surely with his golden touch that would all change. He could turn anything into an overnight success. He was Raphael Baptiste after all.

A box-office failure followed and, crucified by the critics that once loved him, he fell into despair. Overly reliant on drugs and alcohol, he fell into an abyss of substance-abuse which culminated in his then girlfriend – the famous model Sylvie Marot – finding him in a pool of vomit on the bathroom floor. Screaming, she had called the emergency services and what followed was a tabloid frenzy. Pictures of his body being loaded into an ambulance on a stretcher sold for thousands and stories emerged of his debauchery and lifestyle which shocked the world. France's golden boy of cinema had a dark side and now everybody knew about it.

Rehab followed and a strict regime. Days and nights rolled into one and he fell into a deep depression. His beloved Sylvie moved on and all his so-called friends faded away.

Then, after months of reflection and clean living, he was released. Like Orpheus in his famous film, his old self died and he returned to the living world with a new life. Reformed, he vowed to reclaim his standing in the cinematic hierarchy.

This proved difficult. Fickle Hollywood – the place of dreams – had moved on. He was no longer the bad boy of quirky French cinema. He was cruelly rejected and told to claw his way back.

So, here he was. In a soulless hotel in Manhattan making an advertisement for another has-been, Allegra Starr. How he despised this commercial gravy train – he was better than that. He was destined for greater things. Despite everything, he still believed that.

The only upside was that his old friend Bertie had agreed to lend his star quality to this venture. Bertie Wells gave kudos to anything he was part of. A self-confessed 'luvvie', he had made it in the eighties and was now one of Britain's biggest stars. At nearly sixty years of age, he had slightly greying hair mitigated by a surprisingly youthful face. "Oil of Olay," he would joke with a wink. The quintessential English gentleman, his plummy accent and penchant for tweed were his trademarks. Raphael loved Bertie's style – suits and silk cravats – and his apparent *joie de vivre* made him hugely entertaining. If there was scandal around amongst the rich and famous, Bertie knew about it. He knew almost everyone in the industry and was liked by all. Unmarried, his quirky dress sense inspired rumours about his sexuality. Yet he always had a beautiful woman on his arm, ranging from actresses to models.

They had met when Raphael had cast Bertie as Orpheus all those years ago. Together, they had watched Cocteau's version over and over again, drinking wine and discussing how they would portray each scene to make it their own. Then Bertie went on to take home the gong for his portrayal of the Greek lover and the A-list life began in earnest. Drug-fuelled nights followed where seeing the sun come up became the norm. Everywhere they went, people wanted them around. They went to party after party and he drank himself into oblivion. The difference between him and Bertie was that Bertie knew when to stop. He never once crossed the line whereas Raphael wasn't so prudent. The allure of fame and adulation fed his ego and he never refused a drink. Generous and impulsive, he splashed money around and spent it like water. His vast entourage lapped it up and stuck to him like glue, guaranteed a good night in his company.

When it all went sour and he ended up in Clouds House, an exclusive rehab centre in London, all his so-called friends disappeared into the background. All, except Bertie. He visited him and regaled him with outrageous stories. He never once let him believe that all was lost. He promised him that he would be there for him when he got out.

And so he was. The minute Raphael had called and asked for help with the commercial, Bertie agreed to take part. "I'll have to clear it with Harry my agent, old boy. Give me a couple of days."

True to his word, he called back and confirmed. "I'll do anything to get you back on track. Old Louis would turn in his grave."

Raphael's expression darkened. There was only so much Bertie could do to help. The main problem was with himself – he just didn't feel the passion anymore. He felt like a cloud had invaded his brain and he couldn't shift it. At only thirty-eight years of age, he felt jaded.

✎ Chapter Nine ✎

Gabriella followed Isabelle through the glass doors of the studio. Tucked under her arm was a make-shift portfolio she had thrown together the night before. It was filled with sketches and photos of her various designs. Oberon was big news. She just had to get close and show him her work. He might be impressed that she was about to graduate from Parson's. He might just give her a chance and let her train with him.

Closing her eyes she prayed to God that the day would go well. She needed something good to happen.

Isabelle handed her bag to the security guard. "Morning, Hank," she said, smiling.

"Morning, Miss Flynn," said the elderly black man in a blue suit. "Just the obligatory check, ma'am."

"Sure, no problem." She gestured for Gabriella to hand over her bag. "It's policy," she explained.

Gabriella nodded and handed her bag to Hank for him to look through.

"And your book, ma'am," he said, holding his hand out for her portfolio.

"Oh, okay." She placed it on the desk and he flicked through it.

"That's fine," he said, handing it back. "Have a nice day."

They walked on down the corridor and through big soundproofed doors. The noise hit them immediately. The crew had already set up and there were about twenty people walking around chatting and moving cameras or sound booms.

Isabelle nudged her and pointed to a tall man standing by a vending machine. "That's Brad," she whispered. "He's the head camera guy. I had coffee with him yesterday and he told me that Bertie Wells might be here today."

Gabriella's eyes travelled round the room. "Where's Raphael?"

Isabelle shrugged. "Probably late. He knows that nothing will start without him." She walked towards a nondescript canvas chair and placed her bag beside it. "Soon you'll see 'Isabelle Flynn' on the back of this chair – I'm not going to be 'the model' for long."

A small Asian girl approached them holding a clipboard. "You're needed in make-up," she said abruptly to Isabelle.

"Sure, I'll be right there." Isabelle gestured to her chair. "Sit here and wait for me if you like, Gabriella. I won't be too long."

Gabriella nodded and sat down. There was no sign of Allegra or Oberon.

The set design looked sparse – only the famous rock was in place and looked surprisingly real. She could see Isabelle draped over it with her long red hair blowing in the wind.

Suddenly there was a commotion over by the double doors and a tall man appeared. With his long brown hair and amazing cheekbones, it could only be Raphael Baptiste. He was speaking in rapid French and towered over everyone else. He drained a polystyrene cup and handed it to the same Asian girl who had spoken to them minutes before.

"Right, where is the model?" he asked, looking around. "I want to see her on that rock." His English was perfect.

"In make-up," said his assistant.

"Well, get her out of make-up." He ran his fingers through his hair. "I want some rushes today."

"Of course." She scurried away.

"Oh, and Kim?" he called after her.

"Yeah?"

"More coffee."

He flopped down on a chair with 'BAPTISTE' printed on the back. How he craved a cigarette. This made him irritable and he resented having to come down and direct this rubbish. A pretty girl on a rock. How original. He had suggested it as a joke and Allegra had jumped at the idea. Then she wanted a yacht scene which meant a few days on Long Island which he really didn't need. That model they had hired looked like Allegra in the old days. He frowned. The narcissism of it all. An ageing star desperately grasping on to the past. The whole shoot shouldn't take too long – it was a commercial after all. He was hoping to wrap in a week.

Kim placed a fresh cup of coffee on a small table next to his chair. "She's just coming now."

He nodded. "Has Bertie arrived yet?"

She shook her head. "Any minute now." She turned to walk away and he called her back. "Kim!"

"Yes?"

He smiled and it transformed his face. "Thanks."

She blushed. "No problem."

Gabriella stared at him in wonder. When God had given out good looks, Raphael had received the lion's share. She remembered him years ago at the height of his fame as his handsome face tended to be plastered across newspapers and magazines due to his party lifestyle rather than his work. She guessed that he must be nearly forty but he didn't look it. Not one strand of grey could be seen in his dark-brown hair.

Isabelle arrived back dressed in a figure-hugging shimmery silver dress. Her long red hair flowed down her back and her eyes were sultry thanks to the heavy kohl and dark shadow the make-up artist had used.

Raphael barely looked at her.

"Right, the model. Sit on the rock, please."

She made her way over to the prop, her tight dress making it difficult to move.

"Lift your skirt," he commanded.

She obeyed and angled her body so as to sit on the plastic boulder. Gabriella could see that she wasn't comfortable as her face looked strained and the way she was sitting looked precarious.

"*Brad!*" Raphael circled the rock, looking at Isabelle from different angles. "Put two cameras on each side. *Kim!* I need my coffee. I forgot it over there."

Such was the force of his personality, everyone scurried around. Brad, along with two other men, wheeled the cameras into position.

Isabelle slipped a little and in a panic tried to grasp onto the plastic surface. Gabriella could see that she was going to fall and stepped forward to help.

"*No!*" Isabelle hissed. "Don't make a scene. I'll be okay."

Like a seal, she moved up the rock, her tight skirt impeding her movement. The strong lights shone down on her and beads of perspiration appeared on her brow.

"What do you think, Brad?" Raphael held up his hands to make a frame. "I think this will work."

Kim handed Raphael his coffee and he drank it absentmindedly. "Where the hell is Bertie?" he said under his breath. "He's always late."

Kim checked her phone. "I can call him if you want."

Raphael shook his head. "He'll be here. Now tell the model to stay exactly where she is while I work on the *mise en scène.*"

Kim walked over to Isabelle and snapped her fingers for attention. "Hey, you!" she said rudely. "Stay right where you are, okay?"

Gabriella tapped her shoulder. "I think she's finding it hard to stay on the rock."

"And you are?" Kim stared at her contemptuously.

"My assistant," said Isabelle, frantically holding on. "Now back off, Kimmy, and let me do my job."

Kim's face tightened and she stalked off.

"Are you sure you're okay?" asked Gabriella again. "Just tell them that you're slipping."

"I'm fine," said Isabelle through gritted teeth.

Raphael had his head bowed, studying the script. Kim was standing by his side, talking into a hands-free kit on her head. Brad winked at Gabriella who was feeling out of place.

Suddenly, Isabelle felt her body slide downwards. With a shriek, she disappeared down the back of the rock and ended up on a heap on the ground. Her beautiful dress had ripped, revealing her long legs.

Gabriella ran to her friend. "Zsa Zsa! Are you okay?"

Isabelle looked mortified.

Brad held out his hand and helped her up. "That was a bad fall right there," he said, shaking his head.

Isabelle raised her head and her eyes locked with Raphael's for the first time. He looked amused.

Kim rushed over and tutted. "Your dress is ruined! Do you know how much it cost? That's Allegra's, you know!"

"I'm sorry, I'm sorry! The rock is slippery and I couldn't perch properly."

Kim rolled her eyes. "We'll have to find another one. Like I don't have enough to do."

"I said it was an accident," said Isabelle icily. "The dress was a stupid choice anyway. You guys knew that I had to practically abseil up that thing."

"Say again?" Kim stared at her in shock. "A stupid choice? Are you for real? Oberon himself chose it."

"So? He made a mess of it." Isabelle was defiant. "To be honest, it looks better like this." She pointed to the slit in the fabric.

"Oh, what do models know!" muttered Kim. "Just stick to what you do best – posing and looking pretty. Now, come with me." She stalked off with her clipboard.

Isabelle straightened her shoulders and took a deep breath. How dare she speak to her that way? Someday people like Kim would respect her. Someday she would be calling the shots. The rock was a disaster and lacked creativity. No one could stay on it – surely they could see that.

Gabriella looked concerned. "Did you hurt yourself?" she asked, rubbing her arm. "You hit the ground pretty hard."

Isabelle shook her head. "Just my ego. Talk about graceful. I'd better do as I'm told, Gabs. See you in a minute." She walked after Kim, her long hair trailing down her back.

"Who's the model?" asked Raphael, watching her walk away.

Brad shrugged. "I'm not sure. Annabelle or something?"

"It's Isabelle," said Gabriella loudly. "Isabelle Flynn."

"*Raphael!*"

All heads swung around. There, standing in his trademark suit and cravat, was Bertie Wells.

"I'm here! Take that annoyed look off your face right now. At least I turned up." He strode over, his brown eyes twinkling. "I now know what Sting meant in that song. I feel like a legal alien."

"Like a what?" asked Brad puzzled.

"'An Englishman in New York'," said Gabriella in delight.

"Bravo, young woman!" Bertie winked at her. "Now, what is this advertisement and what is my part?"

Raphael made a face. "It's for perfume. Allegra wants a retirement fund. She is paying me a fortune so I can't really complain."

"Theme?" asked Bertie briskly, taking off his jacket and hanging it on a chair.

"A redhead on a rock. Lots of waves and wind. Cheesy music in the background. You in a boat. You rescue her, you fall in love, the end."

"Am I to be a sailor?"

"*Oui.*"

Bertie laughed. "Wonderful. I'll need a white uniform."

Gabriella shrank into the background, unsure if she should be listening so blatantly. It was fascinating to see such a famous man in the flesh. He looked smaller than he did on screen, but his aura was undeniable. The whole room was paying attention.

"Right. Let's talk this through," said Bertie. "My agent Harry has only freed me up for a week."

Allegra Starr had been a beauty in her day. Her pale skin and red hair had caught the eye of Hollywood and during the eighties she was top of her game. In 1987, Allegra featured in the top ten baby names in America. She could command whatever movie roles she liked and had two high-profile marriages to famous actors, both of which ended in divorce. Now in her fifties, she no longer had the influence she once had. She didn't get offered big roles like Meryl Streep or Emma Thompson. So, like any businesswoman, she decided to cash in on her brand. She still had fans and perfume was the way to go.

When she received word that Bertie had showed up, she appeared at the studio wearing a white jumpsuit. Her red hair was piled on her head and her face looked shiny from too much Botox. On her right hand she still wore her enormous diamond engagement ring from husband number two. He was long gone, but the yellow stone was too beautiful to sell.

"*Raphael!*" Her voice was high and loud. "*Yoohoo! I'm here!*"

He turned and waved. "Good to see you," he said mechanically.

Bertie rushed over and kissed her on both cheeks. "Allegra, my darling. You look so well. I just love your shoes. Jimmy Choo?"

"Why sure they're Jimmy's. Aren't you the little fashion buff?"

"I do know about some things." He grinned.

Allegra turned to Raphael. "Is Oberon here? He sent me a picture of the dress he chose for the shoot. I just love the silver."

"Well, that dress didn't quite work out …"

"Oh?"

"We're working on it." Raphael walked away.

Bertie offered her a chair. "So tell me about Cannes. I presume you're heading over this weekend."

"Of course. Elton has invited me on his yacht."

"Good old Elton."

Gabriella felt out of place, just standing there with her portfolio. Like Allegra, she was wondering where Oberon was too. Surely he would turn up as promised?

Isabelle appeared again, wearing a white Grecian-style dress.

"Where's the silver dress?" asked Allegra suspiciously. "It's from my personal collection, you know."

Raphael rushed over to Isabelle and took her arm. "We felt that white would work better."

"We did?" Isabelle looked confused.

"Your silver gown blended in too much with the colour of the rock, Allegra." He gave Isabelle a pointed look.

"Oh, of course." Isabelle smiled brightly. "This is a better colour."

"Perhaps." Allegra looked sceptical.

Bertie was staring openly at Isabelle. "Are you Allegra's lovechild?" he asked. "My word, you're exquisite."

"No, I'm not her lovechild." She raised her head haughtily. "I'm Isabelle Flynn."

"My lovechild? Oh Bertie, you charmer!' Allegra tittered.

"Well, Miss Flynn, you've just got to let me take you out this evening." Bertie did a small bow. "You are too beautiful to hide away."

Isabelle blushed and looked embarrassed.

"Bertie!" said Allegra, exasperated. "I thought that we could have dinner together. The paparazzi would love a shot of us *à deux*."

"Bertie!" Raphael looked equally as exasperated. "Make love in your own time. We need to get started." He stalked off, muttering under his breath.

Gabriella nudged Isabelle in awe. "My God, Zsa Zsa, you've just been hit on by an A-lister."

"Keep cool," whispered her friend. "This is where it all begins, Gabs. I told you how it works. If I play my cards right, people like that bitch Kim will be kissing my feet."

Oberon didn't show the next day either. Gabriella quizzed Evie from Wardrobe as to where he was. She was a small blonde girl with a tattoo of Johnny Depp on her arm. Dressed in frayed cut-offs and a tight sleeved top, she ran the costume department.

"Kim said that he picked the silver dress, so he must have been here at some stage," said Gabriella.

"Oh, he picked that on Facetime," said Evie, sorting through dresses on a rack. "I was around like a crazy person with my cell, showing him Allegra's dresses. Of course he picked his first choice after deliberating for twenty minutes."

"So, he hasn't been here at all?" Gabriella was dismayed.

"Nope. Although he'll probably turn up at some stage." She paused and nodded towards Gabriella's portfolio. "Is that why you're hanging around? To show stuff to Oberon?" She looked at her in pity. "He's not very nice. Prepare yourself for rejection."

"Nothing ventured, right?"

Evie shrugged. "I guess." She checked her watch. "In my experience, commercials like this don't take very long. Two or three more days tops. Oberon should turn up before the end. He'll never put his name to something he hasn't checked."

"Really?"

"For sure. He'll swan in at the end and take all the credit." She removed a black minidress from the rail, draped it over her arm and walked away. "See you later."

Gabriella felt deflated. She felt like she was in limbo,

waiting around, standing aimlessly. It would be fine if she weren't so busy herself. Her graduation was in a few days and she still had to finish the gowns for her clients.

She went back out to the set to find Bertie tapdancing around the rock, making jazz hands and singing at the top of his lungs. Isabelle was laughing loudly as she clapped to his tune. They had really hit it off.

There was no sign of Raphael.

"Are you okay?" called Isabelle, blowing her a kiss.

"I'm fine, I'm fine." Gabriella forced a smile.

"Great, let's get some lunch in a minute." Isabelle turned back to Bertie who was trying to juggle with three pens. "Oh, Bertie! You're so funny."

❧ Chapter Ten ❧

Later that evening, Gabriella placed her portfolio on the dressing table in her bedroom. There had been no sign of Oberon that afternoon either. Maybe it was time to give up. God knows, she had tried.

Isabelle knocked on the door. "Gabs? Can I come in?"

"Sure."

Her friend looked elated. "Bertie asked me for my number and he just texted me there."

"Bertie Wells? *Whoa!*"

"I know, right?" She looked thrilled. "He's so normal. It's hard to think that he's one of the most famous actors in the world."

"Why did he text?"

"Oh, it was a GIF of a man doing jazz hands." She giggled. "Did you see him perform today? He's a scream."

"Raphael wasn't impressed when he got back." Gabriella brushed her hair until it shone.

"Raphael needs to lighten up," said Isabelle dismissively. "He's so intense. It's not like the camera was rolling. I mean, he berated Bertie for not staying in character. He's a sailor, for Pete's sake. You'd think we were shooting an Oscar-winning movie or something."

"Well, maybe that's what he's used to," said Gabriella. "It must be hard for him to adjust."

"He needs to chill."

Gabriella yawned. "These early starts are hard, Zsa Zsa."

"Six thirty? Awful," she agreed.

"So I think I'll give it a miss tomorrow," she continued. "I've so much to do."

"Oh, Gabby! What if Oberon turns up?"

"I don't think he will."

"He might." Isabelle frowned. "It would be terrible if you missed your chance."

In the end, Gabriella decided to go in. The lure of Oberon was too much. Deep in her heart, she could feel he was her destiny. She just needed a chance to meet him.

The day passed quickly and efficiently. By lunchtime, Raphael made an announcement.

"We are almost finished, *mes amis*! Bravo!"

The crew cheered.

"We have two more days on Long Island and that should be it."

Gabriella noticed a look of anguish on Isabelle's face. She understood why – once this shoot was over, she would go back to her normal life. She could see that her friend loved being part of the celebrity world.

At the end of the day, Bertie stood on a chair.

"*Attention, everybody!*" he shouted and all heads turned. "As it's Friday and you've all worked so hard this week, I think some drinks are in order."

The crew cheered.

"So, come to Carney's Irish bar on 7th and I'll buy a few rounds!"

More cheering.

Brad hung his earphones on a hook. "It's been a long day," he said to Kim. "You coming?"

She nodded. "You bet."

Gabriella waited patiently for Isabelle to get changed. Slowly the studio emptied and soon Raphael was the only one left. He was watching the scenes they had shot earlier with a frown.

"*Non!*" he shouted, banging the screen. "Bertie looks wrong." He lifted his head and looked around. "You!" he said, pointing at Gabriella. "Come here and tell me what you think."

"Me?" she squeaked.

"Yes, you," he repeated. "Here! Now!" He ran his fingers through his hair. "Maybe I was too hasty. Maybe we're not finished at all."

Gabriella walked over to the monitor and peered at the screen.

"Look at Bertie," he began. "The way he comes into the shot – I think it's wrong."

Gabriella watched Isabelle on the rock, looking like a goddess. Then Bertie appeared in his white uniform and took her hand. He smiled and kissed her palm.

"Well?" demanded Raphael. "What do you think?"

Gabriella bit her lip. It was a disaster. Even Isabelle's startling beauty could not deflect from the fact that it was a cliché – a boring predictable commercial that had been done a thousand times before.

She took a deep breath. "I'm not crazy about any of it." She kept her eyes cast down.

"What?" He did a double take.

"I don't think it works." Her eyes met his.

He looked thoroughly shocked.

135

"There's no real narrative and they have no chemistry."

Raphael ran his fingers through his hair. "Who the hell are you?" he said angrily. "Do you even work here?"

Gabriella shook her head. "I'm a fashion designer. I came with Isabelle, the model. She's my best friend."

"So, Miss Fashion Designer. You hate my work, *non*?"

"No, I don't. I just think you're better than this." She stared at him steadily. "What's the name of the perfume again?"

"Allegra Starr," he answered bleakly. "As original as this advertisement."

"So, go with an Allegra theme. Include clips of different scenes from different films. All her iconic roles. Then Isabelle on a red carpet in a classic gown that she wore. Then Bertie could appear in a tuxedo, looking at home in his natural habitat."

"Go on."

"Well, when Isabelle went for this job, I made a dress for her, the aquamarine gown that Allegra wore to the Oscars one time. Here, I'll show you." She opened her portfolio and flicked onto the page with Isabelle standing on a red carpet looking back over one shoulder seductively. "That looks classy and hasn't been done before."

Raphael stared at the photo. The girl was right – of course he should stick to the theme. Allegra herself should be the main focus. Bertie would look right at home on a red carpet and the model was the image of Allegra when she was younger.

Only prettier, he thought.

"You made this dress?" he asked impressed. "Not bad. Not bad at all."

Gabriella's heart began to thump. This was her moment. This was her chance.

"You see, Oberon designed the original," she said. "That's why I'm here, see? To meet him and ask him to take me on."

"You've been standing around all day waiting for Oberon?" Raphael grinned. "You must be disappointed, *non*?"

She nodded. "I really thought he'd show up."

"Well, if I go with this idea, he'll have no choice but to show up." Raphael switched off the monitor. "We'll need this gown for a start. Maybe Allegra kept the original. Although, she is smaller than the model ..."

"Isabelle," corrected Gabriella. "Her name is Isabelle."

"Oberon should be able to fix it, *non*? He designed it," he continued. "If not, have you still got the one you made?" He started muttering to himself in French.

"I have it," she said joyfully. "I can bring it in. I mean, that's no problem at all."

Raphael smiled at her and her legs went to jelly. "Bring it tomorrow. I need to see the model, I mean Isabelle, wearing it for my vision." Then he left, banging the door behind him.

Gabriella jumped in delight. "*Yes!*" she yelled.

"Gabby?" Isabelle appeared wearing a short green sundress and strappy sandals. "Are you okay?"

"You'll never guess!"

"Guess what?"

"I told Raphael that the commercial didn't work and he agreed and now he wants that aquamarine dress I made and you're going to be on a red carpet and –"

"Stop!" Isabelle held up her hand for silence. "Please repeat everything you just said. Are you saying it's bye-bye, Mr. Rock?"

"That's exactly what I'm saying." Gabriella's eyes shone. "Let's get out of here and I'll tell you all about it."

Bertie was in the foyer when they emerged. A large bodyguard stood nearby, his hands crossed defiantly.

"There you are," Bertie said, checking his watch. "What took you so long?"

Isabelle hoisted her bag onto her shoulder. "Raphael is changing the whole thing."

"*What?*" said Bertie in surprise. "Do tell!"

"He's changing the theme. It's now going to be clips of scenes from Allegra's films and a red-carpet scenario, right, Gabby?" Isabelle turned to her friend.

Gabriella nodded. "That's what Raphael said."

Bertie sighed. "I must admit I thought I looked dashing in my white uniform. Still, the theme was a bit banal." He frowned. "I'm not sure I'll be available for a reshoot. I'll have to call my agent."

"Oh, but you have to be part of it!" protested Isabelle. "You're the key part."

"You're too kind, my darling," he said, winking. "Too kind."

Isabelle looked around the empty foyer. "Where are the others?" she asked. "Were you waiting here for us?"

"But of course. The rest of the crew have been gone ages. I just wanted to make sure that you came along." He held out his hand. "Vladimir over there, my muscle, has been waiting too. Give him a little wave!"

Isabelle and Gabriella waved at the bodyguard who ignored them.

"Huge biceps, I must admit, but no personality." Bertie sighed. "It gets so tedious when one tries to small-talk."

Isabelle glanced around. "Is Allegra coming too?"

Bertie shook his head. "Allegra took off in a strop about my obvious preference for your beautiful face. She's flying to Cannes in the morning anyway."

"And Raphael?" she asked casually.

"Raphael doesn't really go to bars. Anyway, he'll be impossible now if he's changing things around."

Isabelle turned to Gabriella. "What do you think?"

"I shouldn't go," she said ruefully. "I have an early start at the gallery tomorrow."

Bertie waved his hand. "Nonsense, my dear. All work and no play makes Jack an extremely dull boy."

"Well, I'm not going out with you unchaperoned," Isabelle told Bertie firmly. "Even if you are Bertie Wells."

"Quite right," he agreed. "I might lose control and ravish you."

They reached the bar to find the crew on their second round of drinks. Brad was at the counter drinking a beer and Kim scowled when she saw Isabelle approach. The rest of the crew cheered when Bertie appeared.

"They're relieved that I turned up," he said, smiling and waving. "Now I'll pick up the tab as promised."

There was a buzz of conversation and the stereo was playing Luke Kelly's greatest hits.

"Now, ladies," said Bertie, taking a seat at a small table. "Will champagne suit you both?"

Gabriella nodded, wide-eyed.

Bertie called the barman. "A bottle of Bolly, my good man. Three glasses."

"Say again?" said the barman. "A bottle of what?"

"Bollinger! Surely a fine establishment like this has champagne?"

He shook his head. "We got sparkling wine."

Bertie put his face in his hands. "*Quelle horreur!*" he said to the girls. "How am I supposed to impress you beautiful ladies with a second-rate bubbly?"

"We'll survive," said Isabelle, patting his arm. "Just this once," she added, smiling.

Gabriella pinched herself. What would Magda say if she saw her now? Hanging out with Bertie Wells?

Isabelle was equally as thrilled – however, she played it cool. She took a seat and crossed her long legs.

"So, how long have you known Raphael?" she enquired.

Bertie shrugged. "Over ten years? We met when he cast me as Orpheus."

"He's hard work," continued Isabelle, smiling at the waiter as he deposited three flutes on the table in front of them.

"Some say that because of his manner," said Bertie. "However, I know that it's all bravado – deep down he's a lamb."

Isabelle didn't look convinced. "The way he screamed at Brad for the second take? It was barely millimetres out of place. It was uncalled for."

"There's a price to pay for genius," said Bertie simply. "Just you wait – this advertisement will be top class, despite his apparent abhorrence."

"Abhorrence?" repeated Gabriella. "Why?"

Bertie took a sip of his drink. "Raphael hates this kind of work. He only took the job because he needs as much publicity as possible. Hollywood was most unkind after his meltdown."

"Oh." Isabelle looked deflated.

"Not to worry, my darling," said Bertie. "Every cloud and all that. We may never have met was it not for Allegra and her overpowering scent."

"It's pretty awful, right?" agreed Isabelle, laughing. "She sprayed some on my wrist yesterday and despite

140

having a shower and scrubbing like crazy, I can still smell it."

"No doubt she'll make a fortune," he said.

"No doubt."

Gabriella took a sip of sparkling wine and sighed. It tasted bubbly and fresh and she could feel it course down her throat.

"So, young lady, are you a model too?" Bertie stared directly at her.

"Me? A model?" She nearly choked on her drink. "No, no. I'm a dress designer."

"Wonderful! A master of couture. Are you wearing it right now?"

Gabriella giggled. "No. This is a sundress from Walmart."

"Who do you admire in the fashion world?" he asked.

"Well, I like Valentino and of course Chanel."

"I'm partial to Burberry myself," he said.

"Emma Watson looked so great in those Burberry trench coats," said Isabelle wistfully. "Remember that campaign? She modelled for them after she finished the *Harry Potter* films."

"Don't mention *Harry Potter*," said Bertie, fanning his face. "Almost every British actor was asked to star in that franchise. Everyone except *moi*." He bowed his head.

"Really?" Isabelle looked shocked. "Why not?"

"One of life's greatest mysteries," he answered. "I always saw myself as Professor Lockhart but Branagh pipped me to the post."

Gabriella stared at him in fascination. "It must be so cool to be famous," she said.

Bertie nodded. "It is if one manages it properly. Sometimes it can be a curse."

"I can't imagine that."

"The world is strange," mused Bertie. "We're all human yet we put certain people on pedestals. Celebrity culture is interesting. Why are some deemed more important than others?"

"For their achievements, I guess," answered Gabriella.

"I'm not sure that's it," said Bertie thoughtfully. "Anyway, the public think celebrities have a fine old time of it yet the reality is very different. There is a constant pressure to look well and stay on top. It's really quite exhausting."

"I hope I find out someday."

"Oh?"

"I want to be as famous as Chanel."

"I see." He regarded her for a moment. "I sense a burning ambition in you. I sense that you will stop at nothing to get what you want."

Gabriella shifted in her seat uncomfortably.

"Just be careful along the way," he continued. "Don't forget where you came from. That's the best advice I can give anyone."

Isabelle clinked her glass with Gabriella's. "You'll do it without that Oberon, Gabs. No doubt."

"Oberon?" Bertie asked in surprise. "Whatever does she want with him?"

"I want to be his protégée," said Gabriella simply. "That's why I tag along every day."

"Well, good luck there." Bertie shook his head. "He's a tough cookie. From the wrong side of the tracks."

"Really?" Isabelle perked up. "I didn't know that. What with his posh accent and all."

"All put on," said Bertie conspiratorially. "He transformed himself into a brand. The man was born in a council flat near Brixton in London. Not that I judge him for that. Not in the slightest."

142

"Go on," said Isabelle.

"He is a determined fellow and when he made it big he cast aside his roots and became Oberon, the Fairy King from *A Midsummer Night's Dream*."

Gabriella inhaled sharply. It was fate. She too was from the wrong side of the tracks. She too would make it like him.

"Is he very difficult to work with?" asked Isabelle. "Word on the street is that he's a total bitch."

"Oh, awful," said Bertie. "It was rumoured that he made Naomi Campbell cry and that's not easy, I can tell you." He laughed. "If you ever experience his wrath, just remember one thing."

"What?" asked Gabriella curiously.

"His real name is Sidney Brown."

Isabelle laughed. "It doesn't have the same ring to it."

"Quite." Bertie smiled. "Now, who's for a top-up?"

ꬓ Chapter Eleven ꬕ

Later that night, Gabriella hung the aquamarine gown on her wardrobe door and fingered the material lightly. It made her feel warm inside to think that Raphael Baptiste had asked her to bring it along to the set. That she, Gabriella Ruiz Álvarez, had been instrumental in changing the course of the shoot.

It had been out of character for her to speak out so honestly. In truth, she couldn't believe her audacity. Yet, it had worked.

She took off her clothes and put on her nightie. She was exhausted after her day. What with the fashion show coming up and the graduation, she was really busy. Now, on top of everything else, she had to go back to the studio tomorrow with the gown. Where would she get the time?

Isabelle walked into her room with a glass of water.

"Hydrate, Gabs," she commanded.

"Thanks, Zsa Zsa." She yawned loudly as she took the glass. "Thank God we left when we did. There will be some sore heads tomorrow."

Isabelle laughed. "Especially Bertie. He really likes his bubbles, right? Like mother's milk."

"I really like him," said Gabriella thoughtfully. "He's so friendly and genuine. I mean, we've only know him a day and already I feel like he's been in my life forever."

"I know!" agreed Isabelle. "I keep forgetting who he is. I mean, he's super-famous yet you'd never think it."

"Classy."

"You got it." Isabelle put her hand on her heart. "I swear to be as cool as him when I'm a super star."

Gabriella giggled. "But of course." She drank off the water and put the glass on her bedside table. "I can't believe you'll be wearing my gown tomorrow."

"I know, right? Talk about being in the right place at the right time!" She smiled. "Who needs Oberon with you around?"

Gabriella laughed. "I have a fantasy that he'll turn up and be blown away by my talent. He'll see the dress and understand the time and effort that went into getting it right."

"If I'm honest, your version looks nicer." Isabelle crossed her heart. "No kidding."

"Really?" Gabriella laughed. "Well, let's get some sleep. Thanks for the water and I'll see you in the morning."

"What do you think of Raphael?" asked Isabelle as Gabriella got into bed.

"Intense, but cool." Gabriella narrowed her eyes. "What do you think?"

"Oh, he's fine," said Isabelle airily. "He might be in a better mood now the rock is gone."

"Fine? Only fine?" Gabriella grinned.

"Yes, fine. What are you saying?"

"Night, Zsa Zsa." She turned off her reading lamp, lay down and pulled her duvet over her head.

"What do you mean? Gabby?"

"Close the door on your way out, Isabelle."

Raphael was already at the studio when Gabriella and

Isabelle arrived the next morning. He was drinking a cup of coffee and talking on the phone. He waved as they walked by and then continued with his conversation, pacing the floor as he spoke.

Isabelle wore a similar dress to the day before – a simple sundress that fell just above the knee and strappy sandals. Gabriella had opted for a similar look. She wore a dark-red shift dress and black espadrilles. Her lustrous dark hair was hanging loose and her eyes were made up with dark shadow.

She had the aquamarine gown draped carefully over her arm. "Where's Kim?" she asked, looking around. "She'll know what to do with this."

"At the rate she was downing vodka last night, I'd say in bed." Isabelle made a face.

They paused by the dressing-room door and waited for Raphael to finish his conversation. Isabelle straightened her dress and kept fidgeting with her hair.

"You look great," whispered Gabriella. "Just relax."

"What do you mean?" she asked indignantly. "You keep implying that –"

"Good morning!" Raphael smiled at them both. "It's nice to see that you're on time. I sent out a memo last night to the rest of the crew to be here for a briefing and it evidently was a waste of time."

Gabriella held out the dress. "This is what I was talking about yesterday. It's a replica."

"Good. Why don't you and the mod – I mean, Isabelle – go out back and get ready. I'll just telephone a few people and shout a little."

Isabelle stared at him dreamily as he walked away. "Did you hear him say my name?" she whispered as they pushed open the door of the dressing room. "*Eeez*-abelle."

146

Gabriella nudged her. "You're so into him, Zsa Zsa. Don't even deny it."

"I am not," she denied, blushing. "He's just cute is all. And I like his accent. And his hair and he has a great body for his age …"

They emerged fifteen minutes later to find the studio transformed. The set-design crew were measuring a red carpet and pinning it down. Brad was positioning the cameras and Kim was talking on her hands-free set and writing furiously on her clipboard. Even Bertie had turned up, wearing black shades and looking pale. He waved half-heartedly as they approached.

"Morning, my darlings."

Gabriella patted his shoulder. "You look rough."

"Nothing that tons of make-up won't fix." He groaned. "Why didn't I share that taxi with you two last night? Instead I ended up singing a rather terrible rendition of 'Lilli Marlene' while standing on a chair."

"At least you're not a sailor anymore," Isabelle consoled him. "No boat or white uniform or sea spray." She smiled.

"You're quite right. I don't think I could handle some *mal de mer* right now. Not in this state."

Kim marched up and cleared her throat for attention. "Bertie, you're needed in make-up. I've managed to source a tuxedo for you and it will be here in ten."

"Of course, my dear. I'll be right there."

"And you? Apparently you have a dress?" She turned to Isabelle.

"It's right here," said Isabelle. "On me. I just need some make-up."

"Well then, off you go." Kim sighed dramatically. "Time is precious, people."

Bertie stood up and held out his hand. "Let me escort you to the magician's quarters," he said to Isabelle. "Let us be transformed into stars."

"Why the hell is he changing things anyway?" Kim grumbled. "I woke up to see that memo and I knew my day would be chaotic."

Gabriella said nothing.

"At least the rock has been removed," said Bertie.

"Right, listen, everyone!" Raphael clapped his hands for attention. "Change of plan. I will now be creating a montage of clips from Allegra's greatest roles. Then to finish, a red-carpet scenario from the night she won the Oscar – using Isabelle. She will be in the centre with the world looking on and envying her. Cameras flashing and people screaming. Bertie will escort her out of the frame and then we cut to the perfume bottle with the tagline: *Be a Star with Allegra Starr*."

"Do we need to rent a crowd?" asked Kim.

"No, we'll use CGI." Raphael turned around and began to relate his vision to Brad.

Walking up the red carpet, he turned and looked over his shoulder. Just like the shot in Gabriella's portfolio.

"We will start with the red carpet," he announced.

Gabriella took a seat on an available chair. The lights in the studio were so bright she was almost squinting. It was no wonder that Bertie was wearing shades.

Surely Oberon will turn up today. Surely.

Bertie arrived back first, looking dashing in a white tuxedo. His hair was slicked back and he wore a gold ring on his pinkie. "I'm Rick Blaine," he said, taking a bow. "Now where's my Ingrid Bergman?"

On cue, Isabelle appeared. Her hair was curled slightly and pinned up to the side. Her eyes were as dramatic as the previous day with dark shades and kohl. Her lips were glossy and her body was poured into the aquamarine dress. Gabriella gasped.

"You look stunning!" she exclaimed.

Bertie was gaping too. "Such beauty," he said to himself. "Fabulous."

Raphael turned and stopped dead. Isabelle held up her head and walked confidently onto the set. Still, he stared.

Bertie snapped his fingers. "Earth to Monsieur Baptiste! Hello? *Bonjour*?"

Raphael tore his eyes away. "*Oui*?"

"Where do you want me?"

"At the top. You are at the end of her parade."

"Righty-o!" Bertie saluted him like a cadet.

Raphael bounded up to where Isabelle was standing and put his big hands on her small waist.

She stiffened. "Yes?"

"I want you slightly to the right," he said softly, propelling her sideways.

"Okay." Her green eyes were huge.

Suddenly there was a crash. All heads swung around to see Kim on the ground. "I tripped,' she wailed. "Oh my leg!"

Raphael was by her side in flash. "Oh no, you poor thing! Brad, help me!" They lifted her onto a chair and Raphael rubbed her ankle. "Is it here?" he asked, massaging.

"Yes," she said with a smirk. "Just there."

Later that evening, Gabriella was cleaning the make-up from her eyes, sitting in front of her mirror in her bedroom.

Oberon hadn't shown up, despite four phone calls from a furious Raphael. He was in the Bahamas and was not to be disturbed.

Allegra had called from Cannes at lunchtime and demanded to be kept in the loop. How dare they remove the rock without her consent? She wanted the girl on the rock. She wanted the wind machine and the sea spray. How could they disregard her wishes? Raphael took the phone and explained that the most inspiring vision of all would be Allegra herself. Who better to represent the brand than a replica of her heyday? It would give the ordinary woman a chance to be a star. Mollified, she had calmed down.

Then Bertie had cried off sick, citing a tummy bug, but everyone knew he had a horrendous hangover. So, in the end, they had very little to show for their long day. Raphael had pleaded with everyone to work the weekend but to no avail. Even Kim said no. Everyone had plans. It was New York after all.

"*Gabs?*" called Isabelle from the kitchen. "Do you want a cup of green tea?"

"Sure. I'll be right there."

Her great plan wasn't so great after all. With a sigh, she closed her bedroom door and joined Isabelle in the kitchen.

The next evening she was busily sketching a gown when her phone rang. Absentmindedly she took the call.

"Gabby?"

It was her mother.

"Mama! Good to hear from you."

"Gabby, I have a problem."

Gabriella felt her skin grow cold. "A problem? What's the matter?"

"I'm sick."

"Sick?"

"I can't stop vomiting. I thought I'd be over it by now but it's still as bad as ever."

"Oh, Mama. Will I come over?"

"No, no. Teresa and Lita are looking after me. The

thing is, I have Frank's birthday dinner tonight. Gabby, I'm not able. *Mi cariña*, I need you to take my place."

"*What?*" She jumped up. "Me? Waitress?" Hugo's face flashed through her mind. "Are you serious?"

"I tried to get a replacement maid but the agency was closed. I tried everyone I could think of but no one was available. I can't tell Her Majesty now. She'd be so mad."

"But why me?"

"I asked Teresa but she has the girls and I don't know anyone else who knows the house and the staff like you do …" Magda let out a huge sigh. "I don't have the energy to search, Gabby. Please help me out."

"Oh, Mama …"

"Please, Gabriella."

"Mama, I can't. Celine's my friend. It would be weird."

"You're the only one I know with experience. Please, Gabby."

Gabriella's heart ached. Magda must be desperate.

"Of course," she said eventually. "You rest up, Mama. I'll sort it out."

Waitress? At Hugo's house?

She put her head in her hands. Letting him go had been hard. He filled her thoughts and she spent hours fantasising about what might have been. Now, she was going to see him again, but as the hired help. Then there was the gallery – it was very late to let Tara down. It was a busy time of year, what with tourists and all.

There was nothing else for it – she would have to call Tara and tell her of her mother's sickness.

Tara put her at ease immediately. "Of course you should help. Don't worry about the gallery, sweetheart. I'll take care of it. There are a couple of people I can call on to stand in."

❧ Chapter Twelve ❧

Bruno the chef waved at her when she entered the kitchen of the du Maurier mansion.

"How's Magda?' he called as he chopped a bulb of fennel.

"Really sick," answered Gabriella. "So, here I am."

She had decided not to text Celine and tell her the story. Better to just appear and get on with the job at hand.

Maria, the young maid, appeared holding a tray. "I heard about your mama," she said sympathetically. "There's a black-and-white uniform for you in the back room. Her Majesty insists that we all look the same."

"Sure," said Gabriella with a heavy heart. She had imagined meeting Hugo again under different circumstances. As a world famous designer perhaps. Certainly not as a waitress at his parents' soirée.

Ten minutes later she surveyed herself in the stained old mirror in the staffroom. Her frame was slightly curvier than her mother, so the black skirt clung to her bottom and thighs. Using an elastic band, she put her long hair into a ponytail and then she put on some lip-gloss.

Don't think about Hugo, she schooled herself. That ship has sailed. Do this for Mama. What do you care about those people?

Taking a deep breath, she entered the kitchen once more.

"Gabriella!" called Bruno. "You're up. Take those canapés right away."

"Sure," she said, plastering a smile on her face.

The conservatory had been transformed for the dinner party. A long table with a white lacy cloth dominated the room and the chairs were covered in silk. Two candelabra stood at each end of the table and each place was set with silver cutlery and fine china plates. The guests were out in the manicured garden enjoying glasses of Dom Perignon and tiny canapés prepared by Bruno that morning.

Gabriella took a tray of blinis with Beluga caviar and crème fraiche and walked outside. The sun blinded her momentarily and she held up her free hand to shield its rays.

She instantly spotted Tara and Christian Jacob over by the rose garden talking to Luca and Charlotte.

"Gabby!" called Tara. "Come here, sweetie." Her vibrant red hair was piled on her head and she wore a multicoloured dress that fell below the knee.

She walked over to Luca's mother and offered the group a blini.

"Not for me," said Christian, busy on his iPhone. Again, Gabriella was struck at how like Luca he was. Both were tall and he had similar bone structure. Christian looked good for his age which Gabriella guessed must be about fifty.

Luca shook his head too. "Fish eggs are not my thing," he said distastefully.

Only Charlotte took one and smiled in thanks. Then she turned to Christian. "So, talk me through why the subpoena was granted?"

Luca rolled his eyes. "Attorney talk," he whispered to Gabriella.

"Is your *abuela* here, Luca?" she asked, looking around. "I've never met her."

Luca shook his head. "Mimi? No, she was too tired. She's too tired for a lot of things lately." His expression changed and he looked sombre.

Tara put her hand on his arm. "She's old, honey. Can you imagine her out here right now, standing all this time?"

"I guess not."

"Mimi prefers events during the day now," went on Tara. "She likes to go to bed early."

"Lita is like that too," said Gabriella reassuringly and Luca half-heartedly smiled.

"How was the gallery today?" Gabriella asked, changing the subject.

"Crazy," said Tara with a smile. "But we survived."

"I'm so sorry again for letting you down this evening," said Gabriella apologetically. "I just had to cover for my mother."

"Don't give it another thought," said Tara kindly. "A friend of mine was happy to stand in."

Luca nudged her playfully. "Hugo's here," he teased.

"Luca!" She blushed and was glad to see that Charlotte was oblivious to their conversation. "There's nothing going on there and you know it."

"Yeah, right." He looked unconvinced.

She turned to see Victoria glaring in her direction. She had spent too long chatting. "I'll see you guys later," she said hurriedly and walked away, balancing the tray on the palm of her hand.

The Ashley Hamiltons were out in force. Caroline smirked when she spotted her in a maid's uniform. Gabriella groaned inwardly. Of all the guests to serve.

Miserably, she continued on her way.

Maurice, Frank's CEO brother, was drinking whiskey and his frozen-faced wife stood by his side. She was sipping a glass of sparkling water, her fingers festooned with diamonds. Maurice winked at Gabriella as she passed by and she felt her skin grow cold. She hadn't forgotten his lewd comments at Celine's party. His face was as red as ever, indicating that he'd had a fair share of whiskey already.

Celine was chatting to her father and Hugo, her blonde hair blowing in the sea breeze. She gasped when she saw her.

"Gabby?" she said in surprise. "Why are you here?"

Hugo's head swung around. She could feel the mortification rising up within her. She hadn't seen him since that day in the park.

Stay cool, Gabby. You have nothing to be ashamed of. Nothing at all.

She walked towards Celine, the tray on her arm. "Blini?" she asked politely.

Celine pulled her aside. "Gabs! Tell me why you're serving me canapés!"

"Mama is sick," she whispered. "I had to cover for her."

"Oh." Celine looked uncomfortable. "You poor thing."

"Why? It's just serving people some food." She raised her head proudly. "I do this at Brasserie Michel two nights a week."

"I know, but that's to strangers – this is *us*." Celine shrugged. "It's going to feel weird asking you for more water or bread."

"There will be bread at this party?" Gabriella looked mock-shocked, trying to lighten the mood. "Victoria is slipping!"

155

"Oh, she won't eat it," said Celine, relieved the tension had passed. "God forbid."

"Look, I'll see you later," said Gabriella briskly. "I'd better serve these."

"Sure."

"I've lots of news too. Zsa Zsa and I have been living the dream the past couple of days." She gave a small wave. "Talk later."

She could feel Hugo's eyes on her as she moved away.

Bruno put the last scallop on a plate. "Right, go!" he commanded, perspiration on his brow.

Gabriella and the two other maids jumped into action. She had been avoiding the conservatory until now. However, the starter was ready and it was showtime.

Luca, Charlotte and Celine were at the right end of the long table. Hugo was next to them, his broad back visible. Maria headed in their direction with plates and Gabriella sighed in relief. She would take the left end and avoid all eye contact.

Smiling mechanically, she carefully placed each china plate in front of Victoria, Frank, Tara and Christian.

"Thank you, my love," said Tara warmly.

Christian was typing furiously on his phone.

"Chris! Cut that out," said Tara. "Your starter is here."

"It's that goddamn Mackenzie case," he said, throwing his phone on the table. "I've got to talk to Charlotte again later. The gold-digger wife is causing problems."

Chester and Veronica Ashley Hamilton sat opposite with Caroline on their right. Caroline looked at Gabriella disdainfully as she deposited a plate in front of her.

"More wine," she snapped, making sure that Hugo didn't hear her tone. "Make sure it's chilled this time."

Gabriella nodded and hurried away. Typical that Caroline would be there. Typical that she felt inferior again.

Her eyes cast down, she arrived back to the table with a chilled bottle of Pouilly Fumé. Carefully, she refilled Caroline's glass and moved on.

"*Oh, Gabriella?*" Caroline's nasal twang carried over the noise.

Gabriella stopped dead.

"This is lukewarm."

Hugo had been strategically placed on Caroline's right by Victoria. "Does it matter?" he said.

"Get me another glass, please," continued Caroline, ignoring him.

Gabriella felt like walking away, but she didn't. Victoria was watching them.

"Of course," she said. "I'll be right back."

She rushed out of the room and counted to ten.

Do this for Mama, she said silently. *Do this for her*.

Again she came back with an ice-cold bottle. Hugo smiled encouragingly at her as she passed but she didn't reciprocate. This was business and she was a professional.

She poured a new glass of wine and placed it on the table on Caroline's right. "Is this okay?" she asked politely.

Caroline sipped it and closed her eyes. "It's better," she said, "but not perfect. I suppose it'll have to do."

In the meantime, Maria had served the remaining starters and the guests were tucking in.

"*Hey, Gabs!*" shouted Luca. "*Get over here!*"

She obeyed immediately. "Don't call me Gabs," she whispered. "I'm your server tonight."

"Don't give me that," he said scornfully. "How's Magda? Bruno says she's got a stomach flu."

Hugo was watching their exchange intently.

"She's okay," said Gabriella, feeling very uncomfortable. "So, would you like more wine?"

Celine held out her glass. "Fill me up, Gabby. It's going to be a long night."

After the main course had been cleared, Frank made a speech. He clinked his glass with a dessert spoon.

"*Attention, everybody!*" he boomed and the conversation died away. "I just want to say a few words on my fiftieth birthday."

Everyone clapped.

"I told Vic that I didn't want a big party so she organised this." He raised his glass. "I think you'll all agree that it's been a big success. To Victoria, my wife!"

Everyone clapped again and Victoria bowed her head. "Why thank you, sugar," she said demurely.

"To my kids – Charlotte, Hugo and Celine. I'm proud of you guys and hope you'll be as happy as I am."

Caroline nudged Hugo and winked. Gabriella went cold. Caroline was like a predator and he was her prey. There would be no escape for him.

"This year will be full of celebrations," continued Frank. "My baby girl Char is about to marry Luca and then we'll be related to that son of a bitch over there." He pointed at Christian and guffawed at his own joke. Christian, who was still typing an email on his phone, didn't notice.

"*Chris!*" hissed Tara.

"What?" he said irritably.

"Who knows?" continued Frank. "I might be a grandad by my fifty-first birthday. Right, kids?"

Luca choked on his wine.

"Are you okay?" asked Charlotte in concern, patting his back.

"Sure, sure."

"I don't want kids yet either," she said soothingly. "I want to make partner."

Luca's expression darkened. "You don't say."

"So, let's all raise a glass to me!" Frank laughed uproariously.

"*To Frank!*" they all chorused.

"*To my big brother!*" shouted Maurice. "But for Frankie here, I would probably be living in a trailer park. Elena wouldn't be my wife, that's for sure. Not without money."

Victoria pursed her lips. Maurice could always be counted on to lower the tone. No one needed to know the inheritance situation. Especially those Ashley Hamiltons.

"Hardly, Maurice," she said stiffly. "You're a du Maurier after all."

"The black sheep," he said laughing. "If Frank hadn't become an attorney, I'd be sweeping the streets."

"Maurice!" said Elena under her breath. "Enough."

He glared at her. "I'll say what I want, you hear?"

Celine's eyes met Charlotte's in alarm. Uncle Maurice tended to be a loose cannon at family functions. He had consumed a lot of whiskey and the night was young.

Gabriella and Maria headed to the kitchen as Bruno was waiting to serve dessert.

"All good up there?" he asked, adding fruit to the cream-topped meringue.

Maria rolled her eyes. "The usual. The women ate almost nothing – well, except for Celine of course, and the men are hitting the whiskey hard."

"Well, we're almost there, girls. Take these desserts up and we're set."

The guests retired to the front sitting room after the meal.

Gabriella and the rest of the maids cleared the table efficiently. It took about twenty minutes for everything to be dismantled and all the ware brought to the kitchen.

"I'm pooped," said Maria, wiping her brow. "Bruno's lucky to be finished."

"What's up next?" asked Gabriella, consulting the itinerary. "Coffee and petits fours." She sighed. "Will this ever end?"

"Not long now," said Noreen, another maid.

Maria started to load cups and saucers onto a large tray. "We're almost there, Gabby. Almost."

Bruno had prepared delectable Viennese fingers, mini choux swans filled with cream and tiny macaroons in bright colours. Gabriella arranged them artistically on some plates. Noreen placed bowls of sugar on the tray along with the milk. Breda, the other maid, had tea and coffee ready to pour.

Maria heaved the tray of crockery onto her arm and they all made their way upstairs.

Luca and Celine were standing around a seated Charlotte. Luca was telling a story and laughing. Tara and Christian were listening politely to Veronica Ashley Hamilton. Gabriella knew by Tara's face that she was bored. She nodded at opportune times and stifled yawns. Christian didn't even bother to look interested. Instead he was intermittently staring at Charlotte and checking his phone.

Maria served coffee in tiny espresso cups while Gabriella handed around the tiny treats.

"Fabulous," said Tara, taking a biscuit. "Your chef is a wiz in the kitchen, Victoria," she added.

Victoria nodded. "Yes, I'm very pleased with him." She refused a biscuit and had black coffee instead.

Elena did the same.

Gabriella moved on and came face to face with Maurice who was sitting in an armchair.

"Hello, baby," he said leeringly. "Sure, I'll take a cake." He grabbed a fistful of macaroons. Looking closer, Gabriella could see that he was extremely drunk.

She smiled and moved on. Suddenly something slapped her bottom and there was a roar of laughter. She got such a shock, she dropped the plate and it smashed onto the tiled floor.

"*Gabriella!*" Victoria rushed forward, her face furious. "What in God's name are you doing?"

Mortified, Gabriella fell to her knees and started to sweep up the debris with her bare hands.

"I'm sorry, I'm sorry," she said in distress. "I'm so sorry."

Hugo was by her side in a flash. "Don't cut yourself," he said gently, pulling her hands away. He calmed her with his touch.

Her eyes filled with tears and she got to her feet.

"I'm sorry," she repeated. "I got a shock and ..."

"I saw what happened," he said, a muscle flickering in his cheek.

"Don't say anything," she pleaded quietly. "It will ruin the party."

"Go and replenish the sweets," ordered Victoria coldly. "Let's move on."

Hugo turned on his mother. "Did you see what happened?" he demanded, seething. "Maurice –"

"Enough!" Victoria's eyes flashed. "I saw nothing."

Maria appeared with a brush and started to sweep up the mess.

Celine rushed up. "Gabby, are you okay?"

Gabriella backed away. "I'll just get some more biscuits. I'm so sorry, Mrs. du Maurier, I'm so sorry."

The last thing she saw before she fled from the room was Caroline Ashley Hamilton's smug face.

Maria took up the plate of petits fours in the end. "You sit here and have a cup of tea," she suggested. "Stay away from that creep, you hear?"

"Do you think everyone saw?" asked Gabriella fearfully. "Mama will kill me."

"No one saw," lied Maria. "Anyway, it wasn't your fault, Gabby. He's the pig."

She sighed. "It doesn't work that way and you know it. They'll say I provoked him in my tight skirt. It's only tight because I'm too fat."

Maria laughed. "Fat? You're joking, right? You're perfect, girl. Don't forget it."

Luca appeared a few minutes later. "Hey, Gabs, are you okay?"

She nodded and sipped her tea. "Just lying low. I'm guessing that I'm not Victoria's favourite person right now."

"Ah, she'll live." He patted her back awkwardly. "He's always the same. Maurice, I mean. He doesn't know when to stop."

"I know." Her eyes filled with angry tears. "I guess it doesn't matter with someone like me, right?"

"Wrong!" he said angrily. "That guy should get a punch for what he did."

Gabriella smiled. "Look, I'm good here. Go back to your fiancée and enjoy your night."

"And hear about that Mackenzie case? I can't wait." He ruffled her ponytail. "Maybe it was the schoolgirl look that did it."

She stuck out her tongue. "Yeah, yeah."

"Have you got a ride home?"

"I'll take the train."

"You sure you're okay?"

She nodded. "Just fine."

Five minutes later she got up and washed her cup in the large sink. Going into the back room, she grabbed her coat. She couldn't wait to get home. She wouldn't bother to change her clothes now – her mother could bring the uniform back when she returned to work. Pulling down her hair, she shook out her long tresses. The Westbury station was a ten-minute walk and her feet ached from rushing around. She walked out of the back room and bumped straight into Hugo.

"Oh!" She felt her cheeks redden.

"I just wanted to check that you were okay," he said softly.

She felt her heartrate increase. Suddenly every fibre in her body came alive. She willed him to hold her. Oh, how she craved his touch!

Reaching out, he brushed a tendril of hair from her shoulder.

"Gabby," he began, closing his eyes.

She allowed him to draw her head towards his. Closing her eyes, she waited for his lips to brush hers. However, Victoria's voice ruined the moment. It got louder and louder, indicating that she was en route to the kitchen. Gabriella snapped out of it immediately.

"Oh, why are we back to this?" she said in frustration, pushing him away. "It's impossible – just impossible."

"Stop overthinking things ..."

"Goodbye, Hugo."

She walked away, banging the door behind her.

The sky was foggy, hiding the moonlight behind its

murky haze. There were two lamps at the entrance of the estate, but only one was in working order. Still, the light it emitted was poor.

She walked briskly down the driveway, her thoughts racing. Was Isabelle right? Was she crazy to deny her feelings? So what if he was leaving soon? Was it worth it?

She was so deep in thought, she tripped on a stone and almost fell. The darkness was indeed disconcerting.

Her phone! Her phone had a torch. She rummaged in her bag frantically, searching for the familiar shape. Her fingers closed around her hairbrush and her eyeshadow palate, but no phone. When did she last have it? She had texted Isabelle earlier about Caroline and the chilled white wine. Isabelle had texted back calling the other girl a 'stone-cold bitch' with lots of red angry-faced emojis. She had put the phone down when Maria called her to refill the water pitchers.

She groaned. It was on the kitchen counter. Over by the notice board.

Drat. She would have to go back

On her right, a small glowing red light caught her attention. The accompanying smoke indicated that it was someone smoking a cigarette. There was a rustling noise and a small grunt. She stopped dead. The pitch-black night made it difficult to see.

"Hello?" she called fearfully. "Is someone there?"

There was the sound of a twig breaking and the red light disappeared. Someone had obviously stamped it out. Every instinct in her body screamed at her to run. Something wasn't right – something bad was about to happen.

Turning around she started to walk briskly, heading in the direction of the house once more.

The tight skirt made speed difficult. Hiking it up, she

started to half-run, the lights in the distance her destination.

Suddenly something grabbed her long hair and she halted.

"Well, hello," said a voice in her ear.

Terrified, she didn't recognise the voice initially. There was a smell of whiskey and sweat.

"How about we get to know each other a bit better?" he said, rubbing his crotch suggestively against her back.

It was Maurice du Maurier.

She couldn't breathe. She wanted to yell or scream but terror had silenced her. Gasping for breath, she struggled but to no avail. He dragged her towards the rose-garden gate.

"Just a few minutes will do," he said, breathing heavily. "I don't take long."

"No," she protested, but her voice was barely audible. "Please."

He ignored her and started to pull up her skirt.

"*Stop!*" She pushed him violently away but he only laughed.

Shoving her onto the ground, her head hit the surface with a thump. She could hear noise in the distance. Lying on top of her, his weight pinned her to the grass. His hand roamed her body, grasping her breasts and waist.

"Let me go!" she said breathlessly. His weight made breathing difficult.

"Just shut up and enjoy." He kissed her roughly, forcing his tongue into her mouth. His breath was foul and she gagged. She tried to push him away again but he was too big.

With all the strength she could muster, she screamed, "*Stop!*"

He laughed. "Game-playing – I like it!" He grabbed her

white shirt and tore it open, revealing her bra. "Wow, these babies are what I'm talking about," he said, gazing at her breasts.

Tears began to flow down her cheeks. She was a virgin. She had always imagined that she would lose her virginity to someone she loved.

Not like this, she thought in despair. Not like this.

He undid his belt with one hand, holding her down with the other. In her heart she knew that she would never break free. He was too strong. Closing her eyes, she tried to think of something else. Blotting out his heavy breathing and snorting, she tried to transcend reality. She could feel his wet lips on her neck and she started to pray.

Suddenly, the weight disappeared and she heard a voice roar, "*What the fuck are you doing?*"

Disorientated, she sat up, pulling her torn shirt around her. In the darkness she could make out two silhouettes: one was Maurice, she recognised his paunch, and the other was Hugo. Her heart soared.

Hugo.

In slow motion, she watched him punch his uncle and knock him to the ground. Maurice got to his feet and staggered away, wiping the blood from his mouth.

Hugo rushed over to her and helped her to her feet.

"Are you okay? Are you okay?" he asked frantically.

She nodded numbly. "How did you find me?"

"You left your phone. I followed you to give it back and I heard you scream." He closed his eyes and kissed her temple. "Thank God I did. Thank God."

She clung to him. "I was so scared. I thought that he would –"

"Don't say it." He kissed her hair. "Come on. Let me take you back to the house."

"*No!*" She shook her head frantically. "I can't go back there."

Hugo pulled her close. "*Shhh*, don't worry. I got it."

"I've made too much of a scene already," she said, sobbing. "Imagine their faces if they found out about this."

"*Shhh,* let me take you home."

"To Manhattan?"

"Why sure, to Manhattan. You can't be alone right now."

"It's fine, Hugo. I'll be okay …"

"I insist." He put his jacket around her shivering body. "Let's go."

✎ Chapter Thirteen ☙

The apartment was empty when they finally arrived. The train journey had been a subdued affair. Her cheeks were swollen from crying and she couldn't stop shaking. She gestured to the couch. "Make yourself at home. I need to get out of these clothes." She pulled his jacket tightly around her torn blouse.

"No problem." He took a seat on the couch.

"What will Victoria say when she notices that you're missing?"

Hugo shrugged. "I'll text her and say that I went to bed with a migraine or something."

"Caroline will be looking for you ..." She bit her lip.

"Well, she can look." His blue eyes met hers. "I'm staying here."

"What if they see Maurice? He probably has a split lip."

"That's his problem. Hell, I don't care what they think. He's lucky I didn't kill him."

She closed her bedroom door. Taking off Hugo's jacket, she draped it on the chair by the window. Looking in the mirror, she nearly threw up. Her breasts were exposed and her blouse destroyed. When she thought of what could have happened! She could still smell his breath on her face.

She threw the blouse in the bin, followed by the skirt. What if they noticed it was missing at the house? What if her mother asked her about it? She shook her head. She couldn't think about that right now.

She needed to shower. It felt necessary to scour the imprint of his hands off her body.

Hugo was flicking through a *Vogue* magazine when she emerged in a large fleecy robe and clutching a towel.

"Do you mind if I take a shower?"

"No problem. I'm happy here reading about the upcoming fall collection." He grinned.

Minutes later she was standing under the jet of hot water, vigorously rubbing her skin with shower gel. Her mother must never know what happened. No one must know. She had to make sure that Hugo wouldn't take things further.

"Are you okay?" he asked when she came back with a pink face and her hair wound up in a towel like a turban.

She nodded, her brown eyes huge. "I'm pretty tired so …"

He gazed at her. "Do you want company?"

"Isabelle should be back later."

"Gabby, let me help you." He got up and stood facing her. Grabbing her shoulders, he forced her to look at him. "After what happened tonight, I've no intention of trying anything. I just don't want you to be alone right now."

She nodded again. "Okay," she whispered.

"Lead the way."

She jumped under the duvet right away, still with her robe and towel on. He took off his shirt and pants and slid in beside her.

"Will you be too hot?" he asked with an amused expression.

She shook her head. "I'm good."

169

"Gabby," he said, pulling her close, "just relax. I'm not going to bite."

She let him spoon her and grasped his hand with hers. Pulling it upwards, she pressed it to her beating heart.

"My hair is wet," she said apologetically.

"Doesn't matter," he murmured. "It smells good. Like summer."

"I use coconut shampoo."

"*Hmmm*." He squeezed her and nuzzled closer. "Just close your eyes and know that you're safe," he said softly.

She obeyed. She fell asleep quite easily.

Cocooned under her duvet, they remained entwined until morning.

A wailing siren woke Gabrielle as it passed by the building. She jumped and for a moment forgot where she was. Then she felt the arm on her waist and she could hear breathing in her ear. Events of the day before came flooding back and she closed her eyes.

It had been such a close call.

She turned to find two blues eyes staring at her.

"Hey, you," he said gently. "Are you feeling okay?"

She nodded. "I just forgot where I was for a second. I've never had a man in my bedroom before." She blushed. "God, you must think I'm so lame."

"Not at all." He shifted in the bed and put his head on the crook of his arm. "I like it."

Isabelle was banging pots in the kitchen, singing at the top of her lungs. Gabriella giggled. "God gave her amazing looks and a great personality, but he sure held off when it came to musical talent."

"You got that right." Hugo smiled too. His eyes travelled around the room, taking in the multiple dresses hanging from every available hook and door. "Did you make those?" he asked.

"Yes," she answered. She pointed to a white gown hanging off the curtain rail. "That's a dress I designed for Monica, a girl in my class. She wanted an original piece for her graduation party."

"Nice," he said genuinely.

"Yeah, I'm pleased with it."

"So, when's the graduation?"

"Next week." She sighed. "Then it's the real world for me – I'm not sure that I'm ready."

"You'll be great." He stroked her cheek. "I'm sure of it."

She blushed again, unsure of what to do or say. "I'm so hot!" she muttered.

"I'm not surprised. You're still wearing that robe and the sun is shining outside."

She sat up and struggled out of the robe and towel, then threw them over the side of the bed. All she had underneath was a white cotton nightie that Lita had given her two Christmases ago. It was embroidered and had short sleeves. Isabelle always teased her about her nightwear as she herself opted for sexy silk ensembles with matching robes.

She lay down again.

Hugo reached out and fingered the embroidery lightly. "This is pretty."

"Go on, say it," she said hotly. "I look like a frump."

"Not in the slightest," he said. "I love this look."

Suddenly the bedroom door opened and Isabelle burst in. "Gabs, I'm making some ... *oh!*" She stopped dead. "Oh my God!"

Gabriella blushed furiously. "Zsa Zsa, you know Hugo."

Isabelle waved awkwardly. "Hey."

Hugo looked unperturbed. "Hey."

171

"So, you don't want pancakes, I take it?" said Isabelle, raising an eyebrow.

"I do." Gabriella nodded fervently. "Give me five minutes, Zsa Zsa. I'll be right there."

Isabelle smirked and banged the door behind her.

"She looked shocked," he said with a smile.

"I told you – I never bring guys back here."

"Good." He stroked her cheek. Suddenly his phone rang and he checked the screen. Celine's name was flashing.

"Answer it, Hugo," she implored. "She's probably worried about you."

He sighed and took the call. "Hey, what's up?"

Then there were lots of 'yeahs' and 'sures' and then he hung up.

"Momma is having a heart attack wondering where I am." He frowned. "I need to move out fast. I'm too old for this."

"What else did she say?" Gabriella looked fearful. "Did Maurice go back to the party?"

"She didn't say anything about him." His expression grew dark. "Knowing that son-of-a-bitch, no doubt he skulked off."

"Do you think he remembers?" she asked nervously.

"Probably." Hugo's face hardened. "He'll never mention it though. Too much to lose."

Suddenly she felt vulnerable and scared. What a close call it had been. Drawing her knees up to her chin, she pulled the duvet around her.

He understood immediately.

"Look, Celine would have mentioned it if anything had happened. Don't worry about it. No one will know."

"It's just my mama …"

"I get it, Gabby." He stroked her cheek with his finger.

"I won't tell a soul."

Neither spoke for a moment and she was sure he could hear the furious beating of her heart.

"Look, I'd better get back home," he said, jumping up. "Otherwise they'll have the CIA out looking for me." He pulled on his shirt. "Are you busy this week?"

She stared up at him. It was as though their conversation in Central Park had never happened. "Well, I've got Allegra's commercial tomorrow and my show and of course my graduation."

"Can you fit me in?" He pulled up his pants. "For five minutes or something?" A lock of hair fell over his eye and he smiled.

She smiled too. "Maybe."

"Good." He leaned down and kissed her nose. "I'm going to skip the pancakes if that's okay."

Gabriella shrugged. "Okay."

"Call me." He took his jacket from the back of the chair. "Forget what you should do. Just live in the moment."

Then he was gone.

Isabelle was eating her second pancake when Gabriella finally emerged. There was a large mug of coffee next to her plate and *The Ellen Show* was on the television in the background.

"What the hell is going on?" she asked. "I thought the Hugo thing was over."

"It was."

"So?"

"What a night." Gabriella filled a mug with coffee and added some sugar. "Oh, Zsa Zsa, it was awful."

"Awful? Why?"

"Remember Celine's drunk uncle at her party?"

Isabelle nodded. "The creepy guy. Sure, I remember him."

Gabriella sat down and her expression changed. "He attacked me," she said quietly. "In the garden as I walked to the train."

"*What?*" Isabelle nearly dropped her cup in horror. "Oh, Gabs. You poor thing!"

"Hugo saved me. He heard my screams and he saved me."

"Are you going to press charges?" Isabelle looked thoroughly shocked.

"No!" Gabriella looked horrified. "Mama would die if she knew. Plus, no one would believe me."

"What? Of course they would."

"No, they wouldn't! I'm the Hispanic maid – I'm a nobody. People like Maurice du Maurier get away with things like this all the time."

Isabelle banged her cup on the table, her green eyes blazing. "That's the most stupid thing I've ever heard! If you don't report him, he'll do it to someone else!"

"*No.*" Gabriella shook her head obstinately. "There's too much at stake. Mama would lose her job. Victoria would never let her continue to work there."

"Hugo might tell ..."

"He won't." Gabriella looked her straight in the eye. "He knows that it has to be kept a secret. He was so sweet, Zsa Zsa. He wouldn't let me go home alone."

"Good," interrupted Isabelle.

"And he ended up sleeping with me."

"Obviously."

"Nothing happened or anything. He literally just slept with me." Gabriella blushed.

Isabelle held up her hands. "Hey, I'm not judging!"

"So, we've decided to live in the moment." Her eyes glowed. "Just until he has to leave."

Isabelle said nothing for a moment and then leaned forward, taking Gabriella's hands in hers. "I'm delighted for you. You deserve some happiness, Gabby."

"Thanks, Zsa Zsa."

"Just make sure you're okay after what happened. That creep shouldn't get away with what he did."

"I've put it out of my mind," she answered firmly.

"If you're sure …"

"I'm sure."

Later that evening, Isabelle went for a run as the evening time was cooler. There wasn't an inch to spare in Gabriella's dress and she had just eaten a large pepperoni and fries. Raphael had put everyone under huge time pressure with the change of theme, so the objective was for everything to run as smoothly as possible. Secretly, Isabelle was delighted with the elongation of the shoot. She adored being the centre of attention and enjoyed Bertie's company. It was like she was being given a taste of a world she longed to be part of – it only served to whet her desire even more to make it.

Gabriella, who had eaten pizza and fries as well, was lying on her bed when Magda called, asking how it all went.

"It went well, Mama," lied Gabriella. "I wasn't as professional as you, but I did okay."

"Was Victoria pleased?"

She thought of Her Majesty's frozen face. "Oh, delighted, Mama."

"That's a relief. I cannot thank you enough, *mi cariña*."

"No problem. How are you feeling?"

"Much better. I think I'll be well enough to return tomorrow."

"As long as you don't overdo it and get sick again for my graduation."

"I promise I won't. I can't wait to see you up there. We will be so proud."

"Night, Mama."

"Night, Gabby."

She hung up the phone, an uneasy feeling in her heart. If her mother knew what had happened …

She couldn't bear the thought. She would make a big deal and Victoria would side with Maurice. That's how it worked. The rich protected the rich. So what if he attacked the busty maid? Who even cared?

Hugo had promised not to say anything and she trusted him. Isabelle was her best friend and no one else knew.

It could be contained.

Hugo had texted her all evening, making her laugh and she had let it happen. She was sick of being Miss Careful. She deserved some happiness, even if it was only for a few weeks. And long-distance relationships could work if both people were committed. Rather than trying to predict the future, she had to just enjoy the present.

The week ahead was going to be busy. What with the commercial shoot and the graduation, she would barely have time to sleep. She had messaged Hugo and warned him that it would be the weekend before they could meet.

She thought of the aquamarine gown that now hung in the backroom of the studio. Raphael was insisting that it be used as it was made to measure for Isabelle. She wondered what Oberon would make of it. He would hopefully be flattered. He could only be impressed when he turned up, right? Surely he would give her a chance.

⟣ Chapter Fourteen ⟢

The studio was buzzing when they arrived the next morning. All the cameras were set up and ready to go. Kim was tapping her foot impatiently, waiting for Isabelle to go to make-up.

"Finally," she said with a scowl. "They're waiting for you. Bertie's ready for the past hour."

"Nonsense," said Bertie, appearing out of nowhere. "I've only just been released. Stop telling porkies, Kimmy dear."

Kim reddened. "Let's go," she barked, ushering Isabelle away. "Raphael is anxious to begin."

Gabriella melted into the background, watching the crew efficiently work their magic.

Bertie sipped tea from a china cup and saucer. "I don't do polystyrene," he said with utter conviction. "I loathe those giant soulless cups."

Raphael was sitting at a small desk, his dark head bowed over a script. Using a pencil, he added notes and crossed out lines.

"What's he doing?" Gabriella asked Brad.

"Planning the scenes for the shoot. He's been researching Allegra's films all night and deciding which

scenes he'll use. Then there's sourcing costumes and all
that. He has a lot to organise."

"Oh." Gabriella looked at Raphael in awe.

Isabelle reappeared twenty minutes later in her gown.
Raphael looked up and smiled.

"*Bonjour*, Isabelle," he said softly. "Will you stand on
the red carpet, please?"

She positioned herself where he said and waited for
Brad and his team to adjust the cameras. A girl with a
make-up brush rushed out and fixed a tiny blemish on
Isabelle's cheek. Bertie straightened his jacket and waited
for his cue.

Raphael strode up to Isabelle and moved her slightly to
the left, his big hands on her waist. "There you go," he
said, releasing her. "Now, walk slowly and look back when
you get as far as *that* point." He indicated a spot on the
carpet.

She nodded and waited for the music to begin.

Just as Raphael counted down from five, a clipped
British accent interrupted.

"*Could someone tell me what the fuck is going on?*"

Everyone turned to see a man standing in the doorway.
He was six feet tall with a shaved head and a lithe frame.
His skin was dark brown thanks to his Jamaican mother
and his eyes a peculiar green thanks to his English father.
Even though he was in his mid-forties, he looked much
younger. Dressed in a tight white body top, blue faded
Levi's that clung to his narrow hips, a snakeskin belt and
brown cowboy boots, he looked every inch the fashion
icon.

"*Oberon*," said Gabriella in wonder.

"What the bloody hell is happening here?" he said, his
eyes blazing. "Who resurrected that dress without my

178

permission?" He walked up to Isabelle and circled her like she was prey. "It's not even my original. It's a fake." He looked up. "Who made it?" he demanded, scanning the room for competition.

Gabriella jumped forward. "I did!" she said joyfully. "My name is Gabriella and I've been waiting to meet –"

"*Who?*" he said, silencing her with a cold stare. "Who the hell are you? How dare you rip off my design? Well, it's hideous. Just hideous." He stabbed a finger at Isabelle. "You, take it off."

Isabelle looked at Raphael in shock. Gabriella shrank backwards, her cheeks hot with embarrassment.

"*Oberon!*" Raphael stormed up. "Don't come in here and interfere. You didn't answer your phone when I called."

"I was on holiday," he said. "*Vacances*, I believe you call it in Frog Land. Why would I answer a work call on my holidays?"

"Fine, but don't come in here and berate us."

Oberon laughed. "Berate you? Me?"

"Why are you back?"

"Oh, Allegra called and filled me in on the change of plan." He sighed. "Not very original, I've got to say. Better than the rock, but only slightly. She was bleating on about my overseeing the fashion side of things." He looked disdainfully at Isabelle's gown. "Lucky thing I did, yeah?"

"So, Allegra snaps her fingers and you come running?" Raphael asked scornfully.

"God, no." Oberon laughed. "I wouldn't cross the road for that diva. I have a show here next month – that's why I'm in town." He snapped his fingers. "*Riku? Riku?*" he yelled.

A small Japanese man rushed forward. "Yes, Oberon?"

"Coffee. Now."

"Of course, of course." He bowed and rushed off.

"Plus, I couldn't let my name be used freely without checking things first." He grimaced. "I'm delighted that I turned up. That replica is awful."

Gabriella wanted to run and hide. She had planned it all so differently. In her fantasy, Oberon had been enchanted by her attempt at emulating his work and, flattered, had offered her an apprenticeship. Suddenly, the portfolio she had brought seemed pointless as he would surely ridicule that too.

Isabelle felt the anger rise within her. Never one for holding back, her fiery temper matched her fiery-coloured hair. "Excuse me," she said in a commanding voice. "This replica is a damn sight better than yours. How dare you insult Gabby that way?" She raised herself to her full height.

Bertie pulled her back. "Don't rise to it," he said in an undertone. "He's notoriously like this. Just ignore him."

"Who the hell are you?" asked Oberon rudely. "My word, models have really lost their place. Do my ears deceive me or did that ginger Barbie doll over there just insult me?"

Raphael raised his fist. "Don't call her that."

"What? Ginger or Barbie?" Oberon asked silkily. "Both are quite apt, I think." He strolled over to the storyboard. "So she walks up the red carpet and Bertie appears." He turned to Bertie. "Albert, darling. I thought you were better than this. Selling out in your old age?"

Bertie grinned, unperturbed. "Not at all, my good man. Just helping out a friend. And this advertisement will be wonderful, I don't doubt it." He smiled sweetly.

Riku arrived back with a Starbuck's cup. "One skinny latte," he said breathlessly, handing the cup to Oberon.

"I wasn't going to stick around this morning," said

Oberon, ignoring him. "However, I feel that this will be too ridiculous to miss. Carry on, carry on!" He took a seat and crossed his long legs.

"What about the dress?" asked Raphael in exasperation. "Can we use it? I don't want a law suit later on."

"Fire away," he answered silkily. "I'm sure as hell am not making a new one. It's *so* nineties."

"Don't forget this dress made you famous, dear boy," chided Bertie.

"Much to my chagrin," said Oberon, sipping his drink. "Still, the original was much smaller. I don't know about models these days but they are at least three sizes bigger than in the past."

Isabelle glared.

"Calm yourself, my darling," said Bertie hurriedly.

"*Yoohoo!*" came a familiar voice, stalling things yet again.

Raphael groaned. Not Allegra too.

Oberon jumped to his feet and thrust his cup into Riku's hand. "Allegra, my darling girl!" he said, striding to meet her and kissing her on each cheek theatrically. "My word, you look so well. Looking at you now, I'd guess that you weren't a day over twenty-five."

"Oh, stop it," she said, delighted. "You're such a charmer."

"Charmer?" mouthed Isabelle to Gabriella. She made a cuckoo gesture, twirling her finger around next to her head.

"I got your message and took the next flight," continued Oberon. "They're using our dress – the very one that brought us together. I'm emotional."

"Well, I'm afraid the original is long gone," she said apologetically. "Some place in Ireland bought it – a museum called Newbridge or something? They exhibit stars' clothing."

"And what a star you are!" crooned Oberon. "Brighter than any in the sky. I'm sure the exhibition is centred around you, my darling."

"Oh, not just me, Oberon," she said, simpering. "Grace Kelly and Elizabeth Taylor feature too."

"Not a patch on you."

Isabelle snorted and Oberon whipped his head around.

"Are you quite all right?" he said.

She rolled her eyes. "Just fine."

The girl with the make-up brush appeared and touched up Isabelle's face.

Allegra discarded her silk jacket and took a seat by Oberon.

"This commercial will be a homage to me."

"Who better?" he said, taking her hand. "You're still my number one."

Raphael clapped his hands for attention. "Silence, everyone. This is my set and my shoot. No one is to interrupt from now on, is that clear?" Such was the force of his personality, everyone obeyed.

Bertie got into position. "Righty-o! Let's do this."

Brad put on his earphones and the sound engineer tested the microphone.

Raphael counted down from five. "*Lights, camera, action!*"

Bertie took Isabelle and Gabriella for lunch.

"We need an enormous drink after all our hard work," he said cheerfully. "Then another equally enormous one to get us through the afternoon."

"I'm so tired," said Isabelle, yawning. "It's hard work walking up and down that carpet. Why is he so picky about the takes?"

"He's the best," said Bertie simply. "He's a perfectionist and that's why this will be a wonderful advertisement. Far classier than the product."

Isabelle laughed. "Allegra's taken to wearing the perfume now. I smelt her before I saw her. Who came up with it?"

"Oh, she hired some experts in France, near Grasse, I believe. She paid a fortune for that pong."

Isabelle shook her head incredulously. "It's overpowering."

"Just like its namesake." Bertie's hand flew to his mouth. "Good Lord, I must stop being such a bitch. It's not like me." He grinned.

They took a cab to the Four Seasons with Bertie's bodyguard Vladimir in the front seat. Bertie sat in between the girls in the back and it was a tight squeeze. "I'm the filling of a gorgeous sandwich," he said, kissing both their hands simultaneously. "Just fabulous."

They arrived ten minutes later.

"This is where I'm staying," Bertie informed them. "They have a nice menu in 'The Garden' – it's the restaurant there. It's rather like being in an enchanted forest as the tables are situated between fabulous trees."

"Say again?" Isabelle was confused.

"African Acacia trees to be exact," he said. "Large trunks just growing away in the centre of the tables. It's quite extraordinary."

Gabriella said nothing as disappointment flooded her being. She had imagined her meeting with Oberon to go so differently.

God would punish her for being so negative, but she felt utterly defeated.

They got out and Bertie handed twenty dollars to the driver.

183

"Thank you," said the driver with a wave. "Have a wonderful day, sir."

Isabelle regarded Bertie thoughtfully as they walked toward the entrance. "You're so classy, you know? You haven't let fame affect you at all. I can't see Oberon behaving like that."

They entered the hotel through the glass doors.

"Oberon is essentially insecure," explained Bertie, nodding at the concierge. "The reason he acts so abominably is because he feels threatened by everything."

The maître d' welcomed them into the restaurant. "Hello there, Mr. Wells. The usual table?"

"Yes, Bill. Over by the windows." He turned to the girls. "There's a nice view there."

"Great," said Isabelle enthusiastically. "Thank you so much for inviting us." She nudged Gabriella. "We're so grateful, right, Gabs?"

"Oh, sure. Thank you." She felt like she was in a daze.

Bertie took a seat and regarded her thoughtfully. "You're awfully quiet," he said gently. "Surely you're not upset over Oberon?"

Gabriella tried to smile. "Well, I thought it would go well, is all. Our first meeting."

Bertie opened the menu. "Don't fret. He could see that your attempt at his design was terrific and he lashed out. Typical insecure behaviour."

Gabriella was doubtful. "I'm not sure that's true. He was pretty harsh ..."

"Of course he was," said Bertie briskly. "If he thought it was so awful, why then did he let Raphael use the gown? Even though he claims he's embarrassed by it now, he's an attention whore. This ad will remind the world of his breakthrough and thus put him in the spotlight."

184

"So, why be such a bitch?" asked Isabelle.

Bertie shrugged. "Because he can."

"So much for the American dream," said Gabriella miserably. "Oberon will never take me on now."

"He might," said Bertie. "He's not all bad. It's the persona he has created. Did you see the way he treated his personal assistant? You'd wonder why that poor chap stays with him. Well, I know for a fact that Riku is devoted to him. Why? Because deep down, Oberon's a decent bloke."

Gabriella didn't look convinced. "I don't know about showing him my work."

Bertie shrugged. "You've got nothing to lose, my pet. Nothing ventured and all that."

"Raphael seems happy with this morning," said Isabelle lightly. "He's so nice when he's in a good mood."

Bertie smirked. "You talk an awful lot about my dear friend, Zsa Zsa. Anything we should know?"

Isabelle blushed unbecomingly. "No, not at all."

Gabriella laughed. "You protest way too much. I agree, Bertie. She's intrigued."

"My heart is breaking in two," he said dramatically. "I really thought we'd be lovers."

Isabelle gasped. "You're terrible! Bertie!"

"So, is he single?" Gabriella asked. "I know that she's dying to know."

Isabelle made a face. "No, I'm not."

Bertie nodded. "He's single," he affirmed. "There's been no one serious since Sylvie."

"Who?" asked Gabriella.

"Sylvie Marot."

"The model?" said Isabelle. "I idolised her when I was little."

"She broke his heart," he continued with a frown. "To

be fair, he was impossible back then. Out drinking and taking drugs all the time. When he went into rehab, she broke it off. She felt that she had to move on. She was fed up of all the drama. He has never recovered from her."

The waiter arrived with a bottle of Evian.

"Wonderful," said Bertie. "We need to be sensible and have this for hydration. However, we also need a bottle of Nosostros 2007 right away."

The waiter nodded and disappeared.

"Nosostros? What's that?" asked Isabelle.

"A charming Argentinian red. Tastes like raspberries, I find."

"I don't really drink wine," said Gabriella. "Maybe I'll stick to water."

"Nonsense," said Bertie. "Who knows? You might acquire some Dutch courage and win Oberon over with your pitch."

They arrived back to the studio in tearing spirits. Bertie blew a kiss at Kim as he walked by her en route to make-up.

Raphael narrowed his eyes when he saw Gabriella and Isabelle walk in, linking arms and giggling. "You're late," he said, noticing their pink cheeks.

"Sorry!" said Gabriella gaily. "We shouldn't have had dessert."

Unused to wine during the day, she felt ten feet tall. The alcohol raced through her veins and she felt wonderful.

Kim's hands were on her hips. "Hey, you!" she said to Isabelle. "You're late. Coco is waiting in make-up."

"Sorry!" said Isabelle, disengaging herself from Gabriella's arm. "The taxi got stuck in traffic and …"

Kim held a hand up. "Save it. Just hurry."

There was no sign of Oberon.

Gabriella accessed Instagram on her phone. Like lightning, she texted Hugo, telling him about her day so far. Alcohol gave her courage and she added some heart emojis.

Then he sent a separate message with a heart emoji like the one she sent. Her heart flipped over.

She threw her bag on the ground and took a seat on a canvas chair.

Bertie reappeared in his white suit. "Are you okay?" he mouthed to Gabriella. "Have some water!"

She gave him a thumbs-up.

Raphael strode over and picked up his bag which was right next to her seat. It was then that Gabriella realised where she was sitting: on the chair with 'BAPTISTE' printed on the back.

"Oh, sorry! I'll move." She made a move to vacate the seat.

"No need," he said, rummaging around in the leather hold-all. "I need to stand and observe."

"Will Oberon be back?" she asked casually.

He shook his head. "He said that he has seen enough. He needs to work on his own show. He and Riku left an hour ago."

"Oh." She sat back deflated.

"You'll see him at the première." Raphael found what he was looking for and smiled at Gabriella.

"There'll be a première?" she asked.

"Oh, Allegra wants as much pomp as possible. Especially now that the theme is her movies. She'll arrive with Bertie on one arm and Oberon on the other." He grinned. "Should be a good night."

"How long will the shoot take, do you think?"

He ran his fingers through his hair. "Four more days, perhaps more. I need to wrap it as soon as possible. We are over budget and over time."

Gabriella glanced at Isabelle who was laughing at something Bertie had said. Surely she had mentioned the graduation? Raphael seemed blissfully unaware.

She made a mental note to mention it later. She couldn't see Raphael being too pleased when he found out that his star wouldn't be available.

"Raphael does know about the graduation, right?" Gabriella asked curiously the next morning. "You won't be around tomorrow and you're kind of necessary."

"Sure he does," said Isabelle breezily. "Paolo put it in my contract, just in case production went over time."

"If he read the contract."

"Not my problem." She smiled. "Daddy always says, never sign something unless you've read it through. If Monsieur Baptiste doesn't realise that I'll be missing, then it's his problem."

"Maybe text him?" suggested Gabriella.

"Oh, he'll be fine," she said with a wink. "He's always so nice to me."

She couldn't have been more wrong.

Raphael blew a gasket when he heard that she needed a day off.

"You're double booked?" he raged. "How could you?"

"It was in my contract," she said, backing away. "I mean, you signed it."

"What contract?" He threw his empty coffee cup across the room. "Do you understand how much you're delaying us? *Putain!*"

"It's just tomorrow ..."

"*Tomorrow?*" he roared.

Isabelle shifted uncomfortably. "It's my graduation."

"*Graduation?*" He kicked a chair. "I don't fucking believe this. Who the hell hired you?"

Isabelle's legendary temper surfaced. "*I have to graduate!*" she yelled back, her eyes blazing. "*You should have read the small print! This is not my problem!*"

"Graduate on your own time!"

"How dare you! I've worked so hard this past week. Paolo wrote all of this in my contract – the contract that *you* signed – so get over it."

"Do you realise that Bertie's time is limited with us? Do you realise the cost of this studio? Do you realise that I want to finish this stupid commercial so I can do some proper work?"

"Oh, whatever!" She stalked off, her face as red as her hair. "Just get someone else for all I care!"

Raphael began cursing in French and stomped around.

The crew looked on in fascinated delight.

It was Bertie who eventually calmed Raphael down, offering to take him to dinner and discuss his new film.

"Come on, Raph," he said soothingly. "The girl has to have her day. I'll talk to Harvey and ask for some more time. He has a film in Vienna lined up but I'm sure we can work it out."

"We should never have hired her if she couldn't commit," he said obstinately.

"That's not true – she's perfect. The advertisement would be nothing without her."

✇ Chapter Fifteen ✇

"Gabby? Gabby?"

Isabelle shook her gently. "Wake up, sleepyhead."

Gabriella opened her eyes slowly and winced. The sunlight was blinding and she had forgotten to pull her curtains the night before.

"What time is it?" she asked, reaching for some water in a bottle by her bed.

"After ten." Isabelle was already dressed. "Raphael has been texting me all morning that I would be fired if it weren't for the fact that the dress was made for me and me only."

Gabriella took a big swig of Evian. "I can see why he's angry."

Isabelle bit her lip, her beautiful face worried. "I hope he doesn't fire me."

"He won't."

"Contracts mean nothing to guys like him."

"He won't." Gabriella patted her arm. "He has too many takes with you in them. Plus, he'd never find anyone who looks as good as you."

"We both know that's a lie."

"Are your parents here yet?" asked Gabriella, changing the subject.

"No. In about half an hour, I think."

"Magda and Lita are meeting me at the ceremony."

"It's hard to believe that we're finished," sighed Isabelle. "It seems like only yesterday that we were freshmen."

"Time flies." Gabriella stood up and stretched. "I hope to see Noah today. I really want to clear the air."

"Have you seen him since?"

"No. I've been too busy. I meant to text him but I didn't get around to it."

"Just act normally. He'll be fine."

"I hope so." Gabriella had an uneasy feeling. "I didn't mean to hurt him, you know."

"Of course you didn't." Isabelle patted her arm as she walked by. "Now, get dressed. We have to leave soon."

Half an hour later and she was ready. She had made a red dress from a heavy silk that Lita had picked up at a second-hand fabric store. It was knee-length with a full skirt and a fitted bodice. The scooped neckline was modest and the sleeves were short. She picked black stilettos and let her hair fall loosely down her back. In a flash, she remembered her *abuela* teaching her how to sew when she was seven years old. She remembered her soft voice instructing her gently, always praising and encouraging, never demoralising. She had blossomed under her tutelage and had come so far.

Gabriella hugged herself in delight. She couldn't wait for her family to see her on the podium, graduating with honours. It was a dream come true.

Isabelle did her make-up which was minimal.

"You're naturally gorgeous," said Isabelle, applying some blusher. "I would die for that skin tone."

Hugo had messaged her ten minutes earlier wishing her

luck and reminding her to make space in her busy schedule for him before 2020.

She replied saying that she was so happy and felt so blessed to have had the opportunity to attend such a school.

His message back made her heart sing.

The world is blessed to have you in it

Then a heart emoji followed.

She replied, saying that she was free for the weekend. He sent a thumbs-up emoji back.

Grabbing her clutch bag, she checked her hair and make-up one last time in the mirror.

"*Ready, Gabs?*" yelled Isabelle from the hall.

"*Ready!*"

The whole family went for a celebratory lunch in Brasserie Michel.

Gabriella held up a glass of champagne.

"Thank you," Gabriella said to her family. "I know how hard you worked, Mama. All those extra shifts."

"It was nothing." Her mother reddened slightly.

"And you, Lita. All your help and advice. I would be nothing without you."

"Your talent shines through, *preciosa*. I only set you on this path."

Diego finished his champagne and filled another. "I could used to this," he quipped. "How the other half live, right?"

"I'll buy you a crate of this stuff someday," Gabriella promised. "We will *be* the other half."

Teresa shook her head. "You are way too obsessed with money, Gabs. Just be grateful for what you have."

"I am," she protested hotly. "I just don't want Mama working for Her Majesty anymore."

"Hello, Gabby," came a voice and she looked up. The words died on her lips.

Hugo was standing at the foot of the table.

"Hugo?" she said, nearly dropping her glass. "Why … where … how did you find me?"

She said 'Her Majesty'! Did he hear?

"I texted Isabelle … I wanted to surprise you." His handsome face was open and friendly and he tickled Sophia under her chin. She in turn beamed up at him.

Gabriella tried to gauge his mood. He seemed happy and relaxed. He must not have heard her. She thanked God.

"Isabelle told you where I was?"

"Not easily." He grinned. "She was very cagey. In the end, she gave in."

Magda's face was frozen in shock. "Does your mother need me, Hugo? Is that why you're here?" She got to her feet, flustered.

"No, Magda. I'm here to see Gabriella." He smiled warmly at the older woman.

"Gabriella?" Her eyes darted to her youngest daughter.

"I want to take her out tonight. She's been so busy this week, I thought that I'd surprise her."

Gabriella put her head in her hands. She could feel the disapproval coming off her mother and grandmother in waves.

"Take her out? Like a date?" Magda looked horrified.

"Yes," he answered. "But only if you're finished with her." He took a seat in a spare chair next to Teresa. "Hello, I'm Hugo du Maurier," he said, holding out his hand for her to shake. "You must be Teresa."

"Hello," said a wide-eyed Teresa.

Diego held out his hand. "I'm Diego, Gabby's older brother."

Hugo smiled. "Hello."

Magda pulled herself together. "Would you like some champagne?" she asked. "The owner, Giselle, gave us a bottle to celebrate."

"That'd be great." He smiled again.

Gabriella couldn't speak. Now her mama knew everything and it didn't take a genius to work out that she didn't approve.

After Teresa and Diego had left with the children, Magda and Lita made a move to leave also. Hugo had been positively charming, telling the family about his little boat and his travels in Europe. Sophia, enchanted by this dark-haired stranger, had sat on his lap and tickled him under his chin.

"Have a good evening," said Magda, holding out her hand.

Hugo shook it warmly. "Thank you for being so polite," he said, "I know it's a huge faux pas to gate-crash a party without an invitation."

Lita waved his apology away. "You are most welcome," she said. "Most welcome."

"Bye, Mama," said Gabriella, hugging her mother tightly. "Thank you for all you've done. I would never have made it this far without you."

"You make me so proud," said Magda with tears in her eyes.

Lita took Gabriella's face in her gnarly old hands and kissed each of her cheeks softly. "You are amazing, Gabriella. Don't forget it."

Hugo watched this exchange silently.

Magda waved at them both. "Goodnight."

Lita followed her outside, her small frame hunched over.

"So, have you time to hang out with me now?" asked Hugo playfully.

Gabriella's heart soared. "Yes, I think I can fit you in."

They took the subway to South Ferry. It was close to sunset and the sky was darkening.

They entered the terminal and waited in line.

"The Staten Island ferry is about the only thing in New York that's free," Hugo said, caressing her palm. "It's not exclusive – on this trip, everyone is the same. I don't get preference because my father has a few million dollars in the bank."

She gazed at him with her big brown eyes.

"I couldn't think of where to take you on a date. Everywhere seemed so tedious. Then it struck me – a round trip to Staten at sundown. Just you, me and New York."

"I love it." She kissed his cheek softly. "I really love it."

They boarded the ferry.

Gabriella smiled and held on to the railing as the boat chugged through the water.

After a quick turnaround at Staten Island, the boat headed back in the direction of Manhattan.

"Look!" said Hugo, pointing to the skyline of skyscrapers.

They were illuminated and stunning. She could recognise the Empire State straight away.

"It's awesome, right?" he said, leaning on the railing of the boat. "I just love this. I've been so many places and seen so many things but nothing beats my city. Nothing."

Gabriella pointed the Statue of Liberty on the left, all lit up and majestic. "I always look at her and think of the immigrants. She must have been some sight when they arrived. She symbolises the American Dream. I'll bet every person who passed her on the way to a better life felt empowered at the sight of her."

Hugo nodded. "My great-great-grandfather felt that way. He called his company Liberty Designs after her."

She stiffened. Liberty Designs reminded her of Maurice. He sensed it immediately.

"Hey, sorry for bringing that up."

She waved it away. "Forget it."

"Oh Gabby, I'm sorry."

"I said forget it." She pulled her pashmina tightly around her shoulders. In a flash, she could feel Maurice's weight on top of her and the stench of his breath. Involuntarily, she shuddered.

Hugo stared broodily at the water. "It kills me that he'll get away with this."

She hung her head. "It's for the best," she said quietly.

The wind picked up and she shivered.

"Here, take my jacket," he offered.

"No," she answered. "You'll freeze if you take it off."

"I insist." He pulled one sleeve off his shoulder but she stopped him with her hand.

"Leave it on," she said shyly. "Just hold me instead."

He opened his arms and engulfed her in a bear hug, wrapping his jacket around them both. She rested her head on his chest and could hear his heart beating. He smelled of musk. Closing her eyes, the noise around her faded away and she relaxed totally. Horrible thoughts of Maurice disappeared and she felt at peace.

"Are you okay?" he murmured into her hair.

"This is perfect," she answered, tilting her head to face him. "Thank you."

He stared at her steadily. She closed her eyes. His lips felt cool to touch. He kissed her on and on, his hands closing in around her waist. She arched towards him, pressing her soft body against his. Moaning, she ran her fingers through his dark hair.

"You are so lovely," he said, kissing her cheeks and her nose. "Let's enjoy our time together. I know you didn't want to get involved, but I can't stop myself."

"I just don't want to get hurt."

"It doesn't have to end." He took her face in his hands. "We could make things work."

She wanted to believe him. She almost did in the twilight. He spoke of magic and she wanted it.

"Okay," she said, stroking his cheek.

"Can I take you home?"

She nodded, her eyes huge.

"Good." He kissed her forehead. "Now, stay close and I'll keep you warm."

Isabelle wasn't there when they got back to the apartment. Gabriella threw her keys on the kitchen counter. Her heart was thumping in her chest. She hoped that he didn't think she was inviting him up for anything other than a chat. Sometimes she cursed her naiveté – she had agreed without thinking it through. She knew the story. If you allowed a guy upstairs, certain things were expected. That's why she didn't allow Noah up that time.

She felt out of control and nervous. She loitered by the fridge, unsure of what to do.

Hugo stood there, his hands in his pockets.

"Are you expecting Isabelle to come back?" he asked.

She nodded. "She's with her parents so she won't be late. Plus she has an early start at the shoot." She paused. "We both do."

He regarded her speculatively. "Do you want me to leave?"

She shook her head. "Of course not. Why do you say that?"

"Because you seem nervous."

She laughed but it came out as a squeak. "I'm fine, Hugo. Just fine. Would you like something to drink?"

"Gabby ..." He walked towards her.

"We have wine or juice or tea ..."

"Gabriella ..."

"We might have some whiskey somewhere." She opened a cupboard and looked inside. "You like whiskey, right? I'm sure I saw some somewhere ..."

He came up behind her and grabbed her arms. "Turn around," he said, manoeuvring her sideways. "We need to talk."

"We do?"

"We do." He propelled her towards the couch and pushed her gently down. "You must trust me. I'm not going to pounce on you."

"Pounce?"

"I was there, remember? In the garden?"

She stiffened.

"I understand that you want to take things slowly."

"It's fine, it's fine." She plastered a smile on her face. "All that's forgotten about now."

"Forgotten?" He looked incredulous. "You shouldn't bottle it up, Gabby. Talk to me about it."

"No."

"Gabby!"

She shook her head obstinately. "No." She got up and turned her back on him. "You see, it's not just that."

"Oh?"

She faced him. "I'm a virgin. I've never slept with anyone."

He said nothing but she thought she saw a ghost of a smile on his face.

"You walked me home and now you're here and most guys would see that as a definite come-on."

"They would," he agreed, "except I'm not most guys, Gabby. I don't expect sex for walking you home."

"You don't?"

He shook his head. "I don't."

She visibly relaxed. "It's not that I don't want to. I mean, I do, it's just I've never done it and ..."

He put his finger to her lips. "*Shhh*," he said softly. "It doesn't matter."

"No, I want to explain." She pulled his hand away. "I come from a traditional family. Lita, my grandmother, doesn't believe in sex before marriage. She tells me so all the time."

"So, you want to get married?" He looked amused. "Have you morphed into Caroline Ashley Hamilton? Should I make a run for it?"

"No!" She punched him gently on the shoulder. "Not at all."

"Look, I'm not going to lie and say that the thought of taking you to bed hasn't crossed my mind."

She felt her pulse quicken.

"But I get that you've got beliefs. That's okay with me."

She hung her head. "That's not all."

"Oh? There's more?"

"I've never been that confident about my body," she said quietly.

"What?" he said, looking genuinely shocked. "Why?"

"Look at me!" she said hotly. "I'm not a model."

"So? Models are freaky-looking."

"Isabelle's not."

"She's too skinny for me." He took her shoulders and forced her to look at him. "I personally would love to see you naked. You are gorgeous, Gabby. Please believe that."

She tried to believe him. She really did. However, she could never see herself parading around in the nude on front of him.

"Let's take things slowly," he continued. "Let me date you. Let me take you out sailing and things like that."

"Really?" She felt herself relax.

"Really." He stood up and pulled her close. "I'm not going to put any pressure on you, Gabby. Please believe me."

"I do." She smiled. "I really do."

He stayed for a while and then had called a cab back to Long Island.

Together they drank tea and talked about their childhoods. She told him about the Bronx and her friends. How the best Italian food in New York was found on Arthur Avenue and how the Botanical Gardens was one of the coolest places she had ever been.

She mentioned the Yankee Stadium and he shrugged.

"You're not into baseball?" she said, surprised.

"Not really," he answered.

Then he talked about private school and his annual ski trips to Aspen.

"Where's that?" she asked innocently.

"Colorado," he replied.

"Oh, I've never skied," she said.

They had stared at each other.

Two lives, poles apart.

When Isabelle got home an hour later, Gabriella was alone, sitting on the couch.

"Gabs! How was your day?" Isabelle looked at her warily from the threshold.

"Oh, it was good," she answered. "Giselle pulled out all the stops and we had champagne."

"Anything else happen?" She looked guilty.

"Sophia spilt OJ all over the white linen cloth."

200

Isabelle exhaled. "Oh right, that's great." She walked into the room.

"And Hugo du Maurier turned up out of the blue to take me on a date."

Isabelle feigned surprise. "He did? Gosh, how did he know where you were?"

"Cut that right out." Gabriella raised an eyebrow. "I know you told him where I was, Zsa Zsa. Don't deny it."

"I'm sorry!" she exclaimed, rushing over to the couch. "It's just he was so insistent and he seems to really like you and you deserve to have some fun."

"Mama wasn't impressed."

"Yes, that occurred to me afterwards." She reddened. "Sorry about that."

"It doesn't matter." Gabriella smiled broadly. "He's just perfect, you know? He took me to Staten –"

"What? To Staten Island? " Isabelle looked appalled. "What was he thinking?"

"No, no, he took me on a round trip to Staten so that we could see the skyline at dusk." Gabriella looked dreamy for a moment. "It was so romantic. He gets me, you know? He could have taken me to some fancy restaurant but he didn't. He kept it real."

Isabelle smiled. "So you're happy?"

"I'm happy."

Isabelle took off her shoes and rubbed her feet. "Per Se was amazing. Daddy insisted that we have the works. I ate enough for three people." She groaned. "I'll never fit into that dress tomorrow."

"Are you nervous about meeting Raphael again?"

She shrugged. "Not really. I mean, he was awful to me. I was worried about being fired but you're right. He has too much footage already."

"He's just passionate about his work. I don't think he meant it."

"Passionate or not, I'm not falling over him tomorrow. From now on, I'll be professional, but aloof."

"Tea?" asked Gabriella, getting to her feet.

Isabelle shook her head. "I can't ingest one more thing, be it solid or fluid. I think I'll call it a night. Bertie texted earlier saying that the pressure is on. He's only been freed up for a week and we're over schedule. Word on the street is that it has to be wrapped by Friday."

"As in two days?"

"Yep. Then it's the edit and the première." She hugged herself. "This could be my big break, Gabs. Everyone will see that commercial. Fingers crossed."

"Without a doubt," Gabriella said seriously. "With Bertie on board, it will be broadcast all over the world."

"Mom always says not to count my chickens," said Isabelle practically.

"I thought it was eggs in a basket or something?"

"That too." She sighed. "In a way, I'll be sorry for it to end. I like everyone at the studio."

"Except Kim."

She laughed. "Right, except Kim." Her face looked desolate for a moment. "After Friday, they'll all go back to their A-list lives. I'll just have to hang in the balance, hoping that something will happen."

"It will happen, Zsa Zsa. This is your big break. I mean, you have Bertie Wells' cell number! You've hit the big time."

✎ Chapter Sixteen ✑

Isabelle arrived at the studio the next morning half an hour earlier than normal. She presented her bag to Hank the security guard, her stomach doing flip-flops. What if Raphael yelled at her again? He had been so mad.

She entered the studio sheepishly and headed directly towards Evie in wardrobe. Bertie, who was sipping coffee and reading *The New Yorker*, winked in her direction.

There was no sign of Raphael so she exhaled slowly.

Kim appeared with her habitual clipboard and scowl. "Today will be crazy," she complained to Evie, who was rifling through the gown rail. "We've lost so much time."

"To be fair, it would be done right now had Raphael stuck to the original plan," said Evie, extracting the aquamarine dress.

"Or if *certain* people didn't take yesterday off." Kim glared at Isabelle.

Isabelle rose to her full height.

"Do I need to spell it out, Kim?" she asked, her green eyes glittering. "It was in my contract – in the small print. It's not my fault that your precious boss didn't take the time to read it."

"He has no time for such things," retorted Kim. "His

203

brain works on another level entirely – that of a genius. Why would he waste his time reading about you?"

"Well, he's paying the price for his arrogance then."

Isabelle stalked off into the small room at the back of the studio that she and Bertie used to change into their costumes.

"Arrogance?" repeated Kim. "Is she for real? God, models are so stupid." She flounced off.

Raphael appeared at that moment, in a grey T-shirt and blue jeans.

"Is she here?" he demanded, looking around. "Isabelle?"

Evie nodded. "She's in there," she answered, pointing to the changing room.

Before she had time to stop him, Raphael marched up and pushed open the door. Isabelle was inside wearing nothing but her underwear.

"*Jesus!*" she shouted, covering up with Allegra's dress. "Don't you knock?"

"*Pardon,*" said Raphael, looking away. "I did not know …"

"Give me a minute, will you?"

"Of course, of course. I apologise." He shut the door.

He was sitting on an amp when she emerged five minutes later.

She eyed him warily.

"Did you want me for something?" she asked.

"Yes." He stared at her. "I was going to tell you to hurry up." He pointed to his watch. "I have been here for hours."

"But I'm early today," she protested.

"Early? *Ah, bon*?" He laughed sarcastically.

"Yes, early," she said hotly. "My contracts states that I begin at –"

"You mention your contract again, I see." He laughed.

"Let me guess, it's in the small print." He got to his feet. "Go to Coco and fix your face. I want to get finished. Unless you have somewhere better you need to be?"

"You know that I don't," she retorted. "If I had other plans, it would be stated in the small print that you didn't take the time to read."

"Well, I have learned a valuable lesson, Miss Flynn." He glared at her. "Now, hurry please. We are under pressure."

He strode away and Evie gave her a sympathetic look.

"He can be quite mean, right? Just ignore him and get out there."

"Okay," said Isabelle in a small voice.

Bertie was trying to moonwalk on the red carpet when she got to the set. Brad was cheering him on.

"You're awesome, man. How did you learn to do that?"

"Oh, Michael showed me once. Back in the early nineties. I attended a party in his honour in Berlin."

"*Wow!* What was he like?" Brad looked impressed. "'Beat It' is my favourite song of all time."

"Oh, frightfully sweet and gentle. I really enjoyed his company. A genius, of course. I mean, anyone who can write music like that –"

"Bertie! Stop chatting and get into position," Raphael snapped, interrupting their conversation.

"Speaking of genius," said Bertie, rolling his eyes. "Talk later, Brad darling. I'll fill you in on the rest."

Isabelle stood in her designated spot and waited for her cue.

"*No, no, no!*" Raphael walked up to her and moved her a millimetre to the right. "Stay in the position we agreed, okay?"

"I was!" she protested.

Raphael just glared at her.

"*Again, everybody!*" he shouted.

Bertie waited at the end of the carpet for Isabelle to arrive.

She walked gracefully forward and then looked back at the camera, her red hair framing her face. The CGI screaming crowd was to be added later. She smiled and then continued to walk.

"*Stop!*" called Raphael again. "This is terrible. You are turning at the wrong time and the angle is not what we practised. How many times will we have to do this? Haven't you delayed us enough?"

"Raph!" said Bertie smoothly. "Leave her alone."

Isabelle felt hot tears sting her eyes. The tone of his voice was so cold. She'd had a crazy few days and she was exhausted. Suddenly, it all became too much.

"My God, can I do anything right?" she said, her voice breaking. "It's so unfair. It's just so unfair." She hung her head and started to sob. "It wasn't my fault that this shoot ran over time. You changed the vision. I mean, I *had* to graduate. My parents came up especially. Now, I'm the worst in the world no matter what I do."

Bertie bolted towards her but Raphael was too quick for him.

"Hey, don't cry," he said, lifting her chin with his finger.

Isabelle tried to push him away. "You're being so unreasonable. I can't change what's happened."

"Hey," he said gently. "I'm sorry for being so angry. It's just I don't cope with pressure very well."

She turned away, wiping her tears with her hand. "Just leave me alone. If I don't stop crying, Coco will never be able to fix my face."

"Isabelle," he said, pulling her around towards him again. "Let's try again. I'm sorry."

She sniffed.

"I'll be nicer," he continued. "Please don't cry. "

She looked up to find his brown eyes staring at her.

"Please, Isabelle." He stroked her cheek, wiping away a stray tear.

"Okay," she said quietly.

Three days later Raphael stood on a chair and shouted, "*C'est fini!* It's a wrap!"

The crew cheered.

Bertie took Isabelle's hand in his and kissed it. "It was a pleasure, my darling," he said, smiling. "This is only the beginning for you, I'm sure of it."

Isabelle made a small curtsy. "It was a pleasure to work with you too, Mister Wells. You are one of the nicest men I've ever met."

They embraced briefly.

Raphael was staring at the monitor.

"You know," he said to Bertie, "this might not be so bad after all."

"It will be worthy of the Academy, old boy," said Bertie, slapping his back. "Despite the fact that the product is so awful."

Isabelle hung back shyly, unsure of what to say.

Raphael looked up.

"Thank you, Isabelle," he said softly. "On screen, you are truly beautiful. Isa-*très-belle.* "

She inhaled sharply. She didn't want this to end. The harsh reality was that he would be out of her life soon. Sure, there was the première, but after that there was nothing.

"I think some drinks are in order," suggested Bertie. "It's expected, Raph. Now that it's in the bag as it were."

"Of course, of course." Raphael pulled out his phone. "I'll just telephone Allegra and get her to foot the bill."

"Knowing Allegra, she won't donate a penny to our *soirée*," said Bertie dismissively. "She's as tight as they come."

Raphael walked away, chattering rapidly.

Bertie nudged Isabelle. "So, things are all rosy between you two, I see."

"Well, not exactly."

"After your little meltdown, he was positively charming on set today. My word, I could feel the electricity a mile off."

"Oh, stop it!" Isabelle looked delighted. "It's nothing."

"*Hmmm.*"

"Do you think that he'll convince Allegra to cough up?"

"If anyone can, Raphael can. With that accent alone, he could seduce every woman in Christendom." He turned to see Isabelle's anguished face. "But he won't," he added hurriedly. "I haven't seen him with a woman in a long time."

Raphael came back, his face blazing in triumph. "I have good and bad news."

Bertie sighed. "Do tell, my boy. Start with the good."

"Allegra will pay."

Isabelle clapped her hands. "Awesome!"

"The bad? She will join us."

Bertie groaned. "Is it worth it? Shall I just foot the bill myself?"

"*Non!* Are you mad?" Raphael turned to Isabelle. "Maybe you should call your friend – you know, the girl who made the dress."

"Gabriella?"

"*Oui*, Gabriella. She should join us."

"Us?" repeated Bertie in surprise. "Are you coming too? I thought you hated bars and the like."

Raphael shrugged. "I should celebrate with my peers. Just for an hour or so."

"Raph!" warned Bertie. "You have to be careful. I heard about last week and your frightful Peter Sarstedt impression with the ukulele."

"That was a minor setback. I was depressed about the commercial."

Bertie raised an eyebrow. "If you're sure ..."

"It will just be for an hour. I will drink some soda and be sociable."

Isabelle's heart started to pound.

Act cool. Act cool.

"Okay, I'm just going to change," she said brightly.

"Me too," said Bertie. "I look fabulous in my tux but those lights made me sweat like a trooper. I need to freshen up and fast."

They went to the Village Vanguard, a jazz club in Greenwich Village. Founded in 1935, it was one of New York's most famous jazz clubs. The main door had a red canopy jutting out onto the pavement and the interior was a small triangular room with low ceilings.

"I love this place," said Brad, heading straight for the bar.

Isabelle, who had changed into a black minidress, took a seat near the stage. She had tied up her red mane of hair and had applied very little make-up. Her long legs were bare and she wore espadrilles that wound up her legs.

"Drink?" offered Bertie, wearing brown slacks, a white silk shirt and his trademark cravat.

Isabelle nodded. "I'll have what you're having."

"Champagne it is then."

Raphael had stayed behind at the studio to finish off and had promised to meet them later. Isabelle was as jumpy as a cat. She didn't dare think that he would turn up and steeled herself for disappointment.

Gabriella had texted saying that she couldn't make it as she had a date with Hugo. She added that if Oberon showed his face, Isabelle was to big her up as much as possible.

"Right, a bottle of Moët," said Bertie, placing a bottle on the table. "Bottoms up, my dear. This is on Allegra. It will make it taste so much better."

Isabelle sipped her drink and scanned the room. Evie and Coco had two beers and were chatting at a table nearby. Kim was on her phone and her eyes kept darting to the door as if she was waiting for someone to arrive.

Raphael, thought Isabelle. It was as clear as day that Kim was besotted with her boss.

"So, I'm off to London in a couple of days," said Bertie conversationally. "You should visit me sometime. I have a wonderful house in Belgravia."

Isabelle smiled. "That sounds great. Who knows, I might be at London Fashion Week someday."

"I don't doubt it, my dear."

"Bertie?"

"Yes, my sweet?"

"You won't forget me, will you?"

Her green eyes looked fearful and Bertie's heart melted.

He took her hands in his. "You, my darling girl, are on the cusp of greatness. Every woman in the world will see you in that gown and want to look like you. Allegra will probably make a fortune from that scent, entirely because of your beauty. There might be a slight lull, but once that advertisement premières, you will be snapped up."

"Do you really think so?"

He nodded. "One hundred million per cent."

They were halfway through the bottle of Moët when Raphael arrived. For a moment, he stood still in the doorway, surveying the scene.

Kim sat up immediately and shook out her hair.

Isabelle blushed slightly and kept her eyes down.

Please sit with us. Please sit with us.

Raphael strode over to their table.

"May I join you?" he asked.

Isabelle's heart soared.

"Of course, old boy." Bertie go to his feet. "What will I get for you, Raph?"

"Just a water."

"Coming right up."

Isabelle sipped her drink, unsure of what to say.

Raphael regarded her, an amused expression on his face.

"So, do you think you will take a career as a model?" he asked.

She nodded. "It's all I've ever wanted to do. Ever since I was a little girl."

"*Ah, bon?*"

She nodded. "My mother modelled when she was young. Not now, of course. I used to watch George Michael videos and dream of being on a runway."

"You will be famous after this, I think."

"I don't know about that."

"You will. Your beauty is startling. The whole world will see you and that will be it."

She blushed a deep red, her pale skin transforming. Bertie arrived back to the table with a bottle of water and a glass for Raphael.

"My God, Isabelle. Are you having a hot flush? Is it too warm here?"

She blushed even further.

"Here, Raph. I took the liberty of asking for some segments of lime in your glass. Hope that suits."

"That's fine," he said, his eyes never leaving Isabelle's face.

Allegra arrived an hour later as promised. She made a beeline for Bertie and Raphael, deeming the rest of the crew unworthy of her company.

"*Yoohoo!*" she called, throwing her fur jacket on the back of a chair. "Who picked the Vanguard? It's one of my all-time favourites."

Raphael saluted her amicably, but then turned back to Isabelle. They had been discussing a possible film about Napoleon and Josephine.

Bertie summoned the barman, who happened to be passing. "Another glass, my old friend."

"Sure," he replied.

"So, I hear the commercial is to die for," said Allegra. "I'm so excited about the reception it will receive. It's sure to boost sales of my movies."

"Oh, it will," agreed Bertie. "Have you seen Oberon since?"

"No," said Allegra in surprise. "He told me he was flying back to London."

"Oh, maybe he did." Bertie chuckled to himself.

Oberon was still in New York, staying at the Four Seasons, preparing for a show. He often saw him in the lobby, stalking past with Riku in tow.

"*Raphael! Yoohoo, Raphael!*" Allegra snapped her fingers.

Raphael, entranced by Isabelle, didn't react.

"*Raphael!*" she screeched and he turned his head.

"*Oui?*"

"I just wanted to know what kind of time-frame we're talking about."

"Time frame? For what?"

"Starr by Allegra Starr, of course." She pouted. "Surely it's all you think about."

"But of course," he answered smoothly. "I think maybe two weeks?"

Allegra clapped her hands together. "Fabulous. It will be well established before the Christmas rush. What better than a bottle of Starr in your stocking?" she tittered.

"A bottle of arsenic," whispered Bertie to Isabelle and she giggled.

"Raphy," continued Allegra, "you must talk to me for a while. You've been so rude all evening, chatting to my doppelganger."

"Raphy?" said Bertie in an undertone and rolled his eyes.

"Of course, Allegra," said Raphael mechanically. "How are you?"

He caught Isabelle's eye and made a silent apology, but she waved it away.

As Raphael moved closer to Allegra and turned his attention to her, Bertie sidled closer to Isabelle and filled their glasses.

"What are you and Raph talking about?" he asked, leaning in for the gossip. "He's positively addicted to you, my dear. Hasn't looked away in hours."

"Oh, stop it." Isabelle fiddled with her bracelet. "We're just chatting, is all."

"He's just chatting to Allegra as we speak and he looks miserable. Not remotely like the charming man he was a few minutes ago while engaging in conversation with you."

"I think you're imagining it."

"Not in the slightest," he said cheerfully.

Isabelle gulped her drink and coughed. "*Oops*," she said, almost dropping her glass.

"Never gulp champagne," warned Bertie. "Not only is it sacrilegious, it gives one terrible indigestion."

She grabbed her bag. "I'm going to the ladies' room," she announced, getting unsteadily to her feet. All the booze had gone to her head and she hadn't eaten dinner.

"Hurry up," said Bertie. "We need to order another bottle. The objective this evening is to fleece Miss Starr."

In the ladies' Isabelle splashed some cold water on her red cheeks. The evening was passing by in a blur. She felt intoxicated by the champagne and Raphael. The way he looked at her made her feel like the only woman on earth. She'd had flings with boys in the past, but he was a man. It made her shiver in anticipation.

Isabelle gazed at her reflection in the mirror. Her eyes were huge and smudged with kohl and tendrils of hair had escaped from her barrette. Excitement gave colour to her pale cheeks and her green eyes sparkled. He had said he would only stay for one drink but that was hours ago. He had spoken to no one but her. Well, until Allegra had monopolised him.

She straightened her dress and put her shoulders back. It was now or never. After tonight, Raphael would be a memory. Sure there was the première, but he would be busy with the press.

It was now or never.

Bertie was at the bar when she returned. He was regaling Coco with tales about his last movie shoot in India. Allegra had gone outside to take a call and Raphael was on his own.

"Are you okay?" he asked as she sat down.

"I'm good." She took a sip of champagne. "We've been deserted, right?"

"Yes, I think so." He finished his own drink. "I think we should leave."

"Leave? You mean, right now?"

"*Oui*. Do you want that?"

She inhaled sharply. "Together?"

"Well, of course." He smiled and held out his hand. "Come. Let's go before we have to explain ourselves."

She inserted her small hand in his big one and they furtively left the room.

"What about poor Bertie?" she said worriedly. "He'll be all alone with Allegra."

"Bertie knows," said Raphael, hailing a cab. "He told me to go for it."

"He did?" She glowed with pleasure.

A taxi pulled up beside them.

"Hello," said Raphael, "can you take us to the Langham, please?"

"On 5th? Sure thing, buddy."

They got into the back of the car. Isabelle sat upright, unsure of what to say.

As soon as the taxi began to move, Raphael grabbed her neck and pulled her towards him. His lips connected with hers and he kissed her with such intensity she was winded. On and on they kissed, his hands roaming her body.

"You are so lovely," he murmured against her jaw. "It has been a long time for me."

"Really?" said Isabelle, who was delighted to hear it.

"*Oui*, I have avoided the complications of love."

She pressed herself against him. "I'm not complicated," she said softly.

Isabelle woke the next morning to find the sunlight streaming through a gap in the heavy drapes that hung from the windows. The room was large with a big double bed in the centre. Raphael was sound asleep beside her, his long dark hair fanned across the pillow. The sheet barely covered him and she gazed at his muscular arms and chest. His skin was tanned and hers was so pale – they looked like complete opposites.

She stole out of the bed so as not to wake him. Naked, she walked over to the desk in the corner. It was covered with papers, all with his handwriting. Most of the words were in French and many were crossed out. She guessed it was a script he was working on as it had the layout of a dialogue between two people. There was a Mac, covered in post-it notes and an open packet of cookies. She picked up a page carefully, trying to read and understand what was written on it. Someone called Jack featured and then …

She gasped. The female character was called Isabelle. She glanced at Raphael, who was still asleep on the bed.

He had used her name! A stupid smile formed on her face and she replaced the sheet of paper in the exact spot.

She had never felt like this before. He was a dream come true – she'd had many boyfriends in the past, but never in this league. He had made love to her slowly and deliberately, his lips kissing every part of her body. She shivered at the thought as it had been singularly the most erotic few hours of her life. Then, he had taken her in his strong arms and they had fallen asleep together. It was at that moment – when she was secure in his embrace – that she realised that she was falling in love. It didn't fit the profile at all. She was Isabelle Flynn, a girl who went through life with a flippancy that shielded her from heartbreak. She played and moved on and avoided getting hurt. She had never felt deeply for anyone, except her dog Rihanna of course. Yet now, in the space of a few hours, her heart had been claimed. She felt vulnerable and exposed. As she lay beneath him, while he moved inside her whispering endearments in French, she had seen stars.

Corny as it sounded, she had given herself completely to the man in the bed right now.

Climbing back under the sheet, she lifted his arm and snuggled up to him. He moaned and pulled her close. Closing her eyes, she luxuriated in the heat from his body. She never wanted to be anywhere but right next to him like this. Feeling relaxed, she drifted off to sleep.

When she woke up, the other side of the bed was empty. The drapes had been opened and the sun illuminated the room. Raphael was sitting at his desk, wearing a pair of glasses and drinking a cup of coffee. He had donned a pair of jeans but his chest was bare.

She wrapped the sheet around her naked body and stood up.

"Morning," he said, without looking up from the screen of his Mac. "Would you like some coffee?"

She rubbed the sleep from her eyes. "Sure, that would be great."

Suddenly, she felt shy. There was something about the cold harsh light of day that stripped away the magic.

He pressed 'save' on the word document on the screen, then went and put a capsule in the coffee machine. "Sugar or milk?"

She shook her head. "Just black, please."

He pressed the button. The machine hissed and spluttered as it filled the small cup.

He handed it to her and went back to his desk.

"What are you working on?" she asked nervously, sipping the strong coffee.

"A new film," he replied. "It has been so long since I have felt any passion. I didn't think anything would inspire me again." He looked at her directly. "But something has."

She blushed.

"I have so many ideas but no time to write them down. That is the curse of the artist, I'm afraid. Sometimes, due to life and schedules, great work remains locked in here." He pointed to his head. "I need to go home to Picardy and close myself off for a while."

She bit her lip. The reality was that he was going to leave New York. There was nothing for him to stay for now that the commercial was finished.

"So, will you oversee the editing of Allegra's commercial?" she asked casually, taking a seat on the edge of the bed and crossing her long legs.

He nodded. "It won't take long. Two or three days, I imagine."

"And then?" Her green eyes were wary.

"Then the première and after that I return to France." He met her gaze steadily. "I would like you to stay here with me until I go."

"Stay here?" she squeaked, almost dropping her cup in shock.

He got to his feet and walked purposefully towards her. Taking the cup from her grasp, he put it on the bedside table and then took her in his arms.

"Yes, stay here, sleep in my bed and make love to me." He kissed her tenderly. "Last night was wonderful. I think it's time I had a lover. It has been so long."

"But what then?" She pulled back slightly. "When you go back to France, is that it?"

"No pressure, Isabelle. This is all I can give you right now."

Her brain felt muddled as she tried to make sense of his words. He wanted her to stay by his side while he was in New York. He would be here for another week at least.

218

A week was better than nothing. No one had ever made her feel so good.

"Okay," she said, wrapping her slender arms around his neck.

Gabriella raised an eyebrow. "Say all of that again, Zsa Zsa. You're going to live with him in a hotel until he leaves?"

Isabelle did a pirouette around the kitchen. "Yes, that's exactly it. I'm going to live in sin with my lover."

"Lover?"

"*Mais oui!* That's what he calls me." She giggled.

Gabriella grabbed Isabelle's arm and propelled her over to the couch. "Get down off Cloud Nine for a moment, will you? It's like the real Isabelle had disappeared and been replaced with a love-struck teenager."

"Oh, back off, Miss Sensible. Let me enjoy this."

"Isabelle! You can't just move in with a guy you barely know." Gabriella put her hands on her hips.

"Actually, I can," she retorted, her eyes flashing. "He's everything I've ever wanted. When he touches me, I melt." She sighed.

"*Isabelle!*"

"What?" She folded her arms petulantly. "Just stop, Gabby. I'm not as moral as you."

Gabriella snorted. "I thought you were better than this, Zsa Zsa. He's just using you until he leaves. You're going to be the fancy woman of some ancient French has-been."

"Take that back! He's only a little bit older."

"Nearly twenty years, Zsa Zsa. He could be your dad."

"Cut it out! I mean it." Her eyes glittered dangerously. "I want to be with him. For the first time in my life, I feel alive."

Gabriella rolled her eyes. "Oh, please. This is a short-term thing. Long-distance relationships don't work."

"Practise what you preach!" Her green eyes flashed. "What happens when Hugo heads off to Boston, Gabs?"

"It's not the same and you know it."

"Not the same? Why?"

"Because we're dating and getting to know one another before we, you know ..."

"Kudos to you."

Gabriella's expression softened. "Look, I'm not judging anybody. What you do with Raphael Baptiste is your business. I just don't want you to get hurt."

"I won't."

Gabriella looked sceptical. "Just be careful, okay?"

৬ Chapter Seventeen ৩

Luca pressed 'send' and closed his laptop. He had just sent the brochure of his mom's new show to different art dealers in both London and New York.

Gabriella was due at the gallery as normal.

He glanced at his watch. She was ten minutes late.

Odd, he thought. She's never late.

The door opened with a ping and a red-faced Gabriella appeared. "I'm so sorry!" she said, flustered. "I slept out and then the subway was jam-packed and ..."

"Hey, it's cool." He smiled. "Out late last night?"

She smiled. "Maybe."

"With my brother-in-law again?"

"Maybe."

Luca whistled. "Things are getting serious between you two, huh?"

She shrugged. "Maybe."

He laughed. "I get the hint. I won't pry any longer."

Gabriella typed her password into the computer and activated her profile. "Look, things have been awesome. He's so sweet and the perfect gentleman."

"Oh?"

"He's taken me to fancy restaurants and to see a

classical concert. I took him to the Bronx Zoo and showed him the Botanical Gardens. It's been nice."

"Has he taken you home to Long Island yet?"

Gabriella looked uncomfortable. "It's never come up." She shivered at the thought of that house. It reminded her of Maurice and that night. Hugo knew better than to suggest it.

"Anyway," she added, "I don't think Victoria would be thrilled at the idea of me."

"She's a snob." Luca made a face.

"Yes, I'm no Caroline Ashley Hamilton, Luca. It doesn't take a genius to work out that she would be horrified. The maid's daughter?"

"Hugo doesn't care about what Victoria thinks," protested Luca.

"Maybe, but he's not shouting it from the rooftops either."

"He's not that kind of guy, Gabs. He's smart. Plus, the less Victoria knows the better." He rubbed her arm comfortingly. "Don't worry about it. It will all work out." He checked his phone. "Craig, you know, my cousin? He keeps texting me about his wedding."

"When is it again?"

"Next weekend. There's a rehearsal dinner in some restaurant in Cork."

"A what?"

"A practice run. Just the wedding party and a few speeches." He grinned. "It's a good excuse to party before the main event, I guess."

"How's your speech coming along?"

"It's all up here," he answered, jabbing the side of his head with his finger. "I'm keeping it clean – there'll be no embarrassing stories. Just lots of 'thank you's' and toasts."

Gabriella regarded him speculatively. "That girl will be

there, won't she? That Lydia girl."

His face darkened. "So?"

"I'm just wondering. I mean, will it be awkward between you two?"

"All that's in the past now – it's all forgotten. We're just buddies now. Just friends." He turned away and started to stack some papers. Gabriella could tell that he was agitated.

"Luca?" she said softly and he looked around.

"Yeah?"

"Are you sure you're okay?"

His blue eyes looked lost for a moment. Then he smiled. "I'm A-OK, Gabs. Now, let's have some coffee and talk about Hugo."

She threw a pen at him. "Enough! I'm not telling you anything."

Hugo called in at lunchtime, looking handsome in a navy T-shirt and white shorts.

Gabriella's face broke into huge smile when she saw him. "Hey, you. I didn't know we had plans."

"We didn't." He kissed her softly on the lips. "I was at home doing nothing and I thought why not head into town and take my girl for lunch?"

Luca arrived out from the back office. "Hugo! Speak of the devil."

Gabriella glared at him.

"Were you guys talking about me?" Hugo asked, amused.

"Not at all," said Gabriella breezily. "It's just Luca being Luca." She logged off the computer. "Can I go with Hugo?" she asked Luca. "I'll be thirty minutes tops."

"Take your time! Who am I to stand in the way of true love?"

"*Luca!*"

223

For lunch they got two Rueben sandwiches and two bottles of water, and then went to Washington Square Park.

"Do you want to sit on the grass?" asked Hugo.

"Sure."

They sat down in a sunny spot and she unwrapped her sandwich. "I'm so hungry! I was so late this morning, I forgot to eat breakfast."

"Last night was nice though, right?" He trailed his finger up her leg. "That piano player was incredible."

She smiled at the memory. They had gone to the Vanguard on Isabelle's recommendation and watched a jazz band play. The star of the show had been the pianist and Hugo had been enthralled by the musicians and their talent.

"So, I was thinking that we could go sailing tomorrow," he said, unwrapping his own sandwich. "The weather is supposed to be good and I haven't been out in a while."

"Will I be able to do it?" she asked. "Sail, I mean? I've never been on any boat except a ferry."

"I'll do all the hard work," he said reassuringly. "You just sit there and enjoy it."

"Okay then, I'd love to go sailing with you." She beamed at him. "Should I wear navy and white stripes and a captain's hat? Channel my inner Jean Paul Gaultier?"

He laughed. "No. Just bring something warm. It gets chilly out on the water."

Two women passed, all decked out in running gear. A child threw a ball in the air and squealed in delight when her father caught it. The trees were leafy and full and swayed in the breeze. It was a perfect summer's day in New York.

Gabriella tilted her face upwards and gloried in the heat of the sun.

"How's Isabelle?" asked Hugo, taking a swig of water.

"Well, I haven't seen her in almost two weeks. She's been holed up at the Langham with Raphael. She came home briefly for clothes and then took off again."

"Is it serious between them?"

Gabriella frowned. "I think it's more of a big deal for her. It seems to be all on his terms. Like the other day, she called in tears saying that they had had a huge fight and that he had walked off. He didn't come back until the next morning. She has no idea where he went or what he did."

"He sounds like hard work."

She nodded. "I think he's too volatile for her. She's attracted to his passion but I think it might destroy them in the end. It's too unpredictable and, like most artists, he's inherently selfish."

"When's the première of the commercial?"

"It's next week. Allegra wants to launch the perfume as soon as possible. Plus, the editing is done so Raphael is anxious to leave." She unscrewed the top of her water bottle.

"Leave?"

"Yes, back to France."

"What about Isabelle?"

Gabriella frowned. "That's the million-dollar question. My guess is, he's used to loving girls and leaving them. She clams up whenever I ask about it."

"Poor Isabelle."

"I know, right? I tried to warn her." She sipped her water and wiped her lip. "Raphael asked me to come along to the première as they used my dress. I'm so excited."

"It will be a good night to network." He smiled. "I'll be your date if you want."

"You will?"

"Sure, I will."

225

"It'll be black tie."

"I've got it covered. Momma got me fitted for a tuxedo as soon as I left for Harvard."

"I bet you look amazing in a tux," she said dreamily.

He reached out and rubbed some Thousand Island dressing from her lip.

"What?" Her hand flew to her mouth. "I had food on my face? Every time!"

He said nothing. Instead, he pulled her head towards him and kissed her.

"I know I said I'd take things slowly, but it's getting tough," he said, nuzzling her neck. "You're too gorgeous."

She blushed. "You must be blind."

He kissed her nose. "Someday you'll believe me, Gabby. You're so great. I'm lucky to be with you."

The next day, Hugo picked her up at the apartment. She had offered to take the subway, but it took less time to drive. He parked his father's BMW on the kerb and called her phone.

"I'm just outside," he said, putting on his hazard lights.

"I'll be right there," she answered.

Two minutes later, she appeared wearing a multi-coloured sundress and carrying a navy fleece. On her feet she wore bright pink flip-flops and she had a gold chain around her ankle. She got into the passenger seat and kissed him.

"Thanks for picking me up," she said. "The train from here to Sea Cliff takes nearly two hours."

"Hey, it's no problem," he said, indicating out onto the street. "I love driving this thing."

They sped off in the direction of Queens, taking the Midtown Tunnel under the river. After a while, they left the cluttered city behind and the sea came into view.

"Where's that?" she asked, pointing to the blue water.

"Hempstead Harbour," he replied. "We just follow the coast as far as Sea Cliff and we're there."

She opened the window of the car and inhaled the fresh air. Her long dark hair blew in the breeze and she felt exhilarated. She could understand why people paid megabucks to live by the sea. It had a beauty like nothing else. The water glittered in the midday sun and you could hear the call of gulls as they flew past.

Soon, they arrived at Sea Cliff Yacht Club, a white wooden building with a balcony. Blue umbrellas covered the exterior tables and loungers were lined up on the beach beneath it.

"This place looks classy," she said in awe.

"It's not too bad," he said, parking near the entrance. "The staff are nice and I've good buddies who sail here."

They walked in and Hugo pointed to a wooden door. "That's the ladies' room," he said. "You can leave your bag there if you want. I'll just go and get a life jacket for you."

Her bag was a large brightly coloured canvas hold-all that her cousin had sent from Puerto Rico. It was quite large and was made of cloth – if it got wet, it would be soaked through.

She nodded and did what he suggested. Maybe there were lockers she could use.

A blonde woman wearing a white pants and navy blouse was fixing her hair when she walked in. She looked up and swung around in surprise.

"May I help you, dear?" she asked. "Are you lost?"

Gabriella put her bag on the bench. "No, I'm good," she answered politely.

"Are you here to clean? I'll only be a minute."

Gabriella held her head up. "I'm here to sail. My boyfriend is waiting for me outside."

"Are you a member?" she asked suspiciously. "This is a private, members-only club, you know."

"I've got to go." Gabriella backed out of the room, taking her bag with her.

Hugo was outside by the pool, waiting for her.

"All okay?" he asked, smiling.

She nodded. "Perfect."

"You didn't leave your bag?"

She shook her head. "I want to keep it with me. I have some cash in it."

He laughed. "I'm sure it would be safe here."

"No, I'd prefer to keep it with me."

"It might get wet," he warned.

"It's fine."

"Right then, let's make a move."

He rigged the small boat in no time and soon they were out on the water. The breeze had picked up and the small boat skimmed across the surface.

Gabriella, who had never been so close to the water, held on for dear life. Every so often, the boat would tilt right down on its side and she would close her eyes and pray to God that she wouldn't fall in.

"Isn't this amazing?" shouted Hugo, pulling in the rope.

"Amazing," she echoed, feeling terrified.

"I thought it would be calmer today," he yelled over the wind, "I hope you're not scared."

"I'm fine, never better," she answered through gritted teeth.

On and on they sailed, right out into the Long Island sound. The wind was coming from behind them, so there was little or no steering – it was a straight run out.

After about forty minutes, Hugo turned the boat head to wind. This stalled it and it bobbed on the small waves.

"Isn't it the best feeling in the world?" he said, his eyes glowing. "God, I miss this when I'm away."

Gabriella, who was wet and cold, clung to the edge of the boat. "It's great," she managed, her teeth chattering.

Hugo took a Kit Kat out of his pocket. "Are you hungry?" he asked, handing it to her.

Gabriella accepted it gratefully. "Thanks."

The sugar from the chocolate gave her energy and she sat up. When the boat was stationary, it was pleasant enough. All you could hear were the birds and the lapping sounds of the water against the hull.

"When did you learn to sail?" she asked.

"When I was seven. Momma signed me up for a course. I didn't want to go, of course, but after one day I was hooked." He smiled at the memory. "I spent every summer down here, taking part in races and regattas."

"It sounds lovely," she said. "I've never been so close to the sea. The only water I've ever been close to is the river."

"Do you swim?" he asked.

She shrugged. "Not very well. I used to take lessons at the YMCA, but then I moved to the Village."

"I want to live by the sea someday," he said. "I want my kids to have this experience."

She said nothing. His life was light years away from her own upbringing and sometimes she felt like their relationship could never work. Society and its constraints had a powerful hold over people and their lives. It took courage to break the mould. Sometimes it was easier to adhere to the status quo.

"Right, we'd better head." He got into position at the

helm. "We're facing the wind on the way back, so there will be a lot more movement. When I tell you, you've got to move to the other side of the boat and then back again. Wait for my prompt, okay? Otherwise, we'll capsize."

"Capsize?" she squeaked. "You mean turn over?"

"Yep, and the water is pretty cold." He grinned. "Hold on, Gabby! This is the best bit."

It took two hours to get back. The boat had to zig-zag its way through the water, sailing as close as possible to the wind. Gabriella was exhausted when they finally reached the beach. It felt like she had dragged herself across the boat from right to left a thousand times. Or as Hugo called it, starboard to port.

Hugo hopped out and took the rope from the stern. He then yanked the boat as far as he could up the beach. Gabriella willed her aching bones to move and vacate the boat. Her hair was plastered to her head and her nose was running from the wind.

"Wasn't that amazing?" he enthused, lowering the flapping sail. "My God, I really thought we'd flip at one stage."

Gabriella slung her bag, which was saturated, over her shoulder. "Amazing," she echoed.

He noticed her bedraggled state and was by her side in a flash.

"Are you okay, Gabby? You look frozen."

"I'm good," she answered, her teeth chattering.

"Come on, I can de-rig later." He took her hand in his. "Let's get some lunch at the club."

She stalled. "I'm not sure about that, Hugo."

"Why not?"

"I'm not a member …"

"It doesn't matter because I am and you're my guest."

She bit her lip. Maybe she was overreacting. It was wrong to judge these people by the behaviour of that woman in the ladies' room. True to form, her stomach rumbled. Some fries would hit the spot nicely.

"Okay, let's go," she said smiling. "I need some heat."

They dined on burgers and fries with two bottles of beer.

Hugo, high from his sailing trip, told her all about Berlin and Paris. He concluded with how he loved Europe and was reluctant to come home.

"I'm glad I did," he said, stroking her cheek. "Otherwise I would never have met you again."

She wanted to believe him as he seemed so sincere. But a crippling sense of self-doubt lurked in the background. Sometimes she had to pinch herself to prove she wasn't dreaming. That someone like Hugo du Maurier would bother with someone like her.

"Right, I'll get the cheque," he said, getting up. "I must use the men's room too so I'll pay on the way. Meet you at the entrance?"

She nodded. "Sure."

She put her phone in her bag and automatically stacked the empty plates. Draining her bottle of Corona, she got up and brushed crumbs from her dress. Glancing around, there was no sign of Hugo, so she made her way towards the exit. A man with white hair and wearing navy chinos and a pink shirt walked up to her.

"Can I help you, miss?" he asked in his New York twang. "I'm the manager here." He pointed to the gold badge on his shirt.

"I'm fine, thank you," she said politely.

"Are you waiting for someone?" His smile didn't quite reach his eyes.

"Just my boyfriend."

"Oh? Does he work here?"

She cast her eyes down. "No, he's a member."

"Oh, is he?" The man looked sceptical. "Where is this boyfriend?"

She prayed that Hugo would appear. "He had to use the men's room."

"Look, miss. I think it would be better if you waited outside."

Hugo found her standing by the car a few minutes later. He noticed her tears immediately. "Gabby! What's up?"

She pushed past him. "Nothing, just nothing. Take me home, Hugo. I want to go home."

He grabbed her shoulders and forced her to stop and face him. "What happened?" he demanded. "Why are you crying?"

"It's nothing," she said obstinately. 'Let's go."

"Did someone say something to you? Gabriella! Talk to me!"

She stopped dead. "I'm an outsider here, Hugo. It was a mistake to bring me here."

"What?"

"Those people in there don't see me as an equal. They see an immigrant servant girl." She faced him. "I don't fit in your world, can't you see that?"

"Look, we can't talk out here. Get in."

He opened the passenger door and she got into the car. Then he hopped in the other side.

As he placed both hands on the steering wheel, she could see that his knuckles were clenched. "Right, start from the beginning. What the hell happened in there?"

She inhaled tremulously, trying her best not to cry. In a shaky voice, she told him about the woman in the ladies' room and then the manager.

"I'll get that son-of-a-bitch fired!" Hugo fumed. "How dare he?"

"Just leave it," she said quietly. "Don't you see? Things are still as backward as they've always been. We think we live in a progressive world with a new dawn of equality, but it's a lie."

"You shouldn't take it lying down, Gabs. You should've told that man where to go."

"That's easy for you to say. You're white, you're privileged. You have powerful parents to back you up." Her brown eyes met his blue ones. "You know, when Obama got elected and then re-elected, I really thought the world had changed. A black president of America. It was like a dream come true for us minorities." Her expression darkened. "But it's all a dream."

"It needn't be," he said quietly.

"Remember I told you I wanted to be famous?" Her eyes shone. "I meant it. Money is power and without it, I'll just be another nobody. I want people to respect me."

"Then you're going about it the wrong way." He scowled. "Why would you want that man's respect? Do you think money will make it all better? Well, you're wrong. The American class system is more rigid than that. You don't get to transcend the ranks because you've got a million bucks in the bank."

"Then it's hopeless?"

"Be yourself, Gabby. Respect *yourself*. That's the key." He put the key in the ignition. "Come on, let me take you home."

꧁ Chapter Eighteen ꧂

"Celine du Maurier, you get out of bed this instant!" Victoria pulled the drapes in her youngest child's bedroom.

"Jesus, Momma, that's too bright. Close them again."

"Antonia Brent just called. Apparently Hugo is seeing a Hispanic girl."

Celine sat bolt upright. Gabriella had been kept out of her mother's radar for weeks now. Charlotte had advised it as it didn't take a genius to work out that Victoria would not approve of her son's choice.

"I haven't heard anything ..."

"Antonia said he was at the yacht club with her yesterday. Eating lunch." Victoria began to pace the room. "Who is this girl? Celine, you gotta tell me, sugar. This has to be contained."

"I haven't heard anything, Momma," said Celine again. "Are you sure it was Hugo? He told me that he went to the movies yesterday afternoon."

"She was positive. She was going to say hello but he left in a hurry." She twisted her huge diamond around and around her finger. "Who is this girl?"

Celine shrugged. "Who knows? I'm still unconvinced it was him. Antonia Brent is nearing eighty, Momma. She may have been confused."

"Maybe." Victoria pursed her lips. "I can't find him. He's not in his room."

"I can call him if you want."

"I've tried his cell ten times! It goes straight to voicemail."

Celine rubbed her mother's tense arm. "Calm down. Momma. I'm sure it's nothing."

"It better be."

Celine called Hugo as soon as her mother left the room. Mercifully, he answered.

"Hey, what's up?"

"Hugo! Thank God, Momma's been calling you over and over."

"I was at the gym," he said. "I literally just switched my cell on. Why was she calling?"

"Antonia Brent saw you and Gabby at the yacht club yesterday."

"So?"

"She wants to know who the Hispanic girl is."

"So tell her."

"Are you insane? She'll freak out."

"Why?"

"You know why, Hugo. Momma is a snob and she wants you to marry well."

"Oh, watch it, Celine. Marry well? You sound just like her."

"I love Gabby, I do. It's just she's from the Bronx and her mother's the maid and –"

"Stop right there. I don't care who she is or where she came from. You got that?"

"I don't care either but if you want some sisterly advice, keep your little love affair secret from Momma. She'll make your life a misery, Hugo. Keep this quiet, for your own sake."

"It's too late now. Antonia has blown my cover."

"Say you were at the movies yesterday. I already insinuated that Antonia has gone a bit gaga with old age. We can convince Momma that it's all untrue."

"I don't know, Celine. What if Gabby finds out that I lied about being with her?"

"She won't."

"I mean, I really like her. I don't think I can move to Boston anymore."

"*What?*"

"I'm serious. I want to make things work with her."

"Well, now you just *have* to lie. If Momma got those two pieces of news together, she would have a fit."

"Momma needs to back off."

"Hugo, take one thing at a time. Tell her the Boston thing first and then, down the line, tell her about Gabriella."

"Fine, I guess you're right. So what movie did I see?"

"You're on your own there. Just google what's playing in theatres right now."

When Hugo got home, Victoria was on the veranda at the front of the house. She was sitting on her favourite rocking chair, drinking a glass of ice-cold water with sprigs of mint and slices of cucumber. It reminded her of back home, when she and her own momma would sit outside in the humid evening and watch the sunset over the fields of corn.

"Hey, Momma," said Hugo, bounding up the steps. "Beautiful day, right?"

"Hello, sugar. I've been waiting for you."

"Oh?"

"Take a seat." She gestured to the empty wicker chair opposite her. She looked regal in her white trouser suit and silver sandals. Her long legs were crossed at the ankle and her blonde hair was wound into a French roll. The only thing that marred her appearance were her pursed lips.

Hugo knew that meant trouble. He sat down slowly.

"Water?" she asked, picking up the jug.

"I'm good."

She replaced it on the table. "Hugo, I heard something and I want you to clarify something."

He stared at her steadily. "Heard what, Momma?"

"I heard that you were at Sea Cliff yesterday with a girl – a Hispanic girl. Is this true?" She steeled herself.

"Sea Cliff? I haven't been there in a while. Who said that?"

"I heard that you were having lunch there."

He shook his head. "I was at the movies yesterday."

"You were?" A flicker of hope flashed across her face.

"Sure, Momma. I think I have the stub someplace." He got up and started to empty his pockets.

"It's fine, it's fine." She waved at him to stop his search. "You're positive, now? You were at the movies?"

Hugo gave her a funny look. "Are you okay? This is a weird conversation, I've got to say."

"I'm quite okay, honey pie. Now run along. Maria kept some lunch for you."

Hugo got up and pecked her cheek. "See you later."

"Oh and Hugo?"

He stopped at the front door. "Yes?"

"The Boston office called. You have an interview next Monday. I took the liberty of booking you a flight for Sunday afternoon. It's all arranged."

He closed his eyes. "Sure, Momma."

He walked inside and pulled out his phone. He had to act fast. There was only one person who could help him now. He pressed the 'call' button.

"Charlotte? I need to ask you a favour."

The next day, Gabriella got home from a lunchtime shift at the restaurant to find Isabelle in the shower. She waited until her friend appeared with a towel wrapped around her head.

"Why are you here?' she asked in surprise. "I thought you'd be bathing in milk at that fancy hotel right now, preparing for tomorrow night."

"Oh, I needed to pick up some things."

"Where's Raphael?"

"Oh, he had to go and buy a suit so Bertie took him shopping." Isabelle didn't quite meet her eyes.

"Bertie's back?"

"Yes. He flew in this morning," she answered. "Just for two nights as he's starting a new shoot in Vienna."

"God, it's good of him to come all this way."

"He knows how much it means to Raphael that he be there."

"He has you by his side, surely that's enough?" Gabriella poured a glass of juice.

Isabelle felt something clutch her heart. He had been distant for a while now. They hadn't made love in three days and, whenever she mentioned the première or Allegra, he'd change the subject. She would wake in the middle of the night and find him working on his new film, the glow from the computer screen illuminating his face. She could feel him slipping away.

Earlier that day, she had asked Raphael which gown she should wear to the première. Holding up her phone, she had two photos ready for him to judge. He had shouted at her, saying that her dress was of no importance to him and that he needed space to work. Horrified, she had run off.

She knew he was stressed, but there was no excuse for such histrionics.

"What are you wearing tomorrow night, Gabs?"

"A light-blue dress I made last year for Penny's communion."

"Do I know it?" Isabelle frowned.

Gabriella nodded. "It's to the knee with a flowing skirt. Remember I borrowed your black heels?"

"Oh, right! That colour's awesome with your hair."

"What are you wearing?"

"Why, my peacock dress, of course."

"The one I made?" Gabriella's eyes lit up. "Really?"

"Of course. When people ask me who I'm wearing, I'll say Gabriella."

"You'd do that for me?"

"Of course. I only have an A-list boyfriend for a few more days, so I'd better make the most of it."

"You sound awfully flippant for a girl who's about to have her heart broken."

To Gabriella's horror, Isabelle burst into tears. She rushed over and hugged her.

"Hey, don't cry," she soothed. "Oh, Zsa Zsa, I'm so sorry!"

"I can't bear it, I can't bear it," she sobbed.

"What happened?"

"We had a fight ..."

"Over what?"

"He's stressed over the commercial and I asked him a silly question about my dress."

"So?" Gabriella's eyes flashed.

Isabelle wiped her nose with her towel. "I just don't know where our relationship is going."

"Ask him!"

"No, I can't." She sighed. "To be fair, I knew what I

was getting into, Gabby." She straightened her shoulders. "It's just sometimes it's so wonderful. We've spent every waking moment together. He can be so romantic." Her face clouded over. "He's leaving soon, I know it. Maybe at the end of this week. He wants to go back to France so he can work in peace."

"Have you discussed what will happen between you when he leaves?"

Isabelle wiped away a tear. "There is nothing to discuss – this morning sorted all of that out in an instant."

Gabriella snorted. "Yeah, right. All your things are still at that hotel. You'll see him tomorrow night. There's no way he can just take off without some acknowledgment."

Isabelle said nothing.

Gabriella rolled her eyes. "The only thing Raphael thinks about is himself. You need to put him out of your mind. After tomorrow night, you'll be famous in your own right. Strut in there like you own the place."

Isabelle gave her a watery smile.

"You're going to be front-page news after this," went on Gabriella firmly. "You won't need Raphael or Bertie or anyone."

"But what if he calls and says sorry?"

"Ignore his calls. Teach him a lesson, Zsa Zsa. Be strong."

"He might want to apologise …"

"*No!*"

Isabelle held up her hands. "Okay, okay! I get it. I'll let him sweat."

"He will respect you more."

"I guess."

Gabriella patted her back. "Well, I need to have a shower and get the smell of French fries out of my hair. Want to order some pizza when I get back?"

"Sure, I'd love that."

✎ Chapter Nineteen ✑

The next evening, Hugo pressed the bell outside the main door of Gabriella and Isabelle's apartment.

"Yeah?" came Isabelle's voice over the intercom.

"It's Hugo," he said, leaning towards the speaker.

"Come on up."

She buzzed him in and he climbed the stairs. He had so much news. A quick phone call to Charlotte the day before had secured him an interview with Christian Jacob: Luca's father. Charlotte worked at his firm and it was based in New York. All he had to do was ace the interview and he'd get to stay in the same city as Gabby.

He had toyed with asking his own father for a position at his law firm in Manhattan, but then had decided against it. Everyone knew that it was not a good idea to work with family and he would have to work doubly hard to avoid accusations of nepotism and favouritism. That was the rationale for the Boston idea – start fresh on the same playing field as everyone else and work up through the ranks. Not as the boss's son.

He couldn't wait to tell Gabby. Maybe then she would let her guard down. Maurice's attack hadn't helped things and he understood that. However, he also suspected that she was slow to let him close as she knew he was moving away. Now, if the interview went well, they could maybe take things further. He wanted their relationship to go to the next level.

Caroline Ashley Hamilton was sending him message after message, inviting him to barbecues and beach parties. He had declined politely, making excuses, hoping that she would back off. Yet, it only served to make her more determined. He blamed his momma for a lot of it as she had encouraged it from the start.

Isabelle opened the door and he whistled.

"*Wow!* You look sensational!"

She was stunning in the dark-green peacock dress that Gabriella had made for her mother Elaine's birthday a couple of years back. Her red hair was curled and swept up onto her head. Her make-up was dark and dramatic, which contrasted with her pale skin.

"You don't look too bad yourself," she said, taking in his tuxedo. "You should wear monkey suits more often."

"Thanks," he said grinning, thinking of how he had narrowly missed meeting Victoria as he left the house. She would have been all over him like a rash, wanting to know where he was going and with whom. "Where's my date?"

"Oh, fixing her hair." She sipped a glass of Prosecco. "Would you like a glass? I'm just calming my nerves."

Hugo shook his head. "I'm good. So, is that Raphael guy picking you up?"

Isabelle looked desolate for a moment, but then smiled brightly. "No. I'm flying solo tonight. Paolo, my agent, said he'll meet me there and he has put the word out that I'm the next big thing." She said it without emotion.

"That's pretty exciting, right?" said Hugo in surprise. "You must be thrilled."

"I guess."

Gabriella appeared, wearing her light-blue dress and the same black pashmina she had worn to her graduation. Her long dark hair was glossy and fell in a sheet down her back. She had borrowed Isabelle's black shoes again and she wore Lita's gold cross around her neck.

"You look beautiful," said Hugo, drinking her in.

She blushed. "No, I …"

"*You do!*" said Hugo and Isabelle in unison.

"Okay, thank you!" She made a small curtsy. "You both look amazing too."

"Come on, let's go." Isabelle knocked back her drink. "Paolo hates when I'm late and he paid a guy from the E! channel to interview me."

Hugo hailed a cab as soon as they got outside.

"We should have a limo," grumbled Isabelle, sidling into the back seat awkwardly as her dress was tight. "I asked for one but Paolo laughed in my face."

"A cab is extravagant enough for me," said Gabriella. "I was planning on getting the subway."

Hugo took the front seat. "The Paris Theatre," he instructed the driver. "On 58th."

"You got it."

As the car sped along Isabelle examined her red nails which she had painted earlier. Raphael hadn't called. Part of her had expected him to get in touch and apologise for his behaviour, but there hadn't even been so much as a message. It was just shocking behaviour. They had spent almost three weeks together, yet he was like a stranger. Sure, she knew that he had a mole on his left thigh and that he liked one sugar in his black coffee. She knew that he disliked creamy food and his favourite childhood movie was *E.T.* This was all information she had gathered and stored from their conversations lying on his pillow. A few days ago, she had been fully expecting an invitation to Picardy. He had kissed her temple and told her that she was the best thing that had happened to him in years. Then, just hours later, he had shouted at her over a stupid dress.

The lights of the city blurred before her eyes. She had imagined tonight would be so different. She was supposed to arrive with Raphael on her arm. Then the whole world would know that he belonged to her. Cameras would flash and she would be front-page news.

Now, all she had was a crappy interview with some anchor from E! News and a solitary walk down the red carpet.

They arrived about twenty minutes later. The cab pulled up next to a red carpet that led out from the main entrance of the theatre. *'Starr!' by Allegra Starr* was written on the billboard above the door. Paparazzi lined the sidewalk on each side. There were about twenty people with large cameras, all loitering around, waiting for a celebrity to arrive. Security guards lined the entrance and a large muscular man dressed in black with a head piece was waiting to open the cab door when they pulled to a halt. A crowd of fans were waiting behind two railings that ran adjacent to the red carpet, all with phones poised for that all-important selfie if the opportunity arose.

The main focus was Bertie Wells of course. He was big news and always made time to meet and greet the public. But Raphael was still worthy of a photo as he was gaining momentum in the celebrity world once more. Everyone loved a comeback story and tonight was rumoured to be just that. Allegra Starr herself was a Hollywood veteran and was guaranteed to bring glamour to the event. Rumour on the street was that Oberon was in town and had promised to pop by.

The beefy security guard opened the taxi door.

"Names?" he asked abruptly.

Gabriella turned to Isabelle in a panic. "You told Paolo I was bringing Hugo, right?"

"Yes, relax. It's all sorted."

Hugo stepped out. "Hugo du Maurier," he said, smiling. The man checked his list. "Right, I got your name. Move along." He peered into the back seat. "And you two?"

"I'm Gabriella Ruiz Álvarez and this is Isabelle Flynn." He scanned his list again. "Got it. Right, head on in."

"Gabs! How's my make-up?" said Isabelle, trying to see her reflection in her phone screen. "Is my mascara still intact?"

Gabriella nodded. "You look incredible."

Gabriella emerged first and the photographers barely looked up. They were waiting for the big names and someone had received a tip that Allegra was on the way. The crowd screamed anyway. Sure, they didn't recognise her face but she could be somebody. Gabriella blushed and stumbled slightly in her heels. Luckily, Hugo was there to hold her hand.

"Shall we?" he said.

She nodded. "Let's go in."

"*Are you an actress?*" shouted someone in the crowd of journalists.

"*Who are you wearing?*" shouted another.

Gabriella kept her head down, unused to such attention. As fast as she could, she hauled Hugo along the carpet and into the foyer of the theatre.

Paolo, Isabelle's agent, appeared. He was a small man of about fifty with a shock of black hair and a big bushy moustache. He had been in show business for years, managing different Broadway actors, hoping that one of them would make the transition onto the big screen. Then, when they all disappeared into obscurity, he realised that he would never make a million bucks with the theatre. So, five years ago, he set up a modelling agency and Isabelle, fresh from high school, became one of his clients. He liked her with her unusual colouring and fiery temper. The perfume job had been a major coup and he was determined to milk it for all it was worth. Who knew when she would be in the company of such stars again?

"Please tell me she's here!" he said frantically. "I've lined up two interviews and a photo with Allegra."

"She's just on her way in," said Gabriella consolingly. "Don't worry."

From the darkness of the car, Isabelle searched the crowd for a familiar face. All she could see were photographers and a couple of presenters with large microphones and a cameraman following them. There were fans with banners saying: *Bertie Forever!*

She felt her stomach churn as she prepared to exit the car. What if she tripped and fell flat on her face. What if she made a mess of the interview? Paolo had given her the pre-prepared questions and had suggested answers. She had been told that there would be no surprises.

"Hey, lady! You getting out or what?" The taxi driver looked back. "I gotta make a move."

"Of course, I'm sorry." She took a deep breath. Sure, she was a nobody now, but after tonight that would change. It had to.

Plastering a smile on her beautiful face, she stepped out of the car.

One paparazzo shouted as she stood up straight. *"It's Allegra!"*

Another photographer snorted, "Yeah, like a million years ago." He turned away and lit a cigarette.

The guy who had called her Allegra lifted his camera and took a shot. The flash blinded her momentarily but she was gratified that he had bothered. Slowly, she began to walk, making sure that her posture was correct. She was a model after all.

People began to point and one little girl, who was waiting to see Bertie Wells, shouted out, "*Look, Mom! She's so beautiful!*"

She kept walking, her eyes trained on the giant potted plant outside the door. There was a murmuring in the crowd. With her elegance and grace, she had to be a star.

"*Isabelle!*" called Paolo from the theatre entrance. "I have someone here from E! News Daily."

She smiled and continued on her way. Blotting out the noise and the nerves, she held her head high.

A few of the photographers began to take shots of her as she walked by. "*Look this way, babe!*" one called. "*Right at my lens, gorgeous!*"

She ignored them and kept her eyes trained on the plant. She was almost there …

Suddenly, Raphael appeared, looking handsome in a black tuxedo. He strode towards her on the carpet. Taking her face in his large hands, he kissed her tenderly on the lips.

"Forgive me," he murmured.

The photographers immediately perked up. There was that Baptiste guy and he was kissing the stunning redhead. She must be somebody. This was definitely worth a shot.

Isabelle gazed at him. Raphael took her small hand in his and together they walked the red carpet, pausing sporadically to sign autographs and take photos. They looked eye-catching together – with his dark hair and eyes and her pale skin and Titian hair.

When they reached the main entrance, they turned and posed for a photograph. *"This is my muse!"* called out Raphael, kissing Isabelle's hand. *"She is a star in the making!"*

The cameras flashed and flashed, making her squint. Tilting her chin upwards, she soaked it up. This was what she yearned for – this was the end goal. Fame was teasing and tantalising her and she wanted every bit of it.

"What's her name?" called one man from behind a giant lens.

Before Raphael could answer, Isabelle herself said, "I'm Isabelle Flynn."

The man scribbled it down on a piece of paper. "Well, Miss Flynn, here's my card. Check out my website later and you'll see some pictures." He smiled. "Until we meet again."

Paolo appeared, his face red with excitement. "Fabulous, darling!" he exclaimed, kissing her on both cheeks. Then, when Raphael turned away to chat to a fan, he leaned in closer. "Great move, Zsa Zsa. Now the whole world will know your name."

She flushed with pleasure. It had been a surprise but what a wonderful surprise. Raphael looked gorgeous in his tuxedo and she felt her heart fill with love.

"Come on, you need to do that interview." Paolo pulled her along. "Remember, your right side is your best and don't say anything controversial."

Gabriella was sipping champagne in the foyer with Hugo by her side. Isabelle and Raphael were talking to some journalists and there was a string quartet playing the scores from Allegra's movies. Suddenly there was a roar from the crowd.

"Bertie must have arrived," said Gabriella, straining to see.

A large limo had pulled up and three big bodyguards got out. One held open the back door and sure enough Bertie Wells emerged. He was wearing the same white tux from the shoot and waved madly at the screaming crowd.

"*Good to see you, my darlings!*" he called to his fans, blowing them kisses.

A woman followed, dressed in a full-length black-velvet dress and white gloves.

"*It's Mia Sutherland!*" shouted a woman wearing an *Orphée* T-shirt. "*Mia! Mia! Can I get a photo?*"

Mia waved regally at the crowd, her dark-brown hair cascading down her back. A classic English rose, she was one of Britain's most famous actresses. Back in 2002, at the age of seventeen, she had been cast as a young Mary Wollstonecraft Godwin. The movie was about the period in the novelist's life where she holidayed near Lake Geneva with Lord Byron and her soon-to-be husband, Percy Bysshe Shelley, and of course where she was inspired to write the gothic masterpiece, *Frankenstein*. A dark film filled with debauchery and spookiness, it earned Mia countless awards for Best Newcomer, and she now commanded ten million pounds a film. Her next role was alongside Bertie in Vienna, playing a young Jewish art curator in the thirties. Both she and Bertie shared an agent, the infamous Harry Finkelman. It was through Harry that they had met and were now close friends. When Bertie had asked her to be his date to the première, she had accepted. The acting world tended to stick together and Raphael Baptiste needed the boost.

She followed Bertie up the red carpet, smiling at the cameras and waving at fans. The paparazzi were on high alert. No one had tipped them that Mia Sutherland was turning up. It was turning into a veritable celeb-fest.

Bertie relished the walk of fame towards the entrance to the theatre. He stopped over and over again for fans to take selfies and sign autographs. The paparazzi took photo after photo and three journalists interviewed him for CNN, E! Entertainment and Sky News.

"So, are you and Mia dating now?" asked one.

"It would be my greatest pleasure to call his exquisite creature my own," he answered. "However, alas, it not the case. We are, sadly, just friends."

Gabriella was on her second glass of champagne when Bertie and Mia finally appeared. "Hello, my love!" he said, beaming. Then he grabbed the arm of a passing waiter. "Two glasses of champagne, my good man. *Pronto!*"

Gabriella smiled warmly. "Hello," she said to Mia. "I'm Gabriella."

Mia smiled. "Lovely to meet you," she said in her clipped British tone.

Bertie kissed Gabriella's hand. "This is the budding designer I spoke about in the car. It's just wonderful to be surrounded by such young talent."

Mia smiled. "Bertie was raving about you all."

"And who's this young man?" asked Bertie, turning to Hugo.

"This is Hugo," Gabriella said shyly, pushing him forward.

Bertie raised an eyebrow. "Your better half?"

Gabriella blushed. "Well, I'm not sure ..."

"Yes," Hugo cut in, shaking his hand. "I'm Gabriella's boyfriend."

"Charmed," said Bertie. "Are you a designer too?"

250

Hugo shook his head. "I'm an attorney."

"Oh?" Bertie looked surprised. "What an odd combination: a fashion designer and a lawyer. Still, I suppose opposites attract and all that."

"My brother is a barrister," said Mia helpfully. "We get on very well, despite our differences."

Hugo smiled tightly.

"Why did you call me your muse like that?" Isabelle faced Raphael, two glasses of champagne giving her courage. "You didn't contact me all day and then you do that."

"I'm sorry." He shrugged. "I cannot handle pressure. It is my biggest flaw."

"You hurt me," she said quietly.

"I know." He cupped her face in his hand. "I don't deserve you."

"So, don't do it." She kissed his palm. "Don't be mean to me."

"I'll try, I promise that I'll try."

A woman from *Esquire* magazine appeared and smiled. "Monsieur Baptiste!" she said in a nasal voice. "Have you got a minute?"

Isabelle excused herself and walked over to Bertie. She was sick of the press and the repetitive questions. She kissed him on the cheek.

"Nice to see you, Bertie."

"Isabelle!" He kissed her hand. "Meet Mia, my wonderful companion this evening."

Mia smiled. "Hello."

Isabelle shook her hand in awe. "Wow, I can't believe I'm meeting Mia Sutherland!"

Bertie laughed. "Be cool, Isabelle. You'll never hobnob with the rich and famous if you get tongue-tied."

Isabelle nudged him gently in the arm. "Hey, I'm allowed. I'm not used to this."

Mia smiled. "The first time I met Leo, I did the exact same thing."

"Leo?" Isabelle's eyes widened. "As in di Caprio?"

Mia nodded. "I idolised him in *Romeo and Juliet*. I was exactly like you are now."

"You get over it pretty quickly," added Bertie. "We celebs are just mere mortals like you, except with pots of money and egos the size of Africa." He placed his empty glass on a small table. "I'm in dire need of another drink," he said, wiping his brow. "Working the red carpet is exhausting at the best of times. Still, it's over now." He glanced around. "Has Allegra arrived yet?"

Isabelle shook her head. "Not yet."

"Typical the old boot would attempt to upstage me." He rolled his eyes. "She's probably parked across the street, waiting for the most opportune moment to arrive."

"So what's the story with Raphael?" asked Gabriella, sidling closer to Isabelle. "He seems very attentive."

Isabelle held up her hands. "You tell me. He's like Jekyll and Hyde. One minute he's shouting and super-mean, the next he's calling me his muse."

"Just be careful," Gabriella warned. "Remember how he made you feel. Make sure things are on your terms from now on."

Isabelle didn't answer. Instead she looked at the man she had been sharing a bed with for the past couple of weeks. He was talking to Brad the cameraman, his handsome face smiling. Oh, how she wanted to call him her own! She wanted definition to their relationship – she needed to know that she mattered to him. Sure, he had called her his muse, but that was only to placate her for his despicable behaviour. A statement like that could only help her on her way to fame and he knew it.

Allegra had arrived ten minutes after Bertie, flanked by four huge bodyguards. Her thin body was eye-catching in a white strapless gown. Her signature red hair was hanging loose and she had a white fur stole around her shoulders. She had opted to come alone, fearing that an A-lister date would deflect from her moment.

"*Be a Star with Allegra Starr!*" she repeated over and over again with a brilliant smile.

There was another roar from the crowd outside.

"*Oberon!*" they heard over the din. "*Take a selfie with me, Oberon!*"

Isabelle watched Gabriella gulp back her champagne. Despite her friend's sang-froid, she could see that she still carried hope that Oberon would give her a chance.

Privately, Isabelle couldn't see it. He just didn't seem to be interested in anything or anyone but himself.

Oberon walked into the foyer wearing a sharp black suit and a purple silk shirt. He wore no tie, but left the collar open. His bald head gleamed in the lights and a diamond ring glistened on his forefinger. His dark skin was exotic and his chiselled cheekbones gave him a proud demeanour.

"Allegra!" he said, hugging her.

"You came!" she simpered.

"Of course, of course. I wouldn't miss your big night." He accepted a glass of champagne from a passing waiter.

"We're almost ready to go in," said Allegra. "The theatre is ready."

"I'm sure it will be a triumph." Oberon's eyes sparkled from the hit of cocaine he'd had a few minutes earlier in the back of his limo. "Let's go and see the greatest advertisement ever made."

✆ Chapter Twenty ✇

The press who had been allowed to the screening emerged from the cinema, all chattering loudly.

"Did you see Bertie?"

"She's the image of Allegra ..."

"I loved the music ..."

"The *mise en scène* was just awesome ..."

Raphael, who had opted not to attend the screening, stood in the foyer, anxiously waiting for feedback. He had been pacing for twenty minutes, doubting himself and then giving himself a mental shaking and then doubting himself again.

"*Baptiste!*" shouted one journalist. "*It's fabulous, just fabulous. Congratulations!*"

Allegra appeared, minus her stole, and walked straight up to Raphael. Theatrically, she kissed him on each cheek twice. "Darling, it's just superb! Terrific!"

Cameras flashed.

Bertie came out next, clapping his hands. "Wonderful, Raph! Bravo!"

Slowly the fear and trepidation faded away and he began to relax. People seemed to like it. They really did. He had always handled pressure badly. His mother had often chided him for being a perfectionist. "Life is never perfect," she had warned him time and time again. "You must accept flaws."

Isabelle sauntered out with Gabriella and the press made a beeline for them immediately. "*Miss Flynn!*" one called. "*Isabelle!*" called another.

"This is it," whispered Gabriella squeezing her arm. "Enjoy it."

Isabelle took a deep breath.

"So, your dress is beautiful. Who are you wearing?" The small girl with a dictaphone waited for Isabelle to answer.

"This is an original piece by *Gabriella*," she answered.

"Who?"

"*Gabriella*. Surely you've heard of her?"

The small girl shrugged. "I have now."

"She made my dress in the commercial too."

'She did? I thought that was a piece by Oberon. I googled it and it said that it was the gown that made him famous."

"That's exactly what it is," came a voice from behind. "And don't you forget it." Oberon's haughty face appeared. "It's so retro now, but I have to admit that it's taking me back to the past. That dress made me a star."

"It still looks as fresh as ever," said the girl, turning towards him. "Is that the original?"

Oberon nodded. "In all its glory."

"Hey!" interrupted Isabelle. "Gabby made that …"

"We decided to recreate that iconic night Allegra took home the golden statue," went on Oberon, glaring at Isabelle. "I'm honoured to be a part of it."

After a few more minutes of small talk, the girl walked away, desperate for a chat with Bertie.

Isabelle whipped around and grabbed Oberon's sleeve. "How dare you?"

"On the contrary, how dare you?" He removed her hand calmly.

"Gabriella made that dress."

"Yes, but I designed it."

"So? She deserved a mention."

"Nonsense. It's entirely my baby. Now run along."

Isabelle rose to her full height. "My friend is super-talented."

"Fascinating," said Oberon in a bored tone.

"Look!" Isabelle accessed her camera roll. "Her portfolio is filled with amazing designs. Her best ones are based on iconic royal couture through the ages."

There was a picture of Isabelle wearing a Grace Kelly ensemble which was a mid-calf-length mint-green satin dress, based on the full-length version that Kelly wore to the Oscars the night she won. Then a gown worn by Princess Margaret – a pink organza affair with a fitted bodice and one strappy sleeve, leaving the right shoulder bare. It fell to mid-thigh and resembled a long bell-shaped tutu. Finally a Princess Diana inspired knee-length affair, modelled on the infamous wedding gown designed by the Emanuels. It even had the wrinkled silk and taffeta, complete with bows. However, unlike the original, it didn't have puffy sleeves. Gabriella had sewn on a long train at the last minute for effect.

Oberon glanced at the screen. "More imitation," he said, rolling his eyes. "*Yawn*."

"What did you say?"

"You heard me." He sipped his drink. "That girl is a charlatan. All she does is imitate. Her designs are rip-offs of others' great work. She has a talent for copying, but there isn't an original bone in her body."

"*Oberon!*" Isabelle was at a loss. "That's not true and you know it."

"It *is* true," he said calmly. "She copied me and in that show she imitated others. Do I need to dumb it down anymore? Blimey, you models are stupid."

Isabelle clenched her glass tightly. "The dress I'm wearing tonight is a Gabriella original. What do you say to that?"

He looked her up and down. "Not bad, if I were a peacock. I might fancy you with all those feathers."

"Oberon!" she said again. "You're despicable."

"No, darling, I'm a realist. Tell your little friend to go back to the barrio or wherever she comes from. She will never make it unless she sticks her neck out. She has to be inventive and break the rules."

He walked off and replenished his drink.

Isabelle frowned. Break the rules? Gabby never did that.

She looked across the room at her friend. She was hand in hand with Hugo and laughing.

Gabriella must never know what Oberon said. It would crush her.

Raphael steeled himself not to drink alcohol. If one more waiter offered him champagne, he would explode. The high from the success of the screening had awakened a thirst. He wanted to celebrate – he wanted to let go and enjoy himself.

However, he knew that it was a fantasy. A few glasses of champagne would turn into a three-day session. He wouldn't be able to stop. His counsellor at rehab had warned him – never think that you can control it. Don't be fooled.

He sipped his water miserably. Life seemed so empty sometimes. Sure, he had his work and his friends, but it wasn't the same. Staying on the straight and narrow was exhausting as it required huge effort. The past few weeks had been bearable as he had been busy.

Then there was Isabelle.

Raphael stared at her. She was certainly something. He tried to see an imperfection, but failed. He knew that he had been particularly bloody to her over the past few days, but that was par for the course. He was always the same before a première. What was it with him and models? With her poise and grace, she reminded him of Sylvie. Something clutched his heart.

Sylvie Marot. France's answer to Kate Moss. He had fallen in love with her instantly. He remembered it like it was yesterday. It was nearing Christmas in 2007 and he had attended a party thrown by a French advertising guru. Amongst the guests were the newly elected president, Nicolas Sarkozy and his wife-to-be, Carla Bruni. After lots of champagne and conversations with countless people, he had noticed Sylvie standing by the window, with her blonde hair and classic beauty. He had kissed her for the first time that night and within weeks they were official. They had been the golden couple of Paris. Everyone wanted them at their party and everyone knew their names. Then, after his very public breakdown, she left. Pushed to her limit, she had walked away.

He knew things weren't easy. He understood that living with him had been hard. Yet, her abandonment had scarred him irrevocably.

He stared at Isabelle once more. He liked sleeping next to her, her slim body nestled in his arms. She was funny and sweet and he liked having her around. It was high time he settled down. Sylvie was history. He had to forget.

"So, there's a party at the Plaza," announced Bertie, his cheeks pink after five glasses of champagne. "There's plenty of room in my limo."

Isabelle clapped her hands. "Great! I'd love to take a ride with you. I've never been to the Plaza. Gabs, are you coming?"

Gabriella nodded. "You bet." She nodded in Oberon's direction. "He seems to be in a great mood. I hope he comes to the party too. I think I might try and talk to him later about taking me on."

Isabelle shook her head in alarm. "No, no. Let it be for tonight. You know what they say: don't mix business and pleasure."

"But he seems so happy and friendly."

"That's the coke, darling," said Bertie. "It makes one very affable indeed."

"Oh." Gabriella's eyes were wide.

Isabelle pulled her aside. "Don't try and talk to him. Not tonight. He's as high as a kite and won't focus."

"Look, I'll see how it goes. If I get the opportunity ..."

"*No!*" Isabelle shouted and Gabriella started. "I mean, just listen to me, Gabs. Oberon is not for you. He's not the mentor you want."

"Why are you so against him?" Gabriella looked suspicious. "Do you know something?"

Isabelle sighed. "All I know is that he is not the path for you. Just forget him."

"Why, Isabelle?" Her brown eyes were beseeching. "Tell me."

"He ... I ..."

"Off we go, girls!" Bertie interrupted. "Your carriage awaits outside. Brace yourselves for the screams as my diehard fans are still faithfully waiting outside for a glimpse of their idol."

Two bodyguards appeared and walked on either side of Bertie, with Vladimir bringing up the rear.

"Hello, boys," he greeted, blowing them kisses. "Mia?" he called. "Come along, my sweet."

Mia placed her empty glass on a table. "I'm coming."

Gabriella linked arms with Hugo. "We'd love a ride to the party. Thanks."

"Where's Raphael?" asked Isabelle, looking around. "He was talking to Allegra a minute ago."

"He was on the phone the last I saw of him," said Bertie. "Just give him a ring and ask him to meet you at the Plaza."

"No, I should wait ..."

"Not at all," said Bertie briskly. "This is your night, sweetheart. Allegra may think that it's all about her, but the world is fed up of her face."

"I guess," she said doubtfully.

"Raphael is a big boy. He will follow."

Isabelle took out her phone and dialled Raphael's number. It rang out so she tried again. Again, it rang out. Typing furiously, she sent him a message, asking him to follow her to the party. Bertie was right. This was her chance to mingle and shine.

"This will be your night, my sweet," said Bertie to Isabelle, taking her arm. "The world will know your name by tomorrow, thanks to social media."

"Do you really think so?"

"I do." He straightened his bowtie. "Now, let's go and enjoy the party."

Raphael blew a smoke ring and stared moodily at the passing traffic. After a particularly boring conversation with Allegra, he had slipped upstairs and was now sitting on the fire escape smoking a Gauloise. He hated evenings like this. After the stress and pressure of the première, all he wanted to do was go back to the hotel and sleep. He didn't want to eat expensive food at the Plaza and he certainly didn't want to have to sit there and watch his cast and crew get progressively drunker while he remained sober.

He inhaled deeply and sighed.

He didn't want to be alone either. He could work on his new film, that was an option. However, making love to Isabelle was preferable. He could close his eyes and drift away, warm and sated in her arms.

Stubbing his cigarette, he stood up.

Allegra was holding court in the Grand Ballroom of the historic hotel when they arrived. It had been decorated like an Oscar ceremony, in keeping with the theme of the night. The two chandeliers glistened in the lights and the neoclassical white-and-gold murals gave an old world feel. The round tables had been set for dinner, all covered in white cloth with gold chairs. In the centre of the room was a giant Oscar statue, a gold Academy Award with '*Allegra Starr*' engraved on it.

Isabelle checked her phone for the tenth time. There was still no message from Raphael.

"I kept seats at the head table for you, Bertie!" called Allegra. "You, me and Raphy. Where is Raphy by the way? He's the genius behind it all."

Bertie pretended not to hear. He turned to Gabriella and Isabelle. "Right, the main objective here is to save me from Miss Starr. I cannot sit beside her during dinner."

"Put Oberon beside her," said Isabelle. "The drugs will make it bearable."

"Wonderful idea," said Bertie. "I'll orchestrate that right away."

Brad the cameraman, looking smart in a tuxedo, waved as he walked by. Kim, dressed in a silver dress and with sparkly eyes, looked completely different. Her petite frame had the added bonus of Jimmy Choo stiletto sandals. Due to their four-inch height, she stumbled slightly as she walked. She kept glancing around furtively, desperately looking for Raphael. Isabelle found herself doing the exact same thing.

Evie and Coco looked demure in black cocktail dresses and the rest of the crew looked like they were going to their Senior Prom.

"Everyone scrubs up well," observed Bertie. "It's hard to think that that dashing young man in the suit over there is Mike who holds the sound boom."

Isabelle took a seat at a round table to the left of the statue. Gabriella and Hugo joined her and Mia gracefully sat down. Bertie strategically placed himself directly behind the giant statue, impeding Allegra's view of his whereabouts.

"Say nothing," he said, putting his finger to his lips.

"Will I keep a seat for Raphael?" asked Isabelle. "Or will he be forced to sit with Allegra?"

"Oh, keep him a seat," answered Bertie. "He will never sit up there with her."

"If he turns up," said Isabelle bitterly. "He seems to have gone missing."

Bertie put his hand on hers. "Don't fret, my love. He's probably gone for a walk, relieved that it all went so well. He needs to come down from all of that."

The waiters filled the water glasses. The sommelier appeared and asked the table to look at the menu so as to pair the appropriate wine to their choice of food.

Isabelle tried to focus, but the champagne had gone to her head and she had a pain in her chest when she thought of Raphael's absence.

"May I be excused?" she asked politely, getting up. "I need to use the ladies' room."

Hugo and Bertie stood up immediately and resumed their seats when she had left.

Minutes later, she stared at her reflection in the mirror of the opulent bathroom. This up and down was affecting her mental health. After the muse comment, she had been sure of his affection. Now, his refusal to return her calls had awakened a fear inside her that threatened to engulf her. The door opened and Kim appeared.

Isabelle groaned inwardly.

"Isabelle," she said with a fake smile. "How are you?" She opened her clutch bag and took out some lipstick.

Isabelle smiled coldly and started to walk towards the door.

"Has Raphael gone home?" asked Kim, blotting her lips on a piece of tissue.

Isabelle shrugged. "I don't know ..."

"You don't know?" she echoed.

Isabelle closed her eyes.

"No."

"I guess you two aren't as close as you think."

"I guess not."

"Aw, poor Isabelle. You're not the first dumb model to fall for his spin. Still, you lasted longer than most." She snapped her bag shut. "You see, models and actresses come and go but I remain. He would be lost without me." She laughed. "Enjoy your night now!"

She pushed past and the door shut behind her.

Isabelle felt her eyes fill with tears. She couldn't fight it as Kim was right. She had been a distraction and nothing more.

Oberon ordered a vodka and checked his emails on his iPhone. He had sent samples of his dresses to Kensington

Palace in the hope that the Duchess would wear one or two. Everyone knew that whatever she wore ended up in every fashion magazine on the planet. Not that he needed the publicity, but it couldn't hurt.

His show was almost ready and he only had a week left in New York. The timing of Allegra's gig had been fortuitous to say the least. His appearance tonight would guarantee him some publicity and he got a free dinner. The minute his show was over, he was gone. He disliked Americans and preferred his native London. He and Riku had their flights booked and were ready to go.

There was nothing of interest in his inbox – just a few promotions and a few from Riku regarding the models. His new range was what he called tribal chic. He had travelled to Jamaica to trace his roots and had been enchanted by the colours and the tropical atmosphere. Then, he had researched the Ethiopian roots of his grandfather and found even more inspiration. What had followed was a whirlwind of design and after a year of drawings and modifications, he was ready to show it to the world.

Was he nervous? Of course. Like any artist, he still felt the stomach-churning dread prior to the unveiling of his vision. What if the public hated it and turned on him? What if the dream ended?

Allegra's laugh resonated in his ears. He wished that he could turn her on mute. Sure, she had given him a leg-up at a crucial time by wearing his design, but she was so annoying. Her American twang grated on his nerves. Still, he kept her on side. He was no fool – the secret to staying on top was to keep everyone sweet.

The waiters served the lobster-tail starter and filled wineglasses with cold Chablis.

Gabriella, who had never tasted lobster, attacked her food with gusto.

Hugo sipped his wine and watched her in amusement. "You seem to like it," he observed.

"It's awesome," she said, buttering a slice of bread. "I love the sauce."

"So, I have news," he said in her ear. "I've an interview at a firm in New York next week."

"What?" She almost choked on her lobster. "You mean …?"

He nodded. "It means no Boston. If I get it, that is."

She beamed at him. "Of course you'll get it. You're wonderful."

"You're blinkered," he said, smiling.

She kissed his cheek. "This is just the greatest news, Hugo. It means so many things."

"I know."

Suddenly, his phone started to ring. Taking it out of his pocket, he saw Celine's name flashing on the screen. He decided to ignore it, but she kept calling. In the end, he gave in.

"Excuse me," he said, leaving the table. Walking out into the hall, he accessed the call.

"What's up?"

"What the hell are you doing at Allegra Starr's première?" Celine sounded angry. "You idiot, Hugo. Now you're all over social media."

"So?"

"Caroline rang me and said that she saw you on a red carpet with Gabriella! She saw it on Facebook and Instagram. Now you've blown it."

"I don't care, I really don't. You were the one who made me lie, Celine. I don't see the point. Momma will have to find out eventually."

"Hugo! Have you lost your mind? Remember when I

hooked up with that guy from Montauk? The mechanic's son? She put a stop to that right away."

"Look, I'm moving out soon. She can't control my life. I love Gabriella and –"

"What did you say? Love? Are you serious?"

"Yes, I'm serious." He smiled. "I want to be with her. Charlotte set up an interview with Luca's dad so I'm hoping to start work pretty soon. Then all I have to do is find an apartment and I'm all set."

"You're her only son! Can't you see? She'll have a heart attack."

"She'll have to get over it. I'm going to ask Gabby to Char's wedding as my date."

"*What?*"

"I'm asking Gabby to the wedding. This is how it's going to be. Was there anything else?"

"Hugo!"

"Right, then I'll talk to you tomorrow."

"Hugo! Don't hang up on me."

He ended the call.

"Everything okay?" asked Gabriella when he got back to the table. He kissed her forehead.

"Perfect."

Bertie stood up and clinked his glass. "*Attention, all! I think it's time I said a few words.*"

The conversation died away and all faces turned in his direction.

"First of all, I want to thank Allegra for creating such a wonderful legacy: Starr by Allegra Starr. I shall buy some for my mother immediately."

Everyone clapped politely and Allegra blew kisses.

"Liar!" mouthed Isabelle to Bertie and he smirked.

"Next, thank you to myself for lending my star quality

to such a production. I channelled my Rick Blaine and I think I did a jolly good job of it."

There were a few laughs and some clapping.

"To Oberon for letting us use his design…"

Oberon stood up and bowed.

"And to Gabriella for painstakingly sewing each bead onto the dress. You are a star in the making, my darling. The future Chanel."

Oberon scowled and sat down again.

Hugo kissed Gabriella softly on the lips. "He's right, you know. You're going to rule the fashion world someday."

"Cut it out," she said, blushing.

"To all the crew for giving extra time so we could change the theme of the advertisement. The shoot took longer than expected and no one complained. Well done to all of you on the ground."

The whole room clapped loudly.

"To Isabelle Flynn, my beautiful partner on the carpet! Your beauty dazzles me every day and I can see that today is only the beginning for you. Watch this space, ladies and gentlemen. This girl will be front-page news from now on." Bertie raised his glass and took a sip.

Isabelle felt the colour rise in her pale cheeks.

"And finally, *in absentia*, I want to thank the man behind the whole thing, my *bon ami,* Raphael Baptiste. He dislikes social events and so opted not to attend …"

Bertie was cut off by a scuffle at the door.

"*Let me in!*" came a roar and the security guards were pushed aside.

Raphael, looking belligerent and determined, marched into the room.

"*Raphy! Yoohoo! I saved you a seat!*" Allegra jumped up and waved.

Bertie laughed. "Let me start again. Raphael Baptiste, the director and producer of this wonderful project, has just arrived and if you'd all raise your glasses ..."

Raphael ignored everyone and walked straight up to Isabelle. Taking her arm, he pulled her to her feet. She could smell his musky scent as she looked up at him. His dark eyes bored into hers.

"Let's go," he said softly. "Come away with me. I don't want to sit here talking to people I don't really like."

"But it's a party, it's my big night!"

"Come with me." His gaze was so intense, she felt her legs give away. "Now, Isabelle."

"Okay," she said breathlessly. Taking her clutch bag from the table, she gave a small wave. "Night, everyone."

Raphael took her hand and walked purposefully towards the door.

"*Zsa Zsa!*" called Gabriella. "*You can't leave! The night is only beginning!*"

Bertie raised an eyebrow. "And he's gone! Well, that was a flying visit."

The diners laughed.

Allegra squealed. "Where's Raphy going with my doppelganger?"

Kim looked desolate. She knocked back her wine and coughed.

Gabriella turned to Hugo, her eyes flashing. "Typical behaviour from him! It's a big night for her and he takes her away. Why is it always on his terms?"

"Don't let it upset you," he said soothingly. "She's a big girl and she made a choice."

"It does upset me. He treats her like dirt yet she goes back for more. Raphael will break her heart, I guarantee you that."

⟪ Chapter Twenty-One ⟫

Raphael trailed a finger down Isabelle's smooth thigh and then kissed her shoulder blade. They were lying naked in his huge bed at the hotel, her slender body nestled into his large one, both facing the window.

"Come back to France with me," he said softly.

She stiffened. She had dreamed of these words, imagining herself in a large house in the French countryside, eating baguettes and brie under the summer sun. She wore a big wide-brimmed hat in this vision, as with her pale skin she would burn. Raphael was relaxed and happy, walking around barefoot on the grass, back in his native country. Oh, how she had dreamed of these words!

Yet now the game had changed. There were three emails from Paolo already with auditions. One in L.A. and two in New York. The world had taken notice and opportunities had started to open up. A quiet life in Picardy didn't have the same allure anymore as she'd had a taste of fame. She liked the flashing cameras and people calling her name. If she went across the Atlantic with him, she would fade into obscurity in her own right, and only be known for being Raphael Baptiste's lover.

Did she want that? To be defined by a man?

She closed her eyes.

It was too late. His offer had come too late.

Disentangling herself from his strong embrace, she walked over to the window. Her long hair trailed down her back and her white skin was luminous in the dusky light.

"You are so beautiful," he murmured. "I look at you and I see a goddess, do you know that? A wild Celtic goddess."

"You do?" she said distractedly.

"Yes, I do ... Now come back here. I want you again."

"Raphael?"

"*Hmmm?*"

"I can't go to France with you." She turned to face him. "My life is here. I can't give up my career and future for you."

He sat up and ran his fingers through his hair. "But you would be my muse! The whole world would know your name. Things are beginning for me again and you could be part of it."

"For *you*! It's always about you!" She started to pace. "From the beginning, it has been on your terms. How can you expect me to give up my life to live with you in the middle of nowhere? Don't you see? I'm going to be famous. Allegra's commercial is going to make me a celebrity. I'm on the cusp of everything I've ever wanted."

"I thought you wanted me," he said quietly.

She rushed over to him and wrapped her arms around his neck. "But I do, I swear that I do. It's just I can't move to France with you. We have to compromise."

"I don't compromise."

"Raphael!"

"*Non!*" He pushed her away. "You have to make a

270

choice. Long-distance relationships never work. We either stay together or we finish it." His eyes challenged her.

He looked so handsome on the bed, with his smooth torso and muscular arms. He truly was gorgeous and she loved him. Yet he was selfish and was asking too much.

She picked up her discarded peacock dress. "I'll leave you to it." Her green eyes burned.

He stared at her defiantly. "Goodbye then."

She put on her underwear. Then she yanked the dress over her head and zipped it up. Bending down, she put on her shoes.

Then, taking her clutch bag and shawl, she fought the tears welling up in her eyes as she turned to go.

Walk away, Isabelle. Just walk away.

"Goodbye." She slammed the door.

The apartment was quiet when Isabelle got back. Gabriella's door was closed and her black shoes were near the sofa. Glancing at the clock on the wall, she could see that it was close to four o'clock in the morning.

Miserably, she entered her room and kicked off her shoes. She was exhausted from the emotional merry-go-round that was her relationship with Raphael. Ecstatic one minute, devastated the next. He had given her an ultimatum and she had made her choice.

Why then did she doubt herself? Maybe she should leave with him and try and make it work. Was fame too high a price to pay for a broken heart? Would seeing her face on the front of magazines make up for not waking up in his arms?

She started to sob, her shoulders hunched. She needed to sleep. Maybe things would seem brighter in the morning. Her mother always said that.

Hanging her dress on a spare hanger, she picked up her nightie.

She would call him in the morning. He might change his mind. He was impulsive and might see things differently after some time to think. He had to see things from her point of view. He just had to.

As Isabelle woke up the smell of toasted bread filled her nostrils and she felt her stomach rumble. With all the drama from the night before, all she had eaten was a tiny bit of lobster and half a pumpernickel roll.

There was a text from Raphael on her phone. She read it eagerly and her heart froze.

Grabbing her robe, she padded out to the kitchen to find Gabriella making toast and Hugo drinking coffee. He waved and smiled.

"Morning!" she said as cheerfully as she could.

"Zsa Zsa!" Gabriella looked surprised. "I didn't expect to see you back for a few days." She began to butter the toast.

"Yeah, well, things didn't quite work out."

Hugo looked at Gabriella in alarm. Isabelle's lower lip was quivering and he could see that she was about to burst into tears.

"Hey, you guys, I'll make a move." He stood up.

"Sure, I'll call you." Gabriella handed him his jacket.

Isabelle didn't notice him leave.

Gabriella pushed the plate of toast towards her friend. "You might as well eat it."

Isabelle picked up a slice and started to pick at the crust.

"So, what happened?" asked Gabriella.

Isabelle sighed. "He asked me to go back to France with him."

"He what?"

"I said no."

"You did?" Gabriella looked surprised.

"Sure I did. Why would I go to a foreign country now? Paolo has three auditions lined up already."

"What did Raphael say?"

"He told me that he doesn't compromise. He told me to make a choice."

"Oh, Zsa Zsa!" Gabriella walked over and hugged her friend. "I'm so sorry."

"I love him, Gabby. I love him so much." She started to cry.

Gabriella held her close and rubbed her back. She hated to see her so broken.

"Maybe he'll call you later and say it was a huge mistake?"

Isabelle shook her head sadly. "He texted me this morning asking for my address. He wants to send my things over before he leaves." She rubbed her nose. "It was a cold, formal message, Gabby. He's done with me."

"Maybe it's for the best."

"That's not what I want to hear right now."

"Yes, but you have to focus on you from now on. This is your moment! You have to keep your head."

Isabelle sniffed. "I guess."

"Remember all those conversations we had over a bottle of chardonnay? Our dreams of making it? You are so close, don't let someone like Raphael mess it up for you."

"You're right. I've got to let him go."

Hugo arrived home to find his mother in the kitchen, sitting on a high stool by the breakfast bar.

"I've been waiting for you," she said coldly.

"Me? Why?"

"Oh, Veronica Ashley Hamilton called. She wanted to know why you were all over social media with Magda's daughter."

Hugo rolled his eyes. "What business is it of hers?"

Victoria pursed her lips. "I guess I want to know too. What the hell is going on? Why did you lie to me?"

"Lie? When?"

"You said you were at the movies. Now I realise that you were at the sailing club with that girl."

Hugo looked uncomfortable.

"Are you seeing this girl? Hugo? Are you dating the maid?"

"Yes," he said angrily. "Yes, I am. Her name is Gabriella and she's not a maid – though that is beside the point. She's talented, beautiful and kind. I'm happy."

"Land's sakes, Hugo, you're leaving next week. Plus she's not in your league. What in the world do you have in common? This is not suitable."

"We have lots in common. We like the theatre and riding the Staten Island ferry at night …"

"Have you lost your mind? You're my only son. You're Hugo du Maurier! You can't marry a maid!"

"Oh, leave it, Momma. You're a goddamn snob."

She sprang over towards him and grabbed his shirt. "Damn straight I'm a snob! I didn't raise you to throw your life away on a nobody. It will end in tears and you'll be disgraced. When I think of all the lovely girls I lined up for you!"

"I don't like those girls. They're one-dimensional and boring. Gabby is interesting and bright and I enjoy her company. Now that I've an interview with Christian, I'll get to stay in New York …"

"A what?" His mother let him go and clutched the counter. "You have a what?"

"An interview at Christian's law firm. Charlotte set it up ..."

"Are my children conspiring against me? Is that it?"

"No, Momma."

"How dare you go behind my back!"

"I didn't want to say anything until it was in the bag."

"Hugo! Daddy went to a lot of trouble to get you that Boston position."

"I don't want to go to Boston. I want to stay here and be with Gabby."

Victoria had to sit down. She smoothed a lock of hair off her forehead and started to breathe deeply. "What if you don't get the job?"

"I will."

"But what if you don't?"

"I'll try Daddy's office. I know he doesn't like working with family, but I'll make him change his mind."

"And this Gabriella. When were you going to tell me?"

"I'm taking her to Charlotte's wedding as my plus-one. I guess I was going to tell you then."

"To the wedding?" she whispered, feeling faint. "You're taking her to the biggest society event of the year?"

"Yep." He faced her head on, his blue eyes steely. "And there's nothing you can do about it."

"You can't! She'll be out of place. What will Marcheline Jacob say?"

"I don't care."

"She'll probably wear something provocative again. She looked like a tart that last night, all busty and tight. No wonder Maurice slipped up."

Hugo, who was walking out of the kitchen door, stopped dead. "What do you mean, slipped up?"

"Smacking her sizable derrière. I saw what happened

and I don't blame him. She was putting it out there, there's no denying it." Victoria looked scornful. "She broke my good china plate. It was worth a week's wages to her kind and not one offer to pay for it."

Hugo bounded across the room and banged his fist on the table. "Maurice should be in jail for what he did."

"Oh, grow up. It happens every day."

"No, Momma. You didn't see what happened afterwards. He assaulted her in the garden."

"*What?*" Victoria narrowed her eyes.

"He assaulted her and I saved her. He's out of control."

"Maurice? I don't believe it."

"I saw it with my own eyes. He's lucky I didn't kill him." Hugo looked fierce. "She's not pressing charges, if that's what you're worried about. She didn't want to make a scene."

"Thank the Lord for that small mercy."

"I tried to convince her otherwise."

"Why?" Victoria looked shocked. "Why would you bring shame on the family?"

"Because he's a creep and deserves to be punished."

"Oh, wake up, Hugo! This is the real world. Girls like her ask for it. Maurice drinks too much is all. He probably didn't realise what he was doing."

"Momma! Are you for real?"

"I'm very real. Now, this isn't over, sugar. You best believe that. We'll talk again."

"Oh, back off." Hugo strode away. "You can't do anything about it. I'm staying in New York with Gabby and that's final."

❧ Chapter Twenty-Two ❧

The next day, Victoria dialled Tara Jacob's number.

"Tara! How are you?"

"Oh, hello, Victoria. I'm well. How can I help you?"

"Luca and Charlotte got to Ireland okay?"

"Yes, he texted me earlier. He's nervous about his speech, even though he won't admit it. I'm sorry I didn't make it over now. Craig, the groom, is my cousin, you know. It would have been nice to catch up with the Irish side."

"Tara," Victoria cut her off, "are you available for lunch on Saturday?"

Tara paused. "Well, Gabriella is manning the gallery as Luca is away so I guess I could slip away for an hour. Where are you thinking?"

"I don't know. Maybe some sushi? I'll text you."

"Sure, that sounds good. Say around two?"

"Perfect."

"Is everything okay?"

"Why sure. I just wanted to touch base about our own wedding. Not long now."

Tara laughed. "Not long at all. Just a few weeks, right? God, time has flown."

"I'll be in touch with reservation details. Bye, Tara."

"Bye."

Hugo rang the doorbell of Gabriella's apartment later that evening. He needed to see her and hold her. His conversation with his momma the day before had troubled him. Celine had been right – she nearly had a fit. His interview was scheduled for next Tuesday. Charlotte was due back on Monday so he planned to call her and ask for tips. After all, she had been the interviewee a couple of years back, with a stern Christian Jacob asking questions.

He just had to succeed. Working at his own father's firm wasn't an option. He had to break away and be independent.

The door opened and a sleepy Gabriella stood before him in her pyjamas.

"Hey, you," she said with a yawn. "I was just napping."

"Still tired from the party?"

She nodded. "I'm not used to all that champagne."

He followed her into the sitting room. "Where's Isabelle?" he asked.

"Oh, gone for a run. She's pretty miserable. Raphael sent all her things over by courier without even as much as a note. God, I'd punch him if I saw him."

Hugo said nothing. Instead he pulled her into his arms and held her close. He started to kiss her neck and then her cheeks, like a feather, before taking possession of her mouth. Crushing her to him, he deepened his kiss, pressing against her.

"Oh, Gabby, I can't wait much longer," he moaned. "I want to be with you. It's too tough to be good."

She wrapped her arms around his neck. "Me too," she said, kissing his stubble. "I think I'm ready."

He pulled back in surprise. "You are?"

She nodded, a smile on her lips. "I feel like I'm on fire when you touch me. I want to give myself to you, in every way. Does that sound lame?"

He grinned. "A little."

"I mean, Lita wants me to be married before I, you know, but I can't wait."

"At this stage, I'd almost marry you to hurry things along. Want to fly to Vegas?"

"There's no need." She took his hand and put it under her top. She encouraged him to cup her bare breast and he groaned. He stroked her nipple gently with his forefinger and then his hand moved lower down to her belly. Pulling the elasticated band of her oversized pyjama bottoms, he teased the lace of her panties. "Can I touch you there?" he asked, his eyes cloudy with desire.

She nodded, her brown eyes huge. "Hurry," she said, arching towards him. "I feel like I'm going to melt inside."

"We should go to your room," he suggested.

She nodded.

"Are you sure?" He kissed her bruised lips again.

"I've never wanted anything more. You will be my first and I couldn't think of anyone better."

He took her hand and they were about to head to her bedroom when the door burst open and a sweaty Isabelle appeared. She was dressed in bright-pink running gear which clashed gloriously with her red hair.

"Gabs!" she said, yanking the earphones out of her ears. "I need to talk to you."

"What's up?"

"I've made a huge mistake." She headed into the kitchen.

"I'll be right there," said Gabriella to Hugo. She pushed him into her room and closed the door.

Isabelle was doing lunges in the kitchen, oblivious that she had interrupted anything. "You see, I have to see him. Raphael, I mean. He put his heart on the line and I rejected him. He's obviously hurting and I'm sure if I call over now he will be more amenable."

"Really?" Gabriella wasn't convinced.

"Of course. He's a big kid. He didn't get his way, so he ended it all. He wasn't in the headspace to compromise. I'm sure, after reflection, we could work something out. The world is a small place now, Gabs. We could make it work."

"Is he still here?"

She nodded. "He flies out tomorrow. Bertie gave me all the details when I rang him earlier."

"Has Bertie gone back to Vienna?"

"Yeah. He and Mia flew out yesterday. He was so positive. He definitely thinks I should try and make things work."

"So? What's the plan?"

"I'm going to take a shower and dress up and head straight over there." She did one final stretch. "It's now or never. Once he flies back to France, I've lost him."

"Just be careful," said Gabriella. "He may not have calmed down."

"I'll convince him," she insisted. "You should see the way he looks at me sometimes, Gabs. He's in love, he just doesn't realise that he can't live without me."

Hugo was flicking through a *Marie Claire* magazine when Gabriella finally got away from Isabelle.

"Sorry!" she said, lying on the bed beside him.

"Hey, you didn't know that she'd need counselling."

The bathroom door banged and next thing all they could hear was a discordant version of 'Rolling in the Deep'.

"*Ouch*," said Hugo as Isabelle screeched out the chorus. "That noise is not conducive to lovemaking."

Gabriella sighed. "I guess."

He pulled her close. "How about we make plans for Saturday? I could book us into a nice hotel somewhere."

"Really?"

"Sure. Somewhere with great room service. Then we won't be disturbed."

She felt the adrenaline run through her veins. "I have to work at the gallery until six. Luca's not around."

"I'll pick you up."

She stared at him. "Okay."

"Gabby?"

"Yes?"

"I love you."

She felt her heart soar. "I love you too."

Isabelle took a cab to the Langham. In a violet fitted dress and black high heels, she had wound her hair up into a chignon. Large black sunglasses covered her eyes and red lipstick painted her lips. Why couldn't she have her cake and eat it? She shouldn't have to give up her life in order to be with the man she loved. Feeling confident, she smiled at the concierge as she walked by. He was accustomed to seeing her walk in and out.

She took the elevator to the twentieth floor and walked out onto the corridor. Pausing outside his door, she took a deep breath. She really had no idea if he was in or not. This was all on a whim and she was banking on fate to be kind. She knocked on the door with three short raps. Straining her ears, she listened for some movement behind the large door. There was nothing.

Lifting her arm, she was about to knock again, when

the door opened and a blonde woman appeared. She was about thirty, dressed in a jumpsuit and Christian Louboutin kitten heels.

"*Oui?*" she said.

Isabelle gasped. 'You're Sylvie Marot!" She felt the world spin.

The other woman smiled. "Can I help you?"

Isabelle pulled herself together. "I'm looking for Raphael."

Sylvie raised a perfectly manicured eyebrow. "Oh? Well, he's in the shower. Can I be of assistance?"

Isabelle shook her head. "No, I need to speak with him."

"Well, we're late for a dinner reservation …" Sylvie looked pointedly at her watch. "Can it wait?"

Isabelle stared at the other woman. Late for a dinner reservation? In the shower? What the hell was happening? It had only been a couple of days.

She felt her eyes fill with tears.

Sylvie put her head to one side. "I recognise you. You're the girl on the red carpet."

Isabelle nodded.

"You got to know Raphael quite well," she said matter-of-factly.

"He asked me to go to France with him …"

"I'm sure that he did." Sylvie looked at her pityingly. "You see, Raph would do anything to fill the void that I left. I'm sorry that you got caught up in this. Will I tell him that you called over?"

Isabelle shook her head furiously, wiping away her tears. "Don't say anything. Please."

He must never know.

"As you wish." The door closed.

Isabelle walked down 5th Avenue in a daze. Never in her

wildest dreams did she expect to meet his ex-girlfriend. It made no sense. Why would she turn up after all this time?

She felt winded with misery. Bertie had told her about Sylvie Marot – how she was the one woman to break Raphael's heart. How he still held a torch for her, even after all these years. She had never considered her a threat as she thought she was out of his life. Yet now she was spectacularly back and he had obviously fallen straight into her arms.

The conversations she had imagined having with him seemed silly and pointless now. She was going to pass on the job in L.A. and base herself in New York. That made the journey to Paris more manageable and she was going to suggest that they share the burden by flying over to see one another once a fortnight.

None of that mattered now.

Picking up her phone, she dialled Paolo's number.

"Isabelle?" he said immediately. "Have you got an answer for me?"

"Book me on the next flight to California," she said. "Accept every audition you get, Paolo. I want to be busy."

"You got it, honey."

The phone went dead.

Isabelle stopped in the middle of the moving crowd. Some elbowed past her and others scowled as she obstructed their path through the *mêlée*. Staring up at the Empire State Building, she made a vow. She would never let a man affect her like this again. From now on, she was going to focus on her career. She would be the greatest model that ever lived.

◖◗ Chapter Twenty-Three ◖◗

Gabriella sat in the back room of the gallery, eating her lunch. She had taken her break earlier than normal, as Tara had a lunch date with Victoria du Maurier and she needed Gabriella to cover the front desk.

Gabriella's heart had jumped at the mention of Victoria's name. She knew it was inevitable that she would have to meet her eventually as Hugo's girlfriend. Especially if he got the job at Christian's firm. To say that she wasn't looking forward to it was an understatement.

Her own mother, although shocked, had eventually come around to the idea of Hugo. She wasn't thrilled but she respected Gabriella enough to trust her judgement. To prove this, she had suggested inviting Hugo over for some of Lita's pork stew. He was a nice polite boy and she hadn't seen her little Gabby this happy in years.

Gabriella had warned her mother not to say anything at work. "We'll tell them soon, Mama, but not yet."

Magda understood, as she could see the troubles they would face.

Chewing on her cheese sandwich, Gabriella scrolled through Instagram looking at the different photos that people had posted. There was one of Sophia eating an ice cream, posted by Teresa, and a lovely black-and-white photo of the New York skyline added by Hugo. He had included #staten and #love. She felt her stomach flip over. It was a message for her – it had to be. All she could think about was six o clock that evening. He was picking her up and they were going to a hotel. He had booked somewhere but had kept its whereabouts a surprise. She hugged herself in delight. She had packed a bag with silky lingerie and a bottle of Prosecco. It would make it all even more special. Taking their relationship to the next level was exciting and scary and wonderful all at once. She prayed to God that Hugo would be successful in the interview with Luca's dad. Then they could stay together.

She kept scrolling and saw photos added by Luca. It was of the bride and groom at the wedding in Ireland. His cousin looked great in a grey suit and the bride had a full-length gown and a stunning veil. #goodtimes followed. From his posts on social media, it looked like he was having a great time. There was a great shot of him drinking Guinness in a bar and a beautiful one of Charlotte in a blue dress.

Tara popped her head around the door. "Are you almost done?" she asked. "I have to run. She booked a table at Masa, that sushi place at Columbus Circle. Anyway, I have to take a cab – I'm pressed for time."

"Sure, sure. I'm ready." Gabriella crumpled up her sandwich wrapper and threw it in the bin.

"If the MoMA call, tell them the end of the month is fine and maybe sort out those emails from the London realtor." Tara grabbed her bag.

"No problem. Enjoy your lunch!"

"See you later."

Gabriella opened the emails from the estate agent

dealing with the Canary Wharf property. Frowning, she made a list of what they needed. She would have to go through some bank statements and files in the back office. The price was still too high – they were looking for almost two million – and Tara was insistent that they bring it down. Luca was better at this kind of thing, but he wasn't due back at the gallery until Tuesday and the sale was not yet agreed.

She didn't notice her come in.

"Gabriella." Her southern drawl was instantly recognisable.

Gabriella's head shot up. "Vic– I mean, Mrs. du Maurier."

"Victoria, please."

"Can I help you? I mean, Tara left fifteen minutes ago. She took a cab as she thought she was meeting you there."

"It's you I'm here to see."

The colour drained from Gabriella's face. "Me?"

"Yes." Victoria smiled but her eyes were cold. "I understand that you are dating my son."

Gabriella nodded dumbly.

"How long has this been going on?"

"Um, a few weeks, a month maybe? I'm not sure ..."

"He seems smitten with you."

Gabriella shrugged helplessly. "I guess."

Victoria picked up a brochure with her manicured hand. Her large diamond engagement ring glittered in the sun streaming through the bay window of the gallery.

"Your momma is a great lady," said Victoria, flicking through Tara's latest collection. "She has such a work ethic. I swear that the house would fall apart without her."

"Without her?"

"Why sure. She has been in my service for about twenty years, give or take. It'd be a damn shame to end it all."

"I'm sorry?" Gabriella's heart started to pound.

"She supports y'all financially, am I right?" asked Victoria. "Wouldn't it be terrible if she lost her job? I mean, she wouldn't be able to pay for her apartment or for food. Your grandma is too old to work, I understand."

"How? I mean, she has rights. You can't just get rid of her like that."

"Oh, there are ways and means, sugar," said Victoria softly. "Some jewellery might go missing or some of the silver. Then I'd have to get the police involved and get legal advice ..."

"What?" Gabriella's hand flew to her mouth. "You wouldn't."

"I sure as hell would." Victoria's face hardened.

"Please, please don't fire my mama!" Gabriella pulled at the sleeve of Victoria's dress. "Please."

Victoria stood back and brushed her sleeve where Gabriella had touched it.

"There's also the matter of Maurice."

Gabriella froze. "Who told you about that?"

"Why, Hugo did of course. We're so close, he tells me everything."

"He promised ..."

"Oh, darlin'. The first thing you've gotta learn about men is that they never keep promises."

"Don't worry, Mrs. du Maurier. I'll never say anything." She crossed her chest.

"Well, I can't take that chance." Victoria took out her chequebook. "It's simple. I want you to break it off with my son. There is no future for you two. I also want your guarantee that you'll never mention that incident with Maurice." She wrote rapidly with a gold pen. "Here's some money to sweeten the deal."

"What?" Gabriella went pale.

"You heard me. Now, will ten thousand do it?"

"I don't want your money."

"Oh, grow up. You'll never see a sum like this again. Take it and enjoy it."

Gabriella's face was ashen. "No."

"No? You're sure?"

"I'd rather die."

Victoria shrugged. "Fine. It's your choice. I'm not going to offer it again." She put the cheque book away and clicked her pen.

Gabriella felt a thundering in her ears. She couldn't believe that in a matter of minutes, everything had changed. She stared at the older woman.

"How can you do this?" she whispered, holding the desk for support.

"I can do it because you do not fit in our world," answered Victoria simply. "You would be out of place and would suffer for it. I'm doing you a favour, honey pie. You don't see it now, but you will."

"What if I refuse?"

"You won't." Victoria snapped her purse shut. "You don't want your momma to lose everything, now do you?"

Gabriella wanted to scream. She wanted to hit Victoria's smug face. She knew that she had no choice. That Magda couldn't survive without her job.

"Fine. I'll sort it."

"Good. I knew that you'd see sense." Victoria smiled frostily. "Now, not a word to Hugo about my involvement, do you hear?"

"How will I convince him?"

"You'll come up with something." She walked away.

"Goodbye, Gabriella."

Hugo arrived at the gallery at five to six, a huge grin on his face.

"Are you ready?" he asked mischievously.

Gabriella had her back to him. She had managed to control her tears for hours. Even when Tara had arrived back, grumbling that Victoria had rolled up an hour late, she had acted normally. It was like she was in a trance. Her muddled brain was desperately trying to process what had happened. Now, Hugo was here and she had to make an excuse. She couldn't make love to him now. Not when there was no future for them.

"I'll be right there," she said in a muffled voice.

She took her bag from the back room and waved to Tara in the office. Hugo held out his hand but she didn't take it. Instead she walked out into the evening sun and wrapped her arms around her abdomen protectively.

"Gabby! What's up?" he said, noticing her sombre mood.

"I can't go with you tonight."

"What?"

"I can't, Hugo."

"What? Why not?"

Gabriella didn't answer.

"Talk to me, Gabby!"

She closed her eyes and willed herself to sound convincing. "I'm not ready. I thought I was, but I'm not."

He ran his fingers through his dark hair. "You texted me earlier saying that you couldn't wait. You sent me heart emojis and said that you had some fancy underwear."

"I know, I know." She turned her face away. "It's just I remembered what happened with Maurice and I got freaked out ..."

He took her hand. "You've got to forget about that," he said gently. "We can never move on unless you try and forget."

"I can't." Her eyes filled with tears. "I'm sorry."

"You can't?" He looked weary. "Jesus, Gabby, you are blowing hot and cold. I don't know what to say."

"I'm going home, okay?" She backed away. "I'm sorry, Hugo."

"But I booked us a room. It's all paid for …"

"I'll pay you back."

"It's not about the money," he said angrily.

"I've got to go." She backed away and turned. Walking purposefully, she headed for 7th Avenue.

"*Gabby! Gabriella!*"

She kept walking.

Isabelle zipped up her suitcase and sighed. It was two days later and she was getting ready to go to the airport. Gabriella was lying on her bed, still dressed in her pyjamas. She hadn't ventured outside the apartment since that conversation with Hugo. She couldn't face it. She had called in sick to Brasserie Michel, claiming to have a stomach bug. Giselle had been so nice and understanding that she'd felt guilty for lying. However, she couldn't imagine dealing with diners in her present mood.

"It's going to be so hot in L.A," said Isabelle.

"How long will you be gone?"

"Three weeks, maybe more. Paolo has a few things lined up." She checked her handbag for her passport. "I don't care how long I'll be away. New York has too many memories for me now."

"I know what you mean."

Gabriella looked glum. She couldn't avoid Hugo forever.

290

There were fourteen missed calls on her cell and about twenty messages. She had deflected him by telling him the same lie she had told Giselle. She had a contagious stomach bug and had to be isolated. She knew it sounded lame and that it was only a matter of time before he would be standing on her doorstep, demanding an explanation. How then would she explain things without implicating Victoria? He would be furious and confront her. Then her own innocent darling mama would be fired and she couldn't let that happen.

"What the hell am I going to do?" she asked Isabelle, who had just called a cab.

"I don't know," she answered honestly.

"Please, Zsa Zsa. I have to get away from here."

"If it were me, I'd tell Hugo the truth."

"No! Mama would be fired."

"She has rights, Gabby. Employee rights. Victoria just can't fire her for no reason."

"Oh, she'd find a reason or invent one." Gabriella put her head in her hands. "She's truly evil."

"Then, I don't know."

Gabriella played with a loose thread on the blanket. "Maybe I could ask Oberon if he'll take me on. He's still in New York. Sure, he's mean but he seems to be like that to everyone."

"No!" Isabelle shook her head. "Are we back to this again? Oberon is bad news."

"So? I have nothing to lose."

Isabelle thought of Oberon's cruel comments at the première. She had to protect her friend from him.

"Come to L.A. with me instead," she offered. "Forget about him."

"No, I don't have any money."

"I can lend you some."

"No, thanks."

The intercom buzzed.

"I'll get it," said Isabelle, walking towards it. "Hello?"

"Taxi for Isabelle Flynn."

"I'll be right there." She turned around. "That's my cab, Gabs. I've got to go or I'll miss my flight."

"Just go. Don't worry about me."

They embraced briefly.

"Call me when you land."

"Will you be okay?"

"Of course."

Isabelle put on her Dior shades. "Stay away from Oberon, do you hear? He won't help you."

Gabriella didn't agree. Oberon was her ticket. If she had a fresh start, then she could try and forget about Hugo. She couldn't stay in New York anymore. Not now.

Grabbing her phone, she googled Oberon and saw that his show was due to be held at Lincoln Center, the favoured spot for New York Fashion Week. He would surely be there organising it all. She checked the dates. The show was in two days. That gave her time.

She marched into the bathroom and switched on the shower. Determination flooded her veins. She would lay her cards on the table and force him to listen. It was her only chance. She had to leave New York. Leave America. She had to protect her mama. If she got a good job, she could pay Victoria back the debt and help her family. There were no more 'what ifs'. The time was now.

The Lincoln Center for the Performing Arts was a cluster of buildings in Manhattan. It boasted the Metropolitan Opera House, the David Geffen Hall and the David H.

Koch Theatre to name but a few, all centred around a plaza with a fountain in the centre. Oberon's show was to be held in the Claire Tow Theatre, a small venue that held about one hundred and thirty people. It was the newest addition to the complex, built on the roof of the Vivian Beaumont Theatre. It had an auditorium and some offices, and a lobby that led out onto a terrace on the roof.

Gabriella took the subway and walked purposefully towards the entrance of the theatre. She hadn't brought her portfolio as she knew it didn't matter. Everything rested on this one conversation.

She walked up to a security guard at the door.

"I'm looking for Oberon," she said authoritatively.

"And you are?" He gave her an unfriendly look.

"Gabriella."

"Right, Gabriella." He snorted. "Are you like Madonna or Cher or something? Don't you have a second name?"

"Gabriella Ruiz Álvarez." She glared at him.

"What do you want with Mr. Oberon?" His shiny face sneered at her. "You don't look like a model, no offence."

She raised her chin. "I'm a designer. I need to talk with him about the show."

"Get outta here, lady. I don't have time for this." He waved her away.

Desperately, she looked around. There were sound engineers and models, carpenters and electricians. She searched the faces for someone she recognised.

Suddenly, she saw a small Japanese man inside the building. "*Riku!*" she yelled. "*Riku!*"

He turned around quizzically.

"*It's me! Gabriella!*"

He approached the door, squinting. "Who?"

"Gabriella. The girl who made the dress for Allegra."

He narrowed his eyes. "Oh, right. The commercial. What do you want?"

"I need to see Oberon."

"Why?" He looked suspicious.

"It's my last chance to convince him to mentor me. Please get me in."

He paused for what seemed like an eternity.

"Cody?" he said to the security guard. "Let her through."

"What?"

"Let her through."

Begrudgingly, Cody stood to the side and let her through.

"You've got five minutes," said Riku, leading her down a corridor. "He'll kill me for disturbing him."

"Why are you helping me?"

Riku stopped. "Everyone deserves a shot. Oberon himself was given a chance and you should too. He may not listen, but at least you can try."

Gabriella smiled gratefully. "Thank you."

"You did a good job of replicating that dress too. I think you have talent."

He knocked on an office door and a surly voice yelled, "*What now?*"

Riku opened the door. "Oberon, there's someone here to see you."

"*Who?*" he barked.

Riku ushered her through.

"Good luck," he said, bowing his head.

Oberon was sitting at a desk covered with drawings. He stared at her contemptuously.

"To what do I owe the honour?"

Gabriella faced him. "I want you to take me to London."

"Oh, you do." He laughed and sat back. "Why the hell would I do that?"

"Take me on. Show me the ropes. I need your help."

"You have a screw loose, my girl. I'm not taking anyone on. I don't need a fledgling two-bit wannabe designer following me around. Now, get out."

She stood her ground. "Please. I need to leave New York."

"Why?"

"For personal reasons."

"Oh, please. Did you break up with your little boyfriend?"

She nodded. "Something like that." Turning away, she took a deep breath. "You see, Hugo and I, well, we're in love."

"My heart bleeds."

"But he's from a rich family. His mother wants someone better for him." She hung her head. "I'm from the Bronx. She sees that as unsuitable. I'm a poor immigrant nobody and that isn't good enough for her son."

Oberon said nothing.

"My mama, she works for his mother at the big house. She's been the maid there for twenty years. Can you imagine, the son and heir dating the maid's daughter? So his mother, she threatened me."

"Threatened you?"

She gazed at the green terrace outside. "She told me that she would fire my mama if I didn't end our relationship. My poor innocent mama who has done nothing wrong."

"So, tell your little boyfriend the truth."

"I can't. Victoria, his mother, warned me that if I said anything about her involvement, she'll fire Mama anyway." She took a shuddering breath. "I can't win. I have to convince him that I've lost interest and disappear. So you see that I need to leave. I need to leave New York."

"Stand up to that cow," he drawled. "Call her bluff. She's probably lying."

"I can't!" she said, whirling around. "*You* don't understand what it's like to live on the breadline. *You* don't get it." She clenched her knuckles. "Without my mother's income, my family would be on the streets. She's the main earner, you see. My papa died when I was a baby." She turned away once more and stared out of the window. "I've got to protect my mother," she said quietly. "She's everything to me."

Oberon stared at her hunched back. In a flash he was transported back to his mother's flat in Brixton. The damp peeling walls, the heroin addicts on the corridor. His father had left when he was two years old, leaving them destitute. His mother was discriminated against because of the dark colour of her skin and found it hard to find work. Left with little choice, she cleaned offices late at night, forced to leave her son alone in the dingy flat. He would cry himself to sleep, frightened when he heard sirens and screams from outside. There was many a night he soiled himself, too small to reach the toilet in time. Then he would lie wet and cold in his bed until his exhausted mother returned. Most days, he ate Rice Krispies for dinner and vomited as the milk was sour. He remembered his mother's tears when she couldn't afford to send him on school trips. The disappointment he felt when Santa couldn't find his address or when the bike he had been hoping for didn't arrive on his birthday. He worked every hour God sent in the early days, determined to be the best. Then he could protect his mother. Then he could give her the life she deserved.

His face hardened.

She died just before his big break. A month before the

famous Oscar ceremony that catapulted him onto the world stage, she succumbed to breast cancer. No amount of money or fame could bring her back. He would have died to save her – he remembered that.

"So, you want to be my protégée? Is that it?"

Gabriella wiped away her tears with her sleeve. "What?" she whispered.

Oberon sighed. "Please tell me I won't have to repeat everything."

"No, no. I heard you." She nodded. "Yes, yes, I'd love to work with you."

"Then you've got to stop ripping people off. Your designs have to be original. Channel your hopes, your dreams, your desires." He got to his feet. "I can't promise you anything. You'll have to work doubly hard as everyone else and show me that you're serious. We leave in a few days. I'll get Riku to send you the details."

"I can't afford the flight ..." She blushed.

"I'll pay for it, but you'll work it off. I'm not a charity."

"Of course."

"I'll sort out a working visa from the embassy. That might take some time." He waved her away. "Now, piss off. I have a show to plan."

"Thank you, thank you!'

"Yeah, yeah." He turned away.

Gabriella closed the door of the office, a huge smile on her face.

Riku raised an eyebrow. "Well?"

"I'm in!"

❧ Chapter Twenty-Four ❧

Hugo was standing outside her apartment when she got back. He had his hands in his pockets and was dressed formally in a navy suit.

"Hugo!"

"I've been waiting for you. Why didn't you answer my calls?"

"I haven't checked my phone in a while …" She took her key out of her bag. "Do you want to come up?"

"What do you think?"

She opened the door and her heart started to thump. He would want answers. Victoria's face filled her head.

"Juice? Tea?" She filled the kettle with water.

"I'm good."

"Sit down."

He stayed standing. "So, I had my interview today. That's why I was calling and calling."

She cursed silently. She had forgotten about that.

"And?"

"He'll let me know at the end of the week." He shrugged. "I think it went well. It definitely helps having Charlotte in the firm. They seem to love her."

"Really?" She popped a teabag into a mug.

"Yeah, Christian spent most of the interview talking about her and how great she is."

"Cool."

Her stomach started to churn. She would have to tell him.

"I have news," she said in a strangled voice.

"Oh?"

She faced him. "It's Oberon. He called me and asked me to go to London with him."

"Sorry, say again?" Hugo looked shocked. "Oberon? I thought you hated him?"

"He called and said that he's going to give me a chance. He's flying out early next week and he wants me to go with him. I'm going to be his protégée."

Hugo stared at her. "Are you joking?"

She shook her head.

"You're leaving?" He walked towards her and grabbed her shoulders. "What do you mean?"

"Please don't be mad ..."

"Gabby, this is unbelievable. I do everything I can to get a job in New York so we can be together. I do everything in my power not to go to Boston and then you throw it back in my face."

"I'm sorry." She couldn't look at him.

"You're sorry? *You're sorry?*" He released her and stood back.

"I am. It's just this is a once-in-a-lifetime opportunity and I can't let it go. If I don't go to London now, I'll regret it forever."

"I can't believe it ..."

"I'm sorry."

"Quit saying that."

"Hugo, I ..." Her eyes shone with tears and she ached to touch him.

"Yes?" His blue eyes were cold.

"I'm so sorry. I'm just so sorry. A long-distance relationship would never work. It wouldn't be fair. We need to end it now."

"End it? What do you mean?"

"It's over, Hugo. You and me? It's over."

"What? Why?"

"It won't work. Not now."

"I thought you loved me."

"I'm sorry."

"Fuck you, Gabby. I can't believe I fell for it. You treated that Noah guy like dirt and now you're doing it to me." He backed away. "I wish you the best in London. I hope you get what you always wanted: a life filled with money and fame."

"Hugo, please!" She reached out and touched his arm, but he flinched.

"But mark my words, you'll regret this. When you get what you want, or what you *think* you want, you'll find that it's all empty. That you gave up on the one thing that could make you happy."

He stalked off.

Gabriella stood motionless in the kitchen, her heart breaking in two.

Half an hour later, the intercom buzzed. Gabriella's heart leapt. Maybe he wanted to clear the air before she left. Maybe she could have one more stolen evening with him before she gave him up.

"Hello?"

"Gabs? It's Luca. Can I come up?"

Disappointment flooded her being. Of course it wasn't Hugo.

300

"Come on up," she said, buzzing him through.

There was a knock on the door. She opened it and gasped.

A dishevelled, drunk Luca walked past her and flopped onto the couch.

"Thanks for letting me in."

"What's happened?" she asked in concern.

"Have you any whiskey?" he asked, ignoring her.

She shook her head.

"Any liquor at all?"

"No," she lied. He looked like he'd had more than enough. "What's going on? Where have you been?"

He put his head in his hands. "Oh Gabs, I've made a real mess."

"What? Why?"

He sighed. "I slept with someone else."

Gabriella sat down in shock. "Jesus, Luca," she said, her brown eyes wide.

"I know, right? A month before my wedding."

"Who? Where?"

He looked up, his face etched with misery. "Remember that girl I told you about? That Lydia girl from Ireland?"

She nodded.

"She told me that she loves me, Gabs. At the wedding. She said that she made a mistake when she left me that time."

"Oh, Luca." She bit her lip. "That's tough."

"I was drunk … she looked so good … when I touch her, I feel alive."

"Does Charlotte know?"

He shook his head miserably. "She was in bed at the time."

"So, she doesn't know anything, right? You can move on and pretend it never happened."

301

He shook his head. "I wish it were that simple. I can't stop thinking about her. Lydia, that is. I'm so confused right now."

"Luca!" She sat up straight. "You're engaged. You can't just jilt Charlotte at the altar. You have to get a grip."

"I'm in love with her ..."

"*With Lydia?*"

"I don't know." He banged his fist against the coffee table in frustration. "I was happy, you know? I was doing just fine and then she comes back into my life and messes with my head."

"Luca, you've got to think clearly about this. You're getting married. It's all arranged."

"Yes, but Charlotte doesn't make me feel the way Lydia does. No one in the world measures up, do you get that?"

Gabriella said nothing. She understood. Hugo's handsome face flashed through her mind. How she had hated hurting him. Would she ever feel the same way about anyone again?

"You need to sober up, okay? You need to think this through."

He shrugged. "There's nothing to think about. I know what I've got to do."

"Which is?"

"I've got to go back to Ireland and find out once and for all."

"Luca! You can't!"

"Watch me. I'll just say I'm going upstate for a couple of days."

"That's a terrible idea. Everyone will be so worried."

"You could cover for me." He gave her a small smile. "Please, Gabs. I need to see Lydia and talk this through. If she truly does want to be with me, then we can make it work. I have to know. Imagine if it was Hugo ..."

Her face tightened. "Don't mention him."

"Why?"

She bit her lip and steeled herself not to blurt out the whole sorry tale. Luca was too close to the du Mauriers. He would definitely blow her cover and tell Hugo. Then she would be back to square one and her mama would be fired. Oh, how she wished she had enough money to support her family. London was her only chance. Then, when she was rich, she would come back and put Victoria du Maurier in her place.

"It's over. We've split up." She faced Luca. "I'm going to London."

"London?"

"To train under Oberon." She tried to look excited, but she felt dead inside. "There's no future for me and Hugo now. Not anymore."

"I thought he was going to get a job at Papa's firm."

"Maybe he will, but I won't be here."

"I thought you two were in love." Luca looked genuinely shocked.

She closed her eyes. "Sometimes love isn't enough."

"Gabs! Are you sure you're doing the right thing? It's pretty sudden."

"Like you can talk." She raised an eyebrow. "I need to tell your mom. I'm not giving her much notice about the gallery."

"She'll understand." He reached out and took her hand. "Just make sure you're making the right decision, Gabs. London is very far away. Is this what you truly want?"

She closed her eyes. Being with Hugo was impossible.

303

Not until she was successful enough so people like Victoria du Maurier couldn't bully her. The end would justify the means.

"Yes. This is my destiny, Luca. It won't be easy, but it has to be done." She squeezed his hand. "Looks like we're both at a crossroads, huh?"

He squeezed her hand back. "Just make sure you take the right road, that's all. There's no going back."

Three days later, Gabriella zipped up her suitcase and sighed. Her bedroom looked empty. Diego had driven up especially the day before to help her move the boxes of her things and take them back to her old bedroom in the Bronx. She had instructed Isabelle to rent out her room as she had no plans to come back to New York for a long time.

Isabelle had been suitably shocked when she heard that Gabriella was off to London.

"He took you on?" she kept repeating in disbelief. "Did he have a personality transplant or what?"

They promised to meet at Fashion Week as Paolo, Isabelle's agent, had a show lined up for his newest star.

A taxi was booked to take her to the airport. Riku had organised it. Glancing at her watch, she could see that it was almost time to go.

For a moment, she felt winded. It had all happened so fast. One minute she was madly in love with Hugo du Maurier and the next she was heading off to London with Oberon. A battle of emotions raged within her – grief at the loss of her great love but also excitement at what the future might bring.

Suddenly there was a knock on the door of the apartment. It echoed down the hall to her bedroom and she jumped.

Odd, she thought, as she hadn't buzzed anyone in.

Gabriella went to the door and called, "*Yes?*"

No one answered.

Unlocking the door, she tentatively opened it and looked outside. The corridor was empty except for a bouquet of red roses on the ground.

She immediately thought of Hugo. It was exactly the type of romantic thing he would do.

She picked them up, her heart thumping in her chest. However, as soon as she picked it up, the heads of the flowers fell to the ground. Peering closer, she could see that they had been cut off. All that was left were the thorny stalks in her hand.

"Jesus!" she exclaimed, getting a fright.

Who would deliver damaged flowers? Each rose had been beheaded.

Gabriella gasped and retreated back into the apartment straight away. She placed the stalks on the table and sat down, her whole body shaking.

Who would send something like this? She put her head in her hands.

Maybe it was some kind of sick joke? Oh, how she wished that Isabelle were here!

Should she call her? She'd know what to do.

She'll tell you to call the cops, Gabby. Do you really want to deal with that now? You're leaving anyway.

She sat up and straightened her shoulders. This was just a stupid prank. Maybe the flowers were meant for someone else. There was no card and the corridor was shared by two other apartments. Yes, someone had knocked at the door, but that could have been a mistake, right?

Purposefully, she got a plastic bag from under the sink and put the stalks into it. Next, she put in the flowerheads in the corridor and sealed the bag.

Out of sight, out of mind.

She had no time for this now. She was too weary. The intercom buzzed.

"Hello?" she said guardedly.

"Taxi for Gabriella Ruiz Álvarez?"

"I'll be right there."

❧ Chapter Twenty-Five ❧

London
2017

Gabriella stirred in her sleep. Something was disturbing her slumber, an incessant alarm or a siren. On and on it went until she blearily opened one eye. The screen of her cell phone was flashing and its ringtone echoed in her ears.

Reaching out, she grabbed the offending phone and saw 'Boss Man' on the screen.

Oberon? Why was he calling at this early hour? Focusing in, she read the time. It was eleven thirty. She sat bolt upright.

Eleven thirty?

She knew now why he was calling. She was over three hours late.

The body in the bed next to her groaned slightly and turned over, refusing to be woken up. She reached out and stroked his back. "Sorry, baby, I'll try and be quiet."

He grunted in response and pulled a pillow over his head.

She answered the call and tried to sound like she had been up for hours. Yet, despite her efforts, her voice sounded husky, like someone who had just opened their eyes.

"Morning," she said with faux cheerfulness, despite the pounding in her head.

"Where the fuck are you?" came the bitchy clipped tone. "Do you think appointments like this fall out of the sky?"

"No, no," she said, desperately searching the ground for her clothes. She found her skirt thrown on the radiator and her black string top over by the door.

"Or wait," he continued. "You believe that a band of elves come in at night and perform magic tricks so that all the hard work is magically done?"

"I get it – I'm late. Jeez." She extracted her bra from under a pair of jeans and, balancing the phone under her ear, she clipped it into place.

"Gabriella, I don't object to your having a social life. In fact, after your hermit lifestyle in the beginning, I welcome it. However, one does not go out and get shitfaced before a day like today, do you understand me?"

"It's just there was a party and –"

"Save it," he cut her off. "Your life is of no interest to me. Now, be here in ten. No compromise." He hung up the phone.

Gabriella clutched her head. The spectacular mix of drinks the night before was creating a monstrous pain in her head. There was no way she would be there in ten minutes. Oberon's offices were at a large warehouse in Hackney Wick, right next to Regent's Canal. She would have to take a bus to Green Park, then a train and finally walk for about half a mile. All of that would take nearly an hour. She groaned inwardly. Oberon would kill her.

The man groaned in the bed beside her. She had been seeing him on and off for three weeks.

"Jake?" She bent down and kissed his shoulder. "Do you have paracetamol?"

"In the bathroom, on the shelf above the sink," came the muffled reply.

"Thanks."

Minutes later, she was ready to leave, having brushed her teeth and combed her long dark hair. Her eyes were still circled with smudged black liner, despite her attempts to clean it away. Her clothes smelt of smoke and her nail varnish was chipped. Oberon was right – she should never have gone to that party last night.

"Bye, Jake. I'll call you."

"Bye."

When she got outside, she winced as the sunlight blinded her. Shielding her eyes from its rays, she walked down Sloane Street towards the bus stop. She imagined Oberon prowling around the office like a panther about to strike. She upped her speed and pulled out her oyster card.

Riku pointed to the clock on the wall. "The one day he needed you here, Gabby! What were you thinking?"

"Aw, give me a break already." She dumped her bag on the ground. "Where is he?"

"On the phone to Kensington Palace. The Duchess will be here in an hour."

Oberon's offices filled a huge warehouse in the trendy area of Hackney Wick in East London. It was spacious yet minimalist, allowing space for the cutting of fabrics and patterns. Huge windows afforded them bright light and three podiums stood at the centre of the room. His numerous awards and achievements were framed on the wall and pictures of him with royalty and celebrities were next to those. The first time she had seen the picture of Oberon with Obama, she had been bowled over. Now, she barely noticed it.

"I'll just get the gowns ready," she said, heading for the

storeroom. Oberon's precious never-been-worn-before dresses hung on a rail, each individually packaged in a zip-up bag. "How many does he want to show?"

"Seven. The ones we discussed yesterday. I'd start with the white fur and go from there." Riku's phone started to ring. "I've got to take this, Gabs. Are you still okay for dinner later?"

She nodded. "I'm looking forward to it."

Riku nodded and disappeared out onto the wrought-iron balcony that overlooked the river.

She and Riku had become close over the past three years. She had never forgotten how he had given her a chance that day at the Lincoln Center and they had become firm friends. He and his partner of fifteen years, Jimin, often invited her to their apartment. Jimin was an excellent chef and owned his own Korean restaurant. She adored sampling his food, especially the kimchi. Riku, who had a penchant for gin, would serve large glasses and their soirées would last until the early hours. Whenever they travelled, she and Riku were put in economy while Oberon flew first class. Sitting together for hours on a plane, they had become close, talking for hours about their past and dreams for the future.

Humming a Selena Gomez tune, Gabriella rifled through the gowns. She had to hand it to Oberon, he was truly talented. His keen eye saw loose threads from a mile away and he could create clothes that flattered the female body beyond anything she had ever seen.

When she had first moved to London, he had helped her find a small flat in Tottenham and demanded that she be at work by seven thirty each morning. He was often there before her, drawing designs or cutting cloth. She realised very quickly that his work ethic matched her own.

Over the first year, she learned invaluable lessons. His attention to detail was second to none and he didn't let anything slip. "You have to give one hundred percent to be the best," he said a thousand times. "Nothing less."

Her first Fashion Week season, a couple of months after she had arrived in London, was an eye-opener. The Spring/Summer collection of major designers was showcased in the 'Big Four' – New York, London, Milan, and Paris. Oberon had chosen to début his new collection in Paris. Riku loaded up a truck with gowns and sets, and took the tunnel to Calais. Gabriella and Oberon flew to Charles de Gaulle where a taxi picked them up and took them into the city. Hanging around backstage was an amazing experience as she mingled with assistants and designers alike. She met Stella McCartney and ended up helping with her show, organising models and lining up outfits.

Then came Oberon's turn. Dressed in a silver tunic and black pants, he stood by her side, checking everything twice or three times. Together, they unleashed his Jamaican vision on the world.

Despite his trepidation, his new collection was a huge success. Orders came flying in and Gabriella's eyes widened when she saw how much he charged for a dress. Seeing the money being thrown around by the rich women who lined the runways made her even more determined to be successful.

Chanel's closing show at the Grand Palais really inspired her. Karl Lagerfeld opted for a feminist theme and had Cara Delevingne leading a protest, complete with banners and megaphones, calling for equality. That theme struck a chord with her and she filed it away in her brain. Women deserved a voice. Zadie Smith's address at her graduation echoed in her ears – how she could tackle problems like inequality through her visions and designs.

While in Paris, she had limited spare time, what with the show and last-minute amendments. Yet any chance she got, she took the metro to Trocadéro to see the Eiffel Tower or to Pigalle where she climbed the hill to Montmartre. Taking selfie after selfie, she showed Oberon afterwards who rolled his eyes.

"The photo diary of a singleton," he said scornfully. "A veritable selfie fest. Don't upload it to Instagram, darling. It's far too lonely-looking."

He needn't have said anything as she had deleted her Instagram account after leaving New York. She had done the same for Facebook and Snapchat, and urged her friends to email her if they needed to contact her. Social media rendered the world a very small place and she needed to break away from her old life. Plus she couldn't bear to see posts from Hugo or Celine as it teased her with a life she had believed was within her grasp.

When she arrived in London, she got a new phone with a British number and only gave it out to a select few. Starting again meant cutting as many of the old ties as possible and she was determined to forget the past.

Celine still contacted her now and then. She had finished in LA and was now working at the Art Institute of Chicago. She had been suspicious when Gabriella had broken it off so suddenly with her brother and kept asking questions in the beginning. Gabriella had mechanically answered them, always making out that she had sacrificed everything to selfishly take off with Oberon. When Celine probed about Victoria and if she had been involved, she had brushed it off. She was true to her word – if anything else, she wanted to put the whole thing behind her.

Gabriella consoled herself with the notion that if she had stayed with Hugo, she would never have asked Oberon for a chance. Then she would have missed a huge opportunity.

She remembered studying a poem in school by Robert Frost. It had been about a road and making decisions. Once the choice had been made, there was no going back. She took the road less travelled and she had to let go of what might have been.

It still hurt like crazy. Sometimes she dreamed about him and woke with tears in her eyes. She would never forget him – Hugo du Maurier had been her first love.

An hour later, Gabriella tied up her long tresses and applied some mascara. Her hangover had subsided thanks to the painkillers, and she felt elated and nervous about meeting the Duchess. All her life she had pored over magazines of the royal family – her first business had been 'Couture Royale' after all. She smiled at the memory. Look at how far she had come. Oberon had been right – she had been too careful. She had played it safe and copied the greats. There was no future in that.

"You need to find something that inspires you," Oberon told her one day. "Something that ignites a fire inside you – a vision that you want the world to see. Couture tells a story, Gabriella. You must find that spark and go with it."

She had taken his words to heart. Where better than Puerto Rico? It was her heritage and its culture was in her blood. However, the sketches she produced felt clichéd and boring, like they had been done a thousand times before.

So, she spent her days helping Oberon and following

him around the globe, holding back until she was ready. She had already been to Tokyo and Sydney, as well as most of Europe. Never in her wildest dreams did she think that she would travel like this. She remembered her conversation with Hugo – the time she didn't know where Aspen was. Oh, how times had changed.

Oberon paid her a minimum wage in the beginning. "If I pay you a lot, you'll get lazy," he explained. "I want you to be hungry for it."

Opportunities to make a bit extra arose over the years. Luca, after a short marriage to Charlotte, had divorced and moved to Cork in Ireland. Now he was married to Lydia, the girl he really loved, and they had a little girl called Sienna. When Gabriella had heard about Luca and Charlotte's divorce, she had not been surprised. In her heart she had known that it was doomed from the beginning. The first time she had met Luca after Sienna's birth, she felt like she was meeting a different person. He bounded exuberantly into the restaurant and refused wine with his steak, instead opting for water. What followed was a long conversation about the baby and Lydia, and how happy he was. She had to scroll through at least fifty pictures of Sienna on his phone and coo at the right moments. It was only when they were having coffee that Hugo came up in conversation.

"What happened there?" Luca asked. "I thought you two were perfect for each other."

Gabriella, her tongue loosened after a glass of wine, proceeded to tell him about Victoria. She knew that he no longer was in contact with the du Mauriers so she felt safe.

"She threatened you?" he said in disbelief. "That woman is unbelievable. She meddled in my relationship with Char too. She forced her to lie and drive Lydia away. It was months before I found out the truth."

"Are you serious?" Gabriella was shocked.

He nodded. "She wanted a wedding and nothing was going to stand in her way."

"Yet it all worked out for you in the end, right?"

"Yes." He took her hand and squeezed it. "It will work out for you too. Why don't you call him up?"

She snatched her hand away. "Are you crazy? My mama will lose her job. I'm not earning enough to support her."

"Call Victoria's bluff, Gabs. She'll never fire her. The house would fall apart without Magda at the helm."

"It's too late," she said sadly. "It's been too long."

"Karma will get the old bag in the end," said Luca cheerfully. "She is due some serious retribution."

Luca and Lydia had only married the year before in Venice when Sienna was about eighteen months old. Lydia had asked Gabriella to design her wedding dress and what followed were trips to Cork and London for fittings and lots of wine. Gabriella could see why Luca was so hooked – Lydia was simply lovely. She had a beautiful warm smile and seemed genuinely interested in Gabriella as a person. They had hit it off immediately.

Designing a wedding dress was a dream come true. Delighted but nervous, Gabriella had asked Oberon for advice. What they co-created was stunning – Lydia had been a vision as she glided up the aisle in the small Venetian chapel, her full-length lace gown billowing out behind her. Most of the five-thousand-pounds fee Gabriella had received had gone straight to her mother. Oberon had refused a cut, despite his help. "I only oversaw proceedings," he lied, delighted that his protégée

315

had become so good. He didn't need the money and he knew that every penny mattered to Gabriella.

Luca and Lydia lived in an apartment in Cork city in Southern Ireland. Lydia's first cousin, Colin McCarthy, lived right across the hall. Gorgeous, with brown curls and chocolate-coloured eyes, he was an only child and had grown up in Dublin with his successful parents, Oscar and Diana. Both lawyers, they had pots of money and Colin was subsequently used to the best. When he had decided to study at the university in Cork, his father had purchased a small apartment for his son. It was there, while doing an English Master's with Lydia, that they had met Luca for the first time years before. Now, they were one big family and Colin doted on Sienna, his goddaughter.

Colin's fiancé, Val, was an actor based in Cork and had carved out a nice little career for himself. His latest venture was playing Gar in *Philadelphia, Here I Come!*. He was the complete opposite to Colin. He wore jeans and plaid shirts, loved a can of beer in the evenings and watched sport on the television. "He's the yin to my yang," Colin would say.

The year before, they had bought a dog – a Pom called Britney – named as a homage to Colin's idol, Britney Spears. Lydia called her "Princess Britney" as she was spoilt beyond belief. Colin chopped up free-range chicken fillets each day and cooked them for his baby, and she never drank tap water, only Evian. Britney had a winter and summer wardrobe, filled with Burberry suits and fur-lined jackets, all designed for her breed. Colin spent a fortune online, buying couture for his pooch, and loved taking her for walks into the city centre as people pointed and stared.

Three months ago, Colin had called Gabriella. Impressed with Lydia's wedding gown in Venice, and priding himself as being on the pulse of the fashion world himself, he commissioned Gabriella to design the bridesmaids' dresses for his own wedding which was coming up. Gabriella was delighted with the request – Colin worked for a fashion magazine called *Papped!* – and he had promised to do a piece on her rise to fame in the September issue. Beautiful, spoilt but with a heart of gold, Colin was a tough customer, demanding the best for his wedding entourage: Lydia, his mother Diana, his goddaughter Sienna, and his beloved pooch, Britney. He wanted full-length silk gowns akin to Grace Kelly's wedding dress to match his Armani suit. Gabriella had been delighted as it was right up her street.

The wedding was in two weeks so the pressure was mounting. Colin had been dying to get engaged for years and was obsessed with his Big Day. It was to be held in his parents' garden with a large marquee. They lived in a sizable house in Killiney, an expensive suburb in South Dublin. Bono and Enya lived down the road and it was situated by the sea. Crates of Cristal had been flown in from France and an inventive menu had been created. Colin prided himself on being a great cook so his wedding lunch was going to be second to none.

Gabriella had been invited to the wedding but she had declined. She didn't have a date and even though flights were cheap from London to Dublin, she really couldn't afford it. She had also missed Luca's and Lydia's big day, mainly due to not having the funds to fly to Italy.

She was getting tired of living on the breadline. What with rent, transport costs and food, she barely had twenty pounds for herself at the end of the week.

Oberon straightened his shirt and held his head high. His nostrils flared as he waited for the Duchess to arrive. Five bodyguards had already scanned the room and the corridor for explosives. There were two men at the entrance of the building and it was now in lockdown – no one was allowed in or out during the visit.

Oberon could feel his heart thumping in his chest. Sure, he was top of his game, but it always irked him that he had not been commissioned to design couture for the royals. When he had received the call, he had experienced that same gut-churning excitement he had felt in the old days. He had a challenge and the world would be watching.

Nights followed where he stayed up drawing and sketching. He had just split from his partner of two years, an Italian model called Massimo, so he had the space to work at any hour. His apartment in Kensington was minimalist like his offices. A white leather couch and a walnut coffee table stood in the middle of the huge space he called a living room. There was no television and a large painting hung on the wall. The big windows on the south-facing end of the apartment gave it much light and he liked that. Darkness frightened him and made him feel caged. It reminded him of his childhood.

"Her Royal Highness, the Duchess of Cambridge," a man announced and the door opened.

ᥤ Chapter Twenty-Six ᥩ

"Isabelle Flynn!" Bertie held his arms open. "Well, if you aren't a sight for sore eyes!"

Isabelle turned around at the sound of his voice. She was standing on the steps of the Hôtel de Paris in Monte Carlo. Dressed in a light grey Balmain dress, her legs looked even longer in stiletto gladiator sandals. Her long red hair was tied up loosely and her green eyes sparkled.

"Bertie!" Laughing, she hugged him fiercely. "It's so good to see you!" she said, kissing his cheek.

"What brings you to this part of the world?" he asked. "This is my favourite spot to holiday but I find it frightfully hot this year – far too hot for little old me." He fanned his face with his straw hat.

"Oh, Angelo wanted to visit his mom so we went to Italy and then decided to take a few days here."

"How is your lovely boyfriend?"

"Busy. He's obsessed with beating Lewis Hamilton in Belgium next week."

"I presume you mean Spa-Francorchamps? Tricky bloody circuit. So windy and hilly. Where is he now?"

"Having a shower. He is just back from a run. I was on my way to the bar."

Isabelle had been dating the Italian Formula One champion Angelo D'Agostino for almost a year. Dubbed the next Sebastian Vettel for his achievements on the track, Angelo was fast becoming the world champion. He and Isabelle had met in Milan at a party thrown by Donatella Versace. He was tall and dark with brown curls and was instantly attracted to her pale beauty. In broken English, he had asked her out, but she had declined. At that time, she was going through a messy break-up with an American model called Johnny Martell. Two weeks later, Angelo turned up at her hotel in Paris and asked her out again. She was in town for Fashion Week and had been recruited by Chanel to showcase their Spring/Summer collection. She accepted his offer of dinner and they dined at Alain Ducasse's three-Michelin-starred restaurant at the Plaza Athenée. Over langoustine tartare, he told her of his humble upbringing near Treviso and how he had always wanted to drive fast cars.

She asked him if he feared death and he shook his head. "*Dio* watches over me," he said solemnly. "God is good."

After winning his first major race, the first thing he did was to buy a bigger house for his family. They had insisted on staying in the same town so he found a modern detached place in a nice area. His father was dead, so his mother had worked all her life at a local factory to support her children. The day he told her to hand in her notice was the best day of his life. Now, his mama didn't need to work and he could give her the life she deserved.

"You remind me a lot of my best friend," Isabelle mused over a glass of Chianti. "Her goal is to give her family a better life."

"I salute that!" said Angelo, holding up his glass.

After a few more dates in glamorous locations around

the globe, Angelo took her home to his family in Treviso. The visit was a big success except when Angelo's old grandmother made a Sign of the Cross at the sight of Isabelle's red hair.

"*Sfortuna*!" she said dramatically.

"What's that?' asked Isabelle curiously.

"Nothing," he answered, ushering her out the door. "Take no notice of her, she's very superstitious."

"Tell me or I'll put it into Google Translate!" she said, looking fierce.

He kissed her nose. "It means 'bad luck'. She's just being dramatic. We don't see many redheads around here and the old folk believe it's unlucky to meet one."

"Drink?" asked Bertie. "I'd love a catch-up."

Isabelle checked her gold watch. "Angelo should be down in a minute."

"Then he is most welcome to join us." Bertie took her arm and propelled her towards the bar. "Thank God security is tight in this place. Not a pap to be seen. They'd love a shot of us two. We're like Kate and Leo, forever connected."

"Over Allegra?" Isabelle giggled. "I'm not ungrateful and I know it made me famous but, my God, the perfume!"

"I smell it in my nightmares," said Bertie, wrinkling his nose. "Awful."

They took a seat outside at Le Grill, the rooftop bar of the famous hotel. A waiter appeared wearing white gloves and asked what they would like.

"Champagne?" said Bertie.

Isabelle nodded. "What else?"

She looked out at the sparkling blue Mediterranean. There were lines and lines of boats, moored side by side. The bigger yachts remained off-shore – huge sleek boats with helipads and pools on the deck.

She remembered the long conversations that she and Gabby used to have about being famous and how they would party on yachts off Cannes. Now, that dream was a reality for her and it felt surreal. It had all been too easy in the end. The world had stood up and paid attention after Allegra's commercial and then what followed were high-profile jobs for famous companies. A month after Allegra's première, Chanel had called. She went on to model in Paris and then the rest just fell into place.

They sat companionably for a while.

"How have you been?" asked Bertie then. "The last time we had a proper chat was at my birthday party, I believe."

"I'm good, real good." She smiled. "Busy, but I like that."

"I heard that Hollywood called you."

"Who said that?" She blushed.

"Oh, nobody." He grinned. "But do I predict a transition onto the silver screen? Shall I have the pleasure of acting alongside you someday?"

She shrugged. "They called, but I'm not too hot on the idea. I mean, I'm a model, not an actress. I don't think I'd be any good."

"You don't know until you try, my dear."

"That's what Paolo says."

Bertie regarded her thoughtfully. "You seem melancholy, Miss Flynn. Is everything quite all right?"

Isabelle sat up straight. "Of course, of course. I'm perfectly fine. Why do you ask?"

"You seem detached somehow. The Isabelle I met a few years ago would have been jumping at the thought of being in a film."

"I suppose I'm used to a new life now," she said

carefully. "It's funny, when you want something so badly, you imagine it to be the best thing in the world."

"Go on," said Bertie.

"Bu then when you get it, it doesn't quite measure up." She sighed. "Fame is a weird thing. I read awful comments on social media about my hair. You know, the ginger thing."

"Don't ever ego-google, my love. It's toxic."

"Yes, but I come across it and then I obsess about the negative."

"Perfectly natural."

"Sometimes I wish I could fade into the background and escape judgement." Isabelle sighed. "I mean, I like modelling and all, but I'm getting tired. Don't get me wrong, being a supermodel is incredible but –"

"What makes one super?" interrupted Bertie. "When does one make that transition?"

"When you can command ten thousand dollars before getting out of bed. When the whole world knows your name. When you've been accused of being a coke addict."

"Are you happy?"

Isabelle regarded him thoughtfully. "Sure, I'm happy."

Bertie took her small hand in his. "Have you any close friends?" he asked gently. "Have you anyone to talk to?"

She shrugged. "Modelling requires a lot of travelling so I don't get a chance to form close relationships."

"Are you still in touch with Gabriella? You two were great old pals."

Isabelle shook her head. "Not as much as I'd like. She's busy with Fashion Week season coming up."

"As are you, I'd imagine."

The waiter appeared with a vintage bottle of Moët and two glasses on a tray. "Shall I pour, sir?" he asked in perfect English.

Bertie nodded. "Thank you."

Isabelle smiled at the young boy as he handed her the flute filled with amber liquid.

"Gabriella has stayed under the radar, so to speak. I keep expecting to hear about her at galas or on the red carpet, but so far nothing." Bertie took a sip.

Isabelle frowned. "She's playing it safe. She wants to learn as much as she can from Oberon, but I think she's lost her nerve. Confronted with huge famous designers all over the world, she feels inadequate."

"Surely she could cash in on Oberon's name."

"Nah, she has no interest in that. She's so independent. I keep offering to showcase her work, but she says she's not ready."

"Pity," he said lightly. "I was always rooting for that kid."

"Me too."

"How are things with Angelo?" asked Bertie, changing the subject.

"Great, wonderful. He's just wonderful."

"A beautiful specimen, I must admit. With his dark eyes and hair, he reminds me of my dear friend Raphael."

Isabelle's face tightened.

"Whatever happened between you two? If you had stayed together, he would never have jumped back into that unsuitable relationship with Sylvie."

"That was what he wanted ..."

"I'm not sure about that."

"Oh, it was." She took a vicious sip of champagne. "I'll bet he was carrying on with her while I slept beside him."

"I doubt it."

"Oh please. He was in love with her – you told me so

yourself. I never stood a chance." She laughed bitterly. "When I think of how he treated me! I'm glad I got away."

Bertie said nothing.

"I have Angelo now. He's everything I want."

"Raph liked you a lot, my sweet. It was you that rejected his offer, remember?"

"I was going to compromise ..."

"He probably would have met you halfway. However, with expert timing, his ex arrived back into his life. It was a comedy of errors."

"I can't understand it. Why did she just turn up like that?"

"Oh, she sensed a comeback. He was all over the news. It was the perfect time to reignite their affair. She's getting too old for the runway and needed to cement her position."

"Bertie!"

"What?" He shrugged innocently. "Years ago, she left him at his darkest hour. I know he was hard to deal with, but she left and didn't look back. Then, when he starts to turn his life around, she turns up. Quite convenient, I think."

Isabelle stared at the glittering sea. This conversation was stirring up old feelings – emotions she had suppressed and locked away.

"Of course, they didn't last kissing time. You read about it, I presume."

She nodded. Of course she had seen it, splashed across every media platform imaginable. They had lasted a year and a half and then it was over. The engagement ring Sylvie had worn disappeared and Raphael threw himself into finishing his latest film. It was the week she had first met Angelo and she remembered it as clear as day. She wasn't stupid – it just wasn't meant to be.

"There you are!' Angelo, looking relaxed and tanned,

appeared at the table. His dark hair was wet and curling from the shower. He wore a simple black shirt and tailored brown pants. He beamed at them both.

Bertie stood up and shook his hand. "Hello, *signore!* Join us, join us!"

Angelo kissed Isabelle and took a seat.

"Champagne?" asked Bertie, summoning the waiter.

"Not for me," said Angelo, shaking his head. "I rarely drink."

"Angelo likes to keep a clear head before a race," explained Isabelle. "I wish I could be so abstemious."

The waiter appeared. "Yes, sir?"

Bertie gestured at Angelo to order.

"A San Pellegrino with a slice of lime," he said, smiling.

The waiter nodded and disappeared.

"I love this view," said Angelo approvingly. "Someday, I will have a boat like that." He pointed to a massive yacht moored off the headland.

"Keep driving like you're driving and that will be a reality," said Bertie. "My word, you're doing well."

Angelo shrugged. "I'm doing okay. I still haven't reached my target."

"Angelo wants to be the fastest man on the planet," said Isabelle. "He wants to go down in history."

"I salute that!' Bertie raised his glass. "To the Grand Prix and beating Lewis Hamilton! I feel very unpatriotic as he is a fellow-Englishman, but I'm rooting for you, Angelo."

Later that evening, Isabelle stood in the huge shower in the bathroom of their hotel room. She let the water beat down on her head and rested her head against the wall. She and Angelo had just made love like they always did in the huge bed. He was a caring and attentive lover and she liked sleeping beside him. However, the dreaded familiarity had taken its hold on their relationship and she found that they had slipped into a routine.

She rubbed some shampoo into her hair and scolded herself for even thinking such things.

Seeing Bertie like that had stirred up old memories. It was funny, even though it was over three years since she had seen Raphael Baptiste, she could still remember the texture of his skin or how warm and safe she felt in his big arms. Time had passed quickly and their brief affair was frozen in time.

In retrospect, she could see that he had controlled everything. She had been grateful for any scrap of attention he had bestowed on her.

God, she had been pathetic.

She switched off the water and squeezed out her hair. Best to forget him completely. All he ever did was hurt her. Angelo was her future now.

∝ Chapter Twenty-Seven ∾

Three days after the royal visit, Gabriella was sewing beads onto Sienna's flower-girl dress under the bright lights in Oberon's warehouse. Squinting, she finished a row and cut the thread. Each small bead had to be handsewn and it was taking a lot of time. Lydia's gown was ready and Diana's was two hours away from completion. It meant a few late nights but Gabriella didn't mind.

Colin had called the night before, arranging a final fitting the following week for everyone but the dog. "Britney can't fly over," he said with a sigh. "She has a tummy bug. We'll have to wing it, I'm afraid. I'll make sure she doesn't put on an ounce of weight between now and the wedding."

Oberon had allowed her to use his studio for the last fitting, as he had podiums and mirrors, so she tapped on his office door. He was weird about consent and she knew better than to presume.

"Hey," she said, standing on the threshold. "Would it be okay if some clients called for a fitting tomorrow? They're flying over from Ireland especially and my flat is too small."

"The same group as last time?" he said, without looking up from his computer screen.

"Yes."

"Fine. Just tell that curly-haired bloke to keep his voice down."

Gabriella smiled to herself. Colin chattered incessantly and the first time he had seen Oberon's place, he had been bowled over by the photos on the wall. "Look! That's him with Seán Penn! Oh, and Tom Hanks! I'm all over it!"

"Thanks," she said, closing the door quietly. Oberon had been working every hour since the royal appointment. Riku kept bringing him skinny lattes and reminding him to eat. He hadn't seen his boss this intense since the old days.

Gabriella gathered her belongings and waved to Riku. "See you tomorrow," she said.

"Have a good evening." He bowed his head.

Walking out into the August sunshine, she headed towards the tube station. She hadn't really mixed with many people since coming to London. In the beginning, it was all work and no play. She had stayed at the office every hour she could, learning as much as possible. When Oberon had a deadline, she had stayed by his side, helping him to finish.

Idly, she toyed with the idea of calling Luca.

Pulling out her phone, she found his number. He answered on the fourth ring.

"Gabs! What's up?"

"Hey, you. I was just wondering if you're in London and if you'd like to meet for a drink later?"

"You must be a mind-reader! After the day I've had, I need to let loose a bit."

"Great. Will we say Soho? I can meet you on Leicester Square and we can take it from there?"

"Sure. Give me half an hour to get sorted."

"Great, talk then."

Luca was standing outside the Odeon when she arrived.

329

He looked as good as ever, dressed in a smart suit. His blonde hair gleamed in the summer sun and his blue eyes were warm. They embraced and he stood back to take a look at her. "Wow, Gabs, you look great!"

She waved him away. "No, I don't. I need a serious haircut and I ate way too many pastries this week."

He put his finger to his lips. "Just take the compliment," he said, rolling his eyes. "Hell, some things never change."

"Where do you want to go?" she asked, ignoring him.

"Bar Américain? Just for nostalgia's sake. I miss New York."

"Sure, why not?"

They headed in the direction of Piccadilly Circus. Manoeuvring their way through the tourists, they reached the famous neon lights and then turned up right onto Shaftsbury Avenue.

"So, how's the gallery on Canary Wharf working out?" she asked. "I read about Tara's exhibition at the Tate Modern. Things are really happening for her, right?"

Luca nodded. "She's doing really well, I guess. I sold three pieces this week alone." He frowned. "The only thing is, she works all the time, Gabs. Ever since the divorce, she has thrown herself into the business. I think she needs to balance it a bit better."

Gabriella shrugged. "She's passionate – I get that."

"I don't know," he said. "She's bordering on obsessed. Ever since Papa married Laura."

Tara and Christian had divorced after a long, tempestuous marriage. Never suited, they had battled on throughout the years. After their granddaughter Sienna's birth, they had attempted to make a go of it again. However, after a few months, the cracks started to show. Then Christian met Laura Dixon and that had been it.

Within a year, he and Laura got married in Antibes, despite the twenty-five-year age gap. Now, Luca had a stepmother the same age as him, and Tara, who had taken the divorce hard, had turned into a workaholic.

"Christian is happy now, right?" said Gabriella.

"Oh, he is," agreed Luca. "He and Mom were never suited. They came from different worlds. It never works."

Gabriella thought of Hugo and something clutched her heart.

They reached Brasserie Zédel and walked into the foyer. They followed the red sign with Bar Américain on it and walked into the famous cocktail bar. Hundreds of bottles lined the wall and the lighting was dark and atmospheric. The art-deco fittings gave a 1930's feel and the lounge was elegant.

"Cocktail?" asked Luca.

Gabriella shook her head. "I'll stick with a beer."

Luca ordered two beers and they took a seat at a small round table.

"Does Lydia mind your being away a lot?" asked Gabriella. "You're only in Ireland at weekends, right?"

Luca shrugged. "She's good. We live in the same building as Colin so she spends most of her time with him." He sipped his drink. "They're really close. He cooks for her and cleans our apartment. She'd be lost without him."

"He's good fun."

"Yeah, Colin's great." He sipped his beer. "That wedding will be awesome. He has waited long enough for it." He smiled. "His fiancé Val held out for years. Colin put so much pressure on him to propose, but he stood firm. The Irish voted for gay marriage a couple of years back and still he didn't crack. It drove Colin crazy."

"Why? Why did he hold out for so long?"

Luca shrugged. "He wasn't ready, I guess. Plus he thinks that Colin gets everything too easy. He's a cool guy, Val."

"So what happened then?"

"Out of the blue, he popped the question last Christmas. We were down in Lydia's parents' place. Colin fainted with the shock and when he came to, he became Bridezilla in a matter of seconds. I swear to God, the whole thing was organised in forty minutes. Down to the priest, the band and the canapés."

"I get that he's organised," admitted Gabriella, taking a sip of her beer. "He emails me constantly looking for updates on progress and photos."

"That's Colin," said Luca. "Don't get me wrong, the guy is great, but I'd like for me and Lyd to get a bigger place. You know, a house or something. She wants to stay where we are because she's across the hall from Colin. She's never lonely with him around and he's great with Sienna."

"Well, I can understand that. Imagine her stuck in a big house on her own?"

Luca said nothing.

"Why change things now?" she continued. "You guys have enough room, right?"

"Well, I want another kid. Sienna's two and a half now, and I want to try for a boy." Luca traced the rim of his glass with his finger. "The apartment is too small for four."

"How does Lydia feel?"

"She's not into it. She loves her job and doesn't want things to change."

"Give her time. She might change her mind."

"I was an only child and it was hard. I don't want that for Sienna."

"Just give her time." Her brown eyes were warm. "I

never took you for the family-man type." She giggled. "Luca Jacob, Daddy Cool."

"*Shaddup,*" he said smiling. "Things change."

"They sure do."

Luca eyed her speculatively. "Are you heading to New York in September for Fashion Week?"

She nodded. "Oberon wants to go Stateside this year. Zsa Zsa said I can use her apartment again."

"She still has that place?"

"Oh yeah," said Gabriella, nodding fervently. "It's rent-controlled so it's a steal. To be fair, she spends a lot of time in New York so the place is rarely empty."

"You've got to introduce me to her boyfriend, Gabs. I'm a Formula One mega fan."

"Angelo? I've only met him once or twice. He seems pretty nice."

A waiter appeared and asked them if they wanted refills. Luca nodded and handed him a twenty-pound note.

"So, when's your big début?" he asked. "You can't stay in Oberon's shadow forever."

Gabriella's face darkened. "Oh, don't start. I get this every day from Riku."

"What's the problem?"

"No inspiration," she answered glumly. "I just can't find my muse. Isabelle is waiting in the wings to model for me, but I can't get it together."

Luca nudged her playfully. "You'll get inspired soon."

"You think?" She looked doubtful.

"Sure. Everyone experiences a lull every now and then."

She inhaled deeply. She hadn't felt the same since Hugo. It was like a black cloud had invaded her brain and she found it difficult to get excited about anything.

"So, Colin wants us all to go for dinner after the

333

fitting on Tuesday," he said, changing the subject. "Any suggestions?"

"Well, Sienna will be there so we should go somewhere like Nando's."

Luca laughed out loud. "You've met Colin's mom, right? Diana?"

Gabriella pictured the beautiful blonde lady with the dark-brown eyes and nodded. "Briefly."

"Well, let's just say, she's not a Nando's type of lady. Come to think of it. Colin won't be impressed either. Those guys are choosy."

"So what do you suggest?"

"I'll message Colin. Knowing how organised he is, he probably has a reservation made already."

Luca was right. Colin had booked them all into Le Gavroche, a two-Michelin-starred restaurant run by Michel Roux Junior.

"Sienna can't go there!" Lydia complained. "She won't eat pea velouté or frog's legs!"

"I'm sure they'll have *frites* on the menu," said Colin haughtily. "It *is* a French restaurant after all."

The dress-fitting was a great success. Diana and Lydia had identical gowns made of silk, full-length with heavy skirts. Gabriella gazed at Lydia as she twirled around in her dress. She really was lovely and she could see why Luca was so crazy about her. Small and slim, she had long brown hair and pale skin. Sienna, on the other hand, was a mirror image of Luca. Small and sallow-skinned, she had blonde curls that bounced when she moved. The only feature she had inherited from her mother was her green eyes. Dancing around the room, she looked enchanting in a tiny white fairy dress with a taffeta skirt and a beaded waist.

"I coot," she called, running around the podium.

"Yes, you're very cute," said Colin approvingly. "Only good-looking people in the wedding party, people. Like, hello?"

Diana, his mother, looked regal in her gown. In her late fifties, she looked amazing for her age. Her hair had blonde streaks and her brown eyes were identical to her son's.

"Only ten days to go," said Lydia in excitement.

Colin fanned his face. "I can't believe it, I just can't believe that I'll be walking up the aisle."

Luca met them outside the restaurant. He had come straight from the gallery and was wearing a dark-blue suit.

"*Daddeeee!*" shrieked Sienna, desperately trying to escape from Colin's arms.

Luca reached out and took her from Colin's grasp. Lifting her high up into the air, he whirled her around and around.

"*Stop!*" She called in delight. "*Daddy bitch!*"

Lydia wagged her finger at her daughter. "Sienna!' she chided. "We talked about that word. Don't say it."

Sienna smiled mischievously. "Sobby, Mama."

Diana's eyes had widened in shock. "Where did she pick that up?"

"Oh Mom, kids are like sponges," said Colin. "Sienna here is a genius too, so she picks up language very quickly."

"Hardly a genius, Col," said Lydia.

"Oh, she is," he argued. "She can use the Nespresso machine all by herself. I caught her making coffee the other day."

"She *what?*" said Lydia in horror. "She could've burned herself, Col! Why didn't you stop her?"

"It's a life skill, Lyd. Better she picks these things up now."

Luca put Sienna down. Then he turned and pulled Lydia into his arms. "Hey, you," he murmured, kissing her thoroughly.

"Ahem," said Colin, tapping his foot. "We have a reservation, you know!"

Diana took Sienna's hand and led her into the restaurant. Gabriella, who had been watching everything in fascination, followed.

"I have a booking under McCarthy," said Colin in an authoritative voice. "Table for five and a half."

"Follow me, sir," said the maître d'.

The meal that followed was lovely. Gabriella chose the duck with a beetroot Tatin. Colin had the rabbit and couldn't stop raving about it. "Wonderful," he enthused, "just wonderful." Lydia and Diana both had grilled Dover sole and Luca opted for beef. Sienna, as Colin predicted, had a plate of chips and tomato ketchup. The waitress kept winking at her and tickling her under her chin. "So adorable," she said, when she was clearing the main courses.

"Bitch," Sienna replied, pointing at her.

"Gosh, I'm sorry," said Lydia, flustered. "She doesn't know what she's saying."

Luca tried to look stern. "Sienna! You've got to cut that out."

"Daddy best," she answered, smiling sweetly.

Luca's expression softened and he grinned. "You got that right."

"Oh, please," said Colin in a bored tone. "I've seen you repeating 'Daddy is the best' over and over to her. The child is indoctrinated."

Gabriella soaked up the banter. It reminded her of her own family. Looking at Sienna, she reminded her of her niece, Sophia. When she had left New York three years before, Sophia had been a similar age. With a pang, she realised that she missed her home. The way of life in London was so different. The food, the accent and the weather were all so alien to her. How she yearned for Lita's pork stew or her mama's orange cake. She would have to make sufficient time to visit Melrose when she went back for Fashion Week.

"So, this girl called Niamh did my highlights last week." Colin flicked his brown curls that were now streaked with blonde. "She's new at the salon but so good. I mean, I look great."

"Is that an Irish name?" asked Gabriella.

Colin nodded. "It's spelt N-I-A-M-H."

"What?" said Gabriella. "But pronounced 'Neeav'?"

"I know. Mad, isn't it? She was a fairy princess in Ireland years and years ago." Colin sipped his wine. "Gabby, you should read some stories from Irish mythology. It's amazing."

"Oh, I love mythology," she said genuinely.

"Then you should read Lady Gregory's book," interrupted Lydia. "It's really good."

"Who?"

"Lady Augusta Gregory," explained Colin. "She was a friend of Yeats."

"The poet?"

"Yeah," said Lydia. "She wrote the definitive volume. I have a copy at home."

"Hey, I could bring it to London sometime," said Luca helpfully, wiping Sienna's face with a napkin.

"Oh, thanks," said Gabriella, beaming. "I'd definitely read it."

"You'll delve into a magic world of fairies and princesses and queens," said Lydia softly. "You'll see a society where women were powerful and respected. We Irish call it 'Forlámhas na mBan'. It means superiority of women."

"Queen Maeve, the queen of Connaught, led her army into battle against Ulster. All to capture a bull. Then there was the ancient tribe of Ireland called the Tuatha Dé Danann, who had three warrior-goddesses: Banbha, Fódhla and Ériu, the last of whom gave her name to Ireland. And of course, Niamh, the fairy princess who enchanted Oisín and led him to the land of eternal youth: Tír na nÓg."

"Not my hairdresser," said Colin.

"No," agreed Lydia with a laugh.

Gabriella stared at her in fascination.

"Read the book, Gabriella. These ladies give the likes of Andromeda, Daphne and Eurydice something to think about."

"I will," she promised.

"Right, who wants dessert?" asked Colin. "Nothing too calorific, okay? I'm paying a fortune for those dresses and they'd better fit."

"Bitch!" said Sienna happily.

❧ Chapter Twenty-Eight ❧

"Isabelle! It's good to hear from you!"

"Hey, Gabby. It's been so long. I've been meaning to call …"

"Hey, I know that you're busy. It's fine."

"I've been in Italy and France these past few weeks with Angelo."

"Lucky you."

"Yes, it was nice." She paused. "I met Bertie in Monaco actually. He sends his love."

"Oh? I haven't seen him since his birthday party last year. Aw, I miss him. He always makes me laugh."

"He's been busy making movies, I guess. He was asking about your work and when to expect the global phenomenon called Gabriella to be unleashed onto the world."

"Oh, not you too. I get this from everyone."

"It's been three years, Gabs. You need to make a move. You can't stay in Oberon's shadow forever."

"I'm not ready, Zsa Zsa. I have no inspiration. I feel numb."

"Why?"

"I don't know. It's crazy, but ever since Hugo I feel like my spark is gone."

Isabelle closed her eyes. "I get what you mean."

"I'll sort it out soon, I promise."

"Well, I'm waiting to be your model and Bertie is dying to promote you amongst his entourage of celebrities."

"He's so sweet."

"He wants to meet the next time he's back in London."

"Well, I'm off to New York for Fashion Week ..."

"I hear you. I'm modelling for Ralph Lauren. See you at my apartment?"

"You're so good to me!"

"*Mi casa es su casa.* I'd really like us to spend some time together. I miss you, Gabs."

"Well, if you're sure ..."

"I'm one hundred per cent sure."

"So, see you in New York?"

"It will be like old times. I'll get some food from the deli ..."

"I'll get the Chardonnay ..."

"Can't wait to see you. Bye."

"Bye."

Hearing Isabelle's American twang made Gabriella think of home. Lita's image floated into her mind. She was now well into her eighties and getting frail. Guiltily, she recalled the day she said goodbye before leaving for London with Oberon. Lita had taken her face in her gnarly old hands and kissed her cheeks lovingly.

"I hope we meet again, *preciosa*," she had whispered sadly. "Please visit."

Gabriella frowned. Visit? She had only been home three times since that day. Three times for Christmas.

Her phone buzzed. It was a message from Lydia.

Can I give Aurora Sinclair your number? She wants you to design a dress! X

Gabriella started. Aurora Sinclair was the darling of

340

the London stage and was about to make it in Hollywood. She had read an article about her only the other day.

She texted Lydia back immediately giving her consent. Ten minutes later her phone rang.

"Gabriella? This is Aurora Sinclair. Lydia gave me your number."

"Hey!"

"Sorry for ringing you at home, but I was wondering if you had time to make a dress for me? I really need a gown for a gala that's coming up in December. Bertie Wells is organising it and he's asked me to sing."

"Bertie? I haven't seen him in so long."

"Yes, he's been very busy. He's having a big fundraiser for charity."

"That sounds great. Are you in London at the moment?"

"Yes, I am actually. Are you available to meet?"

"Absolutely. Wow, I'm so flattered you thought of me."

"Oh, I sang the hymns at Lydia's wedding and her dress was just stunning. I would love something similar."

"No problem. I'll check my diary and send you some possible dates and times."

"Wonderful. Thank you so much."

Gabriella hung up the phone and smiled. Aurora was so beautiful, it would be a dream to create a dress for her.

She texted Oberon straight away with the news about Aurora and the gown. He replied saying "**Who?**" as he was not familiar with Aurora's work.

Gabriella smiled to herself. Typical of her boss to be nonchalant. Getting excitement or praise from Oberon was rare.

When Gabriella arrived at work the next Monday morning, Riku rushed up to her.

"Oberon wants to see you in his office, Gabs. Right now."

She hung her cardigan on the back of her chair and placed her handbag underneath it. "Am I in trouble or something? You look so worried!"

Riku shrugged. "He's prowling around, you know how he does." He scurried away.

Taking a deep breath, she knocked on Oberon's door.

"Come in," came the familiar voice.

She opened the door. "You wanted to see me?"

"Sit down."

He was working on a sketch for the New York show and three empty espresso cups stood in a neat line by the paper on the desk. She took a seat and waited.

"I googled this Aurora. I see that she's an actress and a singer."

"She's about to go global. She just finished this movie –"

"I know who she is," he cut her off icily. "I just told you that I googled her. I suppose, what I want to know is, why are we back to this?"

"To what?"

"This messing around. This designing a solitary gown for a solitary client. This shying away from the limelight, comfortably lurking in my shadow."

"Hey! I'm not."

"Oh, yes, you are, Gabriella. You're quite content pissing around making dresses for nobodies while I kill myself making couture for duchesses. Do you see what I'm saying? You'll never emerge as a star if you don't put yourself in the limelight."

"But I am!" she protested. "Aurora will wear my dress and ..."

"And what? I mean, no one knows who you are. You don't have a collection. Let's just say someone does pick up on your name and tries to google you or God forbid, attempt to buy something you've designed. You don't have a website and you shun social media. You're going to have to get it together."

"I can't think of a concept."

"Bullshit. You're not trying hard enough."

"No!" she stood up. "I tried the Puerto Rican thing …"

"Too predictable."

"I know!" she argued passionately. "That's why I abandoned it."

"Calm down." He rolled his eyes. "Just shut up and listen to me, okay? You need to get some ideas on my desk by next week."

"But …"

"No buts. It's not a request. Sketches by next week, Gabriella, or you're out."

"What?" she whispered.

"You heard me. You are underutilising your contacts. You're friends with Isabelle Flynn, right? Why then don't you ask her to wear a gown or two to high-profile events. Even dear old Bertie could give you a leg-up. He's best friends with half the actresses in Hollywood."

"I don't want to freeload off people," she said obstinately. "I want to make it myself."

"Oh, get over yourself. Do you think I'd be here today if it weren't for a few leg-ups? This is a tough industry, girl. You have to use every opportunity you can."

Gabriella said nothing.

"The first thing you have to do is get a collection together. I want the basic vision before we go to New York. Work night and day if you have to. Then, if this Aurora whatever her name is, wears your gown and tells the world, you'll have something behind you. No more fucking around, Gabby. I'm serious."

She nodded mutinously.

"Think of the opportunities you've been given. Embrace it. Stop hiding." He waved her away. "Now, get out. I'm busy."

She stood up. "Will you really fire me if I fail?"

He looked her straight in the eye. "One hundred per cent. Now, piss off."

Later that evening, Gabriella got home to her flat in Tottenham and poured herself a glass of wine. Oberon's words rang in her brain and she grimaced. What the hell would she do now? If she presented something substandard, he would throw it away.

Making a Sign of the Cross, she prayed silently. God had always looked out for her and she needed him now.

Rifling through magazines, she searched for inspiration. Everything had been done a million times over. She gulped back her wine and sat back on the sofa. Oberon meant business. She had to come up with a plan.

There was a package on her desk the next morning.

"That gorgeous blonde American dropped it off," said Riku. "My word, he should model."

"Luca?" Gabriella tore at the package and found it was a book called *Lady Gregory's Complete Irish Mythology*. It was the book Lydia had urged her to read. She pulled it out and baulked at its size. It would take her weeks to get through it. Putting it in her large canvas handbag, she made a note to look at it at home.

"*Gabriella!*" shouted Oberon from his office. "Did those sketches turn up?"

She rummaged round her desk. "I've got them here."

It was two days later when she finally got to read the

book. Work had been hectic and Oberon had insisted that she stay late to finish a dress with him. Skimming through a few pages, she recognised the words 'Dé Danann'. Lydia had mentioned a tribe with warrior queens. Frowning, she read through a few paragraphs and found it to be accessible enough. She had always enjoyed learning about Greek mythology in high school. This was a Gaelic version with heroes and queens and battles and magic. Settling into the sofa, she kept reading …

She woke on the sofa, cold and stiff. The big book lay on the ground, fallen as she slept. The time on her phone read three o'clock in the morning.

"Dammit," she said aloud. She had to be up for work in four hours.

Turning off the lights, she went to her bedroom and pulled back the duvet. Her pillows were just how she liked them: one was horizontal and the other vertical. Snuggling in, she closed her eyes and fell asleep.

The alarm woke her at seven o'clock on the dot. Groaning, she switched it to snooze.

Just five more minutes …

Slowly her brain began to wake up and her mind filled with images. Isabelle wearing a torc around her neck and a toga-like gown. White horses and druids in black robes. Her dreams had been filled with snapshots of the stories she had read before falling asleep. She wallowed in the half-reality between waking and sleeping and struggled to remember the rest. A vast green landscape and swords made of gold. Fearless warriors and fairies.

She sat bolt upright.

She could see Isabelle again. This time she was wearing a fur cloak and a red gown. Her fiery red hair was contained with a green band around her temples. She looked fierce and strong and powerful.

Slowly the vision became clearer. These women that Lydia had mentioned were inspirational. They were mighty women who fought alongside their husbands. They were equal. Feminism was everywhere right now. In a flash, she remembered how impressed she was at her first Paris Fashion Week, watching Cara Delevigne protest against discrimination. Chanel's closing show had had women protesting and calling for action. They had rallied together to be heard and had called for change.

Why not design clothes for the dominant woman? The woman who behaves like a queen and gets what she wants?

Gabriella made a Sign of the Cross.

"Thank you, God," she said, closing her eyes. "You've answered my prayer."

"Goddesses and queens?" Oberon sat back in his swivel chair and regarded her thoughtfully. "Go on."

"Well, this woman called Lady Gregory wrote a book about Irish mythology and I had a dream and –"

"A dream? God save us."

"Yes, a dream." She scowled at him. "I saw Isabelle in this amazing dress with a fur collar and a band around her head. She looked fierce and strong. It was amazing."

"Really?" He looked unconvinced.

"Yes, really." She glared at him. "My vision will show a world where women have achieved what they set out to do. They will be equal to men. They will be forces to be reckoned with."

"Will you burn a few bras on the runway?"

"No!"

"Sacrifice a few men at the stake?"

"You're not listening," she said in frustration. "It's not about being better than men. It's not about getting revenge. It's about being equal."

Oberon swung from side to side on his chair, deep in thought. "Timeline?"

Gabriella shrugged. "I don't know. What with Fashion Week season and Aurora's design … a couple of months?"

Oberon clicked a button on his Mac and the screen came to life. He accessed a calendar and frowned.

"Fur screams winter," he said. "I think we should aim to showcase this before Christmas. People are in good form and they are prone to spending money they don't have. There's a sense of bonhomie and extravagance."

He clicked on November and a list of events popped up.

"Look, on the 24th November your old pal Bertie is having a charity gala at the Savoy. It's an auction, in fact. He sent a generic email to every famous person on the planet looking for freebies. I was going to donate a dress, but now I have a better idea."

Gabriella clapped her hands. "That must be the gala that Aurora is singing at. I'm designing her dress."

"*Hmmm*, that's good. Very good." Oberon rubbed his chin. "Maybe you could showcase seven or eight outfits – you know, get your friend Isabelle to round up a few of her model mates and auction them off to the crowd. We could sell it as an exclusive – the first time the world has seen 'Gabriella' couture. After a few glasses of champagne, those A-listers will lap it up. The world press will be there so you'll go viral. Bertie will make a fortune for charity – there's no better man to convince rich people to fork out. It's win-win, darling." He paused. "Well, not for you financially, but that will come afterwards. You have to sacrifice to make it."

"I get that. You've got to speculate to accumulate."

"Right." Oberon looked amused. "Now, run along and call Bertie pronto. You need to chalk this down and get sketching. We leave for New York in a few days."

Gabriella's eyes lit up. "I feel so positive about this. I can't tell you how great. It's like I've finally found a path. I just want to work at it until it's perfect."

Oberon smiled and it transformed his haughty face. So rare was his smile, that it lit up the room. "Now you're talking," he said. "That's the attitude I was looking for."

◖ Chapter Twenty-Nine ◗

Gabriella called Isabelle first.

"Are you available on the 24th of November?"

"Well, hello to you too, Gabby. How are you?"

"Sorry, I'm just excited."

"The 24th, wait a second, that date rings a bell."

"Bertie's gala?"

"Right, sure. The gala. Angelo has a race in Abu Dhabi that weekend, so I'll probably give it a miss."

"No, no. Don't miss it."

"Why?"

"I want you to model for me. I'm going to showcase my work that night."

"What? Are you for real? That's wonderful, Gabs."

"Well, it depends on Bertie of course. Can you send me his number? I need to ask him."

"Sure, sure. I'm sure he'll be delighted. I mean, with the right publicity, it could be huge."

"Do you have any model friends who would help out? I mean, there'll be no fees as it's for charity."

"I'll pull in a few favours. Wow, well done, you! I'm thrilled for you."

"I'll tell you all about it over the weekend."

"You still have your key to the apartment, right?"

"I sure do. Oh Zsa Zsa, I can't wait to catch up."

"Me too, Gabs. Me too."

Gabriella then texted Bertie, asking him to call her when convenient. He rang her straight away.

"Gabriella! My darling girl. It's been so long."

"Hi, Bertie."

"I was only saying to Isabelle the other day that we should all catch up. How have you been? I hope Oberon is treating you well."

"Oh, he is. I have a question."

"Go on."

"You know the charity gala you're hosting in November?"

"Yes? Would you like to attend? I told my P.A. to invite every living celebrity so I'm surprised you didn't get word."

"Oh, Oberon got the email. He never tells me anything."

"Anyway, go on."

"Well, I was wondering if I could showcase some original work for the first time that night. Like a première of 'Gabriella' as a brand. I'll donate all the clothes of course, and you can auction them. Isabelle has agreed to model so ..."

"Stop right there. You have my full permission."

"Really?"

"Of course. We could make it a huge extravaganza."

"That sounds awesome."

"Wonderful. Now, along with a weekend at the Beckhams', a week on Richard Branson's island and a zillion-pound necklace from Cartier, I have the début of the next big thing in the fashion world. This will be a fabulous night."

"Keep in touch."

"Oh, you can count on it. I'm stuck on Phuket at the moment shooting a scene for my new movie."

"That doesn't sound so bad. I'd like to be stuck there sometime."

"After this gala, you will. I promise you that. *Ciao, ciao!*"

Gabriella zipped up her suitcase and heaved it off the bed. Oberon had already called five times telling her to get her 'arse' to Heathrow as fast as possible. A notorious control freak, he insisted that she check in two hours before and no less.

New York Fashion Week was about to start. She was going home. The thought made her smile.

She had packed enough clothes for the week and had stuffed in toys for her nieces and nephews, plus a tin of English tea for Lita and a box of chocolates from Fortnum and Mason's for her mother.

She couldn't wait to eat hot dogs and watch some baseball. She missed America and her family.

Isabelle was in the shower when Gabriella pulled her suitcase through the front door of the apartment in New York.

She popped her head around the bathroom door.

"*It's only me!*" she called over the noise of the water.

Isabelle's slender arm appeared over the shower curtain and made a thumbs-up sign.

Opening the door of her old bedroom, she saw a Hershey chocolate bar on her pillow and smiled.

Just as she kicked off her shoes, her phone pinged.

She unlocked the home screen and gasped. It was an email from Celine du Maurier. Rubbing her eyes, she read the sender's name again.

The subject was 'Hello'.

It read:

I presume you're in New York for Fashion Week. I saw Oberon's name on the list.

Well, I am too. Have two weeks vacation and decided to spend time on Long Island. You are SO not blowing me off this time, Gabriella!!! We're definitely meeting up – no excuses!

Celine xxx

Gabriella sat down on her bed and read the email again.

She had often felt guilty about Celine who had been a good friend to her throughout the years. She had made no real effort to maintain their friendship since the Hugo thing. It was a form of self-preservation – if she didn't hear about him, she didn't really think about him.

Her heart racing, she emailed back saying that she'd love to meet for a beer and to let her know where. She signed it: **Gabby x**

Isabelle appeared ten minutes later wearing a robe and a towel turban.

"Gabby!" They embraced fondly.

"It's so good to see you," said Gabriella.

"Ditto,' said Isabelle. "You look so well. I love your hair like that."

Gabriella blushed. "It's only a few braids."

Isabelle gave her a pained look. "Take the frickin' compliment already." She picked up her phone. "Want to order take-out like old times? The deli was closed when I arrived."

"Sure. Make it pizza though. They don't have proper pepperoni in England."

Isabelle nodded. "I hear you. The only thing I like in London is the cheddar cheese."

Gabriella laughed. "Are you still a cheese fiend? My God, in your line of work, that's pretty incredible."

"I have to hide my addiction from Paolo. He's always banging on about calories and cellulite." She made a face. "I tried that macrobiotic diet once. Never again. Life's way too short."

"You're so lucky that you don't put on weight," sighed Gabriella. "I only have to look at a cream puff and I'm five pounds heavier."

Isabelle shrugged. "It will get me in the end. I probably have clogged arteries. Okay, open some wine and I'll call the pizza place."

She disappeared into her bedroom and seconds later Gabriella could hear her on the phone. Opening the fridge, she retrieved a bottle of Chablis and uncorked it.

"This wine is pretty fancy," she said to Isabelle when she arrived back minus the towel on her head.

"Oh, no more cheap Chardonnay for us, Gabs. We're classy now." She grinned. "It's actually Angelo's. He left it here the last time he visited."

"How is he? Will he make it for your show?" she asked, handing Isabelle a glass.

She shook her head. "He won't make it to New York, but we're hoping to meet in London. He's training at Silverstone next week."

"I feel like I barely know him," admitted Gabriella wistfully. "It's such a shame that we don't meet more often."

"Let's try and make more of an effort. I'll be in Europe for the next month or so. Surely we can make it work."

Gabriella sipped her wine and glanced at Isabelle. "Celine du Maurier emailed me. She wants to meet for a beer."

Isabelle's eyes widened. "Is she in town? I thought she was based in Chicago?"

Gabriella nodded. "She's on vacation. I said that I would. I mean, she's been my friend forever and I've cut ties with her since Hugo."

"I guess." Isabelle raised an eyebrow. "She'll definitely mention him. Are you ready for that?"

"Of course. I'm over it now."

"*Hmmm.*"

"Look, Zsa Zsa, my friendship with her is a separate thing and existed long before my relationship with Hugo."

"Then go for it."

Magda opened the door and gasped. "Gabby! *Mi cariña!*" She pulled her close. "I have missed you so much."

Gabriella savoured the smell of her mother's hair and clung to her like a child. The last time they had met was the Christmas before, nine months ago.

"Come," said Magda, taking Gabriella's hand. "Lita is waiting for you."

They walked into the sitting room to find Lita sitting in her chair. Gabriella gasped. Her grandmother looked wizened and frail. The fact that she didn't see her on a daily basis highlighted the difference a few months had made. Lita was almost eighty-six and was crippled with arthritis. The nimble hands that once sewed intricate designs, now lay crooked on her lap. Her head was bowed as if it was too heavy to hold up and her shoulders were hunched.

"Lita," said Gabriella, rushing over to hug her.

"*Preciosa,*" she said breathlessly. "*Mi Gabriella, graçias a Dios!*" She reached out and stroked her hair. "You look so well."

Gabriella kissed her papery skin. "I've missed you, Lita."

"Me too. I thank God that you are home and I am still here to see you."

"Don't talk that way. You look as good as ever."

Lita's wise old eyes crinkled in amusement. "We both know that is a lie, Gabby." She stroked her hair. "Tell me how you have been."

"Busy! Oh, Lita, I have many ideas for a show. Can I tell you about them?"

"Of course." The old lady's eyes grew alert. "Tell me and I will advise you."

"I want to do a show about equality. I want to create clothes to show the strength of women. Clothes that transcend gender limitations – clothes that will inspire."

"Do you have drawings?" asked the old lady.

"Yes, in my bag." Gabriella rushed over to her handbag. "Here, I'll show you." She pulled out colourful sketches of dresses and suits. She pointed out lines and suggested fabrics. Lita listened, her wise old face looking intently at each design.

"What do you think?" Gabriella looked nervous for a moment while she waited for her grandmother to speak.

Lita frowned and reached out to riffle through the pages. "I like the idea," she said. "I think that it is good. I would add in a dress that symbolises motherhood. A big, floaty dress. I would have a normal model wear it and then I would send that model out again with a bump, walking as confidently as before. Show the world that women can have it all. They have many identities and they can be what they choose. Pregnant or not, life goes on – you are still the same person." She sighed. "When I was younger, having children put a stop to careers and dreams. You were expected to marry and look after your family. Nowadays, women juggle both. Women can be good mothers and be successful. They can nurture and follow their dreams." Lita smiled. "I think this will be wonderful, Gabby. I'm proud of you."

Gabriella's eyes filled with tears. "Thank you," she said, hugging her. "You and Mama are my role models. You two are so strong. You survived after everything that happened to you. You carried on. I hope I'm like that."

"You are." Lita nodded sagely. "You are."

Magda appeared, wiping floury hands on an apron. "I'm making my orange cake, Gabby. I hope it turns out well."

"Oh, it will." Gabriella beamed at her. "I'm so happy to be home."

"Diego and the boys will be over later."

"Teresa?"

"Yes. Sophia has a dance lesson until half five, so she will be here after that."

Gabriella ambled into the kitchen. "Are we having Lita's stew?"

Magda nodded. "I hope I can do it justice."

"She's looking so old, Mama." Gabriella looked at her grandmother through the doorway.

Magda sighed. "Her strength is not like it used to be. Most days she just sits in that chair."

Gabriella's heart constricted. "I hate to think of her like that, Mama."

"I know." Magda looked sad. "Life has a cruel way of catching up on you. That is why I have news for you today."

Gabriella, who had been staring at her grandmother, whipped round. "News? What? Are you okay? Mama!"

Magda held up her hands. "I'm fine, I'm fine. It's not an illness, Gabriella." She leaned against the kitchen counter. "I gave in my notice last week. I'm retiring."

"Retiring?" The world slowed down.

Magda nodded. "Diego checked it out for me. I just turned sixty-six which means that I can claim full security benefit. I'm eligible for Medicare too. I'm so tired, Gabby. I'm tired of working. I think it's time that I hang my apron up and enjoy whatever life I have left."

Gabriella's eyes filled with tears. "Oh, Mama."

"Life has been good to me, but it has been hard. Every day I travelled out to that house and worked until my back ached. I could support myself and Lita on my pension. We won't be rich, but we will have enough. Maybe if I saved a little, I could travel to London to see you. I would love to meet your friends."

Gabriella took a seat at the kitchen table, her mind racing. Magda's retirement was wonderful news. It freed her from the evil clutches of Victoria and it meant that her mama could enjoy her life. She could get up when she liked and go for walks in the sunshine. She would no longer have to answer to anyone.

Magda busied herself scraping the cake mixture into the prepared tin.

"I feel so positive about this, Gabby. I think it will be the beginning of a new chapter. I won't have to answer to Her Majesty anymore!"

Isabelle was out when Gabriella got back to the apartment. Magda had pleaded with her to stay in her old bedroom at home, but she had reluctantly declined. She had an early start in the morning and the event venue was just a ten-minute walk from Isabelle's place.

Dropping her keys on the table, she went to the fridge and poured herself a generous glass of white wine.

Magda's news had knocked her for six. Victoria's threat had disappeared in a cloud of smoke. She no longer had any power.

The only problem was that life had moved on, as it inevitably does, and they were in different places. She had her job with Oberon and Hugo was God knows where. An ocean separated her old and new life and too much time had passed.

She felt unwelcome tears well up in her eyes. His image haunted her. She could see him sitting at this very table, his blue eyes crinkled with laughter. She cursed fate for robbing her of happiness.

It was too late. It was just too late.

Oberon was drinking a skinny latte and ordering models around when she got to work the next morning. Isabelle was late as she had stayed out the night before, partying with the crew from Marc Jacobs.

"*Gabriella!*" he yelled. "*Over here, now!*"

"Jeez!" She waved at Riku, who was on the phone.

Oberon focused in on her. "Blimey, you look awful. Late night?"

Gabriella shook her head. "I went to my mama's place. We had dinner."

"Fascinating." Oberon rolled his eyes. "Now, I need you to –"

"She's retiring soon," she said, cutting him off. "My mama, I mean. She's so happy." She felt something catch in her throat.

He stopped talking as comprehension dawned. "Oh. So, your sacrifice is no longer needed."

She shook her head miserably. "I feel so sad, you know? Like it was all such a waste."

"Hardly a waste, dearie. You got to work with me." He drained his cup and crumpled it with his fist. "Now, enough moping. We've got models to organise. We all know that collectively they have no brain and absolutely no sense of direction."

"Should I contact him?" she went on, not listening to his rant. "Should I contact him and explain?"

"No!" Oberon looked exasperated. "Forget him. Life has moved on. It was never meant to be."

"I don't mean that we should hook up. I mean, he's probably seeing someone by now." She rubbed her temple. "I just want to explain. I mean, what I did was pretty awful."

Oberon grabbed her shoulders and gave her a shake. "Ring him, call to him, hell, marry him for all I care! I'm no Doctor Phil, Gabby. Sort out your own crap. Just get it together and organise those models, or I really will lose the fucking plot!"

Isabelle shook her head. "Don't do it." She was standing in a robe, drinking a cup of green tea. The Alka-Seltzer she had taken was having no effect and she wore huge Dior glasses to hide her bloodshot eyes.

Gabriella sighed. "Why not?"

"You could get really hurt this time. He might not believe you over his mother."

"I'm not going to tell him about Victoria."

"What? You have to. Otherwise you can never move on. He'll always resent you for leaving."

"I just want us to be friends ..."

"Oh, please. This is me you're talking to. You're digging up the past, Gabs. I don't think it's a good idea." She waved at Ralph Lauren as he passed by. "God, he gets better with age," she reflected out loud.

359

"I just feel like it's unfinished business."

"Forget it. The drama that will follow you and Hugo would be immense. It will end in tears. Sometimes you've just got to accept that it was never meant to be."

Gabriella narrowed her eyes. "What if it were Raphael? How would you feel?"

Isabelle lowered her glasses and stared at her. "Why mention him?" she asked dangerously.

"Well, there's unfinished business there," she answered. "Do you not wish it had turned out differently?"

"I have Angelo now. I've moved on." Isabelle took a gulp of green tea. "Take my advice, Gabs. *Do not contact him.* You'll open Pandora's Box and there's no going back."

Gabriella called to Tara's gallery during her break the next day. It had been a couple of years since she'd been in the West Village and sometimes she missed her old life. There had been a safety in the continuity and regularity of her part-time jobs. She went to school, did her work and avoided drama. Now, her life was crazy with unpredictable hours and lots of air miles.

The door pinged and the familiar smell of oil paint and coffee hit her nostrils.

A small dark-haired man was behind the counter. He smiled as she approached.

"Can I help you?" he asked in an Italian accent.

"Is Tara around?" she asked smiling.

He shook his head. "She's in London, I'm afraid."

Gabriella chuckled. "London? That's so ironic. I just came from there."

"Ah, yes, that is, as you say, ironic." He looked amused. "Will I give her a message?"

She shook her head. "I just wanted to say hi. It's no big

deal." She noticed that the coffee machine had been replaced and the old oak desk had been replaced with a mahogany version. The leaflets and brochures were stacked neatly by the Mac and the diary was open on September. It looked much tidier than when Luca was around.

She smiled to herself. Mister Messy was what she called him sometimes. Back in the days when life was simple.

"Well, have a look around while you're here," said the man, snapping her out of her reverie. "We have Tara's new collection on display at the moment." He handed her a brochure. "It's inspired by the ocean. Tara is Irish, you know. She loves nature."

Gabriella smiled. "Thank you."

"She's moving it to London next week," he went on. "Then to Berlin."

"Oh?" said Gabriella impressed. "Thanks, I'll take a look."

She drifted away and looked at the various paintings and sculptures. There were seascapes and mountains. There was a stone carving of some Celtic rings and symbols. They looked wild and mystical and reminded her of her vision.

Suddenly her brain clicked into gear. Maybe she could collaborate with Tara and use images for the sets of her show? Bertie would be delighted to add another big name to his list. It would coincide beautifully with the exhibition in London too.

She made a mental note to message Luca with her plan. It would be good publicity for the gallery at Canary Wharf. Maybe Tara would attend and donate a piece for auction.

She walked down the street, soaking up the evening sunshine. The pavements were full of people, all chattering and moving, giving a buzz and sense of vitality to the neighbourhood. She stopped and looked at a street artist as he worked, sketching a picture of Freddie Mercury. Someone brushed against her and she moved sideways.

"Sorry," she said automatically, turning around to see who she had obstructed. All she saw was a man walking down the street, his frame hunched and his hands in his pockets. From the back, he looked familiar. She couldn't quite place it, but he reminded her of someone.

Suddenly, her phone rang.

"Hello?"

"Gabby! Where the hell is my Estée Lauder cream? I'm late for a meeting with Paolo."

"Try under the pile of clothes on your floor, Zsa Zsa." She hung up the phone and smiled. Her friend was like a walking tornado at the best of times.

ೞ Chapter Thirty ೞ

"So, what the hell have you been up to, Gabby? It's been so long!"

Celine looked the same. Her blonde hair was tied into a ponytail and she wore blue jeans and a Jim Morrison T-shirt. They had arranged to meet at a bar in the West Village as it was close to Skylight Clarkson Square, the venue for Fashion Week.

"I've been working," said Gabriella simply. "Oberon is a tough boss."

"I can imagine." She sipped her beer.

"How's the gallery?"

Celine's face lit up. "Oh, amazing! I love every moment of it. I'm so glad I stood up to Momma and went to Art school."

Gabriella said nothing, but her face hardened at the mention of Victoria.

"Any man on the scene?" asked Celine. "Surely you have some hot British guy by now?"

"No one special. I just have fun."

"What? I find that hard to believe. You were always a one-man kinda girl. Like when you were with my dear brother for example."

Gabriella stiffened.

"God, he was so blue after you took off to London, Gabs. He moped around for weeks."

"Oh?"

"But he's fine now. He's going out with Caroline Ashley Hamilton. Can you imagine? She's ensnared him at last."

"*What?*" Gabriella nearly dropped her glass.

"Yep," said Celine. "She wore him down. He seems happy enough, by Hugo standards, I mean. He's living in Boston now."

"Really?" she said, her brain whirring.

"Yeah, he took that job after all."

"Great," said Gabriella mechanically.

"And Momma told me about Magda! I'm so happy for her, Gabby. She's such a great lady."

"Sure, sure, she is."

"Momma is spitting, of course. She's allergic to finding a new maid. I suggested promoting Maria, but she was having none of it."

"*Hmmm,*" said Gabriella, still reeling over Caroline and Hugo.

"Anyway, how's Isabelle?" went on Celine. "She's mega-famous, right? I see her on TV all the time."

Gabriella pulled herself together. "Oh, she's good. We're staying at her apartment like old times."

"That's nice. I might join you if things get too much at home. Momma is constantly on my back about carbs and refined flour." She made a face. "That woman needs to seriously chill. The things that worry her."

"So, are you seeing anyone?" asked Gabriella, desperately trying to change the subject.

"Not really. There was this one guy in Chicago, but it didn't work out." She sipped her drink. "Hey, I might be in London this fall with work. Can I stay with you?"

Gabriella paused. "Well, my apartment is tiny and ..."

"Oh, it'll just be a couple of nights. We can have sleepovers like old times." She beamed at her.

"Well, okay, if you want ..."

"We must exchange numbers again. Your American one doesn't work anymore, right? I tried to find you on Facebook and Snapchat, but nothing turned up."

"I told you, I don't use social media. I have enough egotistical behaviour in my working day. The fashion world is like a filter on Instagram. Everything is modified and improved upon, creating an altered version of reality."

Celine put her head to one side. "Right," she said slowly. "You lost me at modified."

"So, how's life otherwise?" asked Gabriella. "How come you decided to go home for your vacation? I thought you'd head to Acapulco or somewhere."

"I'm tired of travelling. I have to fly all over the place with my job." She sighed. "Sometimes there's nothing better than your own bed." She rolled her eyes. "The only problem is that Hugo comes home every weekend to sail his stupid boat. Don't get me wrong, I love my brother, but it would be nice to be an only child for once."

"He comes to Long Island?"

"Sure. Hey, you guys should meet up." Celine raised an eyebrow. "You could be friends, right? I'm sure he's forgiven you for taking off that time."

Gabriella lowered her eyes, Isabelle's warning in her brain. "I don't think so," she said quietly. "It's been too long."

"Suit yourself." Celine opened her purse. "Another beer? I'm buying."

The week flew by as the Spring/Summer Collection 2018

was unleashed onto the world. Despite Proenza Schouler and Rodarte giving it a miss, the shows were a triumph. The sportswear by Michael Kors and the American-democracy-inspired outfits by Raf Simons for Calvin Klein had the crowd clapping in the aisles. Oberon's collection of leather-inspired couture got a standing ovation and he had a busy week giving interviews and partying with fellow designers.

Gabriella found that she was exhausted after the week and refused an invitation to a party in the village, hosted by Shayne Oliver. Isabelle had gone of course as she adored wrap parties.

Gabriella took off her clothes and stepped into the shower. She needed to relax and soothe her muscles which ached from hauling rails of clothes from one side of the auditorium to the other. Her mood had been sombre all week to say the least. Hugo filled her thoughts constantly and she tried her best not to think about him.

She had asked Oberon if she could stay in New York for a few extra days. She wanted to spend time with Teresa and the kids. Lita had offered to help her with her sketches and she yearned to walk down Knightsbridge Road and soak up the ambience of her home. She missed the Bronx: the New York twang, the bagels, the neon lights, and the Italian food on Arthur Avenue. She needed to reconnect with her culture and recharge.

Oberon scoffed when he heard her plans. "Reconnect with the Bronx? Bullshit, my love. You're going to meet that rich sailor boy."

"I am not!" she said passionately. "I have no intention of it!"

Drying her long hair with a towel, she put on her robe and some socks. Her phone lay on the coffee table, taunting her.

Suddenly she knew what she had to do. One message would do it. One small friendly note. The game had changed now. Victoria no longer had any power over her or her family. She googled him and his LinkedIn profile appeared. **Hugo du Maurier. Attorney-at-Law.** His handsome face stared back at her, his stance serious and professional. Her heart ached as she stared.

Then she opened her email and started to type.

Hey,

Long time no see! In New York all week with the fashion show and thought I'd say hi. I met Celine for a beer and she told me that you're doing well in Boston. I'm happy for you.

Staying around until Monday if you have a spare minute for a coffee or something.

Hope you're well.

Take care,

Gabby x

She reread the message and pressed 'send'. It was nice and friendly and breezy. Just the way she wanted it. It was just an attempt at a *rapprochement*.

Isabelle appeared in her head, wagging her finger. Hastily, she pushed that image away.

She had no ulterior motives. None at all.

At eight the next morning, she woke up suddenly. She picked up her phone and like lightning checked her emails. There were a few from Netflix and online shops. Nothing from Hugo.

She sighed and put the phone back on the locker.

He may not have seen it yet.

Of maybe he had and just didn't reply.

Closing her eyes, she blotted him from her mind. There

was no going back. The email had been sent and there was nothing she could do to change it.

London Fashion Week started the day after New York's. Five days of shows were scheduled that included designers like Bora Aksu, Burberry, Emporio Armani, and Mulberry. Oberon, flew back to London immediately and attended most of the shows. He liked to clock the competition and take notes. He emailed Gabriella constantly with images and ideas, telling her what to avoid and what to emulate.

He also sent her a plane ticket for the Monday morning and warned her to be at JFK no later than eight o'clock.

She texted her mother and told her that she would be home that evening and to have her bed ready.

She draped a pink chiffon scarf around her shoulders, adding a splash of colour to her outfit. She liked the gypsy look and with her Spanish colouring she pulled it off beautifully.

Ten minutes later, she herself was en route to the subway, wheeling her suitcase behind her. The sunshine was warm on her skin and she tilted her face upwards. It felt good to be home. Even that email she sent didn't dampen her mood.

She crossed the road and walked down the street, meandering through the crowd. Her suitcase hindered her speed, as it was awkward to haul through hundreds of pedestrians rushing by. She paused at some lights and waited for the green signal to walk.

Suddenly someone yanked at her pink scarf and she fell backwards. Stumbling, she fell on her suitcase and then onto the concrete.

"Are you okay, miss?" asked a concerned man in a suit.

She nodded, feeling dazed. He held out his hand and helped her to her feet.

"What happened?" she said in confusion.

"I'm not sure," replied the man. "You just tumbled."

The red light changed to green and the horde of pedestrians started to move forward. Gabriella, left with no option but to move, pulled her bag and walked unsteadily to the other side of the street. It was only when she reached the entrance to the station that she realised her pink chiffon scarf was missing.

Craning her neck, she tried to see if it was on the pavement on the other side of the road. It was difficult to see as there was an incessant sea of people crossing the road.

"Aw, man!" she said in annoyance. She loved that scarf. It must have fallen off when she fell, and blown away. There was no sign of anything pink anywhere.

Lowering the pulley handle on her suitcase, she started to descend the steps to the station.

Lita's old face lit up when she saw Gabriella approach. "You came home," she said, reaching up for a hug. "I'm so glad."

"Oberon gave me the weekend off," said Gabriella happily. "Where's Mama?"

"At the swimming pool," said Lita. "She goes to the YMCA every day now to swim."

"Really?"

"Yes, for the first time in years she has time for herself. She loved the water when she was a girl. She was very good at it."

Gabriella gazed at Lita. "I never knew that."

"Why would you? All you ever saw your mother do was work. Now, her time has come. Now, she can live again."

Gabriella walked into the small kitchen. "Would you like some tea?"

"No, *preciosa*. I'm okay." Lita held out her hand. "Can I see some drawings? I have been thinking about your vision and I think I can help."

"Sure!" Gabriella beamed at her. "I'll just make a coffee and we'll get on it."

Minutes later, Gabriella placed a steaming mug on the small coffee table and sat on the floor. Reaching into her bag, she pulled out a folder and spread some sheets of paper on the ground. Lita bent forward and peered at them.

"Hand me that one," she said, pointing to a sketch of a warrior queen on a horse. Her shrewd old eyes stare at the drawing. "I like the colour scheme. I love the red dress with the embroidery."

"Thanks, Lita," said Gabriella.

Her grandmother pointed to another page. "What's this one?"

Gabriella handed a drawing of a woman wearing a green toga with a golden torc around her neck.

Lita frowned. "Add something else that's golden. Set off the necklace. Maybe a crown or a bangle?"

Gabriella kissed Lita's soft cheek. "You are just the best," she said genuinely. "Thanks so much."

Two days passed like lightning. Teresa and Diego called over for dinner on the second night. Gabriella couldn't believe how tall the twins were. "Miguel is quarterback at school," Diego told her proudly. Salvador, the quieter twin, was excelling at science. Both boys looked at her shyly and proceeded to watch TV in the sitting room while the adults talked. Gabriella regarded her older brother with respect. He had raised those boys so well, despite having to do so alone.

Teresa was there, minus Rico her husband. Penny and Sophia had grown so much, Gabriella couldn't believe it. Even though she tried to FaceTime as often as possible, it wasn't the same.

They dined on fish with rice and a delicious custard tart. Magda, who looked relaxed and happy, thanked God that her family was together once more.

Gabriella told them of her show and Diego whistled. "This is your moment, Gabby. I bet you fifty bucks that you'll hit the bigtime after this."

Then there was a ping on her phone. She unlocked the home screen, expecting another message from Isabelle, and froze.

It was an email from Hugo du Maurier.

"Are you okay, Auntie Gabby?" asked Sophia, pointing at her. "You look funny."

"Oh, I'm fine." Gabriella plastered a smile on her face. "I'll be back in a second." She got up and went to her bedroom. Closing the door, she sat on the bed and accessed the message.

It read:

Meet me at the Vanguard tomorrow night. I'll be there at eight.

Hugo

She read it again and again, a smile forming on her lips. That bar was a place they had frequented when they were a couple. That had to be a good sign.

The thought of meeting him sent electricity bolts

through her veins. Hugging her phone to her chest, she said a silent prayer of thanks. She could make things right. God was giving her a chance to fix things.

She texted Isabelle, asking if she could stay at the apartment again. It saved her getting the subway back to the Bronx late at night. Especially as the Vanguard was in Manhattan.

Isabelle texted back saying that it was no problem and she hoped that she was behaving herself.

Gabriella took a deep breath. It would just be a couple of drinks and a catch-up. Nothing more.

She took the subway to 14th Street Station. She had chosen her outfit carefully: a mauve maxi dress, black strappy sandals and her usual bracelets and necklaces. Her long hair fell loosely down her back and her face wore minimal make-up. She walked into the famous bar through the red canopy at the entrance. The darkness inside made her squint, so it took her a minute to focus. It was half eight, so she expected him to be there. He had always been punctual when they were together. Sure enough, he was sitting with his back to her, over by the piano.

She walked towards him, her heart thumping in her chest.

"Hello, Hugo," she said breathlessly. "Sorry I'm late but it took longer to walk from Isabelle's than I thought."

He turned and she felt her legs give away. He looked exactly the same. The blue eyes stared at her intensely and she held onto the armrest of the chair for support. It had been so long – too long.

"Hi, Gabriella," he said formally. "Can I get you a drink?"

It was only then that she noticed the two glasses on the table. One beer and a glass of wine. White wine.

In a flash, she remembered Frank's party and the cold-white-wine debacle. She heard her before she saw her.

"Hello, Gabriella. Long time no see." Caroline, who had been in the ladies' room, walked up beside them. She looked different. Her blonde hair was tied up and she wore a navy suit that made her look older than her twenty-four years. In fact, her look reminded Gabriella of Victoria. A Louis Vuitton bag hung from her arm and a diamond bracelet sparkled in the dim lights of the club.

"Hi," said Gabriella in a tight voice. "Good to see you."

Hugo stared at Gabriella with an unfathomable look. "Drink?" he asked again.

Gabriella shrugged. "Just a white wine then."

He headed off to the bar.

"So," said Caroline, sipping her drink. "You're based in London, right?"

Gabriella nodded.

"Have I seen your work anywhere?" She smiled sweetly, but it didn't reach her eyes.

Gabriella shook her head. "Not yet."

"Right, *not yet*," Caroline repeated slowly. "Will we ever see it?" She laughed.

"Yes." Gabriella felt her hackles rise. "Definitely."

"*Hmmm.*"

Hugo arrived back and placed a glass of wine on the table. "I got you a Chardonnay. You used to like that ..."

"It's perfect." She smiled beatifically.

Caroline's gaze darted from Gabriella to Hugo and she scowled.

Hugo sat down again. "So, are you rich and famous yet?" he asked. "That was the plan, right? I mean, that's why you left New York."

373

Gabriella shook her head. "No."

"It's been what, three years? I thought you'd be heading Fashion Week at this stage."

She forced a smile. "I'm taking my time."

He raised an eyebrow. "Well, as long as it's worth it in the end," he said pointedly.

Gabriella felt tears well up in her eyes. He was being so cold. What did she expect? That they would lapse back into the Gabriella and Hugo of old? Bringing Caroline along was a low blow, but she could see why he did it. It was designed to hurt her and it had worked.

"So, we're thinking of buying a house on Martha's Vineyard." Caroline put her hand on Hugo's arm possessively, bringing the attention back to her. "Right next door to my uncle's place. Then Hugo could sail his little boat and it's very exclusive."

"That's great," said Gabriella, like a robot.

"Have you ever been to the Vineyard?" she went on. "Gosh, silly me. Of course you haven't."

"Caroline," said Hugo sharply.

"What? I'm trying to make conversation." Her eyes glittered.

Gabriella took a gulp of wine and coughed. "How's Boston?" she asked Hugo directly.

His face darkened for a moment and then resumed its impassivity. "It's great. Charlotte is based there too. She moved after the divorce."

"Is she okay?"

Hugo shrugged. "She was pretty heartbroken for a long time, but she's better now. I guess you've got to get on with things, right?" He stared at her.

"Right," she echoed, feeling uncomfortable.

Caroline stood up. "I'll be right back." She grabbed

her bag and headed up the stairs.

"Cigarette," explained Hugo. "She's addicted."

Gabriella bit her lip. There was so much she wanted to say. Caroline's absence gave her the perfect chance.

"Hugo," she began after they had sat for a long time in silence.

"Save it." He put up his hand. "I know why you emailed me. To ease your conscience."

"No, no, that's not it."

"Then why now?" His blue eyes searched hers.

She wanted to tell him about Magda's retirement. She wanted to explain everything but she couldn't. There was no point in implicating his mother at this stage. It would drag it all up and for what? He was obviously settling down with Caroline, buying houses and things. What good would the truth do now?

"I just miss you, I guess." She met his gaze. "I wish we could be friends. I'm sorry for the way I treated you. I really am."

He said nothing for a moment. Gabriella felt hot waves of mortification rise up her cheeks. Isabelle had warned her. Oh, why didn't she listen?

"Gabby, I ..." he said slowly, but stopped.

"What?" she asked gently. "Tell me, please."

"I ..."

Then his eyes focused on something over her shoulder. Caroline had arrived back already.

Gabriella got to her feet. "I've got to go," she said shakily. She pulled out her wallet and threw ten dollars on the table. "That's for my drink. Good evening."

"You're leaving?" said Caroline with feigned concern. "That's a shame."

"Goodbye." Gabriella turned on her heel.

"Gabby!" Hugo reached out to grab her arm, but she had walked away. Hot tears stung her eyelids.

Never try and recapture the past. It never worked out as you'd imagined.

The apartment building was deserted when she got back. Pressing the button, she called the elevator and rested her head against the cool tiled wall. Disappointment flooded her being. How naïve was she to think that they would pick up where they left off? Hugo was obviously still hurting and he was now with Caroline. That made him off-limits, despite her aversion to the girl. Maybe she should tell him her reasons for taking off that time? It certainly would change his opinion of her.

Common sense told her that it was a bad idea. He would have to choose between her and his mother and all hell would break loose. Maybe Victoria was right – maybe they just didn't suit each other. People liked to believe that love knew no boundaries and didn't care for background or rank, but it was a farce. Social rules and convention governed almost everything, including relationships. If she and Hugo were together, she would face discrimination for the rest of her days. She would never transcend the class divide and it would put huge pressure on their relationship.

The elevator arrived and the door opened. With a heavy heart, she pressed the button for the third floor and waited as it moved upwards. It pinged signalling its arrival at the destination and the doors opened once more. The corridor was dark and quiet. There wasn't a sound as she walked towards Isabelle's door. As she approached, she took her key out of her bag. Then just as she reached up to insert the key into the lock, the door opened slowly on its own. In slow motion she watched it move, her brain too shocked to process it.

She was positive she had locked it before she went out. She always checked it – it was routine.

With a beating heart, she walked into the apartment and turned on the light. The sitting room and the kitchen were deserted. She crept down to her bedroom and flung open the door. Again, there wasn't a soul to be seen. Isabelle's bedroom was empty too.

Puzzled, she walked back to the front door and checked if the lock had been forced open. It worked perfectly. She could have sworn she had locked it.

Closing the door, she pulled the safety latch and put it out of her mind. Everyone makes mistakes, right? Maybe in her excitement she had been careless.

◢ Chapter Thirty-One ◣

Isabelle was sitting by the pool at the Fasano hotel in Sao Paolo, sipping a cocktail and reading the latest Jilly Cooper novel. She had flown in to support Angelo as he prepared to race the Autódromo José Carlos Pace circuit. He'd had three practice runs and had just completed the qualifier. Now all that was left was the race itself which was scheduled for the next day. Brazil was the penultimate Formula One race of the season, with the last being held at the Yas Marina circuit in Abu Dhabi at the end of November.

She had opted for a lounger with a large umbrella as her pale skin tended to burn in the sun. Her red-gold bikini matched her long red mane and people pointed and stared, as she was instantly recognisable. From behind her large Prada glasses, she watched Angelo swim length after length of the pool, his muscles rippling as he moved. Their relationship was going so well. He was attentive and sweet and never told her what to do. Instead, he indulged her every whim and she relished it. Her daddy Patrick had spoiled her rotten as a child, so Angelo's adoration was welcome. It's just sometimes she wished that he would disagree with her. Her fiery temper remained inert and she couldn't remember the last time she'd lost the rag.

The evening before, he had returned from the practice runs of the circuit and they had dined under the stars. It was then, over a coffee for him and a Calvados for her, that he had suggested that they move in together.

Isabelle had been originally against the idea. She travelled a lot with her work and didn't really know where to call home. After some cajoling, she warmed to the idea and suggested living in her rent-controlled apartment in New York. Angelo had refused. He wanted a house with a garden and lots of bedrooms.

"Why?" Isabelle had asked in alarm.

"For the children, of course."

Cue a heated argument where Isabelle said that she had no plans at the moment to procreate as her job depended on her figure and she was pretty sure a baby would ruin that. Angelo had accepted her reasons but had warned her that he wanted kids someday.

They had compromised by choosing London as their base and opting for a large apartment in Kensington or somewhere similar as opposed to a house in the country.

Her phone rang and she saw Gabriella's name on the screen. "Hi, Gabby. What's up?"

"Zsa Zsa, when can you come to London? I need to do a fitting."

"I'm in Brazil with Angelo. I'm currently lying on a lounger by the pool."

"That's just great, but the show is in two weeks and I'm freaking out here."

A waiter appeared with a fresh cocktail and Isabelle flashed him a brilliant smile. "How about Tuesday?" she suggested.

"I guess it will have to do."

"You guess? Gabby! You sound like Oberon!"

"Sorry, it's just I'm super-stressed and I'm expecting a delivery of Tara's set designs today. Riku has the flu and Oberon has disappeared, leaving me to organise everything by myself."

"You're working too hard," chided Isabelle. "You have to stop or you'll burn out."

"I prefer to be busy."

"Gabby, being busy won't make things better. You need to deal with things."

"No."

"Okay, see you Tuesday, okay? I'll come down to Hackney."

"Enjoy your weekend."

"*Ciao.*"

Angelo sprang out of the water like a cat. His small black swimming trunks clung to his muscular thighs and his brown chest had a smattering of black hair. He was in tip-top shape and his dark curls bounced as he dried them with his towel.

"All okay?" he asked, lying down on a lounger beside Isabelle.

"Gabby needs me back in London."

"When?"

"By Tuesday. The gala is in a couple of weeks."

"I'm so sorry I can't make it that night." His brown eyes were sincere.

"I'm sorry that I can't make it to your race. I was looking forward to Abu Dhabi." She kissed him tenderly on the lips. "I hope you understand that I can't get out of it. It's a big night for Gabby and she needs me."

"Of course, of course." He kissed her hand. "You will be beautiful, my love. She's lucky to have you model for her."

"Drink, sir?" asked the waiter.

Angelo shook his head. "No, thank you."

Isabelle watched her boyfriend as he lay back and closed his eyes. He was so disciplined. He never touched a drop of alcohol during race season and stayed as fit as a fiddle. She, on the other hand, had developed a taste for the good life and sometimes found herself counting her units at the end of the week. There was always a party or an invitation somewhere. She knew she should decline, but she loved to socialise and shine. The first few days after the weekend tended to be hard. She found that excessive alcohol and the odd line of cocaine made her irritable and cranky. Then, by midweek, she was back on form again and raring to go.

She had always been a social butterfly – even at Parson's – but since her catapult into fame, she found herself relying on stimulants more and more. It made her feel good and lifted the threat of boredom behind closed doors. Sure, she was happy – she had achieved what she had set out to do. It was just sometimes she felt lost. Like the world was turning at a frantic rate and dragging her along with it. Angelo was away a lot and so she found herself hanging out with people she barely knew. Anything to stave off the loneliness.

She lay back on the lounger and closed her eyes. She needed to get a grip. She had a life most people dreamed of. It was her duty to enjoy it.

Gabriella draped a fur cloak over a headless mannequin in Oberon's storeroom along with the other outfits she had created. She felt a stomach-churning excitement when she thought of the gala. Bertie was back in London and had called the day before. He was busy organising the auction and wanted all the details of the show.

Aurora Sinclair's dress had been completed the week before and had been picked up. It had turned out beautifully. Like the Snow Queen from Narnia, Gabriella had designed a white-and-silver gown with beads and chiffon. Fitted at the waist, it had a full skirt that fell right to the ground. As it was almost Christmas, she felt it was a good look for Aurora, especially as Bertie had instructed her to sing a list of Christmas songs and hymns.

Luca had jumped at the chance to exhibit boards of his mother's work in the background. Her new collection had just hit Europe and needed as much publicity as possible. Tara had promised to fly in for the gala and donated a sculpture for Bertie to auction. It was turning out to be incredible and Gabriella was buzzing at the thought of it.

The only thing that marred her good mood was Hugo and the missed opportunity.

Isabelle hadn't said 'I told you so' when she heard. Instead she listened as Gabriella poured out her heart and lamented the missed chances.

"He shouldn't have brought that cow along," Isabelle said matter-of-factly. "He must have known that her claws would be out."

Gabriella had defended him, saying that she probably would have done the exact same thing in his position. That didn't make it any easier. Her heart ached when she thought of him and she longed to see him.

So, when she returned to London she threw herself into her work. It was the best way to avoid thinking about him. When she was bone-tired, she didn't have time to dwell on what might have been.

The gala was to be held at the Savoy in London and tickets were five hundred pounds each. The show had sold out, thanks to Bertie's tireless publicity and an impressive guest list that enticed others to come, for fear of missing out. The biggest security firm in London had been employed to police the event and a large red carpet was rolled out at the entrance to the iconic hotel.

Gabriella spent the two days before at the Savoy, organising her show. Isabelle had recruited seven well-known models from all over the world to give up their time to take part. Gabriella had lined them up and assigned outfits to each one, going by skin colour and hair style. When she was satisfied, she showed them the runway and instructed them on what to do.

Tara Jacob had flown in to supervise the backdrops which were huge prints of her new collection. Crashing waves and mountain scenery gave a mystical feel and Gabriella was thrilled with it. It had been years since she had seen her old boss and over a coffee at Starbuck's they caught up, gossiping like old times.

"So, you've really hit the big time," said Gabriella, tracing the rim of her cup. "Everyone knows your name now."

"It took long enough," said Tara drily. "I mean, it's twenty-five years since I started training under Marcus Chensky."

Gabriella made a face. "I hope it doesn't take me that long. I've been with Oberon for three years now."

Tara shook her head. "Times are different now, Gabby. Tomorrow night will make you, there's no doubt about that. With social media, you'll be a household name in seconds." She sighed. "When I was with Marcus, publicity was a twenty-four-hour job. We didn't have the advantages you have now."

"I avoid social media. I hate it."

Tara raised an eyebrow. "Well, that's something you'll have to change. It is the way forward, Gabby. Surely you see that. You just have to be on the pulse nowadays. Go home and set up an Instagram, Twitter and Facebook account."

"It's such hassle, Tara. If I do that, then I'll have to check it constantly and upload photos. I'm really not into it."

"That's the price of fame, my love. You have to put yourself out there. Keep it strictly business – only posts to do with your brand."

"Is Luca coming to the show?" asked Gabriella, changing the subject.

Tara nodded. "He's flying over tomorrow morning with Colin and Lydia."

"Sienna?"

"No. Helen, Lydia's mom, is looking after her."

"Colin promised to do a big piece in his magazine." Gabriella made a Sign of the Cross. "I hope he likes it."

Tara took her hand and squeezed it. "He'll love it. He's been tweeting about it all week saying that you're the next best thing."

"Really?"

"Yes, really. You'd know this if you had a bloody Twitter account."

"Okay, okay." She held up her hands. "I'll sort it out."

"Good. Now, enjoy this anonymity. Soon, you'll be papped wherever you go."

Oberon called over after lunch and rearranged the stage. Then, staring at the storyboard, he shook his head. "Leave Isabelle until the end. Couple her entrance with a crescendo of music. She's the star – she's the one people want to see. Send the minions out first and then finish with your best outfit on your best model."

"But if she came out first –" protested Gabriella.

"Gabby!' He glared at her. "No offense, but you're yet but a child in this world. Listen to Daddy. Do as I say."

When Isabelle arrived for a dress rehearsal later in the afternoon, Gabriella tried it Oberon's way. It was perfect. As much as she hated to admit it, he was absolutely right. She knew that he was as nervous as she was. She was his protégée after all. If this show was a disaster, it would reflect badly on him.

Gabriella launched herself on social media and in three hours had amassed fifty followers. She tweeted about the gala and how excited she was and it was retweeted by two fashion bloggers. Encouraged, she posted a picture on Instagram of a rough sketch of her vision and it received lots of likes.

Oberon rang her as she was creating her Facebook page.

"Hashtag everything, darling," he said. "Especially on Instagram. I'll get Riku to set up a website tonight. It will be basic but it will suffice for the initial rush."

"Rush?"

"Of orders, you idiot. People will want your stuff after the gala."

"Oh my God!"

"Now, tweet about me and say how fabulous a mentor I am."

"Are you serious?"

"Of course I'm serious. It's called giving back. I know I don't need publicity but it never hurts."

She giggled. "You got it, bossman."

☙ Chapter Thirty-Two ❧

The day of the gala dawned. The security company that Bertie had hired had been setting up cameras and checking all exits in the hotel since early morning. Dressed in black, they were predominantly big muscular men with earphones. As the guest list was filled with names of the rich and famous, Bertie was taking no chances.

Gabriella's show was scheduled first, then a singing performance by Aurora Sinclair. There was a sit-down meal of tuna ceviche, fillet steak and Eton Mess, followed by the auction conducted by Bertie. It was all in aid of Cancer Research so the donations had been generous.

"Almost everyone I know has been touched by that awful disease," Bertie had said in his press release on Sky News the week before. "The human race has done incredible things throughout history and I'm sure we can defeat this pestilence too, given the right amount of funding."

Riku had posted many updates on Oberon's website about Gabriella's début and there was a buzz in the fashion world. She could quite possibly be the next big thing and she must have talent if she got to showcase her work at such an event as Bertie's gala. Slowly but surely, fashion bloggers and journalists began to tweet about

Gabriella. This only added to her nerves the day of the show. Crippled with anxiety, she refused breakfast and instead opted for a cup of hot water with a slice of lemon. It was make or break time. She was putting herself on the world stage and would have to weather the criticism.

Isabelle met her outside the Savoy at three o'clock, her red hair wrapped in a Hermès scarf and wearing a full-length brown faux-fur coat.

"You look like you're going to hurl," she observed with a grin.

"Thanks," said Gabriella grimly. "You're used to all this attention. What if they hate my work?"

"Then they hate your work," said Isabelle practically. "You can't control other people's opinions, but you'll never know unless you try."

They walked into the foyer and were immediately set upon by two beefy security guards. "Passes?" one grunted.

Gabriella held up the card that hung around her neck. Isabelle retrieved hers from her bag.

"Go on through," said the other, waving them along.

Bertie was in the function room, instructing the waiters on the flower arrangements.

"Darlings!" he said, opening his arms wide. "Two hours to kick off. Are we excited?"

Gabriella tried to quell the butterflies that were racing around her stomach.

Isabelle took off her coat and draped it on a chair. "Gabby here is about to collapse."

Bertie patted Gabriella's back. "Chin up," he said with a smile. "You must have more faith in yourself, my love."

"Thank you for putting me up," said Isabelle, kissing his cheek. "Soon I'll have my own place so I won't have to annoy you any longer."

"Nonsense," said Bertie. "Annoy me anytime, my sweet. I love having guests."

"Angelo is sorry to miss it."

"Perfectly understandable. Wish him luck in the race."

Aurora Sinclair appeared, holding some sheet music and with her dark-brown hair in rollers. Gabriella gasped. Aurora's photos didn't do her justice – next to Isabelle, she was the most beautiful girl she'd ever seen.

"Bertie," said Aurora in her clear voice. "Will I sing 'All I Want for Christmas Is You' as my encore?"

Bertie clapped his hands together. "Why, yes! That would be splendid."

Aurora smiled at Gabriella. "You look like you want to throw up. Don't worry at all. You're so talented. I absolutely adore my gown for this evening."

Isabelle punched her playfully in the arm. "See? You need to chill, Gabs."

Harry Finkelman, Bertie's and Aurora's agent, walked up and nodded at the group. He was a small Jewish man with a balding head, a hooked nose and a gold signet ring on his little finger. Born and bred in New York, he had that hardness that only a true New Yorker possessed. He held up his phone.

"Bertie, I got Meryl Streep on the line. She wants two extra tickets."

Bertie shook his head. "No can do, I'm afraid. We're packed to capacity."

Harry thrust his phone into Bertie's hand. "You tell her."

Bertie turned around, gesticulating as he spoke. "Sorry, my darling ..." he said as he walked away.

"Hey, Lady Mary," said Harry to Aurora. "How many songs you gotta sing?"

"Seven plus an encore," answered Aurora.

"Make it count, kid. This is the night to shine." He walked off after Bertie so as to retrieve his phone.

"Lady Mary?" said Isabelle in confusion. "Why does he call you that?"

Aurora smiled. "What with my posh accent, he thinks I resemble Lady Mary Crawley from *Downton Abbey*. He's always called me that."

"So you share an agent with Bertie?" said Gabriella enviously. "That's pretty awesome."

"Yes, Harry is wonderful," agreed Aurora. "Tough, but fair." She held up her hand and waved. "See you later. I'm off home to get my hair styled and get into my gorgeous Gabriella gown."

Isabelle picked up her coat. "I'd better hit make-up. Get in before the rush of models."

Gabriella nodded. "Let's go backstage and I'll set you up. Your outfit is on a special rail."

Bertie appeared again, wiping his brow. "I loathe disappointing people, I really do."

Isabelle patted his arm. "It would be worse if there were tickets left over."

"True. It's down to the wire though. I hope everyone who bought one will turn up. It would be just like Raph not to show at the last minute ..."

Isabelle froze. "Raph?" she repeated slowly.

Bertie nodded and his eyes were kind. "Raphael emailed at the last minute and said he would fly in. His grandmother died of cancer so it is a cause close to his heart."

"Right." Isabelle looked pale.

"You're okay with that, I hope." Bertie took her hand in his. "You said in Monaco that you were over it all."

"I am, I am."

"Wonderful. Now, I must dash. The ice sculpture is due at any moment and I want to make sure it's what I ordered."

Isabelle stared at her reflection in the full-length mirror backstage.

No one had mentioned that Raphael was coming. No one had warned her.

Raphael didn't like social events. He didn't go to parties. Everyone knew that he avoided nights like this like the plague. Yet, he was coming.

She cursed silently. She hadn't seen him in the flesh since that night she left him. The only images she had seen since had been in newspapers or on social media. Like all shocking news, it had taken a while to sink in. Closing her eyes, she remembered. The sound of his voice, the feel of his warm skin against hers, his large hands exploring her body. Then she cried silently, aching for a man that had broken her heart.

Gabriella called her name and she took a deep shuddering breath. She would not let him affect her like this. She had to be professional. She had to go out there and do what she did best.

If only Angelo was with her. If only he didn't have that race in Abu Dhabi. With him by her side, she could face a thousand Raphaels.

"*Zsa Zsa!*" Gabriella called again. "I need you in make-up."

"Coming, Gabby," she answered, straightening her shoulders. "I'll be right there."

Colin, Lydia and Luca reached the main entrance of the famous hotel. A crowd was outside, all contained behind iron gates. Phone cameras flashed as they walked by. Luca, with his blonde beauty, was definitely someone.

Colin sucked in his cheeks and posed.

A young girl waved. "*Can you take a selfie with me?*" she called.

Colin clapped his hands. "Of course!" He took the phone from her grasp and angled it so as to get his best side.

"Who are you anyway?" asked the girl.

Colin winked at her. "A famous journalist."

"Oh."

A large security guard dressed all in black held up his hand. "Passes?" he boomed, his walkie-talkie buzzing.

Colin held up his pass. "I'm Press," he said haughtily.

Lydia rummaged in her clutch bag for the laminated cards. "Here are ours," she said, flashing them at the man.

"Go on through." He waved them along.

"Has Emma Thompson arrived yet?" asked Colin excitedly. "I adore her!"

The guard ignored him and turned his back.

The crowd cheered loudly, screaming and stamping their feet.

Aurora arrived next. Harry, her agent, had instructed her to mingle with fans and talk to journalists. Hand in hand with her photographer boyfriend James, she walked up the red carpet, smiling and waving.

"*Miss Sinclair!*" shouted a man from BBC News. "*Any information on your set list tonight?*"

Aurora beamed at him. "I will be singing some Christmas hymns and songs, ranging from 'Silent Night' to 'Fairytale of New York'. Bertie wants it to be festive."

"Who will be Shane McGowan to your Kirsty MacColl?"

"Bertie, of course. He's been practising for weeks." She flashed a brilliant smile.

"Who are you wearing?" asked a woman from Sky News.

"Gabriella," answered Aurora, doing a small pirouette. "She's the hottest designer out there. She even donated all the outfits from her show tonight to Bertie so he can auction them off."

"Gabriella? She's showcasing tonight?"

"Yes, she trained under Oberon."

"Oh, right." The woman wrote something down on a notepad. "When's the film out?"

"The New Year," said Aurora, moving along.

George Clooney sidled up behind her, his wife Amal stunning in red. The press surged forward, shouting his name and holding out microphones.

Colin and Lydia stared at Tom Hardy in awe.

"He looks better in the flesh," said Lydia in wonder.

"Totally," agreed Colin.

A waiter handed them a glass of champagne each and they were ushered through to the function room. Bertie had decorated it like Narnia. Huge chandeliers had been adorned with snowflakes and stalactites, the round tables were covered in white cloth and silverware. Gift bags, donated by various companies, sat at each place. Lydia checked the seating plan and was gratified to see that they had been seated with Luca's mother Tara, Oberon, Riku, James Dixon, Aurora Sinclair, Isabelle, Gabriella, and Raphael Baptiste.

"Col!" she whispered loudly. "That French director is at our table."

Colin peered at the list of names. "*Oh là là!*" he said approvingly. "He's a fine thing. This night is getting better and better."

By seven o'clock, the function room was full. Well-known faces sat at each table, chatting and laughing. Wineglasses were full and plates of canapés were circling, distributed by waiters in black-and-white suits.

Tara sat next to Luca, her red hair piled on her head. Her blue gown was fitted and her fingers wore no rings.

"What's first?" she asked conversationally.

"Gabriella's show," said Colin, scanning the menu. "I'm hungry now, I have to say."

"When do you sing?" Tara asked Aurora, who was sitting on her left.

"Right after that," she answered, her beautiful face smiling. "Then we eat, and afterwards Bertie will do the auction."

"I heard that Angelina Jolie gave him a Louis Vuitton special edition bag to auction off," said Colin with a sigh. "I'd love it."

"So, bid for it then," said Luca. "You have enough money."

Colin shook his head. "No can do, I'm afraid. Val has banned me from spending money on designer stuff. Talk about a ball and chain."

"You poor thing," mocked Lydia.

Tara sipped her wine. "There's no sign of Oberon or that Raphael guy," she said, gesturing to the empty seats.

"Oberon is backstage with Gabby," said Luca. "He's helping her organise the models."

"I can't wait to meet Oberon again," said Colin. "What an icon!"

"That icon shouted at you for making too much noise one time," said Lydia. "He seems like a bit of a bitch, if I'm honest."

"Artistic temperament." Colin sighed. "If I had one ounce of his talent!"

Luca pointed to a tall man at the entrance of the room. He had long brown hair and dark eyes. Dressed in a black suit, his shirt was open at the collar. "Isn't that Raphael Baptiste now?"

Colin's head swung around. "It is! *Wow*, he's gorge."

"What would Val say?" chided Lydia. "You're a married man now, Col."

Colin made a face.

Raphael ran his fingers through his hair and looked around wildly.

Bertie, on seeing his old friend, rushed over and opened his arms. "Raph! Good to see you, old boy. I didn't think you'd show."

"You must have more faith in me," he answered in his deep voice.

"Quite." Bertie grinned. "Now, follow me."

They walked over and Bertie pulled out a chair. "Everyone, this is my good friend, Raphael Baptiste. Raphael? This is ... um, everyone." He gestured loosely at the table.

"He so doesn't remember our names," whispered Colin to Lydia.

"Hello, I'm Tara Jacob." Tara stood up and held out her hand. "I loved your last film. Congratulations on the Oscar nomination."

Raphael nodded briefly. Luca stood up and shook his hand and Lydia waved. Colin grabbed Raphael's big hand and shook it vigorously. "*Enchanté!*" he said, his cheeks pink. "I love your work."

"Hello," said Raphael, retrieving his hand and sitting down.

"Wine?" asked a waiter immediately.

Raphael's face tightened. "*Non*," he said quietly.

394

"So, are you working on a film right now?" asked Tara.

Raphael nodded. "It's a story about Napoleon. I've always wanted to make a film about him."

"That sounds interesting," said Tara, "and so patriotic. Will it vilify him?"

"I hope not."

"He was a complex character," said Lydia. "I mean, a genius. There's no doubt about that. But his hubris let him down in the end."

"Perhaps." Raphael tore open a bread roll. "I hope to show both sides and let the audience make up their minds."

Riku appeared, looking frazzled. "I'm done with backstage," he said, flopping down on his chair. "There's nothing else to be done."

"How's Gabby?" asked Luca. "She's been so nervous all day."

"Green," said Riku, accepting a large glass of wine from Colin.

"I hope it goes well," said Lydia. "She deserves it."

"Are you nervous?" Colin asked Aurora.

She smiled. "Not really. I used to sing hymns at Christmas in my local church when I was little."

A dark-haired man with stubble arrived, a camera slung over his shoulder. He was handsome in his suit and waved at the group. It was Aurora's boyfriend, James.

"Hi, everyone."

"James!" said Aurora. "Sit over here." She patted the seat next to her.

He leaned down and kissed her softly on the lips. "Sorry I took so long."

"All okay backstage?" she asked.

"Great. Oberon is ordering everyone around and Gabriella is quite calm. All's good."

Raphael held out his hand. "Raphael Baptiste," he said in his deep voice.

"James Dixon." They shook hands.

"Well done on that Oscar nomination," said James. "You were robbed in the end."

"Thanks," said Raphael.

"How's the photography work?" asked Colin.

"Never better," answered James. "I'm constantly on the move, meeting the rich and famous."

"I love my wedding photos," said Lydia wistfully. "You did such a great job that day."

James grinned. "An all-expenses trip to Venice? Thank *you!*"

Bertie stood up and clapped for attention. "*Silence, my darlings!*" he called. "*Silence! I need to say a few words!*"

The noise died down and everyone turned their attention to Bertie.

"Thank you all for coming this evening. I know I stalked you with emails and phone calls, but it was worth it in the end. We have made thousands in ticket sales alone."

Everyone clapped.

"Tonight we will be entertained in many ways. First with a fashion show by the up-and-coming designer Gabriella. She has generously donated her début collection to the cause tonight and has given me permission to auction off her designs."

There was a gasp from the crowd.

"So, don't hang around, ladies," continued Bertie. "She will be huge," he added from behind his hand conspiratorially.

"That will be followed by a beautiful singing performance by the exquisite Aurora Sinclair!"

The crowd clapped.

Lydia watched Raphael as he drummed his fingers on the table. He didn't seem to be listening to a word that Bertie said. Instead, he was glancing around nervously, as if he expected someone to appear at any second.

"After that we shall dine on a delectable meal prepared by the dedicated staff here at the Savoy."

More clapping.

"Then there will be an auction of terrific prizes donated by many of you here tonight. I will conduct it myself and I urge you to dig deep. Who wouldn't want a private guitar lesson with Ed Sheeran?"

The crowd laughed as Ed Sheeran himself gave Bertie a thumbs-up.

"So, without further ado, I give you – Gabriella."

The lights went down and all you could hear was the beat of a drum. It resonated through the large room and there were surprised murmurs from the audience as they waited for something to happen.

The runway was a red carpet down the centre of the room and had tables of guests on each side. Gabriella straightened the silver dress on her first model, Lola Madero.

Oberon stood in the background, his haughty face impassive. He had been a huge help in those final moments.

Now, she was ready. Now was the time.

"Good luck," Gabriella mouthed to Lola as the music reached a crescendo.

The lights illuminated the room and Lola took off. Staring straight ahead, she strutted down the red path, her posture erect and proud. Her green gown left one shoulder bare. Her black hair was in a long braid down her back and her eyes were painted with silver.

The crowd clapped as she made her way back to Gabriella and then the next model, Andromeda, took her place.

"Thank you," said Gabriella to Lola as she passed by. "You were awesome."

Colin pointed at the fourth outfit and shook his head in wonder. "I'm loving the look!" he enthused. "So tribal. So wild."

Lydia nodded in agreement. "They're really imaginative, yet wearable."

"Oh, totally," said Colin. "Fashion has to be realistic. Remember that bridal show we went to in Dublin with the swan dress? With the tail and the fur? What self-respecting bride would ever walk down the aisle in that?"

James was taking photos of each model as they walked, shooting their outfits from various angles. Every now and then he would pause and check the small screen on the back of his Nikon, making sure that the frame was correct.

Raphael was staring at the runway, a muscle twitching in his cheek. Six models appeared, one after the other, and he didn't take his eyes off them for a second. Then came the finale. The lights dimmed once more and a screen was lowered at the top end of the red carpet. When the lights were switched back on, there was a silhouette behind the screen. It was the profile of a woman, bending down. As the music started to build, the woman straightened up and threw back her long hair. All the crowd could see was her silhouette.

"Isabelle," said Raphael softly.

Slowly the screen lifted and revealed Isabelle dressed in a sleeveless white gown with a silver bodice. Her long red hair was loose with two braids on each side of her head. Her eyes were circled heavily with black kohl and her lips were blood-red. Her bare arms were covered in blue spiral drawings and there was a blue triquetra on each of her cheeks. Two models appeared at either side and handed her a spear and a shield.

Putting her shoulders back, she closed her eyes and waited.

"So cool," said Colin in awe. "She's like a Celtic queen. Look at her body art! I love it."

The music reached a crescendo and then Isabelle began to walk in a straight line. Perfectly in time with the music, her hips swayed as she moved. Her face was haughty and her eyes fixed ahead, the shadows falling on her cheekbones as she walked. At the end of the runway, she paused and turned, her dress billowing out behind her. The crowd gasped as her gown was completely backless and painted onto her smooth back was a huge intricate Celtic design going all the way down her spine.

Raphael stared at her intently. His eyes never left her as she walked.

The crowd clapped loudly. Then she disappeared.

Gabriella threw her arms around Isabelle's neck. "You were wonderful, Zsa Zsa! Oh my God, you owned it!"

Oberon nodded. "Good work."

Isabelle felt her hands shake. Yes, she had been the consummate professional. Yes, she had walked like she was the supermodel she was trained to be. But part of her knew that Raphael was in the audience. Even though she hadn't seen where he was, she knew he had been watching her. She didn't know why, but she knew.

"Great job," said Lola as she walked by.

"Thanks," said Isabelle. She felt her heart sink. She had to face out now and have dinner. Raphael would be there. Bertie had said so.

Suddenly she couldn't face it. She couldn't face him and the past.

"Gabs?" she said, tugging her friend's sleeve.

"Yeah?" Gabriella's eyes were shining with happiness as people congratulated her over and over.

"I'm not feeling so good. Do you mind if I go home?"

"Are you sure? God, is there anything I can do?" Gabriella looked concerned.

"It's just a tummy thing. I'll call you in the morning."

"Aw, Zsa Zsa. Try and stay out. It will be a great night."

Oberon grabbed Gabriella's sleeve. "Come on," he said briskly. "There's press waiting."

"So, I'll see you tomorrow." Isabelle backed away.

"Sure, sure. You go home to bed. Thank you so much for modelling." Gabriella was addled and couldn't focus.

"I wouldn't have missed it."

Oberon tapped his foot impatiently. "Come *on!*" he said in exasperation, yanking at Gabriella.

Bertie was approaching and Isabelle backed away. "I'm going to leave before I have to explain myself."

"I'll text you." Gabriella was being pulled in another direction by a model. "Mind yourself."

Gabriella walked into the function room with Oberon, just as Bertie was welcoming Aurora onto the stage.

"Ah, the wonderful duo Gabriella and Oberon are joining us!" he said, clapping.

Luca stood up, his handsome face delighted. "Amazing,

Gabs," he said, clapping. "This is only the beginning."

She took her designated seat next to Tara and sighed. "Thank God it's over. I hate being in the limelight."

"Too late for that," said Colin. "You're all over Twitter." He brandished his phone at her.

Feeling slightly overwhelmed, Gabriella accepted a glass of white wine gratefully from Lydia.

"Where's Isabelle?" asked Raphael abruptly. "That seat next to you is for her."

Gabriella stared at him for a moment. "She's not feeling too well. She left."

"Left?" he repeated. "Why? Where?"

"Home." Gabriella's tone was final. There was no way she was telling him where Isabelle was staying. Despite Isabelle's denial that she felt nothing for him, Gabriella suspected that there was still unfinished business.

Oberon glanced at the menu. "Oh Christ, they're serving ceviche? I loathe ceviche."

Colin stared at him in awe. "I'm sure you could get something else," he said.

Oberon focused in on him. "Who are you?" he asked rudely.

"Me? I'm Colin. We've met. You told me to shut up one time at your studio. It's so cool to meet you again."

Oberon raised an eyebrow. "Right," he said, uninterested.

Raphael got to his feet and threw down his napkin. "Goodnight," he said curtly to the occupants of the table.

"You're leaving?" said Colin in dismay. "We can't afford to lose an A-lister like you! You are so upping our profile at this event."

But Raphael had already gone. Straight up to Bertie who was standing on a small podium with Aurora.

"So, without further ado," said Bertie into the

microphone, "I give you Aur–"

"Bertie!" Raphael pulled him off the stage. "Where's Isabelle?"

"What? Who?" Bertie straightened his jacket. "Steady on, old boy. You nearly sent me flying."

"Isabelle!" said Raphael again. "Where is she?"

"Getting changed?"

"*Non!* Gabriella said she left. Do you know where she's staying?"

Bertie said nothing for a moment. "She's with Angelo now, Raph. She's happy."

"Bertie!"

"Leave her be."

"Tell me now!' He clutched his hair in frustration. "I just need to speak with her. Please."

Bertie stared at him. "She's at my place," he said finally.

Raphael patted his back. "Thank you."

402

❧ Chapter Thirty-Three ❧

Colin smiled at the Greek waiter as he filled his glass of wine. "Thank you," he said.

Lydia refused a refill and asked for water instead. "I have to pace myself," she said. "I'm not used to all this wine before a meal."

"No soakage," said Colin. "We'll be a disgrace if we're not careful."

"Says he who just got a refill." Lydia shook her head. "You'll be in an awful state, Col."

But Colin wasn't listening. "Look at Raphael leaving. Honestly," he tutted, pointing at the door. "Just as Aurora is about to sing and everything."

Gabriella looked around sharply. "He's leaving?"

Colin nodded. "He's quite odd, isn't he?"

Riku shrugged. "Maybe there's an emergency or something."

Gabriella was about to get up and quiz Bertie when the lights went down and a single spotlight shone on Aurora. A grand piano stood beside her and Elton John began to play 'O Holy Night'. Soon Gabriella forgot about everything else as Aurora's clear voice soared above them. The purity of the notes made the hairs on her skin stand on end.

"She's magnificent," said Tara to James.

He nodded, his eyes never leaving Aurora for a second. "That song is the first thing I ever heard her sing," he said, a faraway look on his face. "I couldn't believe her talent."

The song came to an end and the room erupted.

"What a star!" Bertie enthused.

Aurora smiled beatifically and waited for the room to quieten down. "Next I would like to sing a modern classic. 'The Power of Love' by Frankie Goes to Hollywood."

Gabriella felt something clutch her heart. She loved this song. She loved every word. Hugo filled her mind and she closed her eyes. If only he was here to witness her triumph. If only.

Isabelle stood in Bertie's guest shower and let the water beat down on her head. It had taken ages to clean the blue paint off her skin. She had made the right call. Staying at the Savoy would have been madness. Seeing him again would have been crazy.

Squeezing the droplets from her long hair, she stepped out into the bathmat and rubbed her body vigorously with a large towel. Angelo had called saying that his practice circuit went well and that he had the qualifying race the next evening. The actual Formula One race was scheduled for sundown on Sunday and then the season would be over.

"Then we can start looking for an apartment," he had said, before hanging up.

She felt guilty that she wasn't with him, but she had promised Gabriella that she would model for her début. It was just unfortunate timing.

Bertie had a chef and a housekeeper, but both were long gone home. The house was empty with only the security cameras keeping an eye on things.

Wrapping herself in a terry robe, she took advantage of the solitude and walked downstairs to the living room. There she found a fully stocked bar. Taking a cut crystal tumbler from the shelf, she filled it with vodka and knocked it back.

"*Ugh!*" she winced, grimacing at the taste. Reaching up, she filled it again. A few drinks and she would switch off. A few drinks and she would fall into a dreamless sleep.

Her phone pinged but she ignored it. She didn't want to check the internet. She would be splashed all over it, no doubt.

It was funny – in the beginning she fell on every single mention like an addict, gazing at pictures and reading articles about herself. She lived for the publicity and the coverage. She checked Google every day to see if there were any new references.

Then she started to resent it. She started to fear what she would see or read. One time there was a picture of her crying outside a club, her face streaked with make-up. The headlines had been speculation and gossip as no one knew the real reason for her tears. Everyone presumed it was her public break-up from the rapper Cicero, but in fact it was the night she had heard her grandmother had died. The media was merciless. It took one's life and plastered it across the world without much truth behind it.

Bertie thanked Aurora for the fifth time.

"Now everyone, time for some nosh. I'm sure you're all sufficiently drunk by now to spend obscene amounts of money in the auction later."

The line of waiters stood poised and ready to serve the starters.

"*Bon appétit!*" said Bertie with a small bow. "I will address you anon."

Gabriella waved him over to their table, which wasn't far from the podium. He smiled and walked over.

"How's everyone?" he asked, beaming.

"Bertie! Where's Raphael?" asked Gabriella in an undertone.

Bertie didn't quite meet her eyes. "Why do you ask, my love?"

"He just took off."

"I'm not sure …"

"Did you tell him where Zsa Zsa is?" She regarded him steadily.

He paused and then nodded. "Yes, I had to."

Gabriella threw up her arms. "Jesus, Bertie! You know where he's gone now!"

"Maybe not," he soothed. "I know he's at the Goring. Maybe he's gone back to his hotel room. You know he hates parties."

Gabriella snorted. "Yeah, right. You know that's not true."

"Anyhow, I must dash. My ceviche will get cold."

"Ceviche *is* cold!" shouted Gabriella in exasperation as he scampered away. As quick as lightning she texted Isabelle, warning her that Raphael might call. Pressing 'send', she waited for the habitual instantaneous reply, but none came.

Please see the message, she pleaded silently.

Isabelle lay on the couch with her eyes closed. Her hair was still wrapped in a towel turban and she still hadn't gone back upstairs to change into her nightie. She was on her third vodka and was toasty warm in her robe. This was a million times better than a noisy gala. Maybe one more drink and then bed.

The doorbell rang and echoed through the empty house. She sat upright, startled. Bertie hadn't mentioned any other guests. She got up and walked to the hallway where there were five CCTV screens mounted on the wall.

She inhaled sharply.

Raphael was standing on the threshold.

What should she do? He was probably looking for Bertie, right? Deep down she knew that wasn't the case. Raphael knew that Bertie was at the Savoy. He had come to see her.

The doorbell rang again and she placed her trembling hand on the door handle. Once she opened it, there was no going back.

Using her free hand, she opened the three locks above the handle. Raphael pushed the door in and then he was there, standing in front of her. His dark eyes stared at her intently.

"Isabelle," he said softly.

She closed her eyes. How she loved the way he said her name. *Eeezabelle.*

"What do you want?" she asked guardedly, stepping backwards.

"I wanted to see you," he said frankly. "It's been so long."

"Why?"

"I think about you ..." He ran his fingers through his hair. "I dream of you ... when Bertie asked me to come and I saw that you would be there, I had to accept. I don't know why, but it was time. It was time for us to meet again."

"No," she said, pushing him backwards. "No way. You've got to leave."

"Please ..."

"No, you can't do this. It's over. We're over. I'm happy now."

He grabbed her shoulders with his big hands and forced her to look at him. "Tell me you don't think about me. Tell me that you've forgotten it all."

"I don't think about you," she said mechanically. "I never think about you."

"Liar," he said, giving her a gentle shake.

"You need to leave," she said, trying to break free. "You need to leave me be."

"I can't," he said simply. "I can't, Isabelle. I can't think of anything else."

"No ..."

"You want me. I can see it in your eyes," he continued. "Stop fighting it."

"No ..." she repeated weakly.

He bent his head and kissed her forcefully on the lips, crushing her to him. He pulled the towel from her head and released her long red tresses. "You smell of roses," he said softly. "You always smelled of them."

"Stop," she said, trying to pull away.

He pushed her against the wall and held up her arms. "No."

Her green eyes were huge as he released her wrists. Untying the belt of her robe slowly, he pushed the fabric back off her shoulders to reveal her pale naked body.

"I can't stop it," he groaned, discarding the robe. "Don't resist. Please."

Isabelle arched towards him, her brain fuzzy from the vodka and desire. It was like she had lost control of her senses. Right and wrong became blurred and she surrendered herself completely to him, wrapping her arms around his neck and her long legs around his waist. He fumbled with his pants and seconds later he was inside her, moving slowly and deliberately. She threw her head back in pleasure, lost in the moment, every nerve-ending alive.

"Come back to my hotel with me," he said afterwards, pushing a stray strand of hair from her forehead. "Stay with me."

"Like the old days?" Her face hardened.

"No. Not like that. Come back to France and live with me. I haven't been the same since you left. I need you, Isabelle."

"We barely knew each other," she said dismissively. "What was it, a couple of weeks?"

"That doesn't matter," he said seriously. "There are no rules with love."

"Love?"

He kissed her softly. "I'm in love with you. Everywhere I go, I'm surrounded by your face. I see it in my dreams. I should never have let you go. I'm sorry."

She stood up and grabbed her robe. "It's not that simple. I'm with Angelo now."

"Do you love him?"

"Of course." She reddened slightly. "He's amazing."

"Then why did you give yourself to me? Why did you scream my name?"

Isabelle's eyes filled with tears. "I shouldn't have. It was a big mistake."

He pulled her close. "*Non*, it was not a mistake, *ma belle*. You did what you wanted to do. Deep down, you know that you belong with me."

Isabelle let him hold her. She felt sick with guilt.

"I think that you should go," she said quietly. "Bertie will be back in a while and I don't want to have to explain."

"Come with me."

"No." Her green eyes shone with tears. "Please leave."

Raphael wiped a tear from her cheek. "I will give you time to think. You must break with this man and come to me. You know it."

He bent his head and kissed her passionately. "Until we meet again."

The door slammed.

Isabelle ran to the bathroom and splashed cold water on her burning cheeks.

Angelo. Dear, sweet Angelo. What would he say? They were planning on moving in together. Now, everything had changed. She couldn't commit to him now. Not after what she had just done. Not when she was in love with someone else.

Gabriella arrived back to her small flat, feeling thoroughly exhausted. The night had been a huge success. Bertie had auctioned off everything with the added bonus of his witty repartee and the final sum raised was seven million. All her designs had sold and she had orders for more. Aurora's dress had gone viral and articles started to pop up online where she saw her name in print. There was even a clip of Aurora on the red carpet saying that she was wearing 'Gabriella'.

Wearily, she got into bed, her muscles aching. Her clock read three and the noise of traffic outside was as incessant as ever. That was always the way in cities. They never slept.

Oberon had paid for her taxi home, his face blazing in

triumph. "You're made now," he said, slamming the car door.

She knew it was a big coup for him as he was her mentor. Soon she would fly the nest and continue in her own right. The end was nigh.

The next morning she woke up to find emails from her family and friends, congratulating her on her success. Teresa sent her a clip from E! News with the presenter Jason Kennedy asking, "So, who is this Gabriella?" and then a montage of her dresses from the gala.

She put her phone away and gave herself a shake. It all seemed so surreal. She had dreamed of it for so long and now it was fast becoming a reality. The world was waking up and taking notice. It was overwhelming.

She filled the kettle and popped a teabag into a mug. She needed to see Oberon. He would know what to do next. He had been in the same boat after all. She had to maximise this opportunity and make her mark permanent.

In one way, she liked the safety and security of being in Oberon's shadow. It was safe there. She could fade into the background and observe. Being the focus of attention was nerve-wracking. People were judging her and one size did not fit all. She would get good reviews but also bad ones – it was inevitable. She would have to develop a thick skin and keep believing in herself. She would have to remember the compliments and try and disregard the insults.

Thousands of miles away, in Boston, Hugo du Maurier was out for his morning run. He usually left his apartment at six which gave him plenty of time to cover his eight-mile target before it was time to go to the office. His apartment was in a chic complex in the trendy South End, a revitalised area of the city that mixed old and new. He listened to his iPod as he pounded along the pavement of Tremont Street and then on to Washington Street.

When he got back to his apartment, he headed straight for the shower. Then he made a bowl of muesli and chopped up some mango for the top. Caroline had travelled north the weekend before and together they had walked through the Seaport District where they had beautiful views of the harbour and the sailboats.

He missed his own little boat – he tried to go back to Long Island as often as he could, but life got in the way. Caroline made plans for them all the time without consulting him. One weekend they had a trip to Toronto. The next? A weekend in Vermont. He knew that she was waiting for the big proposal but he just wasn't ready.

His phone rang as he took a big bite of his breakfast. It was Celine.

"Yep?" he said with his mouth full.

"Check out the link I sent you."

He swallowed. "What link?"

"It's Gabby. She's made it, Hugo. She had a show in London and it was a huge success."

He felt his skin grow cold. He knew it was petty but part of him wanted her to fail. She had sacrificed their relationship for fame and fortune after all. Immediately he felt ashamed. Gabriella deserved to shine. She had worked so hard all her life.

"Is that all?" he said quietly.

"Yes, Cranky. My God, Hugo, you're so much fun in the morning."

"Bye, Celine." He hung up.

412

Accessing his WhatsApp, he saw the link. Clicking on it, a newspaper article appeared with a picture of Isabelle in her stunning white dress. The headline read: GABulous! Then there was a synopsis of her show and all the famous people that bought her designs. Under that was a brief biography about her upbringing in the Bronx and a paragraph on Oberon.

He exited out of the piece. She had done what she had set out to do – she had achieved her goal. He, on the other hand, had sold out. He had given up his music to become a boring attorney in a stuffy office. He was going out with a one-dimensional girl from a tedious family and his momma was so proud.

He debated at whether he should email Gabriella and congratulate her. Then he decided against it. She was living a life that was light years away from his.

Back in London, Isabelle woke with a blinding headache at noon. She had eventually fallen into a dreamless sleep after hours of guilt-ridden thoughts. There was no escaping it. She would have to tell Angelo. She was not the type of girl who could live with a lie. Angelo was too good, too sweet. He didn't deserve to get hurt.

She walked downstairs to find empty champagne bottles and overflowing ashtrays in the sitting room. Bertie had obviously brought the party home. Funny she hadn't heard anything. She thanked God that she had slept through it. Lost in the oblivion of sleep, she didn't have to face her duplicity.

Raphael had texted her in the middle of the night, saying that he was at the Goring and that he was waiting for her. The thought of him made her stomach churn from both excitement and disgust at what she'd done. His arrogance both fascinated and annoyed her. He knew that she would turn up. He knew the effect he had on her. He hypnotised her.

She had denied her feelings for so long, it felt like a fog had cleared. She had resigned herself to never feeling real excitement anymore, putting it down to being jaded and bored with the celebrity lifestyle. Now she understood that it was because of Raphael. She had closed herself off as a form of self-preservation.

Angelo was wonderful. She loved him and enjoyed being with him. But now, after a brief encounter with Raphael, she realised that no one could measure up. No one.

Miserably, she switched on the coffee machine, the inevitability of the heartbreak to come threatening to consume her.

ᕤ Chapter Thirty-Four ᕥ

Bertie surfaced at two. The house had been cleaned and there was no evidence of partying left. He found Isabelle hunched in the library with a book open on her lap but a vacant look in her eyes.

"Enjoying Tolstoy?" he asked, lifting the book and turning it the right way around.

Isabelle shrugged. "Not really."

"You look dreadful, my dear. Did our carousing wake you up?"

She shook her head. "Not at all."

"Then why so glum?" He took a seat on an armchair opposite her.

Isabelle sighed. "I've made a terrible mess."

"Go on."

"Raphael called over last night and it went too far and now I have to tell Angelo …"

Bertie held up his hands. "*Whoa!* Slow down there. Tell Angelo what?"

"That it's over."

"Over?"

"Yes." She looked up. "No one makes me feel like Raphael. He wants me to move to France with him."

Bertie's eyes widened.

"Please don't judge me."

"On the contrary, I feel partly responsible. I told him where you were."

"He would have found me anyway. He came to the gala to see me."

Bertie rubbed his chin. "This is a pickle. I mean, Angelo is so wonderful."

"He is, he is." She put her head in her hands. "I can't call him until the race is over tomorrow night and it's torture."

"Call him? Surely you'll tell him face to face."

Isabelle started to sob. "I can't."

Bertie rushed over and rubbed her back. "But you must, my love. News like that would be horrendous over the phone. You must wait until he comes back to London."

"That won't be until Tuesday."

"Then you have to wait until then." Bertie lifted her chin upwards. "It will give you time to reflect and make sure that this is the right decision."

"Poor Angelo." She closed her eyes. "I can imagine him now, getting ready to race in the Qualifier, his heart set on winning. He likes when I'm there, you know."

Bertie nodded. "I can imagine."

"I should have gone with him. I should never have stayed in London."

"Our paths are predestined for us, my darling. Don't dwell on the 'should haves'. As Lady Macbeth said, '*What's done cannot be undone*', or something like that. You have to face this and accept that it was fate."

"But why now? Why did Raphael seek me out after all this time?"

Bertie shrugged. "He regrets letting you go, I presume.

416

After all, as far as he's concerned, you rejected his offer to go to France."

"Yes, but then Sylvie came along and it didn't take long for him to forget."

"True, but he thought you were gone from his life. He needed closure with her."

Isabelle got to her feet and walked to the window. "This is terrible. I hate being this person. I hate the fact that my happiness depends on breaking the heart of another. Why can't things be simple?"

"They never are, Isabelle. They never are." He clapped his hands together. "Right, no more moping. You get dressed and we'll have a long leisurely lunch."

She smiled a watery smile. "Okay, but I'm going to have a bath first if that's all right."

"Of course, my sweet. There are wonderful lavender-scented bath salts on the shelf by the window. Please help yourself."

Isabelle was just getting out of the bath when the news broke.

D'Agostino in Horror Crash
F1 Crash in Abu Dhabi

Bertie knocked on the bathroom door urgently. "*Isabelle!*" he called.

"Is lunch ready? I'm on the way." She held onto the sides of the giant bathtub so as to lever herself upwards.

"*Isabelle! Open up!*" Bertie sounded frantic.

"I'm coming, I'm coming!"

Moments later she pulled the door open.

"What is it?" she asked, rubbing her hair with a towel.

"It's Angelo." Bertie's face was white. "He lost control at the final lap of the Qualifier."

"*What?*" Her hand flew to her mouth.

"He's critical."

"What? You're kidding me, right?" She swayed.

"No." His eyes filled with tears. "I'm sorry."

Isabelle felt the room spin and she fell to the floor.

Bertie called for his housekeeper.

"Get some brandy," he ordered, lifting Isabelle up into his arms. "Quickly!"

When Isabelle came around, the first thing she saw was Bertie's worried face.

"What happened?" she asked weakly. "My head hurts."

A large TV screen mounted on the wall was showing the latest headlines. A red headline along the bottom read: *D'Agostino Critical*

Slowly it came back to her and she screamed. "*Angelo!* What happened? Oh Bertie, it's karma! I've brought this on. *Sfortuna!*"

Bertie shook his head. "This has nothing to do with you. He took the corner too quickly. I took a call from his coach. I've booked you on the next flight out there."

"When?"

"In three hours."

She got up and felt woozy. "I need to pack. I mean, all I have are winter clothes. What will I do?"

"Don't worry. We'll pick some things up at the airport."

"We?"

"Yes." He smiled kindly. "I'm coming with you, my love."

"I need to call my mom." He eyes filled with tears. "I can't believe this. It has to be retribution."

"Stop that right now," said Bertie firmly. "That's absolute nonsense."

418

"I should call his mother, Greta." Isabelle rubbed her temples. "I presume she's on the way out there."

Bertie nodded. "Yes. You should arrive around the same time."

"I can't believe it. Things don't happen like this. They just don't."

Bertie rubbed her back. "I can't argue with that."

"It must be a cosmic lesson. To appreciate what I have."

"Again, that's nonsense. He was driving too fast. What happened last night isn't even a factor in this. No one knows about it."

"Will you call Raphael and explain?" Her body began to tremble. "I can't talk to him right now."

"Consider it done." Bertie sighed. "Although, he'll hear about it, I'm sure. Every news channel on the planet is covering the story. This is big news."

Isabelle felt the bile rise in her throat. She wanted to ask but she couldn't say it.

"Bertie?"

"Yes?"

"Will he make it?"

Bertie's face darkened. "I don't know, Isabelle. I just don't know."

Gabriella stared in horror at the screen. "Angelo!" she said faintly. "Oh, poor Zsa Zsa!"

She picked up her phone and called Isabelle right away. There was no answer.

She tried again, but it rang out.

Gabriella started to pace the room. Surely Isabelle had been told. It was all over the media. She dialled Bertie's mobile and he answered on the fourth ring.

"Does she know?" asked Gabriella urgently.

"Yes. We're on our way to Heathrow."

"Can I speak to her?"

There was a fumbling noise and then Isabelle's voice. "Oh, Gabby."

"Don't worry. Everything is going to be okay, do you hear me?"

"What if it isn't? What if he doesn't make it?"

"He will. Of course he will. He's young and strong."

"I'll call you."

"I'll have my cell with me all the time."

"Bye."

"Bye."

Raphael rang Isabelle's phone over and over again. In the end, she switched it off. She couldn't deal with him. Not now. Not when Angelo needed her.

Bertie's phone rang too but she instructed him to ignore it.

"Please," she implored.

Bertie threw it into his holdall. "Okay."

They looked out the car window to see journalists by the entrance.

"Damn," said Bertie. "They pipped us to the post."

Isabelle wrapped her Hermès scarf around her long hair and put on her enormous Dior glasses. "Let's make a run for it," she said.

"If you're sure?"

She nodded. "We can't avoid it."

Bertie's two bodyguards got out first and attempted to shield them from both curious onlookers and the press.

"*Hey, that's Bertie Wells!*" shouted one woman, pointing.

"*Isn't that Isabelle Flynn?*" shouted another.

"*Isabelle!*" shouted a journalist, pushing forward. "Any word on Angelo?"

"*Isabelle! Tell us the update!*"

"*Isabelle! Is it true that he's left his fortune to you?*"

Isabelle kept her head down and walked purposefully through the main doors and towards the Departure Gates. Bertie followed, also ignoring the public.

"*Isabelle! Bertie! Come back and talk to us!*"

The press followed in hot pursuit.

"*Back the fuck off!*" roared Vladimir menacingly. "*Leave the lady be!*"

The paparazzi ignored him and swarmed around them.

"*Isabelle, have you any news on Angelo's condition?*"

"*Isabelle, is it true that you're secretly engaged?*"

"*Isabelle! Will Angelo make it?*"

Isabelle stopped dead and turned. Lowering her dark glasses, she regarded the faceless mob and said, "He's going to be fine."

"*Now, back off!*" shouted Vladimir again.

Bertie took Isabelle's hand and they walked through the Departure Gates to the security check.

When Isabelle and Bertie arrived at the hospital, Angelo was still unconscious. His mother Greta had arrived two hours before and was praying outside the intensive care unit, wooden rosary beads threaded on her fingers.

"Isabelle!" she sobbed, opening her arms wide.

Isabelle hugged her closely. "Can I go in?" she asked, her green eyes tearful.

Greta nodded. "He no wake," she said sadly.

Bertie gave the old lady a hug too. "Bloody awful," he said, patting her back. "Damn shame."

A nurse appeared and gestured for Isabelle to follow her. She pushed open the heavy door of the unit and led her to a bed.

There, his eyes closed and attached to a machine, was Angelo. Except he didn't look like Angelo. He looked pale and gaunt with dark shadows under his eyes and a huge bandage on his head. His head was tilted backwards and his chest heaved as he inhaled, as if it was laborious.

Isabelle's hand flew to her mouth in horror.

The only sound in the room was the beeping of the machine. She approached the bed quietly and took his lifeless hand in hers.

"Angelo," she whispered.

No response.

"Angelo, can you hear me?"

Nothing. She pressed his hand to her cheek and kissed it. "I'm here," she continued. "I'm here."

His eyes flickered but he didn't wake.

"You'd better wake up soon, okay?" She was openly crying now. "You'd better."

He didn't move.

Holding his hand to her chest, she gazed at him.

"Madam," said the nurse softly. "You cannot stay here."

"Please?"

She shook her head. "You must wait outside."

Isabelle got up reluctantly and kissed Angelo's cheek. "I'll just be outside," she whispered. "I won't be far."

It was dark outside and she had a cramp in her neck from bending it awkwardly. Three chairs had been set up in the hallway outside the intensive care unit for her, Bertie and Greta. Bertie was sound asleep in the seat next to her, his head lolled back and his mouth open. There was no sign of Greta.

Isabelle rubbed her eyes and stretched. The bright lights of the hospital were disconcerting. It was like the middle of the day inside despite the night sky visible from the window.

She had switched off her phone. It was buzzing constantly with messages and calls from concerned friends and relatives. The only call she had accepted had been from her mother who was on her way to Abu Dhabi that night. Isabelle couldn't wait to see her. Bertie was great but he wasn't family. She needed the support of her mother. She felt scared and alone.

Her encounter with Raphael seemed like a lifetime ago. It felt surreal and dream-like. Anytime he popped into her head, she pushed his image away. Her priority now was Angelo. His welfare was her only concern.

She got to her feet and hailed a passing nurse.

"Any news on Angelo D'Agostino?" she asked.

The nurse shook her head. "He's stable, that's all at the moment."

"Let's go to the Ritz," Bertie said the next morning.

"Angelo was staying there," she said miserably.

"Exactly," he said. "I've booked the rest of us in there too. Let's go and freshen up."

"I can't leave," she protested. "He might wake up."

"You need to freshen up."

"I can't leave." She tied her long hair into a ponytail. "Mom is due any minute."

Bertie sighed. "Fine. We'll wait for Mrs. Flynn. However, you must take a break at some point."

Greta appeared holding a polystyrene tray with three

cups of coffee. "*Prego*," she said, handing one each to Bertie and Isabelle.

"*Grazie*," said Bertie. "You read my mind." He turned to Isabelle. "By the way, I took the liberty of booking a flight for Gabriella too. She's due this afternoon."

"What?" Isabelle's eyes filled with tears. "You did what?"

"The poor lamb is broke and she did auction off all her outfits for charity ..."

"Are you serious?" Isabelle hugged him tightly. "Thank you for everything. You're so amazing. Honestly, I really appreciate it."

"Anything I can do." He smiled. "I like helping people. It's my way of giving back."

Isabelle heard her mother's voice before she saw her.

"Mom!" she said joyfully. "I'm sure glad to see you!"

They embraced.

Elaine Flynn was a beautiful woman of forty-eight. She resembled Isabelle in all but hair-colour and height.

"Is he doing okay?" asked Elaine in concern. "Your daddy's beside himself with worry."

Isabelle inhaled shakily. "He's stable. That's all they tell me."

Bertie held out his hand. "Mrs. Flynn," he said formally. "Delighted."

Elaine blushed. "I can't believe I'm meeting Bertie Wells."

Bertie smiled. "Hope I don't disappoint. The reality often doesn't measure up to the fantasy."

He gestured to Angelo's mother. "Have you met Greta?"

Elaine shook her head. "Our kids have been together

for over a year and we've planned on taking a trip to Europe but it never happened." She shook the Italian lady's hand vigorously. "Good to meet you, Mrs. D'Agostino. I wish it had been under better circumstances."

Greta smiled sadly, not really understanding what Elaine had said.

"Gabby's on her way," said Isabelle to her mother. "Bertie booked her a ticket."

"That's good, honey. You could do with all the support you can get."

In the end, it was Elaine who convinced Isabelle to go back to the hotel for a shower and a change of clothes.

"His mom is here and she'll call if there's any change."

Isabelle hugged Greta tightly. "I'll be back as soon as I can," she promised. "Call me, okay?"

Bertie had organised a taxi to pick them up at the kitchen entrance around the back. There was a horde of press at the entrance to the hospital and reporters from all over the world were on standby for news about Angelo.

Wearing her scarf and glasses, Isabelle was ushered out the door and into the waiting Mercedes. Bertie, disguised in a black hat and scarf, followed and then Elaine.

"The Ritz," said Bertie when they were safely in the car.

Isabelle had a quick shower and changed into a long-sleeved trouser suit that Bertie had had sent up from a boutique downtown. She didn't want flesh on display, so she wrapped a scarf around her head and neck. It was the Arab Emirates after all.

Angelo's room was opulent. There was an enormous bed with the softest sheets, a marble bathroom with a giant bath, and two French windows that opened out onto a balcony with a view of the city skyline. His clothes were folded neatly in the large wardrobe and his lucky jersey was hanging on the bathroom door.

She felt something catch in her throat. Why didn't he wear it at the Qualifier? If only he had. If only this hadn't happened.

There was a knock at the door. It was her mother.

"You look awful, Zsa Zsa," she said, pulling her close. "You've got to believe that everything will be okay."

She buried her face in her mother's shoulder, breathing in her perfume. How she longed to tell her about Raphael. She needed to offload her problems and try and make sense of it all. Something told her not to, however. She suspected that her mom would not be impressed with her behaviour. Elaine Flynn came from a strict Presbyterian background.

"Daddy rang," she continued. "He sends his love."

Isabelle sniffed. "I'll call him later."

"It's an eight-hour difference, honey. Remember that, okay?"

"Okay."

Gabriella was at the hospital when they got back.

"Gabby!" Isabelle ran straight into her arms. "Oh, Gabby, tell me he's going to be okay."

Gabriella started to cry. "You stayed in London because of me. I feel terrible. You should have been here."

"No one could've known."

"Poor Angelo."

They held each other for a few minutes.

"You're so good to come. I mean, this is a bad time for you. What with the success of the show and all."

"Oh, Oberon went crazy when I told him I was leaving town. In the end, I just hung up."

426

"He has a point. This is your time to cement your fame."

"You're more important," said Gabriella simply.

A nurse appeared with a clipboard. "I can let you in now," she said to Greta.

The older lady scrambled to her feet and followed the nurse through the heavy doors, sanitising her hands on the way in.

Isabelle gazed longingly at the entrance to the unit. "We only get a few minutes at a time," she explained. "It's so frightening in there, Gabs. All machines and beeping noises."

Gabriella squeezed her hand. "Let me tell you all about Karl Lagerfeld," she said brightly, trying to be cheerful. "He called Oberon and asked if I was under contract."

"*Whoa!* What did Oberon say?"

"He was actually quite possessive. He told Karl to piss off and poach someone else."

Isabelle smiled.

"So, I asked him for my own office space, a huge raise and a section of the website. Just until I'm big enough to branch out on my own."

"And?"

"He agreed." Gabriella beamed. "He even suggested that I exhibit first at his next big show. Like a supporting act or something."

But Isabelle wasn't listening. Greta had reappeared with a huge smile.

"*He wake, he wake!*" she shouted and then started praying in rapid Italian.

Isabelle jumped to her feet.

"Can I go in? Oh please."

The nurse looked unsure. "He's very weak …"

"Please!" Isabelle implored. "I have to see him."

"Okay. Just for a few minutes."

She led her in through the doors and towards Angelo's bed. His eyes were closed and the tube down his throat looked grotesque.

"Angelo?"

His eyelids flickered. She took his hand in hers.

"Angelo, baby. It's me, Isabelle."

He squeezed her fingers in response.

"Open your eyes," she pleaded.

He didn't respond. Instead, his hand relaxed once more and fell from her grasp.

"He's very tired," said the nurse softly. "Come back in a while and we'll try again."

Isabelle had tears flowing down her cheeks. "I love you," she whispered.

Later that evening, the doctor examined him and felt that he could be taken off the ventilator. The tube was removed from his throat and he looked peaceful when Isabelle was finally allowed in to see him. His eyelids fluttered as he slept, his dark hair dramatic against the starched white pillow.

"Angelo?" said Isabelle, taking his hand and kissing his fingers. "I'm here. Isabelle's here."

Slowly he opened his eyes. "Isabelle," he said in a hoarse whisper.

"It's me," she said joyfully. "Oh, I'm so glad you're okay."

He tried to speak, but nothing came out. He closed his eyes again in exhaustion.

"Don't worry," she said soothingly. "You're going to be fine."

His head lolled sideways and his arm went limp. She rubbed his palm rhythmically and felt her lower lip tremble.

"Oh Angelo, I'm sorry," she whispered tremulously. "I'm so so sorry." She burst into tears.

"It's time to go," said the nurse, putting her hand on Isabelle's shoulder. "He needs to rest."

They went back to the hotel in much better spirits. Greta refused to leave as she didn't want Angelo to wake up and be alone.

"I should stay," said Isabelle.

"You need some sleep," said Elaine firmly. "Greta is his next of kin. She will call with any news."

Bertie took them for a quick bite in the hotel restaurant. Isabelle picked at her food, feeling overwhelmed and exhausted. Her mother noticed and ordered her to bed at once.

"I can come and sleep with you if you like."

Isabelle nodded. "I'd like that."

Gabriella stayed at the bar with Bertie and his bodyguards. The Ritz was on high alert with regard to the paparazzi and security was tight. The press knew that Angelo had been staying there and now they knew that Isabelle was too.

Elaine helped her daughter undress. She climbed under the covers and closed her eyes. Images of Raphael floated around in her head but she pushed them away. It was all too much. She needed to focus on Angelo and take one day at a time.

⟪ Chapter Thirty-Five ⟫

Angelo died that night.

The world woke up to the tragic news splashed across every media platform. He was compared to Ayrton Senna and tributes poured in from all over the world. Greta had been there when he went into cardiac arrest and when the doctor called time of death, she had fallen to her knees in grief.

Isabelle was pulled from a dreamless sleep by her crying mother.

"He's gone," she sobbed. "Oh, Zsa Zsa darling, he's gone."

In the beginning, she had been completely calm. It was like she heard the news and her brain delayed processing the information. She had nodded at the right time and managed to dress herself so as to go to the hospital. Bertie had been there along with Gabriella, both with red eyes hidden behind glasses.

"I'm so sorry," Gabriella said, her voice breaking. "It's such a shock."

Isabelle looked at her numbly. It just didn't make sense. He had woken up and they had spoken to each other. She had taken a few hours to catch up on some sleep. That was all.

The press were outside the hotel in their droves. Cameras and sound booms mingled with journalists and photographers. Isabelle was smuggled out the back door and the car sped off with motorbikes in hot pursuit. Cameras flashed as she passed but she didn't register it. Maybe this was a dream. Maybe this was a horrible, horrible dream.

Greta's anguished face verified everything. They fell into each other's arms.

Angelo's body was released two weeks later and flown back to Treviso. The funeral that followed was a simple affair with just family and close friends. Isabelle wore a black suit and huge glasses. Her parents stood by her side, her mother Elaine holding her hand tightly as the coffin was lowered into the ground.

Angelo was buried next to his father.

Gabriella and Bertie stood behind the immediate family, both with white faces. No one could quite believe that he had died. He had been so young and had such promise. Isabelle had gone into a trance, refusing to talk to anybody about his death. She had stayed in Abu Dhabi while they sorted out all the red tape and then had flown back with his body to Italy. Greta had been there too – a mother consumed with grief and disbelief.

Elaine had booked a flight back to New York for the following day and had insisted that her daughter come too.

"You need a break, honey," she said firmly. "Let me look after you and make you Twinkies."

Isabelle barely heard her and didn't protest when she

boarded the flight the next afternoon. In a daze, she took the sleeping pills her father handed to her and slept for most of the journey. She liked sleeping as she didn't have to face reality. Lost in a dream world, she didn't have to face anything.

Going back to Philadelphia was like a journey into the past. Her bedroom looked the same: pink bedclothes, her giant doll's house complete with seven Barbies, her bookshelf filled with the classics like *Pride and Prejudice*, and her posters of Justin Timberlake.

Being an only child, she had wanted for nothing. Patrick, who adored his little girl, had given her everything. Her fairy princess treehouse still stood on the bough of the oak tree in the garden and the garage was still home to her Vespa moped that she used to ride to High School.

True to her word, Elaine baked cakes and made childhood dinners like meatloaf. She pressed dozens of lemons and added them to sugar syrup, chattering constantly about the time Isabelle had made a pitcher of lemonade to sell on the street so that she could save enough money to go to Disneyland.

Isabelle stared into space, not listening. Her meals returned untouched and she didn't react when Elaine unearthed her Senior Prom photos. It was as if she had to remind herself to breathe.

Gabriella called every day, asking how things were.

Elaine lied in the beginning so as to reassure herself. However, after a week of Isabelle's vacant behaviour, she broke down on the phone.

"Oh, Gabby, I feel like I've lost her. She has no interest in anything."

Gabriella was horrified. "Oh, Elaine, I need to see her – but I'm not coming back for Christmas this year. I have a deadline for Fashion Week in London in February."

"Not to worry," said Elaine, sniffing. "I'm not sure there's much anyone can do at the moment."

She went out to the garden and found Isabelle sitting in the snow. She was wearing a nightie and was barefoot.

"*Isabelle!*" shouted Elaine, appalled. "Get in here this instant or you'll catch your death."

Isabelle turned slowly, her green eyes dead.

"*Isabelle!* Right now, do you hear me?"

She didn't move.

Elaine ran out and yanked her by the arm. "You've got to snap out of this. You can't continue this way."

Isabelle allowed her to pull her inside.

"Look at your feet! They're blue." She propelled her into a chair and fell to her knees. "Let me put some life into them," she mumbled, taking one foot between her palms and vigorously rubbing it.

Isabelle reached down and stopped her. "I'm okay," she said softly. "Just leave it."

Elaine ceased immediately and regarded her daughter. "Let me help you."

"I'm sorry, Mom. I'm just in a bad place."

Elaine got to her feet and pulled Isabelle close. "I understand, baby. You just let it all out, okay? I'm right here."

Isabelle clung to her mother, feeling overwhelmed with grief and guilt. No one could know what she'd done. They would be horrified. Angelo's family had been so sweet, treating her like she was family. It made her sick to her stomach. She felt like a giant imposter – a fake.

Elaine rubbed her back. "We're going to get through

this. You and me. Just have faith, honey. Time will heal."

Isabelle nodded mechanically. Losing Angelo was hard, but living with her guilt was even worse.

It was Christmas Eve when the doorbell rang.

"If it's those goddamn Kapowski kids singing carols, I'm going to lose it," said Patrick in exasperation. He was fiddling with the lights on the giant fir tree in the sitting room and cursing when they didn't work. "I'm heading to the garage to find a transformer," he announced, banging the door.

Isabelle was sitting by the fire, staring into the flames. It was snowing heavily outside and the neighbourhood was covered with a thick blanket of white. Elaine walked to the big front door and opened it. Bells that were hanging on the giant wreath jingled as the door moved and a cold gust of air blew into the house. She gasped.

Standing on the front porch was Raphael Baptiste.

"Good evening," he said. "May I speak with Isabelle?"

Elaine's eyes were wide. "You're that director," she said, recognising him. "You did that perfume commercial with Zsa Zsa."

He nodded. "Yes, that is me."

"What brings you here?" Elaine looked truly flabbergasted. "It's Christmas."

"I need to speak with Isabelle," he repeated. "Is she here? Bertie said she was at home with you."

Elaine nodded. "She's just inside." She stepped backwards. "Come in."

He stepped inside.

"May I take your coat?"

He smiled. "Thank you."

He handed Elaine his long cashmere overcoat and his

grey scarf. He shook the snow from his long hair and straightened up.

"She's right in there," said Elaine, pointing to the sitting room.

Raphael walked in and stopped dead. Isabelle was sitting on an armchair, her long legs curled underneath her. Her red hair was wild and hanging lankly around her face and she looked deathly pale.

"Isabelle," he said softly.

She turned around, her eyes widening in shock. Her lips were dry and cracked and her cheeks hollow from not eating properly.

"What? Why are you here?" she asked in a hoarse whisper. "How did you find me?"

"Bertie told me. He's worried about you."

"You can't be here." She felt her cheeks redden. "You've got to leave."

"No!" He rushed over to her. "I need to see you. Don't shut me out." He took her small hand in his and began to rub her palm gently.

Isabelle's eyes filled with tears. "Just go," she said desperately, yanking her hand away. "I can't see you."

Elaine appeared at the doorway and narrowed her eyes. "What's wrong, honey?" she asked suspiciously, surveying the scene.

Isabelle got up and rushed over to her mother. "Tell him to leave, Mom," she said urgently. "Right now."

Raphael ran his fingers through his hair in agitation. "You must listen to what I want to say."

"No!" Isabelle burst into tears. "You've ruined my life. I was happy until you came along."

"I don't believe that."

"I was! Now Angelo is dead and it's all my fault. It's

435

like karma or something."

"Don't be crazy," he said firmly. "You could not have stopped that crash. It was bad timing I must admit, but Angelo's death was nothing to do with you or me."

"What?" asked Elaine sharply. "Can someone tell me what's going on here?"

"Make him leave, Mom!" pleaded Isabelle. "Please!"

Raphael held out his hand. "Come with me."

"On Christmas Eve?" Elaine looked incredulous. "Are you for real, Mister?"

"Come, Isabelle," he said, ignoring her.

Isabelle stared at him for a moment. "I never want to see you again," she said in a trembling voice. "You are as a dead to me as Angelo is."

"I don't believe you."

"I'm serious." She stared at him defiantly. "Just get out."

Raphael said nothing for what seemed like an eternity. They could hear carollers outside singing 'O Little Town of Bethlehem'.

His dark eyes stared at her intensely and she steeled herself not to falter.

Then he bowed his head. "So, we say goodbye," he said softly.

Isabelle buried her head in Elaine's shoulder. "Yes."

"You're sure?"

She nodded again, her eyes filling with tears. "Please go," she whispered.

He walked out into the hall and grabbed his coat and scarf. "Happy Christmas," he said formally. Then he was gone.

Patrick walked back into the room holding a transformer. "Found this son-of-a-bitch under your old trampoline," he said cheerfully. "Now that tree might play ball."

꩜ Chapter Thirty-Six ꩜

Two months later Isabelle went back at work. Gabriella had a show in London Fashion week, showcasing her Fall/Winter collection. "Please model for me," she had pleaded and Isabelle had agreed. She had been taking it easy since Christmas, only doing a couple of shows in New York and a photo shoot for *Harper Bazaar*. Thanks to some anti-depressants and a few therapy sessions, she was on the way back to feeling like herself.

She found the best way to combat the nightmares was to have a few drinks before bed. Just a couple. She always hydrated with water. Sure, her shrink didn't recommend mixing alcohol with the happy pills, but she was in control, right? A couple of vodkas didn't count.

There were also lots of parties to attend and that helped too. When she was out socialising, she didn't have time to think about Angelo. Sure, there were mornings that she didn't know where she was and there was this one time when she fell down some stairs, but she didn't break anything. Just a few bruises on her ribs. Luckily she hadn't been booked for a bikini shoot or anything. No big deal.

She touched down in London three days before Gabriella's show. Wearing dark glasses and a trench coat, she walked out of Heathrow and took a taxi into the city to Gabriella's new place near Notting Hill. It was on the second floor of an old Georgian house and had high ceilings and a small balcony out the back. It also had a spare bedroom so she offered Isabelle a bed.

"I can stay at a hotel," Isabelle said, but Gabriella insisted.

"Stay with me and we can hang out like old times. I got cheese and Chardonnay."

Privately, Isabelle would have preferred to be alone. She suspected that Gabriella wouldn't approve of her nightcaps nor would she like her penchant for amphetamines. Someone always had some pills at parties and they made you feel so good. She liked the euphoria and the feeling that she was invincible. It took about half an hour for the drug to take hold and then it was like the adrenaline built inside you until it reached a peak where you loved everything and wanted to dance. Oh, what conversations she'd had on an ecstasy high! What interesting people she had met at four in the morning in a smoke-filled apartment with trance music booming in the background.

Yet what goes up has to come down too. The next day was never much fun. She would often wake with her heart pounding in her chest, feeling like she had only slept for two minutes. These all-nighters started to take their toll on her skin too. She had never had problems with zits but now she found herself relying on make-up a lot more. Her diet was unpredictable and she sometimes forgot to eat. Even Gabriella had gasped when she arrived at her doorstep for Fashion Week.

"You're so thin!" she exclaimed in horror.

Isabelle didn't care. She had the perfect career for it.

Who would hire a fat model? People needed to chill out.

Oberon stared at Gabriella. "You want to do what?"

"Bring Isabelle onto the stage with two Irish wolfhounds."

"What?"

"My designs are mythical, you said so yourself. I think it'd be cool. She could walk down the runway in her warrior gown, with the giant long-legged dogs on a leash. What do you think?"

"What about Isabelle? Is she okay with dogs?"

"Oh, sure. She had a dog called Rihanna when she lived in Philly."

Oberon rubbed his chin. "It's odd, I have to say. Where will you get the dogs?"

"I've booked two from an agency for animal actors."

"Animal actors? What now?"

"Animals that act for money."

"Do we have those?"

"Why sure," she answered in surprise. "That horse that played Joey in *War Horse* is doing super well."

"Good Lord."

"Anyway, Niall and Fiona are brother and sister –"

"Who?"

"Niall and Fiona. The wolfhounds."

Oberon shook his head. "It's like I'm living in a parallel fucking universe."

"I think it'll make headlines! No one will expect it."

"As long as Niall and Fiona don't go for giant poos on the runway."

Gabriella laughed. "Of course they won't, silly. They're *trained!*"

"*Hmmm.*"

439

She folded her arms obstinately. "Look, I'm doing it anyway so you can either work with me or not."

Oberon raised an eyebrow. "Down, girl," he drawled. "I've created a monster, I see. Fine, we'll try it at rehearsal but I'm going to be honest."

"Fine."

Oberon skimmed through the programme. "So you're on before Mulberry on Friday, right?"

Gabriella nodded. "Just a half-hour slot which is pretty short. That's why I have to make an impact."

"You've got to start somewhere, luv." He grinned. "Now, are Niall and Fiona going to make it to this dress rehearsal or shall we improvise with some teddy bears?"

"They're outside with their trainer." Gabriella glanced around. "But I'm not sure Zsa Zsa is here yet."

"Then she's late." He rolled his eyes. "Can models even tell the time?"

"Hey," she said, glaring at him. "She's smart so cut that right out."

"Sure she is." He tapped his foot impatiently. "So, call her! I don't have all day."

Gabriella rushed over to her bag and pulled out her phone. Before she had a chance to dial, Isabelle appeared, laughing hysterically and holding a lit cigarette.

"*Sorry I'm late!*" she called gaily. She was dressed in a tiny gold dress and her long legs were spattered with mud. Her hair trailed down her back and eyes were smudged with black.

"Zsa Zsa?" said Gabriella in astonishment. "Where have you been?"

Oberon walked over and calmly removed the cigarette from her hand. He threw it on the ground and stamped on it. "No smoking, darling. This isn't the eighties."

Isabelle wagged her finger at him. "Okay, Daddy," she slurred. "I'll be a good girl."

"She's pissed," said Oberon in disgust. "Smells like a brewery."

"*What?*" Gabriella almost shouted. "I thought you came home last night! Your bedroom door was closed."

"*Shhhh*," aid Isabelle giggling. "Of course I was home, all tucked up." She tried to wink, but failed.

Oberon turned to Gabriella. "Good luck with those wolfhounds," he said disdainfully. "I can't see her managing to stay upright."

Gabriella ignored him. "Come on," she ordered Isabelle. "Let's get you some coffee."

"*Coffee? Make it Irish!*" she yelled, throwing her arms up in the air. "*Let's all take the day off and dance!*" She started to shimmy around, swaying her hips and giggling.

"Take her home," snapped Oberon. "She's drunk and high. There'll be no work today."

"But the show's in two days," said Gabriella worriedly. "And Niall and Fiona came all the way from Surrey!"

"Sober her up and call me. We can make it work." He picked up his leather jacket. "Reschedule those dogs for tomorrow if you can. I have to see it before I can judge. It's ballsy, I'll give you that. However, there's a thin line between the ridiculous and the sublime."

"Don't sweat it." She held up her head. "Have some faith."

Riku raised an eyebrow when he heard about Isabelle from Oberon. They were sorting through outfits for the London show and tagging them numerically for the models.

"It's not surprising, given the talk that's going around," said Riku, writing a giant '3' on a tag and attaching it to a gown.

"Oh?" said Oberon, his interest piqued.

"Word on the street is that she has a real problem. Sacha Reeves was shooting a piece for *Vogue* last week and he said that she turned up high as a kite, sang a terrible rendition of 'Wake Me Up Before You Go Go' and then vomited on a pair of Manolos. It was a car crash."

"Look at you with all the news," said Oberon with a smirk. "I didn't take you for a gossip, Riku."

"Hey, I'm not. It's just people tell me things, that's all. Plus they know I'm connected to Gabby and she's her best friend *yadiyadiya*."

"Go on."

"She's gone off the rails, Oberon. Everyone is watching but no one is doing anything." Riku looked grave. "She badly needs a friend. Gabriella seems oblivious."

"Yes, Gabby doesn't seem to know," reflected Oberon. "She seemed as surprised as I was when Isabelle turned up wasted."

"Oh, it mainly happens across the pond. New York is buzzing with stories and embellished tales of her debauchery." Riku narrowed his eyes and expertly pulled out a loose thread from the collar of a pink shirt. "It's a miracle the press haven't published anything. Apparently Paolo her agent has been paying people off all over the city. He doesn't want it to break."

"Understandably so." Oberon looked thoughtful. "I don't think snorting coke would go down very well with her adoring fans."

"Exactly." Riku sighed. "It's only a matter of time though. Before it blows, I mean. Someone will take a picture and sell it for a fortune to some rag. It's a fait accompli."

"I presume this meltdown is a reaction to her boyfriend's

442

death?" said Oberon. "What a cliché. It just wouldn't do to grieve with dignity, would it?"

Riku gasped. "She's hurting! Don't be so cruel."

"I'm not," said Oberon firmly. "It's just I yearn for a bit of stiff upper lip sometimes. Models are always so bloody dramatic." He checked his watch. "Right, let's do a final inventory and then call it a night."

A sheepish Isabelle woke the next morning with a splitting headache and an insatiable thirst. Dragging herself out to the kitchen, she drank a huge glass of water and then refilled it. She felt disorientated and weak, like she had been run over by a bus. Hazily she tried to remember the events of the previous day and then cringed when she recalled her arrival at the Store Studios.

What must Gabby think?

There was a note on the kitchen counter from Gabriella saying that she had gone to the studios to prepare and that she would see her at around noon for a run-through. She underlined the time and said it was imperative that she make it.

Isabelle glanced at the large clock on the wall. That gave her an hour to get ready and make it to the Store Studio on the Strand.

Gulping down her water, she walked into the bathroom and switched on the shower.

"Sorry, Gabs." Isabelle looked at her friend fearfully.

Gabriella smiled, putting her at ease immediately. "Hey, it's no big deal. It happens the best of us. Now, get back there and put on the green dress."

Isabelle smiled gratefully. "I'll be as quick as I can."

Ten minutes later, she reappeared.

"I guess I'll hold off on make-up until the actual show, right?"

Gabriella nodded. "I just want to see you with Niall and Fiona."

"Say again?" Isabelle did a double take.

"The Irish wolfhounds," repeated Gabriella calmly. "I hired them to lead you down the runway. I want you to hold their leashes in one hand, a spear in the other, and let them lead you, like a warrior queen." She didn't quite meet Isabelle's eyes.

Isabelle blinked. "You're kidding, right?"

"No." Gabriella reddened. "I was going to tell you but I figured it would be better not to give you time to even worry about it ..."

"Gabby! I'm not used to big dogs. Rihanna was a terrier. What if they trip me up or go crazy?"

"Please, Zsa Zsa! This is so important. I've spent weeks clearing it with the BFC and the dogs cost a fortune to hire. They're in demand."

"Niall and Fiona? Those are their names?"

Gabriella nodded. "They've been in three commercials already. They're also known for being really chilled, so you've nothing to worry about."

Oberon appeared holding a skinny latte and wearing a tiger-print shirt. The amber and brown combination worked wonders with his dark skin and his shaved head gleamed in the lights. A giant turquoise ring on his index finger added a splash of colour and his lean hips were moulded into blue jeans.

"Are you ready to see my vision?" Gabriella asked him in excitement, clearly anxious to impress her boss.

"I'm about to burst with anticipation," he drawled.

Riku stood at the beginning of the runway, his hands

on his hips. "The dogs are ready, Gabs. Can we move this along? I know they're trained and everything, but if they poop, you know who'll have to clean it up."

"That's what I pay you megabucks for!" called Oberon.

Isabelle appeared in a long green dress with four slits to her mid-thighs. Her long hair fell loosely around her face and she had a golden diadem on her head.

Then Roy Spencer, the dogs' trainer, walked in leading two huge Irish wolfhounds.

Isabelle's eyes widened in fear. "They're ginormous!" she said in horror.

Riku nodded in agreement. "Good luck there, Miss Flynn."

Roy nodded at Isabelle. "Gabriella said that you are a dog lover," he said in a clipped British accent. "Niall and Fiona are nice dogs and should behave."

Isabelle turned wildly to Gabriella. "Are you serious, Gabby?"

Gabriella nodded. "Just try it," she said, handing her a tall spear.

Niall barked and swished his tail. Fiona yawned, showing big teeth.

Isabelle took both leashes from the trainer and walked to the top of the runway. Straightening up, she shook back her hair.

"You look fabulous!" said Gabriella. "*Riku! Play the music!*"

Riku obeyed and the haunting sound of uilleann pipes filled the room.

"It's like the Crufts Dog Show," said Oberon, smirking.

Roy clicked his fingers and the dogs started to move.

445

Isabelle followed, walking down the runway, holding the spear and the two leashes tightly. She could see Oberon's haughty face and Gabriella's beaming one. Holding her head up, she kept an impassive face, even though her heart was thumping.

"When you get to the end, stop and be ready to pose!" called Gabriella. "Just copy the dogs!"

Roy had moved to the side of the runway at the top. At a signal from him, Niall and Fiona turned smoothly sideways and posed in profile, heads raised.

Isabelle stepped close behind the dogs, spear erect, and struck a dramatic pose mirroring theirs.

"Perfect!" cried Gabriella, eyes shining.

Isabelle patted each dog on the head and turned to Gabriella and Oberon.

"Should I attack a random member of the audience now? Maybe impale a few people with my spear? Set the dogs on them?"

Gabriella laughed. "No, you're good." She twirled around. "I knew it would work. If this doesn't go viral, I'll freak out."

Oberon shook his head. "Bonkers!" he said loudly. "I hate it. I don't get it and it's frankly a disaster, darling. Back to the drawing board."

Gabriella's face turned red. "I think it works."

"What works exactly?" he asked rudely.

"It's fierce and strong. She's a warrior and she's a queen."

"Nonsense. It's all nonsense." He waved Gabriella away. "Take my advice, dearie. Lose the dogs and play it straight. Get Isabelle to model like she trained to do. Not as a wannabe Boudicca." He crumpled up his cup. "You've a lot to learn, Gabs. You're not ready to fledge just yet." He snapped his fingers. "Let's go, Riku. It was exactly as I had feared."

Gabriella's eyes filled with tears. "You're so mean to me."

"*Ciao!*" Oberon ignored her and walked off. "Let me know what amendments you make."

Isabelle patted her back. "He's just abrupt, Gabs. Don't be disheartened."

"Do you think it's crazy?" Her brown eyes were huge.

Isabelle paused. "It's just a bit weird, that's all. But weird can be good. Go with it if you want, do you hear? Don't be bullied by Oberon."

Gabriella's slot was at three on the Friday. Isabelle had battled with herself the night before, having only one vodka before bed. She owed it to Gabby to look well and be in control. One night of sobriety wouldn't hurt.

Denying herself was so hard and the minutes crawled by as she desperately tried to fall asleep. She had always prided herself on being in control – why then was she sweating and edgy, craving a drink to help her drop off?

There was a big buzz around and there were rumours that Meghan Markle was tipped to attend. The Fashion World was waiting to hear who had been chosen to design her wedding dress but as yet no one knew. It was a tightly kept secret that would be revealed on the wedding day in May.

"Well, it's not me," Oberon said disdainfully. "Her loss."

Gabriella checked her inventory and made sure the outfits were in numerical order. Isabelle looked fresh and happy as she had her make-up applied. Oberon had texted to say that he would be in the audience and that he hoped she had seen sense.

The music boomed through the speakers. It was time.

❧ Chapter Thirty-Seven ☙

A swarm of press approached Gabriella when she appeared from backstage after the show. "*Class! Total class!*" shouted a journalist from *Marie Claire*. "*Where did you get your inspiration?*"

Gabriella smiled. "My friend Lydia gave me a book about Celtic mythology and the rest is history."

"Do you have Irish roots?" asked a tall dark-haired woman with a Dublin accent. "I'm from *Exposé,* an Irish fashion programme." She held the microphone close.

Gabriella shook her head. "None. Just Puerto Rican. I wish I had though. I love your country."

Isabelle walked up behind her wearing a Stella McCartney dress, but when she saw the journalists, she turned on her heel. They ran towards her immediately.

"*Isabelle, great show, how's life?*"

"*Isabelle, how are you coping?*"

"*Have you a dog at home?*"

"*Any comment on that stairs incident?*"

Isabelle kept her head down and disappeared through security to the backstage area. Gabriella found her hiding behind a rail of gowns. She was sitting with her legs drawn up to her chin and her beautiful face was worried.

"Are you okay?" Gabriella bent down on her haunches. "I'm fine."

"You don't look fine. What were they talking about? A stairs?"

"Nothing." She stared to tremble. "Just the paps sticking their noses in where it's not wanted."

"Oberon wants to take us out for drinks as a 'sorry for doubting you' thing."

Isabelle closed her eyes. "You guys go. I'm pretty tired."

Gabriella rubbed her back. "Really?"

"Yeah. I think I'll head back to your place and crash."

"Aw, Zsa Zsa. It'll be fun."

"No. I've made up my mind." She managed a half-smile. "I'm pretty pooped after my day hunting with giant dogs."

"Have you got your key?"

She nodded.

"I'll see you later. I won't be late." Gabriella kissed her cheek.

Later that evening, Gabriella and Oberon sat in Bouji's club drinking Martinis.

Oberon slid a green olive off a cocktail stick and ate it whole. "Well, Riku had some interesting news about our Isabelle," he said, chewing.

Gabriella stared at him. "Interesting? What do you mean?"

"Oh, just this and that."

"Oberon," she said warningly.

"She's developed a penchant for wild nights out and drugs."

Gabriella inhaled sharply. "What?"

"Oh, it's all over New York apparently. Coke, ecstasy,

meth, anything she can get her hands on. Turning up late to jobs, looking like something the cat dragged in. You saw it yourself the other day, luv."

"She said she had a bad night. She said that sometimes things get to her."

"Sometimes? All the time."

"No, no. You must be wrong. Isabelle isn't stupid."

Oberon snorted. "She's on a downward spiral. The press are baying for blood and it's only a matter of time before we have a scandal akin to those Kate Moss photos in the *Mirror* years ago."

Gabriella took a big sip of her drink and coughed. "Well, she's at home now anyway," she said firmly. "She told me that she was exhausted."

Oberon laughed. "One hundred per cent she's out somewhere. Call her."

Gabriella scowled. "You're such a cynic. I believed her."

"Call her!" he taunted.

Gabriella took out her phone and dialled Isabelle's number. It went straight to voicemail.

"She's probably asleep," she said practically.

Oberon drained his drink. "Wake up, for fuck's sake. She gave us the slip to indulge in her daily vice. I guarantee you that Miss Flynn is currently snorting something up her nose in a dingy toilet."

"No!"

"Gabby, you need to realise that she's lost the plot. She fell down a stairs at a party in New York and almost broke her neck."

"Stairs?" she whispered in horror. "They mentioned the stairs."

"They?"

"The paps."

Oberon rolled his eyes. "Then her protection has ceased. Oh, oh. This will add notoriety to your show now. I thought those dogs might do it but having Isabelle in the loop will really catapult you onto the world stage."

"Oberon!" Gabriella looked fierce. "You're awful."

"Scandal sells. People love it. Now go and get us more drinks. Martinis. Dirty."

Gabriella left after the next drink. Oberon was chatting at a mile a minute about the Spring/Summer collection but she didn't hear a word. She couldn't focus and needed to get home to check on Isabelle.

Was this true? Was her friend in that state and she had no idea? Sure, she had been busy with the show and her New Year trip home had fallen through due to deadlines. In truth, New York was somewhere she wished to avoid, mainly because she it reminded her of Hugo. When she had called Isabelle to tell her, there had been no problem. Her friend had been perfectly fine with the change of plan.

Then they had met for lunch in London in the middle of January and Isabelle had seemed fine. Jumpy, but she had put that down to jetlag. Looking back on it, she had eaten very little and had drunk most of the bottle of wine.

Gabriella had a sick feeling in her stomach. Had she missed it?

She and Elaine had been in regular contact and there had been no mention of any crazy behaviour. Then again, Isabelle had moved back to her flat in New York so she was no longer living with her parents.

Could it be true?

Isabelle had always been sociable but sensible.

Please God she's in bed asleep.

She opened the door to her apartment and dropped her

keys on the table. Purposefully she walked down the corridor to the guest bedroom and pushed open the door. Isabelle was nowhere to be seen and the bed was covered in dresses. Gabriella's heart constricted in her chest. Oberon couldn't be right. Surely not.

She tried Isabelle's phone again and it went straight to voicemail once more.

Cursing, Gabriella ran her fingers through her hair. What would she do now? Isabelle could be anywhere.

Gabriella fell asleep and when she opened her eyes, it was morning. The sun shone through the window pane and she could feel an imprint of a zipper on her cheek. She was still fully clothed and on Isabelle's bed, but there was no sign of her friend. That awful feeling of panic took hold and she frantically dialled her friend's number for the umpteenth time. Nothing happened. It was the same old frustrating story.

Pressing on her Google app, she typed in Isabelle Flynn. Images of her appeared instantly with the wolfhounds and lots of hype about Gabriella. Too stressed to focus, she skipped all the media coverage of the show, she had all day to peruse them. There were some newspaper articles on Isabelle's rise to fame, along with articles from *Vogue* and *Marie Claire*. Angelo featured in a lot of the links and pictures of them as a couple in the South of France looked so happy. It was all such a tragedy – such a waste. She scrolled down and looked for anything damning, but there was no gossip. Just mentions of Isabelle at various shows and starring in different commercials.

Getting up, she went to the kitchen and switched on the coffee machine. Should she call the cops? Was that completely over the top? She threw her phone on the counter in frustration.

Where the hell was she?

When Isabelle didn't turn up by lunchtime, Gabriella had worked herself into a frenzy. All sorts of scenarios went through her head. Maybe Isabelle had been abducted on the way home? She called Oberon in a panic.

"Abducted? Oh, please."

"I'm freaking out here."

"She's probably wrapped around some junkie in a flat somewhere."

"No, no. Isabelle isn't like that. You've got it wrong."

"Normal Isabelle may be, but drug-fuelled Isabelle might be a different story. In the old days, when I partook of such things myself, I turned into a completely different person."

"What? You were actually nice?"

"Ha, ha. Look, keep googling her and checking Twitter. Something will crop up if it's bad news."

"I'm worried."

"Nothing you can do. Just take your mind off it. She'll turn up eventually."

Isabelle came home at nine that evening. Her nose was bloody and her eyes were crossed. She stumbled through the door and collapsed on the ground.

"Zsa Zsa!" Gabriella rushed to her side. "What the hell? Where were you? How did you get home?"

"I took a cab," she said weakly. "Gabby, I think I'm about to have a heart attack."

"What? Why?"

"I overdid it. I took a lot of coke and now I don't feel so good."

"Your nose!"

"It hurts, Gabs. It really hurts. My heart is beating so hard, I think it's going to burst." Her head fell backwards and she passed out.

"*Zsa Zsa!*" screamed Gabriella in terror. "*Jesus Christ!*" She laid her head gently on the floor and rushed over to her phone. She dialled 999 and a voice answered immediately.

"My friend, Isabelle, I think she's OD'd or something."

"Right. What has she taken?"

Gabriella started to sob. "I don't know. I don't know."

Isabelle was taken straight to A&E by ambulance. She woke up in the middle of the journey and vomited all over the floor, screaming to be let go. Gabriella, who was allowed accompany her, held her hand and calmed her down. With sirens wailing, they sped through the streets of London.

When they arrived at the Chelsea and Westminster Hospital, Isabelle had lost consciousness again. A lone biker had followed the ambulance and was dressed all in black. When the paramedic opened the doors of the ambulance, a camera flashed and Gabriella gasped.

"*Back off, buddy!*" she yelled. "*Don't you dare take photos!*"

"That's Isabelle Flynn, luv," he retorted. "Who'd have thought she'd play a blinder?"

Gabriella tried to shield her friend from the lens and the paramedic raised his fist at the photographer as they rushed by.

"*Been following her all night!*" shouted the paparazzo. "*Nice when it works out!*"

"*Fuck off!*" howled Gabriella.

The bright lights of the hospital blinded her as they headed straight down the corridor.

"We'll take it from here," said an Indian doctor kindly.

Gabriella stopped and wiped the tears from her face. "Keep me updated! Please."

The waiting room was packed with crying kids, elderly people on trolleys and a few drunk people roaring abuse at the nurses.

Gabriella called Elaine and Patrick first. Elaine burst into tears. Patrick calmly asked for Gabriella to update them and that he was booking flights immediately.

Bertie rang half an hour later. "Isabelle's trending on Twitter. Please tell me it's a joke."

Gabriella started to cry. "They're pumping her stomach now. Oh Bertie, how did I not see it? She hasn't been okay in a long time."

"We're all to blame, my love," he said sadly. "I carry the most blame, I fear."

"What? Why?"

"Now is not the time for explanations."

"Where are you?"

"Capetown."

Gabriella sighed. " I wish you were here. I've no one to call except Oberon."

"How about that handsome blonde man? Tara Jacob's son?"

Gabriella brightened. "Luca! Of course. I'll see if he's in the city."

She dialled his number and he answered on the fifth ring.

"Gabs?"

"Luca, are you in London?"

"No. I'm at Lydia's parents' place. What's up?

"Isabelle overdosed. I'm all alone and I don't know what to do ..."

"What? Jesus, Gabby."

She started to cry. "I'm so scared."

"I can imagine. Oh Gabs, I wish I was there to help."

"It's okay."

"Keep me posted."

"I will."

The story broke half an hour later.

FLYNN FIGHTING FOR HER LIFE

IZZY DRUG NIGHTMARE

Celine du Maurier called, crying down the phone. "Not Isabelle! She's so lovely."

Gabriella closed her eyes. "She's hurting, I guess."

"Did you find her?"

"She collapsed in front of me. Then I rode in the ambulance with her."

"Oh, Gabby. That's just awful."

"It was terrible. I was so scared. I mean, I was all alone. What if she had died?"

"She'll be okay. I know it. All that cheese over the years will keep her alive."

Gabriella laughed sadly. "I know, right?"

"I'm praying."

"I'll keep you posted."

"Don't forget."

"Bye."

A doctor appeared an hour later with an update. Isabelle's stomach had been cleaned out and she was stable.

Gabriella was allowed in to see her.

Isabelle looked gaunt and pale, her red hair a splash of

colour against the white sheets. She was breathing peacefully, her chest heaving up and down. Gabriella felt her heart ache. Poor Isabelle. Poor sweet Zsa Zsa who had been crying out for help. Tears began to fall and she took her friend's lifeless hand in hers.

"I'm sorry, I'm so sorry," she sobbed.

It was all too much. She felt overwhelmed and isolated. Adrenaline had kept her going throughout the whole ordeal but now that she knew Isabelle was going to be okay, she realised just how close it had all been. She thanked God that Isabelle had made it back to the apartment. She could just as easily be dead on the street by now.

"I'll look after you," she vowed, squeezing her hand. "I'm here for you."

◖ Chapter Thirty-Eight ◗

Elaine and Patrick Flynn arrived in London three hours later. Elaine had called as soon as they had landed at Heathrow and Gabriella had told them that Isabelle was going to be okay. That didn't stop Elaine from crying hysterically.

Gabriella was in the waiting room when they rushed in. "Gabby!" said Elaine in a panic. "Where is she?"

"Down the hall, second room on the right. It's just one person at a time, Elaine. They're pretty strict."

Elaine ran down the hall.

Patrick hugged Gabriella close. "Thank you so much for staying with our girl," he said, his voice breaking.

Gabriella clung to him. It had been so hard being on her own.

"I'm just going to get some fresh air," she said in a shaky voice. "Now that you guys are here, I can take a break, right?"

"Of course, Gabby. Of course. You've been amazing."

"Not really." She backed away, blushing slightly.

"Hey, Gabby!" Patrick called after her. "We got accosted by press on the way in. Those bastards have no heart." He looked fierce for a moment. "My baby's life is hanging by a thread and they corner us like a pack of wolves."

"There's no mercy," she agreed. "I'll try and find the back entrance. Thanks for the heads-up."

"Take your time, honey."

She walked down the corridor, past all the trolleys and machines. The smell of the hospital was cloying and she couldn't wait for some clean air in her lungs. The waiting room was full as she passed, filled with tired-looking people anxiously waiting to be called. Children were crying and parents looked stressed. She walked past them all.

"I'm trying to avoid the press – where can I go for fresh air?" she asked a security guard.

"Keep going and take the lift," he said helpfully. "Go to the basement and you'll see a sign marked 'Deliveries'. You should be okay there."

"Thanks."

Minutes later, she walked outside. There was a large wall that enclosed her from prying eyes. Throwing her head back, she inhaled deeply. The cold air was invigorating and she pulled her cardigan around her. Life was so crazy. One minute you're worrying about something trivial like how big your thighs look in a pair of shorts and the next? Everything is thrown upside down. The show and her success seemed like weeks ago. She had ten missed calls from Oberon regarding a show in Milan. She made a point of not replying.

Luca had called, as had Tara. Even Britney the dog had WhatsApped, holding a card with 'Get Well Soon' between her paws, followed by heart emojis from Colin. Paolo was flying in later that day and he would take over the updates and press releases. Word on the street was that it was a suicide attempt stemming from grief over Angelo. Social media was buzzing with posts and comments from people who either sympathised with Isabelle or condemned her.

She arrived back into the hospital to find Elaine talking to a specialist and Patrick drinking a cup of coffee. Both had worried looks on their faces. Gabriella heard the words 'toxicology' and 'liver' and felt herself shiver. How long had this been going on?

Elaine's face was grim when he had finished. She turned to Gabriella. "She's off to rehab."

"What?"

"This can never happen again."

"Where?"

"America. I'm going to make a few calls." She stalked off.

Patrick put his head in his hands. "She feels responsible. Zsa Zsa was home with us after Angelo died and we should've kept her there. Instead she went back to New York and her lifestyle."

"I feel the same," said Gabriella glumly. "I was so focused on my career, I missed the signs."

"Has she always been like this? Into drugs and things?"

Gabriella blushed. "Not really. Sometimes she would have the odd line of cocaine, but nothing major." She frowned. "I haven't seen much of her lately so I can't say anymore."

Patrick sighed. "Well, all that's going to change. She's coming home with us and she's going to get better."

When Gabriella got back to her flat, she collapsed on her bed. Her phone battery had died so she plugged it in. It turned on automatically and a barrage of emails came through. Wearily, she accessed her inbox and scrolled through them. Invitations to parties, openings and horseraces featured, along with an invitation to appear on *This Morning* with Philip and Holly. There were at least ten from Oberon, demanding that she call him back as soon as possible about the Milan show. His last message was written in shouty capitals, ordering her to reply. She rolled her eyes and kept scrolling. There were a few from online shopping sites and three from the Book Depository. Then she saw 'Hugo du Maurier' and her heart leapt. Sitting up straight, she pressed on the message. Tantalisingly it took a few moments to load and she bit her lip in frustration. Then, the words appeared.

Hey Gabby,

I'm so sorry to hear about Isabelle. I know how worried you must be.

Just to let you know that I'm thinking of you.

Hugo.

Tears welled up in her eyes.

Just to let you know that I'm thinking of you.

Those words, those lovely words, made her heart sing. Oh, how she yearned to see him. Oh, how she ached to hear his voice.

What was stopping her?

Gone was the young immigrant girl without a penny to her name. She was *Gabriella*. She was somebody. She could now meet Hugo on his level and not feel inferior. Victoria's interfering had been despicable and nasty, but she had been right about one thing – their love would have struggled due to their social differences years ago. Now, that had all changed. She had made it. She was important. She could go to that yacht club and be treated with respect.

Couldn't she?

The easy thing to do would be to tell him about his mother's threats. Then he would understand that she acted out of loyalty to her family, not because she didn't love him.

Yet, she knew that that was not the way forward. Driving a wedge between him and his family would end in tears. He also had a girlfriend. Caroline Ashley Hamilton had belittled her at every opportunity but that didn't matter. It wouldn't be right to chase a man who was committed to someone else. God would frown upon such things.

Gabriella deleted the email with a heavy heart.

The media stuck to Isabelle's story for another week. Stories circulated about her penchant for cocaine and the stairs incident. Witnesses came forward and sold their tales about her antics and the world devoured the scandalous material. What followed was a close look at models and their lifestyles. Did the world put unrealistic expectations on mere mortals to look like goddesses? Daily talk shows were filled with experts and their opinions, condemning the fashion world and its power to influence the young. Isabelle was dropped from three clothing lines and Allegra Starr came out and said that she 'regretted' hiring such a girl to advertise her product years ago. Standing in her fur coat, Allegra put on her compassionate face and said she felt responsible for catapulting Isabelle to fame and thus being instrumental in her fall from grace due to the pressures of staying on top. Bertie rang Gabriella and ranted for twenty minutes about Allegra, saying that she would do anything for publicity and that everyone in the industry knew that she regularly snorted thousands of dollars up her own nose.

Gabriella made a point of not reading or watching anything to do with the scandal. She knew Isabelle better than anyone and she understood that her friend had fallen by the wayside from sadness. Most of what was reported was exaggeration. Isabelle may have had a problem, but she wasn't taking ecstasy before breakfast. She had just lost her boyfriend and struggled in the limelight. She wasn't the first to seek fame and then find it hard to cope.

Gabriella's London show was a huge success and featured in numerous fashion magazines. *Vogue* called and asked for an interview and Oberon organised a show in Milan in June. Victoria Beckham emailed, asking to meet, and Vivienne Westwood tweeted that Gabriella was the most exciting thing to happen in the British Fashion Industry in years. America fought back, claiming that she belonged to them. She was from the Bronx after all. However, Gabriella felt her roots were now in London and proudly wore a Union Jack dress on the *Graham Norton Show*.

Each day she sketched and coloured, producing outfit after outfit in dazzling colours. Oberon scrutinised each one and gave her advice, but more and more she found herself disagreeing and disregarding his instructions. Her confidence grew and she found that she wanted things done her way. Oberon feigned annoyance at her rebellion, but in fact he was secretly delighted. Finally, she was finding her voice. At last she was blossoming into her own brand. One day, after a particularly heated argument about a leather sash, he asked her to see him in his office. She walked in and closed the door, preparing herself for another argument.

Oberon took a seat at his desk and crossed his legs.

"The time has come, Gabriella."

"The time? For what?"

"For you to fledge."

"Excuse me?"

"You are no longer welcome here. You need to find your own space and move on."

Her eyes widened. "You're kicking me out? Over a sash? You're kidding, right?"

His eyes crinkled in amusement. "No, not just that. You are no longer my protégée – you are your own woman now. You need to set up your own space with your own brand. You need to take the next step."

"Where will I go?" She started to pace. "I'm still pretty broke. I mean, all the money I have, I spend on rent and I send the rest home to Mama ..."

"Yawn." Oberon rolled his eyes. "So not my problem."

"Oberon!"

"Go to a bank and get a loan. Take control, Gabriella. You're a big girl now."

"And?"

"Rent a space. Somewhere chic. Then find yourself a Riku and set up a website. Do I have to spell it out? *You. Are. No. Longer. My. Problem.*"

"God, you're such a nice guy," she said bitterly. "So, this is really the end?

"Yep." He grinned. "It was nice working with you. We will be linked forever as I will always be the one who gave you your break, but you're a star in your own right now. My work is done."

"Star?" Her eyes widened.

Oberon got up and walked towards her. Taking her shoulders, he forced her to look up at him. "Yes, a star," he said softly. "I'm proud of you, Gabriella Ruiz Álvarez.

Now get out of my office. All this emotion is making me nervous."

Isabelle was sent to Promises Rehab Center in Malibu. Past guests included Britney Spears and Ben Affleck. Situated next to a beach, she spent her days relaxing and staring at the sea. Sipping green tea, she closed her eyes and let the gentle breeze caress her face. She didn't wear make-up and avoided the real world. Elaine took a condo nearby and visited every day. There was no way she was letting her daughter alone.

The first week was hell. She woke up sweating, calling for help as she craved alcohol. Then, the cravings lessened and her sleep patterns improved. Yet, the depression remained and she struggled to stay positive. Every day, she had to find reasons to face the day. She played a game where she would list all the positive things in her life and be thankful. Soon, she became exhausted from this task. The darkness engulfed her and she just wanted to sleep.

A psychologist came every three days to talk and after a while Isabelle began to open up about her feelings. She told him about Raphael and Angelo. How fame had not brought all that it had promised. How she felt so lonely all the time. His kind face listened without judgement and Isabelle started to feel better. She had never spoken so candidly about her personal life and it felt good to let it all out. She described how Raphael had swept her off her feet when she was young and impressionable. How she had given her heart to him and how he had thrown it back in her face.

It was only when she told the story that she realised that both of them were responsible for their break-up. She was the one who had rejected him when he had suggested moving to France, not the other way around. However, he had expected her to give up all that she'd dreamed of and walk away from her career. Maybe, just maybe, things would have turned out differently had she spoken to him that time she had met Sylvie. Maybe he wasn't the heartbreaker she had categorised him to be.

Then she spoke of Angelo but admitted that she started drinking and flirting with drugs during their relationship. She went to great lengths to keep this from him, as he would not have approved. It was through this session that she realised that maybe things weren't as perfect as they seemed. She was unfulfilled and searching for something – something that Angelo couldn't give her. She hung her head in shame when she related how Raphael had called to Bertie's that night. How in a cruel twist of fate, Angelo had crashed the next day. How she took it as a sign that she was being punished.

The psychologist said nothing. He just wrote notes in his journal and nodded.

Isabelle then looked at the story objectively. Angelo was unaware of her duplicity. He crashed because he took a corner too quickly. Sure, the timing was bad, but her actions with Raphael had absolutely nothing to do with it.

Then her psychologist asked her if the crash had not happened, what would she have done?

"I would have ended it with Angelo and moved in with Raphael," she announced.

He raised an eyebrow.

After six weeks, she was released and Elaine took her back to Philadelphia. Again, she slept in her childhood bed and ate the pancakes her mother made in the morning. Her melancholy remained but it wasn't as black as before. Slowly, she was healing. Slowly, she was letting go of the terrible guilt and starting to see that she deserved to be happy.

Taking Oberon's advice, Gabriella searched for a small space to set up an office. She trawled through real estate in the East End, looking for a trendy renovated area that would suit the purpose. Finally, a small space in a warehouse near Shoreditch cropped up. She called up and found that three people were bidding for the same place.

Facing a bank manager was scary, so she asked Riku to practise the interview as she really wanted to come across as serious and trustworthy. She called to his flat one evening, armed with her portfolio and a resumé of sales to date. Dressed in a beige suit and nude pumps, she sat upright in Riku's favourite chair and spoke in a posh voice.

Riku, pouring gin into two giant glasses, asked her ridiculous questions that resulted in the two of them giggling uncontrollably.

"Who's my favourite Beatle?" she repeated, accepting a large glass of gin and tonic.

"I'm trying to teach you to think on your feet," replied Riku, adding cucumber and mint to the glass.

"John."

"Me too!" He high-fived her. "Okay, what are your projections for 2019?"

Gabriella choked on her drink. "Say again?"

"Earnings, Gabby. What do you expect to make?"

She shrugged. "Who can tell? It's a fickle business."

Riku tutted. "Act like you know, girl! That you'll be raking it in. I wouldn't give you a loan, no offense."

"Okay, okay, I expect a fifty-percent profit increase due to Fashion Week and a show in Milan."

467

"Do you prefer Oreos or Doritos?"

"*Riku!*"

Three weeks later, she was sitting in her new office. The only furniture she had was a second-hand mahogany desk that Oberon had been throwing out and a swivel chair from IKEA. As yet, she didn't have framed photos of her with various celebrities on the wall, but she had them in the pipeline. She had met various celebrities at parties and events. Madonna's people had contacted her for a private fitting and the Korean boyband BTS had asked her to design outfits for them. Work was flooding in and she hired two assistants as soon as she could – a young man called Boris and a young girl called Jade. Together, they worked late each evening, designing and sewing prototypes, drinking coffee and singing old tunes.

Boris was blond, in his late twenties and hailed from Gdansk. He religiously went to the gym every morning and as a result was big and muscular. He liked to wear tight T-shirts to emphasise his biceps.

"Wait a second," said Oberon when he saw him. "How come you get a Polish hottie and I'm stuck with Riku?"

Jade was French and hailed from Rouen. She was small with a dark bob and olive skin. She had attended fashion school in London and was eager to work for a designer. All doors had been closed in her face, so she was delighted when Gabriella took her on.

"I remember what it was like in the beginning," Gabriella told her in the interview. "Everyone deserves a shot."

Gabriella was a great boss and often surprised her assistants with doughnuts during a late-night session or a Monday off after a particularly busy week. In turn, they adored her and did everything they could to please her.

ೖ Chapter Thirty-Nine ೞ

Two months later, Isabelle met Bertie for lunch in L.A. She had flown in with her mother for a shopping trip and to catch up with some old friends from Parson's who were based there. They stayed at the Beverly Wilshire and after a morning of shopping on Rodeo Drive, Elaine went back to their suite for a rest. Isabelle went out alone to meet Bertie for sushi.

He looked the same as ever with his twinkling blue eyes, white shirt and silk cravat. He opened his arms wide when he saw her and she hugged him fiercely. Vladimir stood behind him, his massive arms crossed. Cameras flashed and journalists called their names, so Bertie ushered her inside the restaurant, away from prying eyes.

"I can see the headline already," said Bertie rolling his eyes. "'Flynn is Feeling Wells Again' or 'Flirty Bertie'. What do you think?"

Isabelle giggled. "Flynn is Feeling Wells Again? Bertie! Whatever do you mean?"

He winked. "One can dream."

"I have one photographer that follows me everywhere so I'm used to the intrusion. I mean, most of the time it's pointless shadowing me – boring stuff like going for a haircut or picking up some milk at the store. Now he'll have shots of me with an A-lister so he must be thrilled!"

"Bloody parasites, the lot of them," Bertie said cheerfully. "Now, let's order some sashimi and a large bottle of vino."

Isabelle shook her head. "Not for me, I'm afraid. I'm in AA now."

Bertie slapped his head with his hand. "Gosh, I'm such a fool! Of course you are. How crass."

She rubbed his arm. "Not to worry. I'm used to it. Dad handed me a beer at a barbecue last weekend and Mom freaked out."

"I'll have some Evian then," he said, taking a seat at a table. "In solidarity."

She shrugged. "It doesn't bother me, Bertie. You have what you want."

A Japanese waiter appeared with some green tea and bowed his head. Isabelle flashed him a smile and accepted the small cup from his hand.

"Bottoms up," she said, raising her cup.

Bertie clinked his against hers and winked. "So good to see you back to normal."

She nodded. "It's been tough, but I'm so much better."

"Gabby said she called to you a few weeks ago."

"Yeah, she was in New York for a show and an interview with *Esquire*. She came to Philly for a night."

"She's really hit the big time, hasn't she?"

Isabelle nodded. "Totally. I saw Jennifer Lawrence wearing one of her dresses last week at a première."

"I'm delighted for her."

"Me too. She's waited long enough."

Other diners stared over curiously. Bertie was instantly recognisable, but so was Isabelle with her Titian hair.

A young girl of about seventeen approached with her phone. "Can I take a selfie with you guys?"

Bertie sighed. "Is it a matter of life and death, young lady? I'm famished and I need to order."

"Please?" She activated her phone. "Just two seconds."

Isabelle got up and moved to Bertie's side of the table. The girl positioned herself next to them and the camera flashed.

"Nice," she said, looking at the photo. "Thanks, you guys."

Bertie raised his eyes to heaven. "What happened to a good old-fashioned autograph? That one would frame and put on one's wall?"

Isabelle laughed.

The waiter appeared once more with two menus. He bowed his head as he handed one to Bertie and one to Isabelle.

"So, how are you really?" asked Bertie, scanning the list of sushi.

Isabelle took a deep breath. "I'm okay. Well, as okay as I can be."

"Are you sleeping?"

She nodded. "I take pills most nights, they help me drop off. It's my addictive personality."

"Have you come to terms with Angelo's death?"

Her face looked anguished for a moment. "I don't think I'll ever get over that," she admitted. "He was so young and so full of promise."

Bertie nodded and sipped his green tea.

"I had a shrink in rehab," she went on. "He was so nice and it was great to talk. He made me realise, all by myself, that Raphael had nothing to do with the car crash.

That it was coincidental and that I shouldn't blame myself for his death." She felt the tears well up in her eyes. "That time with Raph was so wrong – it shouldn't have happened – but it's not like I was sneaking around for months behind Angelo's back, having a full-blown affair."

"Quite."

"It was once and a mistake and –"

"A mistake?" Bertie raised an eyebrow.

Isabelle blushed. "Well ..."

Bertie regarded her thoughtfully. "He rings me all the time, my old friend Raphael. He asks for you constantly."

She wiped a tear away. "I think about him all the time."

"Then go to him, my sweet. Don't let life pass you by. Angelo's untimely death has shown us all that we should seize the day and embrace happiness."

She fiddled with her chopsticks. "I don't know ..."

"You do know," he said gently. "You two are running around in circles and it's time to stop. I know that he's at home in Picardy for the next month or so. He's working on a new film."

She said nothing.

"His house is not far from Paris. Just a short taxi ride."

She looked up slowly, her green eyes connecting with his. "You think that I should?"

"I *know* that you should." Bertie took her hand in his own and squeezed it. "You're both so lost, you deserve to find one another."

Isabelle touched down in Paris a week later. Charles De Gaulle airport was bustling as she pulled her suitcase through the crowds. Wearing a scarf and large glasses, she kept her head down, hoping that no one would recognise her. The press had tired of her story, mainly because she had been hidden away for over two months, and the world had moved on to other scandals, mainly associated with the U.S. president. She hailed a taxi, her gold bracelet glinting in the summer sun. A white car pulled up and a tall man with a moustache got out and took her bag.

"*Direction Amiens, s'il vous plaît*," she said, smiling. She had downloaded a 'Teach Yourself French' app and had been practising on the plane.

"*Bien sûr, madame,*" he answered, delighted to have such a beauty in his car. With her pale skin and tendrils of red hair peeping out from under the Hermès scarf on her head, she looked like a star. The car sped off down the road.

Amiens, famous for its gothic cathedral and the medieval Saint Leu district, was just over an hour and a half from Paris. Isabelle stared out the window as the taxi sped up the motorway, her mind racing. Her stomach was in knots at the prospect of seeing him.

She had discovered that the Baptiste mansion dated from 1824 and was an impressive stone house on the banks of a lake. After the death of her husband, Agathe Baptiste, Raphael's mother, had moved to a smaller house near Paris, leaving the grand old Baptiste home to her son.

It was there that Raphael wrote screenplay after screenplay in the tranquil surroundings of the estate's huge gardens.

Using her Google maps, Isabelle instructed the taxi driver where to go. When they got to the large gates, she was dismayed to find them closed. There was a security pad on the right of the gate. Bertie hadn't mentioned a code.

"*Madame?*" The driver shrugged.

Isabelle got out of the car and took off her glasses. The

lodge house near the gate was deserted and the front door was boarded up. She knocked on the window but she could see it hadn't been used in a long time. She toyed with ringing Bertie, but he was in Toronto and it was still the middle of the night there.

"Goddamn!" she said out loud.

"*Madame?*" The driver pointed to his watch. "I need go, *madame.*"

"Sure, sure." She pulled out her purse. "How much? *Combien?*"

He looked at the meter. "*Cent cinquante euros.*"

She pulled out three fifties. "*Merci.*"

He smiled. "*Au revoir.*" Then he hopped in his car and drove off.

She took a long shuddering breath. There was nothing else for it – she would have to announce her arrival.

With a trembling finger she pressed the intercom. No one answered.

Then she pressed it again, her heart racing. Would she hear his voice? Would he grant her access?

"*Allo?*"

It was a woman's voice.

she exhaled in relief.

"*Um, bonjour,*" she began, desperately trying to remember her basic French. "I want, *um, je veux, Raphael Baptiste.*"

"May I have your name?" the woman asked in perfect English.

"Sure. It's Isabelle. Isabelle Flynn."

A minute passed – an agonizing eternity – before the large gates began to open slowly. Isabelle activated the pulley handle on her case and walked through the entrance, her bag leaving a trail of dust on the road.

The long drive was tree-lined with a large house at the top. She yanked off her headscarf, letting her red hair fall free, and began her journey under the hot sun.

She didn't notice him at first. It was only when she was halfway up the road that she noticed a figure running towards her, his long dark hair flying.

She took off her sunglasses to be sure and then felt her stomach flip over.

It was Raphael.

She stopped and let him approach her, biting her lip in trepidation. Everything rested on this moment. There were no more chances for them.

When he was about ten feet from her, he stopped. His dark eyes connected with hers and she tried to gauge his mood.

"*Isabelle!*"

She closed her eyes, savouring the way he said her name. *Eeez-abelle.*

When she opened them again, he was standing right in front of her. They stared at each other.

Then, without further thought, she flung her arms around his neck and kissed him. He pulled her close and buried his face in her hair.

"Why are you here?" he asked gruffly, not wanting to let go.

She clung to him. "I wanted to see you. I wanted to tell you something."

He kissed her neck and her lips. "I waited and waited for you …"

She smoothed his long hair back from his face. "I had a lot to deal with."

"I know." He kissed her forehead. "I didn't want to push."

"Can I stay?"

"Of course." He looked at her. "But for how long?"

She stared at him. "I don't want to ever leave you."

"But what about your career?"

"I don't care about that anymore," she said.

"I'm difficult. You know this. I'm hard to live with …"

"I know." She smiled. "But now that we're both teetotallers, I thought we could keep each other on the straight and narrow."

"I called Bertie every day when you were in rehab. I asked everyone how you were."

She kissed his lips tenderly. "I love you."

He hugged her fiercely. "*Moi, aussi.*"

"Let's never be separated again." Her green eyes were serious.

"*Jamais.*"

Bertie called the next day and whooped when he heard that all was well.

"That's a frightful relief, Raph old chap. I always felt so guilty about you two."

"Why?"

"I told you where she was that night and it set the wheels in motion."

"You could not have stopped it, my friend. What is meant to be will happen."

"Perhaps. I'm ecstatic you've worked things out. Restores my faith a bit, I have to say."

"In love?"

"Of course, in love. I had become cynical of late, deeming it all to be nonsense. Now, I'm leaning towards the fairy tale once more."

"Hardly a fairy tale. Rehab is not *Far, Far Away*."

"You know what I mean."

"Yes. Maybe I do."

"Now, I must dash. I have a dinner date with Kim Cattrall. She's in town for a play and is just as funny in real life. Give my love to your ravishing girlfriend."

"I will."

Raphael hung up his iPhone and stared at a naked Isabelle asleep on his king-size bed. Her eyelids fluttered as she slept and her long red mane covered the pillow. Her long legs were curled up and she was lying on her side. Stealing over quietly, he lay down beside her and kissed her shoulder. For the first time in his life, he felt at peace. It was like the jigsaw had come together and he was complete. He hadn't realised how important she was to him until it was too late. Then it took years of yearning and missed chances to get back to this stage.

She stirred slightly and lifted a slender arm upwards to stretch.

"Good evening," he said, nuzzling her neck. "You've been asleep for hours."

She yawned. "Jet lag sucks." She turned and kissed him. "What have you been doing?"

"Working. Speaking with Bertie. Staring at you."

She blushed. "I hope I wasn't snoring or anything. Angelo used to say –" Her hand flew to her mouth. "Oh! I didn't mean to …"

Raphael put his finger to her lips. "Don't worry. It's natural to speak about him."

"I know, but it hurts." Her face grew sombre. "I still can't believe that he's dead. It's all so surreal."

He caressed her arm. "It's okay. Talk to me."

She looked up. "Why did you come and find me at the gala? After all that time? Why?"

He stroked her cheek. "It took me a long time to

realise that I had made the biggest mistake. When I asked you to come to France with me and you rejected my offer, I was so angry."

"I couldn't give up my career and the lucky chance I had been given."

"*Shhh!*" He kissed her nose. "Sylvie arrived the next day and she spoke of our love and her regrets. I didn't have time to think about it."

"I called to your hotel room and I met her," said Isabelle, reddening.

"What?" He started. "When?"

"A couple of days after we parted ways. Sylvie answered the door and said you were in the shower. I ran away, Raph. I told her not to say anything ..."

"I'm sure she did not object." His expression grew angry. "She never mentioned that you called. I was not given a chance."

"I'm sorry." She hung her head. "I was hurt and when I saw her I panicked. Bertie said she was the love of your life."

"*Non*," he said shaking his head. "That is you. It took me a while to realise it."

"But we were only together for a couple of weeks," she protested.

"That does not matter, Isabelle. You changed my life and I was too stupid to see it until it was too late. Sylvie and I, well, we split up."

"I know," she said miserably. "I read about it."

"Then I saw that you were dating Angelo. You looked so happy and successful. Who was I to think I had a chance with you any longer? I lacked the courage to try."

"So, why the gala? Why did you come to see me?"

"I was surrounded by your image. On the internet, on

billboards. I dreamt of you at night and craved you during the day. In the end, I had to act. I am not getting any younger and I had to find out once and for all."

"So, you seduced me."

"It was not difficult." He smiled. "You see, what we have is impossible to ignore. I feel it and you feel it. It is a link – a bond – where you set me on fire and I you. I have burned for you, my love. Let's never part again."

She took his large hand in hers. "You must be kinder then. You must never shut me out."

He crossed his heart. "I promise," he said solemnly.

"If we are to be together, you must treat me with respect."

"Always."

She wrapped her arms around his neck. "Now kiss me before I explode."

⋙ Chapter Forty ⋘

"So, I said to Chelsea Clinton to book it right away! You know how these things sell out."

Caroline laughed and her diamond bracelet shone in the lights of the restaurant. L'Espalier, a sophisticated French restaurant in the Back Bay neighbourhood of Boston, was full to the brim with diners enjoying the delicious cuisine.

Hugo played with his dessert spoon, bored and eager to leave. He should never have agreed to this stupid dinner with his boss at the firm and his wife. Caroline had insisted saying that it would count when it came to promotions. To climb the ladder, one had to be connected socially.

His boss, Winston Chambers and his wife Elizabeth, were both in their sixties and powerful in the Boston set. He was balding and wore a signet ring on his little finger. She was regal in Chanel with impressive diamond jewellery on display. Both staunch Republicans, they spent most of the night pontificating about Trump. Hugo listened and nodded at appropriate times, but he didn't agree. Caroline had warned him not to express any negative views in the Chambers' presence. She wanted that promotion after all.

The waitress cleared the dessert plates and Caroline stood up.

Winston and Hugo immediately got to their feet.

"If you'll excuse me," she said demurely. "I have to use the ladies' room."

The men resumed their seats as soon as she had left. Hugo knew that she was actually heading outside for a smoke but he said nothing. Caroline liked to pretend that she was something very different to reality.

After two brandies and a lot more political talk, they said goodbye and Hugo hailed a taxi.

Caroline lit another cigarette when the Chambers were out of sight.

"God, he can bang on," she said in her nasal voice. "Still, we did good work tonight, Hugo. You'll make partner by sucking up to him."

A taxi stopped and he opened the door. "Ladies first," he said, standing to the side.

"I'm not ready," she said coldly. "Can't you see that I just lit this cigarette?"

"It's Saturday night, Caroline. Taxis are hard to come by. I, for one, would like to get home if that's okay with you."

"Fine," she said, stomping on her Marlboro and pushing past him to get into the car.

They travelled in silence and in no time at all they got to his apartment.

The minute he opened the door, she walked in first and headed straight for the fridge. Pouring a large glass of white wine, she took a big gulp.

"I'm going to have an uninterrupted cigarette outside," she announced, taking her bag.

"Fine," he answered, loosening his tie and sitting on

the couch. He pulled out his phone and opened Google. Typing in 'Gabriella' he waited for the various links to come up. Scrolling down through Twitter, Instagram and Facebook profiles, he gazed at her face. Her happy, open, lovely face.

Caroline opened the sliding door unexpectedly and he threw the phone to the side.

"What were you doing?" she asked suspiciously.

"Nothing."

"It didn't look like nothing." She stalked over and picked up his phone. "Why are you googling her?" Her face hardened.

"Who?"

"Gabriella."

"No reason."

She scrolled down through his search history. "Looks like you've been looking her up quite a bit. Can you explain?"

He stared at the painting on the wall. "There's nothing to explain."

"Yeah, right." She flung the phone on the cushions. "You still have a thing for that maid, don't you?"

"Don't call her that."

"Why? She's nothing, Hugo. An immigrant nobody who got lucky."

"Caroline!' He sat up straight. "She's not like that at all. She worked hard to get where she is and I respect her for it."

"You respect her? Well, it's all coming out now." She started to pace the room. "So, do you dream of Gabby at night? Do you lament the fact that you didn't work out?"

"No."

"Then why are you googling her like a stalker?"

"I'm just interested in how she's doing."

Caroline turned her back to him. "Hugo, we've been together nearly two years. I've given you everything. Why then do I feel that you're not interested? You've been weird for months now."

He stared at the back of her head. Did he see himself growing old with her? It was a picture he couldn't imagine.

"Caroline," he began.

"Save it." She whipped around. "You're going to break up with me."

He paused and then nodded. "It's not working out. It hasn't been right in a long time."

"I've given you two years!" she screamed. "Two years for nothing. How dare you dump me for that piece of trash?"

"*Don't call her that!*" he roared. "You don't even know her."

"I don't need to," she spat. " Girls like that are all the same. She's as common as muck."

He got up and walked to his bedroom door. "You can sleep on the couch, but in the morning I want you to leave."

Caroline stared at him in shock. "Are you serious?"

"It's over."

"*Hugo!*"

He slammed the door.

Two months later, Gabriella frowned as she typed an Instagram post.

Been commissioned to design the #Oscars gown for British nominee @aurorasinclair
#excited

483

She pressed 'share' and placed her phone on her desk. The call had come through the day before from an ecstatic Aurora who had been nominated for her role as Scarlett in Carey McGrath's remake of *Gone With The Wind*.

"Billions watch the Academy Awards, Gabby!" she said in her clear voice. "I want the world to know that I'm wearing your design."

Oberon called over to her office to congratulate her. "It reminds me of Allegra at the Oscars that time. As much as I hate to admit it, it was the making of me."

Gabriella did a little dance around her desk. "I'm bursting with ideas. I mean, she's so beautiful. Anything will look amazing on her." She flopped down on her swivel chair. "Speaking of Allegra, I'm off to France in the morning."

"Oh?"

"I'm flying to Nice and then taking a cab to Grasse."

"Grasse?" Oberon put his hand over his mouth. "Surely not."

She nodded. "I'm making a perfume."

"Gabby! Don't sell out so soon!"

"I'm not! Look at Chanel No. 5. It can't fail."

"Make sure it doesn't resemble Allegra's frightful scent."

"Oh, I will." She made a face. "I swear that Isabelle's apartment still smells of that stuff. Even after the years."

"Horrid," he agreed. "What time are you off?"

"First thing. I'm staying in Cannes and then flying back on Thursday."

He whistled. "You've gone from zero to hero in two seconds. Cannes, if you don't mind."

She blushed. "I've never been and I've always wanted to. Boris and Jade are coming with me so we'll have a laugh."

"Well, think of poor old me in my stuffy office in this

heat while you sip rosé by the sparkling blue sea."

"Oberon! You were in the Bahamas last week!"

"So?"

The next day, Riku was hoovering the multi-coloured Turkish rug at the entrance to Oberon's office when a dark-haired man walked out of the elevator.

"Hello," he said in an American accent. "Is this where I find Oberon?"

"How did you get into the building?" asked Riku in astonishment, turning off the Dyson.

"A woman was walking out as I arrived, and she kindly held the door."

"Did security let you through?"

"I said I was Gabriella's friend."

"Gabby?"

He nodded. "We used to know one another in New York."

Riku stared at him intently. "Have we met before?"

He nodded. "I was at Allegra's première."

"Ah, yes!" Riku smiled. "I remember now."

"Anyway, I'm in town for one day on business. I thought I'd look her up. Is she here?"

Riku shook his head. "Gabby isn't based here anymore. She has her own place near Shoreditch."

His face fell. "Is that far? Can you give me the address?"

Riku shook his head. "There's no point as she's not there. She flew to France this morning. She'll be back next week."

"France? Please say you're kidding."

"No, sorry." Riku took pity on him. "I have her phone number if you want to call her."

He shook his head. "No, no. I wanted to see her in person."

"Yeah, but I'm sure she'd love to hear from you, being from home and all."

He backed away. "Thanks but it's okay."

"Will I tell her that you called?"

"No, don't. I'll catch up with her some other time." He pressed the elevator button over and over. "Come on," he muttered under his breath.

The door opened.

"What was your name again?" said Riku as the doors closed.

Hugo cursed his luck. When the business trip to London had come up, he had put himself forward immediately. It gave him the perfect chance to look Gabriella up and maybe take her out.

He had been nervous in that elevator, wondering how she would react. He had upset her at the Vanguard that time, bringing Caroline along. It had been a cheap shot, but he wanted to hurt her for leaving him behind to further her career.

Then he had emailed when Isabelle was in hospital, but she had never replied.

Maybe she had forgotten him. Maybe she was too famous now – too busy with celebrities to bother with her old life.

She used to always talk about God and his signs. He had laughed at her superstition but now he wasn't so sure. Her being in France was unfortunate, but maybe it was a sign that they were not meant to be. Maybe he should just let it go.

Oberon picked up some sashimi with his chopsticks and dipped it in wasabi. Riku helped himself to some pickled ginger and they ate companionably in silence for a while.

"Gabby sent a picture of her and Bono in Nice. She met him eating lunch at La Petite Maison near the Promenade des Anglais. Remember we ate there one time?"

Riku nodded. "She's really hit the big time, hasn't she? It's crazy."

Oberon took a sip of beer. "The world today is all so instant. Things happen overnight, no one waits for anything anymore."

Riku nodded in agreement. "Everyone is connected."

"I just hope she keeps her head and doesn't end up like Miss Flynn."

"She's too sensible for that." Riku added some soy sauce to his tuna roll. "By the way, speaking of Gabby, this American turned up at the office today."

"Who?"

"He was looking for Gabby. I didn't catch his name but he was the guy she brought to the Allegra première that time."

Oberon nearly dropped his chopsticks. "The rich sailor boy! Go on."

"He was in London on business and wanted to see her. I said she'd gone to France and he just took off."

"Interesting."

"Why?"

"Oh, he was the love of her life. She adored him."

Riku put his hand on his heart. "How sweet!"

"I wonder what he wanted," mused Oberon. "The last I heard he was seeing some posh girl who was nasty to Gabby."

"Oh, he didn't say. I offered him her number but he said he wanted to see her in person."

"Did he say anything else?"

"Nope."

Oberon speared some salmon with the end of a chopstick. "Hugo was his name as I remember. Maybe we should call Gabby and tell her."

"He said not to," said Riku.

"Why?"

"Who knows? I think we should stay out of it." Riku was firm.

"I don't know. They might need a helping hand ..."

"Oberon! This is not *A Midsummer Night's Dream*! You can't use magic to make people fall in love."

"*Hmmm*."

❦ Chapter Forty-One ❧

The day after he returned to the States, Hugo took annual leave from the office and went back to Long Island. It was nearing the end of the summer and he wanted to sail his boat as much as he could before it got too cold. When he arrived home he found that Celine had decided to do exactly the same thing.

"If Charlotte turns up, we'll be a complete set!" she quipped.

No chance of that, he thought. His sister was embroiled in a huge divorce case between two leading Bostonian families and was working seventeen-hour days. He often chided her for working too hard, but she brushed it off. Since her divorce from Luca, she had closed herself off emotionally, despite her startling beauty. Hugo wished she would take some time to date and have a life outside of the office, but so far she had expressed little interest.

He met his mother on the veranda, instructing the gardener.

"Hugo!" she said in delight. "I'm so glad to see you."

He embraced her and took a seat on a wicker chair.

"Your room is ready," she said, sitting opposite him. "I

also took the liberty of asking Bruno to prepare your favourite roast chicken for dinner."

He nodded. "It's so good to be on vacation," he said yawning. "I'm looking forward to taking it easy."

"Caroline is on Long Island too," said Victoria innocently. "Veronica called yesterday and suggested that we meet for a barbecue or something."

"No." He met her gaze steadily. "It's over, Momma."

"But she's a nice girl ..."

"No." He got up. "I'll just grab a sandwich or something."

"You'll have to do it yourself. Maria called in sick today." She pursed her lips. "She sounded fine on the phone. I mean, it's been hard enough since Magda left. Maids can be so inconsiderate."

Hugo walked away. "I'll see you later."

It was over breakfast the next morning that they heard the news.

Elena called in a frenzy saying that Maurice had been accused of sexual harassment. A horrified Frank took the call in the hallway and arrived back to the dining room with a pale face.

"It's Maurice," he said in shock. "He's in big trouble, Vic. Ten women have accused him of sexual misconduct."

Victoria dropped her fork with a clatter. "Say again?"

Hugo immediately thought of Gabriella and his skin grew cold.

Frank took a seat. "Elena's going crazy. She said that she's leaving him."

"She'd better not be too hasty," said Victoria calmly, dabbing her lips with a starched white napkin. "Who says it's true?"

"One of ringleaders is Maria, our maid."

"Maria?" repeated Victoria in disbelief. "How could she let us down so? That's her job terminated right away."

"You can't just fire her," said Hugo.

"You just watch me," answered his mother. "How dare she bring our name through the gutter? No wonder she called in sick."

Celine looked uncomfortable. "Would it be disrespectful to say that I'm not surprised about Uncle Maurice?"

"Celine!" Her mother glared at her.

"I mean, he was always leering at my friends and being inappropriate."

Victoria banged the table with her fist. "Celine du Maurier, you shut your mouth this instant. Can't you see that your daddy is upset? Maurice is his baby brother."

"Sorry, Daddy," said Celine reddening.

Frank rubbed his temple. "It can't be true. I mean, he's always had an eye for the ladies, but nothing like this. It can't be true."

"Of course it's not, sugar." Victoria got up and walked to her husband. Placing her hand on his shoulder, she rubbed it soothingly. "This is a group of women out to make a fast buck. He is a du Maurier after all."

"I hope so, Vic. I hope so."

"I mean, if it's the likes of Maria and that ilk, they're definitely on the make."

Frank put his head in his hands. "I can't believe it."

"We'll hire the best attorney money can buy," she continued smoothly. "We'll save Maurice."

Hugo got up abruptly. "If he's innocent, that is."

Frank glared at his son. "What are you saying, Hugo?"

Victoria shook her head behind Frank's back and put her fingers to her lips. Hugo understood her silent message.

"Nothing. I'm saying nothing." He walked out of the room.

Victoria caught up with him on the stairs.

"*Hugo!*' she hissed, grabbing his shirt. "I presume you're referring to Magda's daughter that time."

"I saw it with my own eyes."

"You saw nothing of the sort." She narrowed her eyes. "You stand by your family, you hear? Don't let your daddy down."

"But Maurice is guilty. I bet my life on it."

"No matter. We stand together."

"How can you defend him?" he demanded.

"Because he's family. Because we don't want a scandal." She let go of his shirt. "Don't rock the boat any further, Hugo. That's my final word."

He turned away. "Message received loud and clear."

Victoria smoothed her hair on her forehead. "Good. I'm glad we understand each other."

Gabriella came back from France and went straight to her office. She was buzzing from her time on the Côte d'Azur – eating and drinking al fresco, going for rides on fast boats, sampling different scents in a factory near Grasse. Her thoughts had been filled Aurora's Oscar gown and she was anxious to begin the design.

Taking out her sketch book, she toyed with calling Lita for advice. Even now, she still relied on her *abuela* for ideas and feedback. Picking up her phone, she noticed seven missed calls from Isabelle. She called her back, drawing a rough outline of a woman's body as she waited for her friend to pick up.

"Gabby! You've heard the news, right?" said Isabelle straight away.

"Well, hello to you too." Gabriella laughed. "What news?"

"About Maurice du Maurier."

"What?" Her skin grew cold.

"He's ruined. Ten women have come forward saying that he assaulted them. It's all over the news back home."

Gabriella dropped her pencil. "What?" she whispered again.

"One of the main women is Maria, from Victoria's place."

"Maria?"

"Sure, there's a clip on YouTube. She did a press release where she urged others to come forward. Apparently, his wife has left him and he's been sacked from Liberty Designs. The rest of the family are standing by him and all that, but he's in big trouble."

"Why are you telling me this?"

"You've got to tell your story, of course."

"What? I can't do that. What would Celine and Hugo say?"

"Who cares? You have to stand by these women, Gabs. It's important."

"No."

"Why? You're famous now. You could really make a difference. Maria is a maid. It took real guts for her to do this. She stands to lose everything she has. They need someone like you to fight. They need you, Gabby. Do it for them."

"My mother ..."

"Doesn't work for them anymore. You owe them nothing."

"I can't, Zsa Zsa. I just can't."

"Think about it, Gabby. If it were me, what would you

tell me to do? Creeps like Maurice get away with it every day and why? Because they have money and they prey on the less fortunate. If Hugo hadn't intervened that night, what would have happened? Honestly?"

Gabriella took a shuddering breath.

"Exactly."

"How will I face them?"

"With your head held high. They have played with your destiny for too long. Do this for all the women out there without a voice. Channel your vision. Think of me with those wolfhounds, marching into battle."

Gabriella smiled weakly.

"Do the right thing, Gabby. Or you'll regret it."

Gabriella called her mother straight away.

"Hey, Mama."

"Hello, *mi cariña*. It's good to hear your voice."

"Mama, is it true about Maurice du Maurier?"

"How did you hear about that?"

"Isabelle."

"Why, yes. It's true. To be honest, I'm not surprised. He was always so creepy at the big house."

"What's happening with it now?"

"He's on bail and awaiting trial. I met Maria last week and she is determined to bring him to justice."

Gabriella closed her eyes. "Will she win?"

Magda shrugged. "Who knows, Gabby? There are different rules for people like him. Money can buy you almost anything."

"His wife left him ..."

"Well, there's no surprise there. They were never close, from what I could see. Frank is trying his best to smooth things over but the other shareholders in the company voted to get Maurice out. He's ruined, I believe."

"So Frank is supporting him?"

"He's family, I guess. Victoria was quoted as saying that it was a mountain out of a molehill and that there was a grey area around consent. God, I'm so glad I'm out of there."

"Me too, Mama. Me too."

"So, I saw you on TV last week. You came across so well."

"Thanks, Mama."

"Stay in touch."

"Give my love to Lita."

Gabriella went online and typed in '**Maurice du Maurier scandal**'. News stories popped up immediately about the group of women who had come forward with accusations of sexual harassment and assault. It went on to say that the women were receiving free legal aid. Gabriella scrolled down to find a YouTube video of Maria, her mother's old friend from work, outside a courthouse. She looked official in a black suit and her expression was grim. Gabriella pressed 'play' and sat back.

Maria began to speak. "*For years I put up with being treated like dirt. Not only by my employer, but also by her friends and family. For some reason, respect is not a word that is known or understood for my people. I am standing here today for all those nameless women who suffered because of the colour of their skin. I am here to fight for those who had no choice – those who had to bury the truth in order to keep their jobs and feed their families. I have lost my job as a result of this, but if it means justice for those Maurice has wronged, then it's worth it.*"

Gabriella pressed 'pause', her heart thumping.

She had kept quiet to save her family. She had been victimised because of her background.

Isabelle was right. She had to go back and testify. Not just for her, but for all the women who never got a chance.

Gabriella instructed Jade to book her on the next flight to New York. Then, on Isabelle's advice, she called Bertie and told him the story. If anyone could help, it was him. He was the most well-connected man in Christendom.

After she related her tale, Bertie was suitably horrified.

"Good Lord, the cretin! We must succeed, my darling! Leave it to me."

He made a few calls and found out as many details as he could.

Maurice had the best defence attorney in the business: Vincent Piccone. Vince, as he was known, was famed for his ability to convince a jury of anything. Of Sicilian descent, he was a small dark-haired man of forty-five, who charged by the hour and arrogantly guaranteed a successful outcome no matter what. He had been hired by Frank right away to save his brother.

The women, headed by Maria, had the services of a young attorney called Marjorie Willis, who had agreed to represent the women *pro bono* on the advice of her seniors. "It'll look good later on your resumé when you go for a promotion," one partner had told her.

Vince, on hearing of the prosecutor he faced, had laughed his head off. "They're taking me on with a goddamn novice? That girl's only out of law school for two minutes."

Bertie then called his agent Harry Finkelman and asked him to recommend a good prosecuting attorney. The only way to win was to fight fire with fire. Vince had to meet his match and Marjorie Willis, although dedicated, did not have the experience necessary. Harry immediately sent the link to a fellow Jew called Marty Kassewitz, a renowned shark in the legal world. Bertie called Gabriella and urged her to act quickly as this Marty was a busy man.

Oberon was sitting in his chair in his office when she walked in.

"What the hell is wrong with you?" he asked, observing her frazzled state. "I was about to call you with some interesting news."

"I'm heading back to America."

"What? Why?"

"Things have gone crazy."

"Do tell." His green eyes gleamed. "Do we have scandal?"

She flopped down on a chair. "Remember I told you about Hugo? That guy I really liked back home?"

"Well, funny you should mention it …"

She ignored him. "Well, there was more to that story. You see, Hugo's uncle, the head of the clothing brand, well, he … he …" She reddened.

"He what?" asked Oberon irritably. "Jesus Christ, Gabby! Spit it out."

"He attacked me. In the garden. He was going to rape me but Hugo stopped him." She took a shuddering breath. "I didn't tell anyone at the time because I was too scared. Mama would have lost her job and no one would have believed the maid …"

Oberon raised an eyebrow. "So, you covered it up?"

She nodded. "Things were different back then."

Oberon said nothing.

"Anyway, lots of women have come forward now and they're accusing Maurice of harassment and assault. I've got to go back and stand with them. I've got to tell my story."

Oberon sat back in his chair. "I'm not sure this is a good idea. It could damage your brand. Do you want to be associated with this going forward?"

She shook her head. "I wish I could hide from it and forget it, but I can't. I owe it to these women. Who knows how many more he attacked after me. All because I didn't act. I have to do this. I have no choice."

"You'll have to testify …"

"I know."

"Have you got a lawyer?"

She took out her phone. "Bertie sent the number of this amazing prosecutor called Marty Kassewitz. I'm going to see if he'll take it on."

After a very short conversation with a secretary in the firm, she hung up. "They're busy until 2020," she said dolefully.

Oberon had watched her in fascination. "Why did you meekly say your name was Gabriella Ruiz Álvarez? No offense, darling, but who the fuck is that? Call back and own it!"

"He may not have heard of me …"

"That secretary will have, so ring her back."

So she did and when they heard who she was, there was a pause and then a promise of a call back.

Marty himself called a few minutes later. "Sure, I heard about this case. He's saying it was consensual. It's a tough one but I'm sure we can make it work."

"Thank you, Mr. Kassewitz."

"Marty, please."

"Okay then, Marty."

"Fire that other attorney, whatshername Willis, and

meet me in a couple of days' time downtown at my office. We need to see what evidence we've got."

"So, you'll take us on?"

"Vince Piccone beat me at tennis one time, the arrogant fuck. I'll help you bury him."

Gabriella hung up.

"He's going to help me," she said.

Oberon nodded in approval. "Go on, get going. You'll miss your flight."

"You said you had something to tell me?"

"It doesn't matter now." He had wanted to tell her that Hugo had come looking for her. "I'll tell you some other time. You have bigger fish to fry." He ushered her out the door.

₪ Chapter Forty-Two ₪

On touching down in New York, Gabriella went straight to Melrose to see Magda. Her mother was delighted that her little girl had come home unexpectedly.

"Gabriella! This is a wonderful surprise. Lita is still asleep – will I wake her?"

Gabriella shook her head. "Don't disturb her, Mama. I need to talk to you."

Ten minutes later, her mother's hand flew to her mouth in horror. "Tell me it's not true," she whispered. "My poor Gabby. My baby girl."

Gabriella started to cry. "I couldn't tell you, Mama. I was so worried that you would be fired."

Magda pulled her close and stroked her hair. "You did what you thought was right, *preciosa*. No one can blame you for that."

"This will go global, Mama. There will be journalists and photographers. They will try and find anything to print."

"We've nothing to hide," said Magda grimly. "Don't you worry about that."

"I need to call Maria. We have to come together on this."

"Sure, sure, I've got her number." Magda got up and wiped her eyes. "Let me just check my phone."

Gabriella stared at the picture of the Blessed Virgin on the wall. The gold frame was slightly tarnished and Mary's eyes were staring up to heaven.

Magda handed her the phone. "Here you go. Maria's number."

Gabriella smiled gratefully.

Gabriella arranged to meet Maria that evening in the lounge of the Melrose Hotel.

She was waiting in the bar when she arrived.

"Gabby!" she said, hugging her warmly. "What brings you here? I don't understand." Her brown hair was tied back and she wore a simple navy dress.

"I'm standing with you," said Gabriella, squeezing her hand. "Maurice? He attacked me too. I got away, but it could've been a lot worse."

"What?" she whispered, shrinking back. "When?"

"A few years back. The night of that birthday dinner . . ."

"You never said ..."

"I couldn't. I had to stay quiet to protect Mama."

Maria nodded. "I understand."

"But now I'm coming forward. I've hired this attorney called Marty Kassewitz to help us. If you don't mind, that is. Apparently he's the best."

"Hired?" Maria's eyes widened. "But it will cost a fortune! We have a woman who agreed to give us free legal aid."

"I can afford it." Gabriella assured her. "We need someone who can fight this Vincent Piccone."

Maria closed her eyes and said a prayer under her breath.

"Are you okay?" asked Gabriella.

"I'm thanking God that you're here." Maria's eyes were shining with tears. "This is a miracle."

Marty Kassewitz's office was on the fifth floor of a building just off Madison Avenue. Both Gabriella and Maria went there the next day for a meeting.

Marty welcomed them at the door of his office, his black hair wet from the shower. Tall and athletic, he had just come from the gym and was bursting with energy.

"Coffee?" he asked, flashing white teeth.

"I'm good," said Gabriella, taking a seat in a leather chair.

Maria just shook her head and followed suit, sitting in the other available chair near his desk.

"I called this Marjorie girl and she brought me up to speed," he began, taking a swig of water. "We've got ten allegations of sexual harassment, three of groping and one criminal sex act, vis à vis, a forced blowjob in the back of his Porsche. Is that correct?"

Maria nodded.

"I've gotta say, these cases are notoriously hard to prove. As yet, we're relying on stories and accounts. Have you got anything that will help?"

Maria's brown eyes were troubled. "There was a girl, a couple of years back. She was hired to waitress at a party at the du Maurier mansion. I found her crying in the wine cellar. Her clothes were ripped and she was shaking real bad."

"What happened?"

"She said he raped her. She called and called for help, but no one heard."

Gabriella shuddered.

502

"I tried to convince her to come forward but she refused. She wanted it all to go away."

"We need her to come forward," he said, rubbing his chin. "She needs to testify. Did she go to a doctor afterwards?"

Maria nodded sadly. "Oh, she did. You see, she got pregnant. She found out two months later."

Marty's eyes lit up. "And?"

"She had a little boy." Maria met his gaze. "She couldn't bring herself to terminate it. She's religious, you see. So, she had the baby."

"Then we need a paternity test right away."

Maria shook her head. "She won't allow it. I've asked her over and over. She doesn't want Henrique to know the circumstances of his birth."

Marty picked up his phone. "Leave it to me. I'll subpoena her if I have to."

Gabriella took Maria's hand. "This is his job. We have to have faith."

The story broke a few hours later. CNN reported it first and then it went global. Oberon sent a text saying that he had been accosted on his way home by paps, demanding information on his protégée. He finished the message with 'The things I do for you' and an emoji with rolling eyes.

Gabriella herself was followed and photographed hugging Maria goodbye. The story hit Twitter and the hashtag #MeToo started to trend once more. Marty gave a press release demanding that Maurice du Maurier surrender to police as there was overwhelming evidence to prove the accusations. Marty went on to say that the further accusations of sexual harassment and assault included a criminal sex act and groping.

Vince Piccone released a statement saying that his client was denying all charges against him and that if sexual relations occurred, they were consensual.

Magda was followed to the drugstore and asked if she had any updates on the case. She called Gabriella immediately and warned her not to come home. There was a group of predatory paps stationed outside their building, waiting to pounce.

Gabriella booked into a small hotel under a fake name and covered her head with hats as she walked in and out. Stories began to circulate about her humble beginnings and her rags to riches tale went viral. Photos of places she used to frequent in the Bronx, her graduation photo from Parson's, pictures of her and Hugo at the launch of Allegra's perfume, and holiday snaps of her in Mallorca, all appeared. Her previous socio-economic status and her delay in coming forward became the subject of much discussion on daytime TV. Celebrities who had bought Gabriella's couture tweeted in solidarity, showing support for her plight.

Weary from an intense meeting with Marty, Gabriella went straight to her hotel room and poured herself a vodka from the minibar.

Her phone buzzed over and over with messages from friends and colleagues, saying how shocked they were and offering support. Her thoughts drifted to Hugo. He must have heard by now. She wondered how he would react. He never seemed to like Maurice very much and he had been on her side when the attack had happened. A long time had passed since and she suspected that he would stand by his father on this.

Miserably she downed her glass and filled another. It had been a gruelling day.

Luca had been stunned at the revelation. "Why the hell didn't you tell me, Gabs?" he asked angrily down the phone.

Throwing her phone on the bed, she kicked off her shoes. She just wanted to relax and sleep, without chatter or noise. Gazing out the window, she sipped her drink and sighed. She had achieved what she had set out to do. Her career was reaching new heights and she had grown so much. Yet, was she happy? Was it all worth it? To the world, she had it all, but in the privacy of the hotel room, all she felt was emptiness.

Victoria du Maurier watched the screen with a frown. "Can you believe this? She went off and hired Marty Kassewitz. Land's sakes, he's a slippery so-and-so. Daddy is going clean out of his mind."

Hugo stirred his coffee contemplatively. "She's doing what she thinks is right. If I hadn't helped her that night, who knows what might have happened."

"I've said it before, she was dressed like a hooker. Poor Maurice was seduced."

Hugo banged his fist on the table. "*Gabby's not like that, Momma, and you know it!*"

He got to his feet just as Gabriella came on the screen. She looked nervous and unsure, biting her lip as the journalist asked her questions.

"That little tramp, I can't believe she's doing this," said Victoria. "I thought I made it quite clear –" She stopped herself just in time.

Hugo whipped around. "You made what quite clear?"

"Nothing."

"Momma?"

"Nothing, sugar. I don't know what I'm saying, is all."

She picked a speck of dirt off the coffee table.

"Did you mention Maurice to Gabby?"

Victoria pursed her lips. "I might have advised her on the matter."

"Momma?"

"I just gave her my opinion, Hugo. I told her not to say anything as it would bring shame on the family."

"You did what? When?"

"After you told me. It was nothing, darlin'. Just a friendly conversation." She turned away.

Hugo narrowed his eyes. "Are you sure that was all?"

"Of course, I'm sure." She laughed nervously. "She had no intention of speaking out anyway. She had made up her mind."

Hugo said nothing.

"Have you plans for today?" she asked brightly. "It's a lovely day outside."

"No." He walked away, meeting Celine on the way out. He strode past with a dour expression.

She rubbed her eyes and headed straight for the sofa.

"What's up with him, Momma?" she asked yawning.

"Oh, he's still hurting over Caroline, I guess." Victoria didn't meet her eyes.

"Caroline? But *he* broke it off with *her*."

"Yes, but it's still gotta hurt, sugar. They were together for such a long time."

"I'm glad it's over. She was hard work."

"Don't say that about your friend. Now, I'm off to town. Do you need anything?"

Celine shook her head. "I'm good."

"Now, don't even dream of trying to meet up with that Gabriella, you hear? She's the enemy now."

"But Uncle Maurice ..."

Victoria held up her hand. "She's lying through her teeth, baby. It's as plain as day. No fraternising with her, okay?"

Celine made a salute like a cadet in the army. "You got it."

"Don't sass me, young woman." Victoria grabbed her car keys. "Magda's daughter has crossed the line. There's no goin' back."

Tara Jacob met Gabriella for a drink on 7th Avenue.

Gabriella had dressed so as to look as incognito as possible. Copying Isabelle's look, a scarf covered her long hair and large sunglasses covered most of her face. Scurrying inside the bar, she glanced around nervously. It looked like normal clientele, eating snacks and drinking wine.

"Gabriella!" came a voice and she turned.

Tara was waving madly. She looked the same with her red hair piled on her head and her bright blue eyes. They took a seat at the bar, perching on two wooden high stools.

"Gabby, darling. How are you holding up?" She hugged her tightly. "I'm reading about it every day."

"It's pretty tough," she admitted, taking off her scarf. "My experience is nothing compared to some of the others."

Tara sighed. "I can imagine."

The barman approached. "What can I get you?" he asked, smiling.

"I'll have a Sancerre," said Tara.

"I'll have a Chardonnay," said Gabriella.

She placed her sunglasses on the counter.

Tara rubbed her arm. "What a nightmare for you, Gabby."

"Oh, I got away lightly." She rubbed her eyes tiredly. "We have a girl, she wants to remain anonymous, who he raped. She had a kid as a result and he made her sign a NDA ..."

"NDA?" Tara interrupted.

"Oh, a non-disclosure agreement." Gabriella explained. "I'm all legal-speak at the moment thanks to Marty."

"Go on."

"Anyway, she refused to talk until we convinced her that no NDA could stand up in court if it was concealing a criminal act. It's morally indefensible. So, she caved but demanded that she's not publicly identified, to protect her son."

"Vince Piccone is saying that Maurice will be exonerated."

Gabriella shook her head. "It's a tough one. It's hard to prove that it wasn't consensual. It was first-degree rape, Tara. We just don't know how we'll prove it. Marty filed new charges this morning against him, citing her detailed account of what happened. He wants Maurice to give himself up."

Tara sipped her juice. "Elena left him and he's been sacked from the firm."

"I know."

"Will he play ball?"

"I think so. Marty has put forward an agreement to Vince."

"Oh?" Tara raised an eyebrow. "What agreement?"

"If Maurice is arraigned, the judge –"

"Arraigned?" Tara rolled her eyes. "You sound like my ex-husband."

"Sorry! Well, if Maurice accepts the charges made

against him, the judge will set bail at $750,000. He can easily afford that."

"Well, I would pay anything to stay out of jail."

"He'll pay. Then, of course, he can't leave the state while the Grand Jury hear all the testimonies."

"Are you nervous about testifying?"

Gabriella shook her head. "No. I can't wait to see him pay for what he's done. Men like him have gotten away with this kind of thing for too long."

"That's for sure." She took a gulp of her wine. "Luca sends his love. I was talking to him this morning."

"How's he doing?"

Tara smiled knowingly. "I shouldn't say anything but I can't keep it to myself. Lydia is three months gone."

Gabriella clapped her hands together. "Oh, I'm so thrilled. Luca must be delighted, right?"

"He's on cloud nine. Lyd is just over her morning sickness so she's in better form."

"Sienna will love a sibling."

Tara raised an eyebrow. "I'm not too sure about that. She's number one in that household."

"My God, how Luca has changed," reflected Gabriella.

Tara sipped her wine. "Tell me about it."

✏ Chapter Forty-Three ✐

Magda called her first thing the next morning. "Gabriella? Are you up?"

"No, Mama. What's wrong?"

"There's a story about you in the *Star*."

"Oh?"

"It's all about you and Hugo."

She sat bolt upright. "What?"

"Is it true?"

"What? Is what true, Mama?"

"That Victoria threatened you?"

Gabriella felt her skin grow cold. "What did you say?"

"Oh, Gabby. I feel so bad."

"I'll call you back." She hung up the phone.

She googled the article right away. There, in black-and-white, was a detailed account of her doomed love affair with Maurice's nephew. In-depth information from an unidentified source saying how she was forced to split up with him because she wasn't good enough and that she still loved him after all these years. The fact that he was Maurice's nephew made it extremely newsworthy and hundreds of comments had been added since early morning online.

Gabriella put her head on her pillow. It was true – every single word was true, like it had come from her own mouth. Who would have sold her out like that? Isabelle? Surely not. Oberon? He would never be so stupid.

She threw back the covers and went straight to the washbasin in the bathroom. Splashing her face with cold water, she blinked away the tears. Fame – that elusive thing she had craved for so long – was a cruel mistress. Now, the world was reading about her heartbreak and judging her for it. Some would say that she should have stood up for herself and told Hugo the truth. Others would understand her dilemma and commend her for it. These people didn't know her nor did they know anything about the situation.

Charlotte du Maurier opened a message from her childhood friend, Ellie Compton. It was a link with a message saying: *Read this now!*

Sipping her coffee, she downloaded an article from the *New York Star*. Two minutes later, she called Hugo. He answered on the seventh ring.

"Char?" He sounded sleepy. "Why are you calling me so early?"

"I just read an article about Gabriella, Magda's daughter."

"Sure, sure. It's all over the news about Maurice. I know about it already."

"No, this is something else. I think you'd better take a look. I'll send you the link, okay?"

"Okay."

"Call me back afterwards."

"You got it."

He waited a minute and then the message appeared on

511

his screen. Clicking on the link, he downloaded the piece. His blues eyes scanned the first paragraph and then he saw his name. He read the article like lightning, his face darkening.

"**A source close to Gabriella said …**"

He called Charlotte back.

"This is a joke, right?"

Charlotte paused for a moment. "I'm not so sure. It makes sense, Hugo. I mean, you two were so in love. Then she just disappeared."

"She got a job …"

"It says in the piece that she went looking for it as a means of escape."

"Momma would never do that."

Charlotte sighed. "Oh, she would. Believe me."

"What?"

"Momma likes to meddle. When Luca came back to New York with Lydia the first time, she forced me to lie. She made me tell him that I was pregnant so that our wedding would go ahead. I told Lydia to disappear and not tell him why. She did and we got married. Then it fell apart."

"*What?*"

"I swear to you, it's true. Momma wanted the wedding to go ahead at all costs. I would imagine you going out with Magda's daughter would not be acceptable. I think you need to find Gabriella and find out the truth."

"I've got to find Momma first."

Victoria was in the sitting room with Maurice and Frank when Hugo walked in. His uncle was pacing around the coffee table, his face red and angry.

"Vince says I've got to hand myself in," he ranted. "I

512

pay him top dollar and he fucking gives up?"

Victoria smoothed her hair. "That evidence from that girl is a game-changer, Maurice. Vince thinks if you hand yourself in it will go in your favour when it comes to sentencing."

Frank banged his fist on the mantelpiece. "Did you rape her? That's what I want to know. I mean, goddamn it, I've tried my best with you. You said it was always consensual."

Maurice looked shifty. "It wasn't rape. I swear. She handed it to me on a plate."

Frank didn't look convinced. "Look, Vic is right. You've gotta do what your attorney says. This is too big now. Especially since Magda's kid got involved."

"Speaking of Magda's kid," announced Hugo and three heads swung around. "Momma, I'd like a word."

Victoria's blue eyes widened slightly. "Oh? Why, sugar?"

"*The study. Now.*" He stalked off.

Victoria got to her feet. "If you'll excuse me."

Hugo was standing by the window when she arrived into the room. "Everything okay?"

"Have you seen the *Star* today?"

She shook her head. "Maurice called over and he's been having a fit over Vince Piccone …"

"You should read it," he cut her off. "Someone sold their story about Gabriella and her past. Makes for interesting reading."

"Interesting?" she scoffed. "Hardly, Hugo. What's interesting about the Bronx?"

He pulled out his phone and handed it to her. "Start at the beginning."

"What is this?" she said annoyed. "I have no interest

in reading about that hussy."

"Read it," he said softly. "Right now."

She focused on the screen and scrolled with a perfectly manicured finger. He watched her face intently. Her face paled and she pursed her lips.

He snatched the phone. "So, it's true."

"No! I mean, this is all lies."

'Did you force her to break up with me?"

"No! You mustn't believe this –"

"*Tell me the truth!*" he roared.

"She wasn't good enough for you, baby. I could see it. You were talking about bringing her to Charlotte's wedding and I panicked. What would people have said? I had to act."

"So you threatened to fire Magda?"

"Not directly."

"Momma!"

"I insinuated as such, but I wasn't serious. You've seen how the house has fallen apart since she retired."

"Gabby knew that her family would be destitute without that job. She knew that her mother would suffer. How could you?"

"It was the right thing to do!" she shouted. "You were blinded by her and you couldn't see that it was entirely unsuitable. I had to act on my instincts. I just had to, Hugo."

"All these years I believed that she ran off to further her career, leaving me behind. All these years, I thought she was a heartless bitch. I could kill you right now."

"Don't say that," she said in alarm. "I was only doing what I thought was right."

"Bullshit. You were interfering in something you knew nothing about."

He made for the door. "I'm done with you all." He slammed the door.

Magda's eyes opened wide when she opened the door to find Hugo du Maurier on the threshold. Photographers were snapping and shouting, asking for a comment on the revelations.

"Hugo?" she said, ushering him inside. "Why are you here?"

"Is Gabby here?" he asked, looking around.

She shook her head. "There are too many photographers as you can see. She's at a hotel in town."

"Where, Magda? I need to see her."

"I can't tell you," she said gravely. "That horde outside will follow you now. A shot of you two together would be worth a lot."

"Please, Magda. I had no idea ..."

"Neither did I." She shook her head. "My poor *preciosa* went through so much to protect me. I feel awful."

Hugo pulled her into his arms and hugged her. "I'm sorry. I'm sorry for how my mother treated you and I hope you'll forgive us."

Magda wiped away a tear. "Gabby is a great girl."

"I know. I need to tell her that. Please tell me where she is."

Magda stared at him. "Are you serious about her?"

"Yes."

"You won't upset her?"

He shook his head. "I need to see her."

Magda went to her phone. "I will call her and ask her to meet me at Isabelle's apartment. I still have a spare key."

"Meet *you*?"

515

"She might not come if she knows it's you."

"I guess."

"Then you go and wait for her there. Hopefully, the press won't see you."

"Thank you."

"Make sure you're not followed, do you hear?"

"I promise."

"I'll say this evening at around five. Put those photographers off the scent. Maybe take the subway somewhere and then disappear. They must not follow you."

"I got it." He took the key from her grasp.

"Oh, and Hugo?"

"Yes?"

"Good luck." Her lined face smiled.

Hugo took the subway to Times Square and then disappeared into the throng of people on the pavement. Cutting back, he got a cab and went straight to Isabelle's place. He entered the apartment using Magda's spare key and placed it on the table. The air was stuffy so he opened the window and immediately the noise of the city invaded the room.

In a flash he remembered the times he had spent there, eating pizza and laughing with Gabby. He walked down the hall to her old room to find it empty. All her things had been removed and the bed lay unmade in the corner.

The intercom buzzed and he jumped. With a beating heart, he walked over and pressed the button to allow access to the building.

A few minutes later, there was a knock on the door. He opened it wide and his expression softened. Standing there was Gabriella, dressed in a long trench coat and a headscarf, huge sunglasses concealing most of her face.

"Hugo?" she whispered in shock. "My mama said that she was ..."

"I needed to see you." He stared at her intently for a moment.

"But why are you here?" She swayed slightly.

"I read that piece in the *Star*."

"I'm so sorry about that article. I don't know who sold me out."

"Doesn't matter." He reached out and grabbed her waist. Cupping her head with his hand, he kissed her deeply, propelling her backwards until she hit the hall. Using his leg, he kicked the door closed.

"Hugo, I –"

"Don't say anything," he said hoarsely.

"But Caroline ..."

"I'm not with her anymore." He kissed her again, his hands roaming her body.

She allowed him to touch her and it felt like heaven. He opened her coat and yanked it off, throwing it to one side. She was wearing a black strapless summer dress underneath, so he pulled it down and exposed her bra. Unhooking it, he threw it to the floor. She threw her head back in pleasure as he bent his head and kissed her breast, sucking gently on her nipple. She reached up and tore at the buttons of his shirt. Pushing it back over his shoulders, she left a trail of kisses along his chest and up his neck. He opened his belt and pulled up her skirt. She nodded, closing her eyes. Seconds later, he thrust inside her again and again. Years of desire and missed opportunities hung in the air as he called her name over and over. It felt so right. She clung to his back and kissed his shoulder as he climaxed.

No one spoke for a while. Hugo had his head on her shoulder and his breathing was rapid. She kissed his forehead and stroked his neck with her finger. Nothing existed but the two of them. She couldn't think of the real world – all she wanted to do was stay close to him and never let go. He lifted his head and stared at her.

"You look the same," he whispered.

She smiled. "So do you."

He kissed her nose. "I thought you'd have a British accent by now."

She laughed. "No, I'm still the same old Gabby."

He brushed her hair off her face and caressed her cheek. "The same old Gabby," he repeated in a whisper.

She stared at him in wonder. She had almost forgotten what he looked like. It had been so long.

"I'm sorry about Momma. I had no idea." He looked troubled.

"You must forgive her," said Gabriella, stroking his cheek.

"Would you stop being so nice for a minute? I know she's my mother but you can be mad, you know."

"There's no point now. It's too late."

Hugo's expression darkened. "Ever since I was born, she's been manipulating my life. Harvard, my dates, where I work."

"She wanted what was best for you, I guess."

"No, that's not true. She wanted what was best for her and her precious reputation amongst those soulless Upper East Side people she wants to impress so badly. If she really wanted what was best for me, she would have let us alone."

Gabriella closed her eyes. "I'll bet that I'm the enemy in your house right now."

"So? Maurice is the one who screwed up. I'm done with him."

"But your dad –"

"Is pretty sick of him too. Maurice has been pretty loose with facts and Dad is slowly realising that he's protecting a real bastard."

"That's hard on your dad, Hugo. He's his little brother."

"Would you cut it out? Stop being so fair to everyone. You deserve to be so angry right now."

"But I'm not," she said simply. "I'm here with you and I feel so good. I know that sounds crazy but I've wanted this for so long."

He kissed her thoroughly, holding her head with his hand. "When you testify, I'll be right there to support you."

"Your family will be so upset."

"Tough. My loyalty is to you. I don't care what they think anymore."

She snuggled close to him, listening to his heartbeat. The heat from his body was comforting and she closed her eyes.

"I'm so happy," she whispered. "The hardest thing I ever did was let you go. I regretted it so much. I threw myself into work to keep my mind off it. When you agreed to meet me that time, I was so excited. Then I saw Caroline and I nearly died."

"I'm sorry about that. I wanted to hurt you like you'd hurt me. I didn't know at the time about Momma." He paused. "Why didn't you tell me?"

"I couldn't, Hugo." Her expression darkened. "Things were different back then. I didn't have the life I have now."

He nodded empathetically.

"When my mama told me that she was retiring, it meant that the threat was gone," she continued. "I

519

wanted to make amends. Then, when I saw that you and Caroline were buying a house together, I tried to forget you." Her brown eyes searched his. "I love you, Hugo. I always have and I always will. I know I'm not the right type of girl for your family –"

"Cut that right out." He looked fierce. "I'm not good enough for you. You're the most beautiful, brave and talented girl I know. You're worth a million of any of those girls I've dated over the years."

"Really?"

He kissed her again. "Really."

"Meet me later," she murmured with her eyes closed. "I'm so lonely in that hotel. Come and stay with me there."

"Of course."

"I'm at Broadway Plaza Hotel under the name Miss Moneypenny."

"Miss Moneypenny?" he repeated.

"Yeah." She grinned.

"I'll head home and grab some things. Then I'll meet you there."

"At three?"

"Perfect."

They snuggled closer and such was her happiness she didn't notice the pink chiffon scarf hanging on the coat rail by the front door.

Victoria was on the phone when Hugo got home. He motioned for her to hang up and she held up her hand.

"Sure, sure, Elena. I'll tell Frank to ring you. Right, talk then. Bye, bye."

She ended the call. "Now, where on earth have you been?"

Hugo stared at her steadily. "I've been with Gabriella."

"You've been *what?*"

"I'm going to pack some things …"

"Pack? Hugo, what in hell's fire are you saying?"

He rounded on her angrily. "I'm going to be with her. We're staying together. I'm going to be her number one supporter when Maurice goes down."

"You wouldn't."

"Actually, I would. I'm handing in my notice in Boston and I'm moving to London with Gabby."

Victoria fell backwards, feeling faint. "Moving to London? Are you joking?"

"No," he answered grimly. "I've never been so serious about anything. I'm sick and tired of living someone else's life. All these years I've done what you asked and how do you repay me? By threatening the only girl I ever loved …"

"Loved? *Loved?*" she scoffed. "Oh, Hugo, you have a lot to learn."

"Cut it out, Momma."

"Love is for fools, sugar. She will drag you down to her level, mark my words."

"Stop!"

"She's a tramp and she'll make you miserable. You'll be cut off from all that you know."

"I don't care."

"No one will invite you over, Hugo. You'll be blackballed by your equals." Her voice started to rise. "And for what? A cheap Mexican slut you barely know?"

Hugo lifted his arm to strike her, but held himself back.

Victoria stood her ground, her blue eyes glittering.

"Don't you *ever* speak about Gabby that way."

"I'll do what I like –"

"*Ever!*" he yelled. "*You've crossed the line!*"

521

"If you leave, Hugo, then you can never come back. I won't have her in this house, do you hear? Make your choice."

He turned on his heel. "Goodbye, Momma."

Celine knocked on Hugo's door as he threw the last of his shirts into a large bag.

She whistled. "*Whoa*, big bro. That was some showdown."

"Get out while you can," he answered grimly, zipping up the bag.

"Oh, I've been out for years. Ever wonder why I chose UCLA?" She sauntered over to his bed. "Where are you going now?"

"To be with Gabby. She's incognito in a hotel. I'm going to stay with her until she testifies."

"Daddy will have a heart attack when he hears."

"There's nothing I can do about that." He walked over and kissed her cheek. "He'll be too busy with Maurice for the next few days. He's supposed to turn himself in at the precinct by Friday."

"Stay in touch."

"Of course I will." He ruffled her hair.

༺ Chapter Forty-Four ༻

A couple of hours later, Hugo arrived at Gabriella's hotel. He walked straight up to reception.

"Hello, I'm looking for Gab– I mean, Miss Moneypenny," he said at the hotel desk.

The receptionist nodded knowingly. "Will I call and let her know that you've arrived?"

"Please."

She dialled the room and waited patiently. "She's not picking up, sir."

"She's definitely there. We arranged to meet at three thirty. Please try again."

The receptionist called the room twice more and shrugged. "Perhaps she popped out. You're welcome to wait at the bar or in the lounge area."

Hugo took out his phone. "I'll just call her." He waited or her to pick up, but nothing happened. After three attempts, he took a seat in the lounge. Where could she be?

He texted Celine asking if she had Gabby's home number in Melrose. Maybe Magda knew where she was. She replied with the number and a smiley face.

He called and Diego answered. No, he hadn't seen

Gabby and she had not made plans to call over.

"Could you call Teresa and see if she called over to her?"

Diego called back five minutes later. No one had heard from her that day.

Two hours later, there was still no sign.

Hugo went up to the desk once more. "I'm worried. Please call the room again."

The girl nodded and once again, there was no answer. "I'm sorry, sir."

Hugo ran his fingers through his hair. "There must be something wrong. She arranged to meet me here. What if she's fallen and hit her head? Have you a master key?"

"I'm not at liberty to –"

"You've got to!" he almost yelled. "Something isn't right."

She bit her lip. "Okay, I'll ask the concierge to accompany you." She called the man at the door. "Can you escort this gentleman upstairs, please? He's lost his key."

Hugo smiled gratefully and she winked.

"Of course, sir." The young man smiled. "Right this way."

They took the elevator to the third floor. The concierge used a master key and opened the door of room 305. "Here we are, sir," he said and then the words died on his lips. The room was wrecked – chairs were thrown around, the desk was upended and Gabriella's possessions had been flung around the floor. Clothes were strewn all over the bed and shoes were scattered all over the carpet.

Hugo pushed past and checked the bathroom. There was no one in the room.

"Call the manager!" he said urgently. "Now!"

524

The man backed out and ran down the hallway to the elevator.

Hugo pulled out his phone and called 911.

"Hello? Yes, there's been a break-in. Yes, my girlfriend's gone. I think she's been abducted."

"Who would do this?" said a tearful Magda at the precinct two hours later. "No one knew where she was. I can't believe it."

Diego hugged his mother. "Try not to worry, Mama. Gabby is tough. She'll be okay, I'm sure of it."

A detective called Dwyer appeared. He was a small man in a grey suit and looked about forty.

"Come this way," he said to Magda. "I'm Detective Dwyer and I'll be working on this case."

"You must find my daughter," said Magda desperately. "Please tell me that you'll find her."

The detective regarded Magda. "We'll do our best, ma'am. Now, please come with me."

"Can I come?" asked Hugo. "I mean, I was the last person to see her."

"And you are?"

"I'm her boyfriend."

He nodded. "Fine. Come with us. We need all the information in order to proceed with the case."

Hugo was grilled by two detectives for an hour. They asked him where he was all day and if he had an alibi. Growing more and more frustrated, he roared, *You're wasting time with me! I'm not the one you're looking for!*

Detective Dwyer said nothing, but wrote something in a notebook.

"Are we done here?" said Hugo, his eyes flashing.

"For the moment," answered the detective.

Hugo walked out of the room, just as his phone rang.

It was Celine. "I just saw it on Breaking News. What the hell happened?"

Hugo sat on a plastic chair and closed his eyes. "I don't know. I just don't know. She was perfectly fine when I left her. It makes no sense."

"Where could she be? Did she mention any plans? There must be some clue."

"Nothing. She was so excited about meeting at the hotel. I just don't understand."

"Do you think she's run away?"

"I don't know."

"It wouldn't be the first time."

Hugo's expression darkened.

"I mean, she's hardly been kidnapped or anything. It's too crazy."

"Look, Celine, I don't know." He felt like yelling. "She could've been."

"The only person she's really pissed off in the past is Caroline Ashley Hamilton ..."

Hugo frowned. "Unless ..."

"Unless?"

"Maurice! He was so mad the last time I saw him. He didn't want to give himself up and was acting all crazy."

"He'd hardly be that stupid," she said doubtfully.

"Why? He has nothing to lose now."

"Jeez, I don't know, Hugo. Don't go saying anything to the police. He's in enough trouble."

Hugo got up. "I'll call you later." He hung up his phone, grabbed his coat and strode purposefully down the corridor.

"Off somewhere?" asked Detective Dwyer, appearing

out of nowhere with an impassive face.

"I'll be right back." Hugo pressed the elevator and waited.

"There's still nothing to tell, right?"

Hugo shook his head and stared blankly ahead. "I just need some fresh air."

After the breakdown of his marriage, Maurice had moved to a motel in Brooklyn. Sacked from the company, he had declared bankruptcy. Frank had given him a few thousand to tide him over.

Hugo took a cab, his heart thumping in his chest. He pulled out his phone and called his father. "Dad! Have you seen Maurice? No? when was the last time you spoke with him? Yes, yes, it's important. No, no, he's not picking up. What room number is he? Great, thanks. Right, call you later."

The taxi arrived at the motel. It was the classic motel – shaped like a square with the rooms adjacent to each other. Hugo paid the driver and went straight to Maurice's door.

He knocked loudly.

"*Maurice!*" he shouted. "*Open up! It's Hugo!*"

No one answered.

"*Maurice! Open up, for fuck's sake!*"

Detective Dwyer appeared behind him, giving him a fright. "Interesting that you show up here," he said silkily.

"What the hell?" Hugo scowled. "I just wanted to check something, okay?"

"It makes sense. She's testifying against him. He's lost his wife, his company and his reputation. He's looking at doing time. Pretty solid motive, right?"

Hugo ignored him. "Maybe not. I'm just ruling it out."

"Cut this vigilante crap right out," said the detective, pulling Hugo to the side. "You need to tell us everything and I mean everything. I checked the minute you left – you're his nephew. With a name like that, you had to be connected."

"So? I had nothing to do with this."

"Then I read an interesting article about you and Miss Álvarez. Forbidden love and all that. Maybe your mother has a motive too."

"Leave my momma out of this."

"You need to tell us what you know, you got that? We're on borrowed time."

Hugo said nothing.

"Stand back, Mr. du Maurier," ordered Dwyer. "Let us do our job."

Two beefy police officers kicked the door in. Maurice's apartment was empty. There were flies buzzing over dirty dishes in the sink and the curtains were closed. The officers checked all the rooms and ascertained that there was no one inside.

Detective Dwyer called the precinct. "I'm putting out an APB on Maurice du Maurier. White male of around fifty. Wanted on suspicion of abduction. Notify all officers."

Oberon stared at Riku. "She's been what?" he said in shock.

"Kidnapped! I saw it on CNN. There's a huge search going on as we speak."

"I take one day off – *one day at a spa* – with no internet or phones and this happens?" Oberon slammed his fist on the table. "*Book me a flight right now!*"

"What?" Riku's eyes widened. "To New York?"

"No, to Moscow!" Oberon rolled his eyes. "*Of course to New York!* We've got to find Gabby."

Raphael rubbed suntan lotion on Isabelle's back as they lay on loungers by a pool. He had rented a small chateau near Sommières in the south of France. It had its own private pool and a small chapel. "Your skin is so pale, we must not let it burn," he said softly, caressing the small of her back.

"Keep going," she said in a husky voice. "You're lost as a director. You should open a massage parlour."

Raphael stood up, his broad chest brown from the sun. "Let's go inside," he said, holding out his hand. "I'll finish the massage in our bed."

Isabelle put on her robe and followed Raphael into the cool kitchen. The chef waved as they passed, adding the finishing touches to a delectable meringue cake with fresh fruit.

"Have you seen my phone?" asked Isabelle, looking around the messy sitting room. "I haven't seen it all day."

Raphael shrugged. "*Non,*" he answered. "Try the bedroom. I'll follow you up."

She walked up the stone staircase and opened the large oak door of their room. Her phone was on the bed, discarded that morning after checking her emails.

She picked it up and saw ten missed calls from her mother, three from Bertie and seven from Oberon.

"What the hell?"

She called Elaine right away.

"Zsa Zsa, thank God!"

"What's up?"

"It's Gabby. She's disappeared."

"Gabby?"

529

"She's been abducted, we think. Check out CNN."

She hung up and picked up the remote control. She turned on the television, just as Raphael appeared in the doorway.

"*Look!*" she said, pointing to the screen.

Pictures of Gabriella and a red headline saying '**Missing**' filled the frame.

Isabelle sat down. Missing? Why? Where?

"Raph?"

"*Oui?*"

"I need to go to New York."

Magda opened the door and gasped. "Isabelle! Oh!" She hugged her tightly. "You're so good to come."

Isabelle and Raphael had got the next flight from Marseilles, with a connecting flight from Paris.

Isabelle kissed her mother's cheek. "Any news?"

"Nothing." Magda's eyes filled with tears.

"She'll be fine, you know," Isabelle said gently. "Gabby's a tough cookie."

Teresa, who was sitting on the couch, stood up. "Can I get you some tea?" she asked politely.

Raphael shook his head. "No, thank you."

Lita sat on her favourite armchair, clutching rosary beads and praying quietly.

"What do they know so far?" asked Isabelle, taking a seat on the couch.

"The prime suspect is Maurice," said Magda. "He's disappeared too. He was supposed to give himself up today. The police think that he's on the run."

"But why take Gabby?"

"Revenge? I don't know. Her involvement in the case turned the tide on him. He was positive that he'd be exonerated until Marty Kassewitz got involved."

"Thanks to Gabby."

"Exactly."

Teresa took Sophia on her lap. "We must not think the worst," she said calmly. "This may turn out to be nothing. He might have a change of heart and bring her home."

Lita made a Sign of the Cross.

Diego walked in, his face taut. "Any word?"

Magda shook her head. "My stomach keeps flipping over and over. It's awful."

Suddenly Oberon appeared on the television.

"Turn it up!" said Teresa urgently.

Diego picked up the remote and turned the volume on high.

"*This is a travesty,*" Oberon was saying in his British accent. "*Gabriella is the sweetest girl I know and wouldn't hurt a fly. Why anyone would abduct her like this is beyond me.*"

"That's a turn-up for the books," said Isabelle in amazement. "I've never seen him gush in my life."

"*So, I want to offer a reward of fifty thousand dollars to anyone who comes forward with information.*"

Isabelle's eyes widened. "That's pretty good money. Maybe it'll work."

Magda let out a sob. "This is just terrible! How could anyone do this?"

The phone rang, its loud shrill tone reverberating through the small apartment.

Diego picked up the receiver.

"Detective," he said. "Any update?"

Two seconds later, he hung up the phone, his face ashen.

"They found a body in the Hudson."

"*A body*?" shrieked Magda.

Lita started to rock to and fro.

"It was a man, Mama," said Diego. "They've identified him as Maurice du Maurier."

Victoria stared at Frank. "What happened? What happened to him, Frank?"

Her husband put his head down on the table and started to sob. "I don't know, Vic. I just don't know. Stab wounds to the neck is what they said. I can't believe it."

Victoria stood immobile, her brain buzzing. The awful news had been delivered by the police ten minutes before. Elena, being his next of kin, had identified the body. There was no doubt that it was Maurice.

Celine rushed into the dining room, tears streaming down her face. "*Daddy!*' she yelled, catapulting herself into his arms. "*I'm so sorry.*"

He clung to her.

Victoria watched them with a frozen look on her face. This was just unprecedented. For the past few days they had harboured such ill-feeling towards her brother-in-law and now he was dead, seemingly murdered.

"They're doing an autopsy now," said Frank. "We should have a report soon."

Celine wiped her eyes with her sleeve. "What about Gabby? She's still missing. If Maurice is dead, then who took her?"

Victoria fingered the huge diamond on her left hand. She had been thinking the exact same thing. To say she felt guilty about the girl was an understatement. Hugo's words had affected her greatly and she felt remorse for what she'd done. Now there was a good chance the girl was dead.

"I don't know, sugar. I just don't know."

Hugo stared at the sea. It had been three days since Gabriella had disappeared.

There were no witnesses. There was no record of her leaving the hotel. Even the paparazzi tried to help, offering photos they had taken of Gabriella over the past week. None gave any clue to her whereabouts. None gave a lead to the police.

Forensics had combed the hotel room for clues. There were no prints besides Gabriella's and no sign of a struggle. The room had been trashed but there was no blood. It looked like a robbery, yet all her jewellery and cash remained.

Hugo closed his eyes and prayed. With Maurice's body in the morgue, it didn't look good. The police had confirmed that he was murdered. Five stab wounds to the neck and then thrown in the river. He had been dead for over eight hours when he was found. Now the media were stalking his family, asking question after question that no one could answer. They were relentless, stalking them like prey with no sense of propriety.

He could see why people tired of fame – it was exhausting being in the spotlight, having your life splashed across every platform imaginable. Gabriella had sought it so badly, believing it to be her golden ticket to happiness.

Hugo frowned. The reality was very different.

"Did she have enemies?" Raphael asked Isabelle as they lay in bed.

Isabelle shook her head. "No way. I mean, she's the nicest girl."

"Any rivals?"

"No."

"I don't understand it. It must be connected to the du Maurier case. Why was Maurice murdered? There has to be a link."

Isabelle sighed deeply. "Losing Angelo was so hard, Raph. I don't think I could cope with losing Gabby too."

He pulled her close and kissed her temple. "Don't think like that, my love. She will be okay. You've got to believe it."

Isabelle's phone rang. "It's Bertie," she said, looking at the screen. "Hello?"

"Frightful news, just frightful. Any update?"

"No. It's like a dead end."

"London is buzzing about it. I'm stuck at a shoot in Lake Windermere, otherwise I'd be there."

"There's not much you can do."

"I saw Oberon on the news offering a reward. I nearly fell off my sofa, Zsa Zsa. The man is notoriously as tight as a duck's arse. He *must* be fond of her."

Isabelle smiled sadly. "I hope it works."

"Me too, my love. Me too."

"Hello? My name is Tatiana. I need to speak to a cop about that Gabriella case. I saw her a couple of days back."

"One minute, please." The secretary covered the receiver of the phone. "Hey, I got a girl here with information on the Álvarez case. Anyone wanna talk to her?"

A junior detective waved her away. "We get twenty crackpot calls a day. I wouldn't waste my time."

Detective Dwyer, who was passing, stopped. "What did she say?"

"That she saw her."

He took the call. "Hello?"

"Hi, there. I saw a picture of that girl who's missing and I think that she was in my store a couple of days back."

"Really? Which store?"

"I run a liquor store off Broadway."

"Right."

"She came in and was looking to buy some fancy champagne. We don't have much of that in stock, we usually sell beer and wine, so I went in the back to find something. When I came out, she had taken off her big glasses and was looking at bottles on a rack near the window."

"Anything else?" He picked a piece of fluff off the desk and flicked it away.

"She was wearing a scarf on her hair. I asked her if she was living locally and she didn't answer."

"And you're sure that this girl was Gabriella."

"She looked Mexican, right?"

"Look, Tatiana, I'm not sure that we're talking about the same lady here ..."

"Wait, Mister, let me finish. Her phone rang after she'd paid. She looked surprised but took the call. She mentioned the name Noah."

Detective Dwyer sat up straight. "Go on."

"She seemed to be arranging to meet him or something. The reason I remember is that my grandson is called Noah and I was about to tell her when she took the champagne and left."

"How can you be sure it was her?" he repeated.

"In your description on the internet, you say that she was wearing Dior glasses. That girl in my store was wearing those. I love that brand and wish I could afford it."

"Thank you, ma'am. We'll need you to come and make a statement."

Detective Dwyer called Magda at nine that night.

"We've got a lead, ma'am."

"What?"

"A woman came forward. She remembers seeing Miss Álvarez in her liquor store the day she disappeared. She sold her a bottle of champagne. The tapes from her CCTV confirms that it was Gabriella."

"Where?"

"Two blocks from her hotel."

"And?"

"She answered a phone call while she was paying. The woman heard her say 'Noah'. Does that name mean anything to you?"

Magda shook her head. "Noah? No, not at all. I mean, I don't think so."

"Think! Did she know anyone by that name?"

Magda called Teresa and Diego, who were watching a baseball game in the sitting room. They both came to her at once, alarmed.

"Does the name 'Noah' mean anything to you?" she asked.

Diego looked confused. "As in the guy in the Bible?"

Magda felt like screaming. "*No!* Did Gabby know a Noah? Please say you've heard the name!"

"Wasn't there a guy in her class called Noah?" said Teresa frowning. "I'm pretty sure ..."

Magda's face lit up. "You're right! He was at the graduation. I remember now."

"Detective?" she said into the phone. "She had a friend at school called Noah."

"I'll be right over."

"Do you have a lead?" Raphael asked Detective Dwyer as soon as he and Isabelle arrived at Magda's after she had called and asked them to come over.

"Possibly," said Dwyer.

Magda motioned for them to sit down. "Isabelle, remember there was a guy at Parson's called Noah?"

"Noah?" said Isabelle in surprise. "As in Noah Brennan?"

Magda closed her eyes and thanked God. "Yes, it must be the same person."

"He was sweet on her at Parson's. She broke his heart."

"Well, she answered the phone to a Noah on the day she went missing. A woman came forward."

"Where is he now?" asked the detective.

"God knows," said Isabelle. "They weren't on good terms in the end so they lost touch." She paled. "You know, he was really in love with her. I used to tease him. Then she hooked up with Hugo and that was that."

Dwyer took out his phone. "This has been really helpful. Thank you." He walked to the door.

Magda rushed after him. "Find my girl, please find her!"

"Goodnight, ma'am. I'll be in touch."

ᎨᏈ Chapter Forty-Five ᏆᏂ

Gabriella willed her eyes to open. She was cold – so cold. It had been days, she was sure of it. Weakly, she yanked at the rope on her wrists. She need to drink something – her throat was so dry and she couldn't move. However, he had tied the knots so tightly that trying to escape was futile.

She struggled to remember. Noah had called while she was buying champagne. She had been surprised as it had been so long. He sounded so cheery and well that she had agreed to meet him for a coffee like old times. Then it got hazy. She couldn't remember actually drinking a coffee – all she could recall was waking up in this dark, cold room with ropes eating into her wrists.

"*Help!*" she called, her voice barely a whisper. "*Help me!*"

There was no answer. Just the sound of running water, tantalising her in her thirsty state.

She dropped off to sleep and, the next thing she knew, a bright light was being shone in her face.

"*Wakey, wakey!*" came Noah's voice.

She could smell cigarette smoke.

"Water!" she whispered hoarsely. "Please."

He stared at her. "You're thirsty?"

538

She nodded.

"Are you suffering?"

She nodded again.

"Good." His eyes glittered contemptuously. "You deserve to suffer." He kicked a bowl on the ground and strode over to the window. The light illuminated the room – it was grey and damp with bars on the window.

"Please, Noah," she said weakly. "Let me go."

He ignored her.

"Noah! This is crazy. I don't deserve this ..."

"Oh, but you do."

"Why?"

"You fucked me over, Gabby. You never knew how much I loved you."

"I'm sorry ... I ..."

"You chose that preppy rich boy over me. I worshipped you!"

"Please!"

"Every time you came back to New York, I followed you. Every single time. I used to go to Isabelle's place and sleep in your bed. How fucked up is that?" He laughed bitterly. "The pillows still smell of you. Even now."

"Noah ..."

"Then I heard about what that du Maurier guy did to you. How he attacked you." He kicked the wall in rage. "I stabbed him like a stuck pig. He won't touch you again, you hear?"

Maurice. Stabbed? Gabriella felt she was about to faint. "Water," she whispered.

Noah whipped around. "Oh, fine. Have some goddamn water." He picked up a bottle and held it over her mouth. The water flowed down her throat as she desperately tried to drink it.

"I like having you in my power," he reflected. "It's nice having you here all the time."

She felt herself gag. "What are you going to do with me?"

He threw the bottle on the floor. "I'm not sure. I mean, no one will find·you here, that's for sure."

"I want to go home ..."

"Oh, poor Gabby! Poor, poor Gabriella." He laughed. "You'll never see your home again."

"What?"

"Ever. I'll make sure of that."

"Are you going to kill me?" she whispered, her heart thumping.

"Kill you?" He looked at her in surprise. "I'd never kill you. I love you, dumbass. You're my world."

"Then let me go."

"Um, no." He grinned. "I want to keep you here. It's better that way. When you moved to London I was so pissed. I couldn't afford a flight, not on my crappy wages. So, I checked the internet a million times a day, keeping track of Oberon's shows and then your own. Every time you came home, I was so happy. You got that? It felt good to watch you and make sure you were safe."

"Noah, this is insane. Let me go."

"No way, Gabriella. If I let you go, you'll end up back with preppy and that can't happen."

"I won't."

"I saw you two," he said, his expression darkening. "I followed you to Isabelle's and then I watched you through the window. He's going to die for touching you like that."

"Stop!"

"No one is allowed touch you like that! No one except me."

Gabriella felt sick. "You?"

He smiled. "Yes, me."

Hugo banged on Detective Dwyer's desk. "*There has to be a lead!*" he shouted. "I mean, he can't just disappear off the face of the earth!"

The detective regarded him calmly. "We're checking everything."

"You say he worked at that pizza place."

"They haven't seen him in days."

"What will he do for money?"

"He closed his bank account last week. Withdrew everything, including an inheritance from his late grandma."

"Where could he be?" Hugo clenched his fists.

"We're working on it."

"He might hurt her."

"He might, but we're hoping that he won't."

"How can you be so controlled?"

"That's my job, Mr. du Maurier. Now, please leave so I can get on with it."

"Noah Brennan, Caucasian male, twenty-five, resident of Brooklyn, only son of a Kathleen Brennan, deceased, and a Gus Brennan, who works for Global Shipping in New Jersey. Father has been interrogated three times. Hasn't seen his son in six months. The suspect has worked at Pizza Haven for the past three years. Colleagues say he's quiet and introverted. His apartment showed obvious signs of obsession with the victim, Miss Gabriella Ruiz Álvarez, leading us to the conclusion that Noah is indeed involved in her disappearance. We have put out an APB across all states and airports, ports and borders are on high alert."

Detective Dwyer looked at the room of police officers.

"Forensics have established that Maurice du Maurier was murdered from multiple stab wounds to the neck. The coroner's report showed that the size of the weapon matches the brand and blade of the selection of knives found at Brennan's apartment. The coroner's report also confirmed Brennan's DNA on du Maurier's body."

He looked up gravely.

"I don't need to tell you that time is of the essence, gentlemen."

Noah lay down on the floor next to Gabriella and stroked her hair. "I always loved your hair," he said softly. "There was always a shine off it."

She stiffened. "Please stop."

"Why? You're mine now. I can do what I want."

"Noah, I know you're a good person ..."

"I know that, too."

"So, let me go. I promise I won't tell anyone."

"I can't do that, Gabby. Every cop in America is looking for you right now."

"Please."

"They have no idea who took you. That makes me laugh." He kissed her forehead and she flinched. "I bashed my phone with a hammer. There's no way I'm going to be traced. It's kind of cool being cut off from the world. I mean, I only ever used internet to follow you, but now you're here. The world can end for all I care. It's just you and me now." He kissed her temple and she flinched. "*Shhh!* Stop talking and enjoy it." He nuzzled her neck. "This is exactly where I want to be."

She closed her eyes and imagined that she was at home. Magda was making orange cake and Lita was telling her about Puerto Rico in her soft voice. There was a self-help talk show on the television and she was sitting on the couch with her favourite cushion under her head.

Home.

"Remember that time we went to the Yankees game? You had mustard on your lip from that hotdog." He chuckled. "You always liked your food."

She refused to listen. She kept her eyes fastened shut and focused on her family.

"Wake up!" He shook her. "Wake up and listen to me!"

She shook her head defiantly, her eyes still closed.

"Gabby! Open your eyes, goddammit!" He sat up. "Now!"

She began to hum to herself, keeping her eyes fastened shut. The next thing she knew, he had slapped her hard across the face.

"Open your eyes! Now!"

Her eyes watered at the pain, but she stood her ground. "No!"

He slapped her again, harder this time. She turned her head away.

He got to his feet in rage.

"Open them!"

"*No!*"

He kicked her in the ribs. Then he kicked her again. Her arms were tied behind her back so she curled up into a ball to protect herself. He kicked her once more and she screamed.

"Gabby!" He stepped backwards, clutching his head. "Gabby!" he repeated and bent down to hug her. "I'm sorry, I'm so sorry. I didn't mean to hurt you. I'm sorry." He rocked her to and fro.

She started to sob loudly.

"Stop crying," he said, kissing her hair. "Don't cry like that."

She tried to suppress the tears but she couldn't. Waves of panic engulfed her and she started to shake.

Hugo stirred some sugar into his coffee. Victoria watched him, her blue eyes sad.

"Would you like a biscuit with that?" she asked softly.

He didn't answer. Instead he continued to stir – round and round, his eyes staring blankly ahead.

"You're getting skinny, sugar. You've got to eat."

He didn't react. Instead he carefully placed his spoon on the saucer of his espresso cup.

"She needs you to be strong, Hugo. You're no good to her like this."

His blue eyes met hers. "She's gone, Momma. I can feel it."

Victoria put her arm around his shoulders. "Hey now, you don't know that. Hugo, come on, stay positive."

He rested his head on her shoulder. "I love her so much. I feel so powerless."

"I know, I know." She kissed his forehead. "The police are doing their best."

"It's not good enough."

"They have pictures of that cretin all over the country."

"Yet no one has come forward."

"They will, baby. He will slip up and, when he does, we'll bring Gabriella home."

Oberon received an email the next morning from a man in New Jersey. It simply read:

I think I've seen that man. Give me the money and I'll tell you more.

"*Riku!*" he yelled and his assistant appeared. "Call that detective. We might have a lead."

Detective Dwyer arrived at the Four Seasons fifteen minutes later. He read the email.

He nodded. "Say you'll meet him somewhere. Tell him to come alone and that you'll have the cash in a bag."

"Me? Can't Riku do it?"

The detective raised an eyebrow. "It has to be you. He trusts you and your offer."

Oberon inhaled and his nostrils flared. "Oh, fine. I'll do it then. Make sure you have at least ten snipers ready to fire. The world needs me."

"Right."

Oberon typed exactly what was said and pressed 'send'. "I hope he replies."

"He will."

Sure enough, five minutes later an email appeared with an address and a time.

Oberon replied and confirmed the meeting.

"It's Newark Container Trucking Terminal," said Oberon.

Detective Dwyer raised an eyebrow. "Noah's dad works there." He called for back-up. "Yeah, at seventeen hundred hours. Right, yeah, call the father again, there has to be a connection." He hung up.

"Can you give me a bulletproof vest?" Oberon asked. "I mean, even pre-schoolers have guns in this country."

"That can be arranged."

The trucking terminal was closed when Oberon arrived. He had a bulletproof vest and a wire concealed under his green silk shirt. Hundreds of containers lay stacked in a large yard, different colours ranging from orange to pale blue. The streaks of rust down the sides of them was almost artistic.

I could channel this look, thought Oberon irrationally.

The email had stated that they would meet at the front gate. Oberon was to hand over the bag of cash first and then he would receive the information.

Walking towards the gate, he felt his heart thump loudly. What if this informant was Noah himself? What if he came out and opened fire? Oberon closed his eyes. He was in his prime. There was no way he was dying today.

He placed the bag on the ground and straightened up. The yard was deserted. He felt so alone even though he knew he was wired up and the police were monitoring his every move. Five minutes passed, and then ten. He felt his skin grow clammy and he checked his Rolex.

Suddenly he heard a noise. A small man in overalls appeared from behind a stack of crates and scurried over.

"Is that all the dough?" he asked in a thick New Jersey accent.

Oberon nodded.

The man opened the zipper and his eyes gleamed when he saw the rows and rows of cash.

"So, what information have you got?" asked Oberon in his clipped tone.

"That Brennan guy. I seen him yesterday. He bought water and cigarettes in a store on Wilson Avenue."

"Which store?"

"The Mini Mart."

"How do you know it was him?"

"I know his dad, Gus. Noah used to help out during the summer when he was a kid."

"Was he alone?"

The man nodded. "There was no sign of the girl."

"Any idea where he would be hiding?"

He shook his head. "It could be anywhere. There are lots of abandoned warehouses around here. He can't be too far, that's what I'm guessing." He smiled and Oberon shuddered as his top teeth were missing. "Thanks for the cash," he said gleefully. "This is my lucky day."

Oberon regarded him in disgust. "That money will bring you nothing but misfortune. You've just cashed in on the life if a young girl. Shame on you."

"Do I look like I care?" he said, suddenly fierce. "It's fine for you, making crazy amounts of cash for a goddamn dress. Shame on *you!*" He walked away, muttering to himself.

Oberon held up his hand which was a signal to hold back. This man wasn't a danger. He had come for the money and got what he wanted.

By the time he walked back to the car, Dwyer had gone to Wilson Avenue to check out the CCTV. The tape from the day before indeed showed Noah wearing a hood, buying a pack of Marlboro and a large bottle of water. When he exited the store, he turned left. Cameras mounted on the street corners showed him walking down the avenue and then turning off. After that, there was no more footage.

"The area is closing in," said Dwyer later to Hugo and Magda. "We're searching the warehouses as I speak."

Hugo clutched Magda's hand. "Do you think we'll find her?"

"I'll be in touch." Dwyer walked away.

"I'm heading out for some food." Noah put on his hoodie. "I'll be about half an hour."

Gabriella stared at the wall, lost in thought. Her wrists

ached from the ropes. They were cutting into her skin and her muscles kept going into spasm involuntarily.

She dozed for a while and woke to find Noah pulling her up into a sitting position.

"Get up," he said. "We have to move."

"What? Why?" she asked, disorientated.

"The cops, they're looking for me. Those bastards figured it out. God knows how, but they did."

"What?" she said, a glimmer of hope appearing in her eyes. "How do you know?"

"I saw it on a TV screen. They're looking for me. We've got to go."

"Give yourself up," she pleaded. "You'll never get away."

Suddenly they heard sirens.

"*Get up!*' he roared. "They're here. We've got to go." He pulled her by the hair.

"Untie me then," she said. "I can't move with my arms like this."

He grabbed a knife and slashed the rope, cutting her hand in the process. "Now, *move!*"

She baulked at the sight of blood. "I can't, Noah. I'm too weak."

"Oh, come on." He pulled her in the direction of the door.

"Please let me go."

"Are you fucking crazy? We are *never* going to be separated, do you hear me? *Ever.*"

"*No!*" she screamed. "*I'm not going with you!*"

He pulled a gun out of his pocket. "Do what I say!" he ordered, pointing it at her chest.

Her eyes widened in fear. Then they heard a voice through a megaphone.

"*Noah Brennan! Come out with your hands up. It's over, Noah. Come out now.*"

He started to pace the room, the gun in his hand. "*Shit, shit, shit!*"

She backed away slowly, making for the door.

"*Where do you think you're going?*" he yelled. "*Get back here!*"

"*No!*" She bolted but tripped on a bag.

"*Gabby!*"

She pulled herself up. "*No!*" she screamed, stumbling forward.

Noah pulled the trigger.

"Get in there now!" Dwyer ordered when he heard the shots.

The officers beat down the door and barged into the dilapidated building. All the ground floor was empty so they climbed the stairs, their guns poised.

"All clear," said one, before turning down a corridor. There was a door at the end of the hallway. He nodded in its direction. Four armed guards followed and they kicked it down. Gabriella was lying in a pool of blood on the ground. Noah had his back to them.

"*Turn around!*" yelled the first policeman.

"*Now!*" yelled another.

Noah turned slowly and regarded them, his eyes dead.

"Drop your weapon and put your hands on your head," ordered the first policeman.

"Fuck you," he said, placing the gun in his mouth and pulling the trigger.

❦ Chapter Forty-Six ❧

One year later

Isabelle pulled at her dress. "I look so different, Raph."
She stared at her reflection in the mirror of her New York
apartment. The empire line of her green dress flowed
elegantly over her bump, falling to the ground with a
slight train. At nearly five months pregnant, she carried it
well.

Raphael, handsome in a suit, walked up behind her
and kissed her neck. "You are my wife and you're
carrying my child," he said, wrapping his big arms around
her waist. "You look beautiful."

Isabelle craned her neck to kiss him back. "Thank
you." She took her clutch bag from the bed. "Come on,
we'll be late. It takes over an hour to get to the Bronx
from here."

St. Jerome's Church on Alexander Avenue was the church
where Gabriella had been christened and where her
father's Requiem Mass had been held. This made it the
natural choice for her wedding ceremony.

The wedding itself had been a closely guarded secret –
there were rumblings in the press about possible dates and
locations and photographers were on high alert.

Gabriella's dramatic abduction and rescue had dominated the headlines for weeks. Then, a few months later, she had designed Aurora Sinclair's iconic dress at the Oscars. Despite the fact that she didn't take home the golden statue that night, Aurora still made the front pages across the globe for her inventive gold gown with a ten-foot train. Then when Gabriella announced her engagement to Hugo du Maurier, all the old stories resurfaced. Maurice's name was thrown around again and people speculated on how long the marriage would last.

Oberon took it upon himself to design Gabriella's wedding gown himself. The dress itself was made of heavy silk with a full skirt and a train. The bodice was embroidered with lace and the neckline was high. The cathedral-length veil was trimmed with lace and kept in place with a diamond clasp. The whole ensemble was simple and traditional.

As it was a low-key affair, a small number of guests had been invited. Gabriella only wanted close friends and family, especially after the events of the previous year. Hugo had not objected and Victoria had been secretly delighted that it was not a huge society affair that would be splashed across newspapers and social media. Yes, her only son was marrying an immigrant girl from the Bronx. Yes, he was happier than she'd ever seen him. However, the less people knew, the better.

Celine arrived at the church wearing a green dress – the exact same colour as Isabelle's – however, hers was tightly fitted. Both girls were bridesmaids along with Teresa's girls as flower girls. Sophia looked enchanting in a white dress, her brown hair styled in ringlets with flowers threaded through them. Penny, at thirteen, had blossomed into a beautiful young girl and wore a dress similar to her sister's. Miguel and Salvador looked handsome in their matching suits. Their role in the ceremony was to bring up the rings at the right time.

Luca and Lydia had flown in especially with their children – Sienna and the new addition, Xavier, who was nearly five months old. Tara Jacob had been invited, as had Colin and Val.

Aurora had been asked to sing and James was the photographer. Aurora arrived at the church to flashing cameras and shouts from journalists.

"*When's the new film out, Aurora?*" shouted one.

"*Where's James?*" yelled another.

"Where is James, actually?" asked Val, looking handsome in his suit.

"With Gabby," she answered. "He's been taking photos all morning." She headed for the vestry. "I'm just going to warm up my voice."

The du Mauriers were seated on the groom's side. Frank looked proud and Victoria looked stricken. Her only son was getting married. It still hadn't hit home. She clutched the front of the pew for support.

Charlotte looked beautiful in a silver dress, her tall willowy beauty as unchanged as ever. She had come alone, despite having a boyfriend in Boston. He too was an attorney and was busy with a case. She knew better than to tear him away from his case files. He, like her, was obsessed with his work and wouldn't rest until his current case was closed.

Colin and Val took a seat on the bride's side. Raphael was already there, reading the order of service. Elaine and Patrick were on his right, looking great in yellow and grey respectively. Luca, Lydia, Sienna and the baby were just behind them. Lydia was rocking Xavier back and forth, pleading with him not to cry.

Sienna held out her hands. "I want Colin!" she said.

"Oh, come on then." Colin picked her up and put her on his lap.

A muscle twitched in Luca's cheek. He hadn't seen Charlotte or Victoria since the divorce. To say things were awkward was an understatement.

Tara arrived, looking beautiful in a pale-blue suit and hat. "May I join you?' she asked.

Lydia moved to the left. "You look great," she said.

Tara smiled. "Thank you! I wasn't sure about the colour."

Boris and Jade arrived and took a seat. Riku waved at them and took a photo.

Suddenly there was a roar from outside.

"*Thank you, my darlings!*" came a voice.

"Bertie!" said Raphael, turning around with a grin.

Sure enough, Bertie arrived up the aisle with Vladimir in tow. He looked dashing in a pink suit and a green cravat.

"Raph!' he exclaimed. "Good to see you, old boy."

He took a seat next to his friend.

"Thank God I got here on time. One should never be later than the bride." He picked up the order of service and scanned it. "Wonderful! Aurora is singing. I'll look forward to that."

He looked around the church. "What a mixture of people! You can clearly see the two sides of the family." He pointed to Lita. "That's something old." Then he pointed to Oberon. "Look at his nose! That's definitely something new."

Colin giggled.

Then Bertie pointed to Victoria, who looked desolate. "And there's something blue. Look at the face on her! My word, it's like she's at a funeral."

"He's her only son," said Raphael fairly.

"*Hmmm*," said Bertie. "My guess is that there's more to it than that." He looked around at all the faces.

Xavier started to cry. "Oh, Xav!" said Lydia desperately. "You just had some milk. What's the matter?"

Tara offered to take him. "It's probably wind," she said. "Let me try."

She put him on her shoulder and patted his back.

Charlotte, on hearing Xavier's cries, looked back and her eyes met Lydia's. Like lightning, she turned away.

Magda sat in the wedding car with Gabriella and blinked her tears away. She thanked God that her *cariña* was okay and that she was happy after all that had happened. When she had heard about the gun! And then there was those first twenty-four hours at the hospital ...

She shuddered. It could have turned out so differently.

She grasped Gabriella's hand. "Are you nervous?" she asked.

Gabriella nodded. "It's silly, I know, but my heart is racing."

"Soon you will be married and you won't even remember the nerves."

"I guess."

James took lots of photos and then hopped into the front seat. "Right, let's go," he said to the driver. He then spent the journey going through the shots he had taken, deleting any that were sub-standard or out of focus.

The car pulled up outside the church. Despite their

efforts to keep it under wraps, there was a group of journalists and photographers waiting. On Bertie's advice, Gabriella had hired a security firm to police the ceremony. Her wedding would be as private as possible. The paparazzi would not be permitted inside the church.

Cameras flashed as she emerged from the hired Mercedes.

Celine rushed forward and fixed her train. "You look so lovely," she said genuinely.

Isabelle wiped away a tear. "I'd bend down and help, but I'd probably topple over."

Gabriella giggled. "It's so weird seeing you with a bump. It's like the cheese has finally caught up with you."

"Ha, ha!" Isabelle stuck out her tongue. "Just a couple of more months and I'll be back to myself."

"*Good to see you up and about, Gabby!*" shouted one pap, snapping like crazy.

She smiled and walked unsteadily forwards. The bullet had been removed from her thigh, but she still hobbled slightly.

Magda, who was giving her away, took her arm. "Lean on me," she offered.

"Thanks, Mama."

Suddenly a woman came forward and was stopped by security. "Let go!" she protested. "I just want to wish the bride well."

Gabriella looked and saw that it was Giselle, the owner of Brasserie Michel.

"It's okay," she said and the guard let go. "Giselle!" she said warmly. "It's so good of you to come."

Giselle handed her a small leather pouch. "It's a rabbit's foot for luck," she said. "I hope you are very happy."

Gabriella's nieces were waiting at the entrance to the church, surrounded by beefy security guards.

Sophia shrieked when she saw her aunt. "You look awesome, Gabby!" she said in wonder.

"Beautiful," agreed Penny.

Oberon appeared and ordered everyone out of his way. Standing back, he looked at Gabriella. "Right, the veil is all wrong, needless to say. I would've thought that you of all people would get it right. Have I taught you nothing?"

Gabriella smiled as he fiddled with the diamond clasp.

"You know, I wouldn't be here today if it wasn't for that source that leaked my story to the tabloids."

He ignored her and adjusted the veil.

"I never found out who spilled the beans," she said.

"Really?" he said blandly, avoiding her gaze.

"Really." Her eyes were warm.

Oberon changed the subject. "Now! You don't look so bad if I do say so myself. Maybe I should specialise in bridal wear?"

She hugged him suddenly and he stiffened. "Thank you," she whispered into his ear. "For everything."

'Clark's Trumpet Voluntary' boomed through the church, played by a local organist that Magda had hired. Oberon rushed up to his seat next to Riku and Jimin. The flower girls and the bridesmaids started to walk up the aisle, smiling at the guests as they passed. Penny and Sophia took a seat in the same pew as their parents, Sophia doing a small pirouette as she sat down. Dressing like a princess was right up her alley and she was enjoying every moment. The music resounded through the church, making the hairs on Gabriella's neck stand up. She could see Hugo at the top, waiting for her to join him.

Hugo du Maurier.

She couldn't believe that they had made it this far. After everything that stood in their way. Surely that must mean that it was meant to be. Surely that meant that God blessed their union.

He glanced backwards nervously and their eyes connected. Then he smiled and it transformed his face.

The organist started to play 'The Bridal March'. Taking a deep breath she clutched her mother's hand. "Let's go, Mama," she said.

She smiled at the faces as she walked by. Bertie waved and blew kisses. Vladimir nodded with a stern face. Luca made a 'thumbs-up' sign and Lydia beamed at her. Sienna clapped her hands and pointed. "*She's a princess!*" she called loudly. Tara, who had a sleeping Xavier in her arms mouthed, "Good luck, honey." Colin took a photo with his phone and waved madly. Val winked as she swept by.

Elaine and Patrick took photos as she passed and Elaine wiped away a tear.

Gabriella's family occupied the front pews. Teresa and Rico stood with their daughters and Diego stood with his sons. Lita sat in a wheelchair, her small body hunched.

Hugo turned and their eyes met. For a moment he stared at her, his blue eyes intense. She smiled and so did he, and Magda put her hand in his.

"Look after my girl," she said softly.

"Always," he answered.

THE END

Now that you're hooked why not try

Echoes of Grace
also published by Poolbeg

Here's a sneak preview of Chapter 1

Chapter One

The rain beat against the window pane, causing rivulets to fall down the old lattice at tremendous speed. The Big House of the estate had weathered many a storm; for over three hundred years it had faced the wrath of the Atlantic, its grey granite stones defiantly protecting its inhabitants within. Its sheer size was enough to stop any wind in its track. The fourteen-bedroomed mansion stood regally on the cliff's edge. Today, its strength was being tested; the sky was dark-grey and the sea a murky green with waves crashing against the rocks of the Cornish shoreline.

Aurora picked up her Barbie and bent the doll's rigid body into a sitting position. Then she carefully placed it on a dining-room chair in the banquet hall of her large doll's house. The little girl's dark-brown hair fell down her back, the long tresses tied with red bows. Her large brown eyes, fringed with black lashes, dominated a pretty heart-shaped face and her slim frame was dressed in an old-fashioned plaid frock, chosen as always by her nanny that morning.

'Now, Princess Grace,' she said sternly to her doll, 'eat your broccoli so you'll grow to be big and strong.'

The doll stared into space, her back straight and her blonde hair carefully pulled back into a ponytail. Aurora always christened her dolls 'Grace'. It was the name of her dead mother. The game never varied either: Princess Grace, the beautiful blonde heroine, was rescued from her lonely tower by a handsome prince. She had lived all of her life alone and was desperate for company. Then her prince would arrive and take her away in his red Barbie Ferrari to a new life.

Aurora sighed. She was just so bored. Being nine was hard enough without being bored stiff as well. Her father, though attentive, was just too old to play. He was nearly sixty-two and constantly complained of a bad leg. 'Not today, my darling,' was the habitual reply when she begged him to play ball with her or take her to the beach. He was always sitting in his study, writing on paper and frowning. He refused to have a TV in the house and so she had to content herself with making up stories and singing to her teddies. Maggie, her nanny, would explain that her father was writing plays and must not be disturbed. Aurora understood that he was famous. Her teacher at school always talked about the great playwright Henry Sinclair, but Aurora had no interest in reading his books. The words were too long and she didn't understand any of it.

Her older brothers lived in London, not that it made a difference. In fact, they tended to ignore her. They were the product of Henry's first marriage – their mother Marcella had died of breast cancer fifteen years before. They had no interest in their half-sister, from what they deemed Henry's unsuitable marriage. Nor did they lament Grace's death – her dark beauty and mane of wild hair had made her unconventional and they resented her association with their upper-class father. In their eyes, she had pounced on Henry when he was grieving for their own mother and, despite being almost thirty years his junior, had trapped him into marriage by getting pregnant with Aurora. To top it all off, she had been an actress – in their opinion a two-bit singer. This, for George and Sebastian, was just lurid icing on the ghastly cake. Her death during childbirth had been tragic and they had helped their father through his loss, but it definitely was in their favour when it came to inheritance and the estate.

Aurora got to her feet and stretched. Her tummy rumbled so she bounded down to the big kitchen where Maggie was rolling out pastry for an apple pie.

Maggie was an elderly lady of about sixty-five with a shock

of white hair. She was small and wiry with sallow skin. Her wise eyes were as blue as the sky and her hands were rough from manual work throughout the years. She had worked for the Sinclair family since the age of fifteen, just like her mother before her. She still cycled around the Cornish countryside as she had never learned to drive.

'Alright, little 'un,' she said lovingly as Aurora took some orange juice out of the fridge. 'Daddy 'as visitors comin' today.'

Aurora drank thirstily and wiped her mouth with her sleeve. 'Is it that Gloria lady?' she asked, her brown eyes wide.

'It is, my lovely,' said Maggie. 'It's the third time this month. She must like your daddy to drive all the way from London.'

Aurora tilted her head to one side. 'Are they kissing, Maggie?'

Maggie started. 'I don't know about that, my darlin'. Don't be worryin' about things like that.' She started to slice cooking apples into the waiting pie dish. 'Your father needs friends, that's all. It's lonely down 'ere without company.'

Tell me about it, thought Aurora, frowning.

She was still too young for boarding school so her father had hired a tutor to teach her every day. He was a stuffy man of fifty-five, a Latin scholar with a love for the classics, and so Aurora was an expert on Dionysus and Ariadne, but had problems with basic mathematical problems.

Oh, how she yearned to play with children her own age! There was only Freddie, Maggie's nephew, who visited on weekends. He was a farmer's son from the village and was a whole year older than Aurora. He had sandy-brown hair, a ruddy complexion and sea-blue eyes. He took her to the beach sometimes and explained in his Cornish drawl about periwinkles and sea-monsters. He related tales of smugglers and pirates and showed her the dark caves beneath the cliff where treasure was supposedly hidden.

Aurora adored Freddie. Not only was he a year older and infinitely more sophisticated, he was also kind and didn't mind that she was a girl. They had become firm friends and she craved his company. His visits were more frequent in the winter, as the summer and harvest were busy times at the farm. He would arrive around noon and they would run off down the road, making the best of the limited daylight.

'Freddie,' said Aurora once, as they sat on the rocks and trailed their fingers in the lukewarm water of the rock pools.

'Yeah?' he answered, splashing her gently.

'You'll always be my friend, won't you?'

He nudged her. "'Ere, why do you ask?'

'Because you're *my* best friend,' she said seriously, sitting up and brushing her hair back from her face. 'Without you, it would just be me and Daddy and Maggie. Don't ever leave.'

'What about Seb and George?' he asked playfully. 'Your dearest brothers?'

'*Ugh!*' She made a face. 'They're horrible and you know it.'

'Look,' he said, grabbing her shoulders and staring into her dark eyes, 'you're cool, as girls go. I'll be your friend forever. Do you believe me?'

She stared back. 'I believe you.'

'Now, come on. Auntie Maggie has 'ot chocolate for us when we get back.' He pulled her to her feet. 'I'll race you, Sinclair!'

'*Aurora!*' Henry Sinclair's booming voice resonated down the corridor. '*Aurora, darling! Come and say hello to Gloria!*'

Aurora sighed and put a bookmark in her worn copy of *Harry Potter and the Chamber of Secrets*. She was just at the good part. Now, she would have to smile and pretend to be interested in grown-up conversation that she didn't understand.

This Gloria lady seemed nice enough; she always brought sweets and smelled like lavender. Her blonde hair was short and wavy with streaks of grey, her blue eyes merry and her tall frame dressed beautifully in couture. Aurora could tell she was nearly as old as her father, by the lines on her face. Maggie had mentioned that she was a widow and that she had pots of money. Why did she visit then? Surely she and Daddy were too old for kissing and hugging and things?

She could hear laughter from the drawing room as she trudged down the stairs. The oak staircase dominated the main hall and had a threadbare red carpet on the steps. The house, though majestic, was badly in need of refurbishment. The paint was peeling in some parts of the walls and the heating was Victorian. Aurora was quite accustomed to seeing her breath as she exhaled on cold winter nights. Her bed had two duvets and she had fluffy socks for her feet. Her hot-water bottle was her favourite possession and she cuddled it each night, luxuriating in the heat it emitted. Sometimes she wished she had a house like those people in the village: a small, warm terraced house with double-glazed windows and central heating.

She entered the drawing room quietly, shutting the old door with a click. Maggie's apple pie was on the dresser. A jug of cream stood near it and a stack of china plates.

Her father, Henry, was standing by the old fireplace, his handsome face smiling down at their guest. He was a striking man with his tall slim frame and grey hair. His blue eyes were warm and he had a soft voice that was rarely raised. Gloria looked as groomed as always, her legs crossed elegantly at the ankle.

'Aurora, darling,' said Henry, gesturing for her to come closer. 'Gloria has brought you a gift.' He pointed to a bag on the coffee table. 'Come and say thank you.'

Aurora approached the smiling lady and gave her an awkward peck on the cheek. Then she picked up the bag and peered inside. It was filled with sweets and chocolate bars.

'Oh!' she said in delight. 'Thank you!'

'You look lovely today,' said Gloria, brushing a long tendril of dark hair from Aurora's shoulder. 'Such a pretty child,' she added to Henry.

'You look nice too, Gloria,' said Aurora dutifully.

Gloria squeezed her hand. 'You're so good to say so,' she said with a laugh. 'It was such a long journey, I was sure my hair would be flat on arrival.'

'Did you drive, ma'am?' asked Maggie, appearing out of nowhere with a tea tray in her hands.

'No, my son James brought me down. He's nineteen and desperate to practise his driving.' She smiled. 'His Volkswagen

Golf is his pride and joy. Any excuse and he's off. The opportunity to drive hundreds of miles was too tempting so he came along.'

Maggie poured two cups of tea and placed them on the coffee table with a jug of milk. 'Sugar, ma'am?' she asked Gloria, knowing that Henry preferred his tea without.

'Not for me, thank you,' replied Gloria, smiling.

'Where is James now?' asked Henry, accepting a cup of tea from Maggie.

'He's just popped down to the beach to take some photographs,' said Gloria, adding some milk to her cup.

'Photographs? Whatever for? The weather is frightful.'

'He's studying photography as you know,' she said, placing her cup and saucer carefully on the small mahogany table near her chair. 'He saw the stormy sea as he was dropping me off and scooted down to take a few shots before he loses the light.'

Maggie placed a plate with a slice of apple pie and a fork on the table by Gloria's chair. 'Cream?' she asked politely, holding up a small jug.

Gloria nodded. 'I shouldn't but I will.'

Henry refused a plate of pie and sipped his tea.

'Have you other children?' asked Aurora politely.

'Yes,' she replied. 'I have three children: James, William and Laura.' She smiled. 'Laura is only a few years older than you. She's thirteen.'

'Did she come today too?'

'No.' Gloria shook her head. 'She was at a friend's house last night and she stayed over.'

'Oh,' said Aurora in disappointment. 'Will I ever get to meet her?'

Henry's eye met Gloria's and he cleared his throat. 'Well ...'

Suddenly, the front door banged loudly and they all jumped. Maggie scuttled out to the hall and reappeared seconds later with a young man, drenched to the skin.

'James!' exclaimed Gloria, jumping to her feet. 'You're saturated! Oh, for goodness' sake!'

He pulled back the hood of his jacket to reveal dark hair and eyes. His skin was sallow and he had light stubble on his chin.

Maggie took his soaking jacket from his outstretched hand and held it at arm's length.

'I'll put this by the Aga,' she said, walking out of the room. 'It's bleddy soakin', it is.'

'James! You said you would take those photos from the car,' his mother fussed. 'You'll get pneumonia, being out in this weather.'

'Relax, Mum! It was worth it. I can't wait to develop them.' He ran his fingers through his hair and droplets flew everywhere.

Henry held out his hand. 'Good to see you again, son.'

They shook hands formally and James smiled.

'Did you see the rugby yesterday?' he asked. 'It was a close one. Will nearly blew a gasket when that Kiwi kicked the drop goal.'

Henry nodded. 'I thought we had them. It was a tragedy in the end.'

Aurora sidled behind an armchair and gazed at Gloria's son. His eyes were warm and he winked at her. Blushing, she smiled back, unsure of how to react. He was the opposite of her stern haughty brothers who habitually ignored her completely.

'This is Henry's daughter, Aurora,' announced Gloria, gently pulling her into view.

James held out his hand. 'Charmed, I'm sure,' he said, shaking hers firmly. 'Are you a princess with a name like that?' His brown eyes crinkled in amusement.

Aurora giggled. 'Sleeping Beauty was called Aurora.'

'Is she the one who ate the apple?'

'No!' She shook her head furiously. 'That was Snow White. Aurora hurt her finger on a spinning wheel and fell asleep.'

James scratched his head. 'I'm pretty sure my sister Laura has subjected me to every Disney film that has ever been made, yet this does not ring a bell.'

'She sleeps and sleeps and then the prince kisses her and wakes her up.' Aurora's brown eyes were wide. 'He saves her and takes her back to her real family.'

'Is she happy?' he asked softly.

'At the end,' she sighed. 'She's happy at the end.'

James winked at her again. 'Sounds like a great film.'

Henry cleared his throat. 'Gloria, darling, will you two stay the night? That storm is going to get worse before it gets better.'

Gloria got to her feet and looked out the window at the black sky and incessant rain beating against the pane. 'Well,' she began, glancing at her son, 'James has a date later with this girl ...'

James shrugged. 'It's not that important. It was only a few drinks.'

'I would really prefer if you didn't travel.' Henry's tone was firm. 'Wait until morning.'

'I didn't bring anything ...' Gloria gestured to her clothes.

'I'm sure Maggie can produce a nightgown for you,' Henry said with a smile.

Aurora put her head to one side. She was unaccustomed to seeing her father behave like this. His head was always intent on a computer or a page; now he was beaming and speaking in a strange voice.

Maggie bustled back in and poured a cup of tea for James. He gratefully accepted it and took a sip. Then, placing the cup and saucer on the coffee table, he sauntered over to the bookshelves that lined one wall. 'Are some of these first editions?' he enquired, running his finger over the faded volumes stacked closely together.

'Why, yes,' answered Henry. 'My father flirted with being a writer at times. He loved Thomas, Eliot and Frost in particular. He was also a good chum of Teddy Hughes.'

'I really enjoyed your play about Cocteau.' James pulled out a worn copy of *La Machine Infernale*.

Henry shrugged. 'It was in my head for years. I just had to take the time to write it.'

'I went to see it with Dad that time. Do you remember, Mum?'

'Yes, I do,' she answered sadly. 'I took Laura to see *Toy Story* at the Odeon. We had ice cream afterwards.'

'Master James,' Maggie interrupted, 'your apple pie's 'ere on the table for you.'

'Thanks, Maggie,' said James, moving back to the coffee table.

Henry took Gloria's hand in his own and stroked her wrist. 'It's odd how it can hit you sometimes – the grief. It's almost ten years since Grace passed, but sometimes it feels like only yesterday.' He gestured towards a huge portrait by the bay window. It was of a beautiful dark-haired woman wearing a white dress with a faraway look on her face.

All the occupants of the room gazed at it for a moment.

'She looks just like you!' exclaimed James, his eyes moving from Aurora to the painting. 'It's uncanny!'

Aurora said nothing. She was used to people saying that: she strongly resembled her mother. She often wished she could see her and touch her and hear her voice: just once.

'Yes, Aurora looks exactly like Grace,' agreed Henry sadly. 'I can't quite believe it sometimes.'

'She was very beautiful,' concluded Gloria.

'Right,' interrupted Maggie. 'Are you two stayin' for a bit of dinner? I 'ave stew and dumplins, followed by cherry puddin' and cream.'

'Sounds great,' said James, smiling. 'I'm famished.'

Also available on Amazon from Caragh Bell
The 'Follow Your Heart' 3 Book Series